THIS
SUMMER
WILL BE
DIFFERENT

TITLES BY CARLEY FORTUNE

Every Summer After
Meet Me at the Lake
This Summer Will Be Different

THIS SUMMER WILL BE DIFFERENT

Carley Fortune

BERKLEY ROMANCE
NEW YORK

BERKLEY ROMANCE
Published by Berkley
An imprint of Penguin Random House LLC
penguinrandomhouse.com

Library of Congress Cataloging-in-Publication Data
Names: Fortune, Carley, author.
Title: This summer will be different / Carley Fortune.
Description: First edition. | New York: Berkley Romance, 2024.
Identifiers: LCCN 2023049231 (print) | LCCN 2023049232 (ebook) |
ISBN 9780593638880 (paperback) | ISBN 9780593638897 (hardcover) |
ISBN 9780593638903 (e-pub)
Subjects: LCGFT: Romance fiction. | Novels.
Classification: LCC PR9199.4.F678 T48 2024 (print) |
LCC PR9199.4.F678 (ebook) | DDC 813/.6—dc23/eng/20231023
LC record available at https://lccn.loc.gov/2023049231
LC ebook record available at https://lccn.loc.gov/2023049232

First Edition: May 2024

Printed in the United States of America
1st Printing

Book design by Ashley Tucker

To Meredith, of course.
I shucking love you.

THIS
SUMMER
WILL BE
DIFFERENT

PART ONE

Isn't it nice to think that tomorrow is
a new day with no mistakes in it yet?

—L. M. Montgomery, *Anne of Green Gables*

PROLOGUE

I cupped my hands over my eyes so I could gulp down the view. A sun-drenched bay. Water glittering like sapphires beneath rust-colored cliffs. Seaweed lying in knotty nests on a strip of sandy shoreline. A wood-sided restaurant. Stacks of lobster traps. A man in hip waders.

Sea brine filled my nose and the *putt-putt* of a fishing boat my ears. A salt-kissed breeze sent the skirt of my dress flapping against my calves, and I smiled. It was everything I imagined my first Prince Edward Island vacation would be, minus one crucial detail. Bridget may have missed her flight, but I was here. And I was hungry.

It took a moment for my eyes to adjust when I stepped inside Shack Malpeque. My attention went straight to the girl wearing fake red pigtails and a straw hat. She sat at a table by the window, and while her older brother watched the mussel farmers on the water, she plucked a thick French fry from his plate. She popped it into her mouth as she caught me staring, and I gave her a thumbs-up.

"Your problems will seem smaller once we get to the island," Bridget had promised yesterday. I was slumped at the kitchen counter in our apartment, forehead on the granite. She rubbed my back. "Don't listen to your parents. You've got this, Bee."

Bridget never used my given name. I was Lucy Ashby to most everyone in my life except my best friend. To Bridget, I was Bee.

I stood beside the hostess stand and a hand-painted sign that read SHUCK IT UP, the tang of malt vinegar in the air making my mouth water. The mismatched wooden tables were full, and no one looked close to settling their bills. It was that kind of day.

As I was about to leave, a server with salt-and-pepper hair and three plates of lobster rolls balancing on the length of her arm called over to me.

"Take a seat at the bar, sweetie." I twisted my neck to find a row of empty stools behind me.

And him.

He was on the other side of the counter, head tipped down, shucking oysters. His white T-shirt strained against his arms and shoulders as he worked. His hair was a shade darker than mine— a deep chocolate brown, thick and wavy—short enough that it didn't fall into his eyes but long enough for disorderly conduct, tumbling over his forehead. The urge to dig my fingers in it was sharp.

I watched his forearms flex as he sank a small wood-handled knife into an oyster, watched his wrist twist, prying it open. He wiped his blade on a folded tea towel and then slid it through the middle of the shell. The top was tossed aside. There was another flick of his knife, and then he set the oyster on a bed of crushed ice.

As I walked closer, he cleaned his blade again. Instead of plunging it into the next oyster, he paused and glanced up at me.

I almost stumbled. His eyes were the most dazzling shade of

iceberg blue, striking against his deep tan. A cleft parted the center of his chin. His face hadn't seen a razor in at least two days, and it was a study in contrasts. Strong jaw. Soft pink lips, the bottom fuller than the top. The bright eyes trimmed in black lashes.

He held my gaze for less than a second. I saw him, and he saw me, and in that blink of time, something passed between us.

A knowing. A need. A want.

Electricity.

My pulse raced, loud and insistent in my eardrums, and the weight of all the worry and fear and shame I'd been carrying since I told my parents about quitting my job slipped from my shoulders like silk.

He went back to work and didn't acknowledge me when I pulled out a stool. I stared at his hands as he undressed one oyster after another with incredible speed. He dismantled a full dozen and set the platter at the end of the bar.

He looked straight at me then, and for a moment we both stared. There was something guarded about his gaze, a wariness that lingered under those bright pools. For a second, I saw a flicker of sadness, but just as I was wondering where it came from, it was gone. Up close I could see that his right iris had the smallest smudge of brown below the pupil. A tiny, perfect flaw. Suddenly it didn't seem tragic that Bridget had missed our flight. It felt like destiny. This was, without question, the sexiest guy I'd ever seen.

"Hungry?" he asked.

"Starving," I replied, and I thought I saw his lip twitch.

"Where are you in from?" His voice was deep and as dry as birch bark. His accent was thicker than Bridget's—his *you* more like a *yah.*

"How do you know I'm in from anywhere? I could be local."

He held my eyes. Again, an exchange. A current zipping along a live wire. His focus drifted to my hair—copper brown and braided into a crown around my head—and then to my outfit. His brow sketched up. When I planned my holiday wardrobe, I thought the dress was appropriately pastoral—an off-the-shoulder number in oversized red-and-white gingham. Anne Shirley with a modern twist. But maybe the puffed sleeves were a little on the nose.

He shrugged a single shoulder, a gesture that felt familiar. "Most islanders don't dress like tablecloths," he said, deadpan, as the server scooted behind him, batting him on the shoulder with a tut. I smoothed my hands over the cotton, frowning, then straightened the neckline.

He picked up another oyster and, after taking it apart, said, "It's a nice tablecloth."

"It better be. This tablecloth stretched my credit card within an inch of its life."

"Don't mind him, sweetie," the server said as she took two platters of battered haddock from the kitchen pass. "He's rusty. Thinks he can get by on those eyes alone. Women appreciate manners, I keep telling him."

I laughed. His gaze swung to mine at the sound, and I felt it again. Lightning down my spine.

"Is that what women appreciate? Manners?" His voice was low, brushing across my collarbone, my shoulders.

I knew that tone. A flirtation. He was subtler than what I was used to—lacking the blatant pickup line and *you can't resist me* swagger—but it was there. An invitation to play. A scene partner's opening line in an improv. I could flirt. *Flirting*, I was good at. My lips tingled; a grin played on one side of his.

"I don't know about other women, but this one would appreciate a menu." I leaned in closer. "Please."

"Fair enough."

But he didn't obey my request. Instead, he grated a knob of fresh horseradish, which tickled my nose, and he placed it along with two lemon wedges in the middle of a ring of oysters. He set the plate and a bottle of hot sauce in front of me. Six glossy Malpeques.

"It's on me."

"Really?"

He moved down the bar. He wore jeans, dark denim and cuffed at the bottom, and a pair of black-and-white-checkered Vans. I watched his biceps as he poured a pint. He placed the frosty glass in front of me.

"Here you are . . ." He drifted off.

"Lucy."

"Here you are, Lucy."

"Thank you . . ." I gestured to him.

He wiped his hands on a tea towel, eyes fixed on mine like he needed to decide something before giving me his answer. "Felix," he said after a moment.

"I'm not usually a beer drinker, Felix."

"It's a blueberry ale, made here on the island. Try it."

I took a sip. It was ice cold and slightly tart.

"Thanks." I set the glass down. "And you were right earlier—I'm not from here. I live in Toronto," I said, picking up an oyster.

"Toronto," he repeated, though it sounded more like *Terranah*. He nodded once, solemn. "Sorry about that."

I gave him a crooked smile. "Don't be. I like it. Most of the time. Have you been?"

"Once," he said. "I was only there for a night, but it was long enough."

I hummed. Toronto could be an acquired taste, and even though I'd lived there for seven years, I wasn't certain I'd entirely acquired it. I topped the oyster with a pinch of horseradish and a squeeze of lemon and lifted it toward Felix in salute before tipping it back with my eyes shut. Fresh ocean salt hit my tongue, and with it a memory.

Bridget and I in our apartment last fall. We'd just moved in together and had spent the weekend unpacking and assessing. How did our stuff fit together? How did *we* fit together? By Sunday evening, we'd determined we had two can openers, no coffee table, a futon with an aggressively uncomfortable frame, and a lifetime supply of IKEA tea lights.

We were covered in dust and lying on our backs on the floor when Bridget jumped up and skated to the kitchen in her socks. She pulled a box of PEI Malpeques from the fridge. Bridget was a rare twentysomething with her own shucking blade, but I'd never had an oyster. She couldn't find the knife in the chaos of newspaper and plastic wrap and cardboard, so she jimmied the whole batch open using a screwdriver she'd dug from her toolbox, face scrunched pink with effort.

"If you ever meet my family," she'd said as I fished out a shard of shell, "swear you'll never tell them what a shit job I did with these."

We'd been friends for a year, and aside from my aunt, she was already my most treasured person in the world, but I fell a little more in love with Bridget that night.

She should be here for this. My first oyster on PEI. I'd seen her just that morning, but I suddenly missed her with such intensity, my throat ached.

When I opened my eyes, Felix was staring at me. I could have sworn I'd seen a hint of pain—a melancholy swimming beneath the blue surface. But it vanished again before his mouth hooked up at one corner.

"Good?" he asked.

"Very."

I shifted on my seat, crossing my legs. I could feel the beginnings of a blush. I wore my strongest emotions on my chest in bright red. It started between my breasts and crept its way to my neck. Felix's eyes skated down, landing on the trio of moles below my collarbone.

"So what brings you to the island?"

"Girls' trip."

It had been Bridget's idea. I would finally tell my parents I'd left my PR job, and then we would take a vacation to her family's home on the island. Two weeks of oysters, sand, and sea. Two weeks to unwind, with nothing to worry about. It felt like we'd reached a new level in our relationship. We'd been roommates for a year, and friends for a year before that, but you never really know someone until you meet their family. And I couldn't wait to meet Bridget's. She was the most confident, most capable, most bighearted person I knew, and I wanted to see where she came from.

Felix made a show of looking at the empty seats beside me. "Did you lose your friend along the way?"

Bridget's parents were visiting friends in Nova Scotia until the following week, and her younger brother hadn't responded to her texts or calls about my solo arrival. I was supposed to drive to their place and let myself in. "Go around the house to the deck," Bridget had instructed. "There's a spare key under the ceramic toad."

I hated being alone as much as sitting still, and I didn't want to spend the rest of the afternoon lounging around the Clark house by myself, my parents' displeasure reverberating in the quiet. I drove the rental car directly from the Charlottetown Airport to Shack Malpeque.

"My friend's arriving tomorrow," I said, holding Felix's gaze.

He processed this information, head slanted to the side, squinting, and then he picked up his knife. I watched him shuck three dozen oysters in minutes, his hands moving with impressive speed. I was starting to think I'd read him wrong, when he spoke, eyes finding mine from beneath his lashes.

"Do you have any plans before your friend gets here?"

Maybe it was the beer or the buzz of being somewhere new, but I wasn't usually so forward, so sure about what I wanted. "No," I told Felix. "I'm wide open."

His eyes expanded and then he cursed. A ribbon of blood unspooled down his arm. I grabbed a handful of paper serviettes from the dispenser, hurrying around the bar.

"Are you okay?"

He lifted his hand over the wound on his left wrist, and I covered it with napkins.

"I think you might need stitches."

"It's just a nick."

I stepped closer, holding his arm, applying pressure to the cut.

"For the love of Mary," the server called. "Clean that up, then get out of here."

Still clutching his arm, I followed Felix into a tiny office, where he found a first aid kit in the desk drawer.

"Does this happen a lot?" I said as I wrapped his wrist with gauze. I could feel the warmth of his breath on my skin.

"No, Lucy. Beautiful women don't tend to tell me they're wide open while I'm holding a sharp object."

I smiled. "How about blunt ones?"

"Afraid not."

"That's a shame," I said, not that I fully believed him. His face was the intersection of breathtaking and rugged. Plus, the hair and the biceps. I'd taken a good look at his backside, too, and it was outstanding. I bet Felix had heard one or two pickup lines involving shucking puns. I'd come up with at least five since I'd walked into the restaurant.

I fastened the bandage but couldn't make myself let go of him. "Do you want to get it looked at?" I asked. "I can drive you to a hospital."

"My arm's fine." Felix ducked to meet my eyes.

Spark. Fizz. Crackle.

"How about taking me home instead, Lucy?"

WE HARDLY SPOKE ON THE DRIVE, BUT THE AIR INSIDE the car was buzzing with anticipation. I could feel Felix's attention roaming from my cheek to my shoulders. Lower. I'm sure he could see the pulse in my neck.

I was nervous, my stomach swooping and diving like gulls through an open sky. At twenty-four, I was familiar with no-strings hookups. Flings, dalliances, a night of fun, a few weeks of fooling around—casual was my specialty. But this felt different. Riskier. We hadn't shared a meal, or a drink. I hadn't googled him. I didn't know his last name or how old he was. Early twenties? All I knew about Felix was that he was hot, made shucking oysters look like foreplay, and he wanted to have sex with me.

I turned down his driveway, a red dirt squiggle through a celery-green field. Sprays of pink and purple grew in a fringe along the ditch. I rounded one bend, then another, and a house came into view. It stood proud in the distance, with graying cedar shingles and a roof that soared in two dramatic peaks at either end. The trim was fresh white, the front door a happy yellow. The ocean sprawled behind it, a shimmering plain of blue.

"This is where you live?" I asked once I parked. The flower beds were fantastic. Peony season was over in Toronto, but here they were in full bloom. There must have been at least a dozen. Roses galore. Magenta clematis climbing a trellis. Snap dragons. Black-eyed Susans. I turned to Felix. "Is this your garden?" But he was already getting out of the car.

He walked around the hood, opened my door, and held out his hand. Atlantic air filled my lungs as a strong breeze whipped my skirt around my legs. I laughed, trying to hold it in place, but Felix tugged me close. I forgot about the peonies. He was an inch or two taller than me, and we lined up perfectly, nose to nose, chest to chest, hip to hip.

"This is not how I expected today to turn out," I said.

I caught the wink of a dimple in his left cheek as he smiled, no trace of the sorrow I'd sensed at the restaurant.

"No?"

His lips brushed against mine before they trailed down to my neck. I tilted my head back, gazing at a heron that flew above.

"Nuh-uh."

His stubble tickled my skin as his mouth found its way to the triangle of moles. He placed a kiss on top of them, then tasted them with his tongue. I shivered.

"You mustn't have done your research," he said, lips moving to my ear. "This is how we always welcome gorgeous women from away—a traditional islander greeting."

It pulled a laugh from my throat. "If I'd known that, I would have come sooner."

His hand curved around the back of my head. "I think your timing is impeccable."

There was a thread of air between us, and we watched each other for one charged second, before snapping it closed. I wanted to go fast, but it started slow and soft, tentative, until Felix's tongue slid past my lips. I leaned into him, my fingers migrating to his hair. He sucked my bottom lip, and I let out a moan. And then his teeth were there, dragging over my lip. His bite wasn't hard, but it surprised me enough that I opened my eyes.

He inched back, gaze heavier than it had been moments ago. "Too much?"

I touched my mouth, shaking my head. "More."

Felix led me into the house, and before I had time to gape at the view, we were kissing again. I reached for the hem of his shirt as I heard the metallic *snick* of my zipper, and then we were undressing and tripping over our clothes, climbing upstairs to his bedroom, a frantic tangle of limbs and laughter.

We fell onto his bed together, already naked. Felix's body was all hard lines and shadowed ridges, as if it were designed for aerodynamics. His shoulders were broad, his chest solid and dusted with dark hair. I skated my fingers over his bronzed skin, marveling at the tight packs of muscle covering his stomach.

I didn't notice much about his room, just the worn copy of *Wide Sargasso Sea* on his nightstand that caught my eye as he kissed his way down my body. It struck me, briefly, as unusual reading material for a guy in his twenties, but then his jaw scraped against the inside of my thigh, and I stopped paying attention to the decor.

The sun was setting, stripes of royal blue and orange rippling across the sky, when we decided we needed to refuel. Felix made dinner. Thick slices of crusty bread slathered with butter. A plate of juicy tomato rounds, salted and glistening with olive oil. Another of cold rotisserie chicken. Cheddar cheese. Corn on the cob. We assembled open-faced sandwiches with the tomatoes and cheese and demolished the entire plate of chicken on the deck overlooking the gulf, him in a pair of boxer briefs, both of us wearing white T-shirts he'd retrieved from a drawer full of them.

The next time, we didn't make it upstairs. We didn't even make it inside. Felix tasted like the summer-ripe tomatoes we'd eaten at supper—a fresh burst of sun and salt.

More, I kept saying. *More.*

I WOKE IN THE MORNING WITH FELIX'S ARM OVER MY middle, his body wrapped around mine. We must have fallen asleep like that, though I had no memory of it. I lay still, not wanting to rouse him, not wanting to confront the inevitable awkwardness of morning. We had been frenzied last night. We were strangers who'd acted like long-lost lovers. I think Felix had needed to cut loose as much as I had. Surely we'd both be embarrassed in the daylight. But then I felt the rasp of his jaw on my shoulder and the whisper of his lips on my neck. And it wasn't awkward. It was slow and lazy and sweet, like warm caramel sauce sliding down a scoop of ice cream.

When we eventually pried ourselves apart, when I said I better get going, Felix told me I didn't have to rush away.

"Have a shower if you want," he said. "Do you drink coffee or tea?"

So I stayed. I showered. Felix had tea, and I had coffee.

"When do you need to leave to get your friend from the

airport?" he asked. We were on the deck, he in the armchair and I in the corner of the outdoor sofa where we'd ravished each other the night before.

"Soon, I think. Her flight lands at twelve."

Felix blew into his tea, and steam curled from the mug.

"I had a great time last night," he said, lifting his eyes to mine. "I know you're here for two weeks, but——"

I cut him off. "Felix, last night was . . ." Explosive. Hot as hell. Ruinous, probably. Legitimately the best sex I'd ever had. "It was . . . well, you were there. You know what it was."

His eyes dipped to the flush blooming across my chest, pausing on the trio of moles. "I *was* there."

I wanted him to know that we were on the same page. We didn't have to have *that* talk. "What I'm trying to say is that I agree—it was tremendous. Five stars. But I know it was a one-time thing."

"It was more of a four-time thing." His single dimple flashed.

"Right," I said, my eyes catching on his.

Spark. Fizz. Crackle.

He cleared his throat. "Where are you staying? If you want, I can give you some suggestions for places to check out. I have a list for when someone asks at the restaurant. I left my phone in my buddy's truck the other night, but I'll text it to you when he drops it off today."

"That would be great, actually." I reached for my phone and opened my text chain with Bridget. "My friend grew up here, but she's been living in Toronto for years now." I read off the address she'd given me for Summer Wind, then glanced at Felix.

He watched me, unblinking, his face suddenly pale.

"What?"

It took him a few seconds to speak. "Are you sure?"

"I think so?" I read the address again. "Why? Do you know it?"

His eyes darted around my face. "You're Bridget's friend," Felix said. "I thought you were coming next week."

I opened my mouth to reply, but then I spotted the green ceramic toad next to the sliding door. My stomach dropped, fast and hard, like an anvil from a cliff's edge.

"Oh my god."

Bridget gave me just three rules for the trip.

Number 1. Eat your weight in oysters.

"You're Bee," Felix said.

I was shaking my head, even though he was right. I was Bee.

Number 2. Leave the city behind.

I tore my sight from the toad, under which I knew was a set of keys.

"You're Wolf," I murmured. "You're Bridget's . . ." The nausea hit me with such dizzying force, I couldn't finish the sentence. I covered my mouth with an unsteady hand.

And *Number 3. Don't fall in love with my brother.*

"Yeah," Felix said. "Bridget's my sister."

1

Now

Nine Days Until Bridget's Wedding

I study the illustration on the table in front of me, frowning. It's more detailed than my typical sketches. Sometimes, just to show off, I'll whip up a simple line drawing while a client watches. But I've been working with flowers for more than five years, and I don't need to mock up the archways and chuppahs anymore. This time, though, I've carefully rendered each leaf and petal, shaded them in greens and blues and whites. But it's still not right. Floral archways are my specialty, and this one has to be spectacular. Breathtaking. Perfect. Because this is the arch Bridget will stand beneath when she and Miles promise to love and cherish each other, forever, in front of their friends and family. It's where they will share their first kiss as a married couple. Bridget's dad is walking her down the aisle, but I feel like I'm giving her away, too. My best friend, soon to be married.

"I think something's missing. It needs more drama," I say to Farah. She's my second in command at In Bloom and has worked here almost as long as I have. She's a poet with an impeccable eye and a creative soul that was catnip to my aunt. Farah says arranging flowers helps her art. She likes her eyeliner smudgy and black and her clothing bright. Today it's neon orange bike shorts.

I spin in my stool to face her. "What do you think?"

She hums, then shuffles the papers so that all my sketches of Bridget's flowers—the centerpieces, bouquets, boutonnieres, swags, and various other arrangements—are lined up together. "You've got so much plant material here, there may not be room for the guests."

Farah has a manner that oscillates between indifference and disdain. It took months of working together before I saw her full smile, the cute gap between her front teeth, and months after that to learn the attitude is mostly bluster. Farah brings her black Lab, Sylvia, to work with her, and she's a doting dog mom. Sylvia's sleeping under the table now, her nose on my foot.

"You think it's too much?" I ask.

She slits her espresso eyes my way. "You don't usually over-think the design like this."

It's true. Aunt Stacy showed me how to properly care for flowers, both in the garden and the vase, and she delighted in handing down her tricks. But my sense of balance, of color and form—that's innate. And once I'm flowing, the way my hands take over for my brain is magic. The quick snip of shears against stem is my favorite sound.

"You have an eye, my darling," my aunt used to say. "A gift that cannot be taught." Stacy was an actor before she was a florist. Her claim to fame was a recurring role as a busybody Italian relative on the Canadian teen drama *Ready or Not* and three seasons with the Stratford Festival. She was full of proclamations, and she doled them out with grandeur.

"I know," I say to Farah. "But . . ." I drift off.

"It's Bridget," she finishes.

"Yeah. It's Bridget."

My best friend has the mouth of a sailor, the heart of a mother lion, and a frightening passion for lists, label makers, and spread-sheets. And in true Bridget fashion, she's overseen wedding planning with surgical precision. There's a color-coded binder and a shared Google calendar for the myriad appointments—both her fiancé, Miles, and I have access to it, as well as her files with vendor and bridal party contacts, a day-of schedule, and ceremony musical selections.

The flowers are the only thing she's abdicated control of. She's given Farah and me free rein, and we've spent hours schem-ing about how to make the Gardiner Museum look like the most magnificent greenhouse. Peonies and roses, lilies and ranuncu-lus, trailing ivy and asparagus fern and magnolia leaves.

Bridget will love whatever I do. She's my most vocal advo-cate, my loudest cheerleader. My only cheerleader now that my aunt is gone. She's the one person in my life whose love and sup-port come freely and without conditions. She believes in me more than I believe in myself. Her wedding day flowers are a chance to say thank you, to pay her back for everything she's done for me. They will surpass anything I've ever done. They're my gift to her. And I want my gift to make her cry.

I give my forehead a gentle, frustrated *bonk* on the table, star-tling Sylvia. I offer her a scratch behind her ear, and she settles back down.

The bell over the door chimes, and I bolt upright, smiling at the young man who's just walked in. He's dressed nicely and looks nervous. A first date, I'm guessing. Maybe it's an important date. A proposal? I have a nose for this sort of thing, and Farah and I run an unspoken contest to see who guesses right. Maybe he's asking his partner to move in with him?

"Hello," I say. "Can we help you with anything in particular?"

"Yeah. I want to get some flowers."

I can feel Farah resisting an eye roll.

"Well, you're in the right place. Is it a special occasion? Who are you shopping for?"

"They're for my boyfriend's mom. I don't know what she likes."

"Meeting the parents?" Farah asks.

"Yeah."

She looks at me, smug. I was close.

"We have a reservation at six at a restaurant down the street," he says. "I saw your sign and realized that I should probably bring her something."

I glance at the clock. It's five forty. That's odd. Bridget should be here by now. She's supposed to meet me in five minutes, but she's usually early. Her final gown fitting is this evening, at a boutique a block west. We're walking there together, getting the dress, then grabbing dinner.

"Let me help you," Farah says, standing. She speaks to the customers with a tone that manages to sound both resigned and wise. I could never pull it off the way she does. I'm bubbly, my smile full of teeth.

She leads him to our hand-tied bouquets. There are only three left, but he's lucky he has any to choose from. We're often sold out at the end of the day.

As she helps him pick, I go back to the drawing. I squint one eye, imagining Bridget in ivory, Miles in his suit. Her dress is elegant, simple. It's one of the reasons I feel the archway should make more of a statement. If her gown were extravagant, I would make sure the flowers didn't undermine it. The dress is stunning, but there's not a flourish on it. There's not even a train.

A train.

I pick up my pencil and begin a rough sketch of an archway that cascades to the floor in a waterfall, extending over the ground. It will be a river of flora. A train of flowers.

I don't notice Farah standing over my shoulder until I hear her say, "Elaborate."

"Perfect."

"Perfect," she agrees.

The next step is figuring out what I need to order, but I've got time. The flower auction, where I do the bulk of my buying every week, is first thing Tuesday morning so I still have five days to decide. And now that I have the archway design nailed, I can turn my attention to tomorrow. I chew on my lip.

As if reading my mind, Farah asks, "Is there anything you want to go over before your meeting?"

I'm having breakfast with Lillian, the events manager of Cena, one of Toronto's poshest hospitality groups. She'd read about the shop in the newspaper and has asked In Bloom to take on florals for all of Cena's restaurants. There are eight of them, one of which is inside the swanky hotel where we're meeting. My Friday will begin with a thirty-dollar omelet and a contract that could change my life.

"I think I'm good," I tell Farah.

I'm certain I'll be signing that piece of paper tomorrow, but I can't deny it makes me uneasy. I'm not sure if I'm having second thoughts because corporate orders don't fill me up—dozens of uniform vases, uninventive, impersonal. Or if I'm worried that I won't be able to handle the increase in volume. Right now, I have Farah and two part-timers, but if I go ahead with Cena, I'll need two or three full-time staffers. And while I love arranging flowers, I do not love being a manager. I find difficult conversations difficult. But if self-doubt and fear are holding me back—it's more reason to jump in headfirst. That and taking the contract mean I can give Farah the massive raise she deserves.

"I'm excited," I tell Farah. "I'm also tired. I haven't slept well in weeks." I've been overthinking when I should be sleeping.

"Maybe if you took a day off . . ."

"You know I can't do that." We're already running at full tilt.

She growls. "Then don't stay out late tonight. You're trash when you don't get enough rest."

Farah moves toward the front door and turns the deadbolt. I glance at the clock, surprised to find that it's already six. Bridget is ten minutes late. Bridget is never late. She's the most reliable person I know.

We've been best friends for seven years, and in all that time, she's been late precisely once. That first trip. The time that counted.

"That's strange," I say, trying to keep fear from seeping into my voice. Bridget's fine. She has to be.

"She must have got caught in rush hour," Farah says. But I can hear the uncertainty in her voice.

"Maybe."

Bridget works as the VP of publicity at Sunnybrook Hospital, and she was going to leave right at five so she had plenty of time even if traffic was heinous, which it usually is.

I send her a text, but she doesn't reply.

At ten after six, panic sets in. I unlock the front door and step into the muggy August evening. I look up and down Queen Street East, searching for a head of white-gold corkscrews. I fell in love with Bridget's hair, staring at the back of her head in a company all-staff before we ever spoke. She's dyed it platinum for the wedding, but I prefer her natural, softer shade. It reminds me of late summer haystacks.

Like the rest of Toronto, Leslieville flexes its charm on hot nights. I see three red streetcars traveling west in a row, an elderly basset hound in a stroller, and a toddler holding a melting ice cream cone, his face and hands coated in glossy green mint chip. But I don't see Bridget.

When I step back inside, Farah is counting the arrangements for tomorrow's delivery, so I grab the broom from the back and begin sweeping the leaves and flowers and scraps of ribbon.

Farah points a long finger in my direction, its sharp nail tipped with a stripe of acid yellow. "Stop what you're doing. I don't need your help."

"I know you don't, but I'm here . . ." And I need a distraction.

"Sit. Relax for thirty whole seconds. Your stress stresses me out."

I look at the clock again. Six eighteen. My heart is pounding. Bridget wouldn't miss something as monumental as her last gown fitting. "We were supposed to be at the store at six."

I call the boutique. Maybe we got our wires crossed, and I was supposed to meet Bridget there? But no, the aggrieved sales person who answers the phone tells me, Bridget isn't there. In fact, she is twenty minutes late, they close at seven, and it's a very busy time of year, don't I know? I apologize, assuring her we'll be there soon.

I finish sweeping and pull out a stool. I send Bridget another text, fingers beginning to shake, then check CP24, searching for news of accidents on her route.

"Lucy," Farah chides. I don't like the softness in her tone, either.

I've already lost my aunt. I can't lose Bridget, too.

Something is very wrong.

I stand again. Begin to pace. Sylvia watches for a moment, then leaves her spot under the table to walk beside me.

The longest five minutes of my life pass, and then my phone vibrates in my palm. The sound that leaves my throat when I see Bridget's name on the screen is guttural, somewhere between a sob and a gasp of relief.

"Bridget, where are you?" I say. "Are you okay?"

Her voice cuts in and out, barely audible over the wind blowing into the microphone.

"I can't hear you. Can you hear me?"

"Bee?"

The line crackles. I hear the *whoosh* of a sliding door, and then the blowing stops.

"Bee?" My best friend's voice comes clear through the other end, but it doesn't sound right. It sounds broken. Small.

"What's going on? Where are you? We were supposed to be at your fitting half an hour ago."

"I'm home," she says. "I'm at Summer Wind."

It takes a second for her words to make sense. "You're . . . what?" My pulse has become a jackhammer in my ears. "Is your family okay? Your parents? Is—" I stop myself from using the wrong name. "Is Wolf okay?"

I hear her sniff, and I hold my breath. "Yeah. They're fine. But I thought they'd be here. They didn't tell me."

"I'm not following, Bridge. They didn't tell you what?"

"They decided to drive to Toronto for the wedding. They're making some kind of vacation out of it," she says, her voice pitching upward. "You know how they are."

I do know how they are. Bridget's parents are spontaneous,

the opposite of their daughter. It drives her bonkers. Which is why it's not just highly unusual that Bridget has up and left for the island. It's deeply troubling.

"Okay. But, Bridget, why are *you* in PEI? Your wedding is in less than two weeks."

There's the fitting tonight. I'm supposed to go over to her condo tomorrow. Miles was going to make a fancy dinner while I helped Bridget finalize the seating chart and a shot list for the photographer. I'm throwing the bachelorette party this weekend.

"I know. I know. I know. But I needed to get away, Bee. I needed to come home." She's speaking in staccato bursts, fast enough that I almost miss what comes next. "And I need you here with me."

"You need me *there*? On Prince Edward Island?"

Farah's eyebrows reach to her hairline.

"I really, really do. Please come," she says. Another sniff. "There's a flight leaving tomorrow that still has seats. I'm looking at the website now."

"You want me to come to PEI *tomorrow*?" I gape at Farah. Sylvia sits next to her, head cocked.

"Please, Bee. Please come out. I need you."

The list of excuses I have for staying is long. There's the Cena meeting tomorrow. The flower auction Tuesday. I don't know if our part-timers will be able to pick up extra shifts. There's also Bridget's wedding to prep for.

But Bridget never asks for help. She's never had to. She loves me to Neptune and back, but she doesn't need me the way I need her. Until now. I'd travel anywhere if she asked for my help. Saying no isn't an option.

I look to Farah. "Go," she whispers.

"Okay," I tell Bridget, shaking my head. I can't believe I'm doing this.

"You're coming to PEI?"

I swallow. "Yeah," I tell Bridget. "I'm coming."

Even though there's one very good reason why I should never set foot on Prince Edward Island again.

2

Now

Eight Days Until Bridget's Wedding

I stare out the oval window at the tarmac, watching as my pink suitcase is thrown onto the conveyer belt. It travels the ramp into the belly of the aircraft. A flutter worries in mine.

"We'll be departing for Charlottetown, Prince Edward Island, in a few minutes," the captain says over the speaker, and I twist my fingers in my lap. I wasn't sure whether I'd hear those words again.

As the plane lifts off, I take a long breath. In and out. And then another. I shouldn't be nervous. I'm going because Bridget is in crisis. It has nothing to do with him. I probably won't see him. He's probably in a car with his parents, making his way to Toronto. I didn't have the courage to ask Bridget, but it doesn't matter. I shouldn't be thinking about him at all. Bridget is my only concern.

She was so shaken when we spoke and wouldn't say anything about why she'd gone home. All I know is that she arrived on the island yesterday and that she wants me by her side.

"Bridget is your life's true fairy tale," my aunt Stacy once said, and I agreed.

I thought I'd make all these amazing connections when I

moved from St. Catharines to Toronto for school. They say university is where you meet your people, but I drifted through four years of my professional communications degree never finding someone who fit.

After we became close, Bridget told me she was sometimes loneliest in a roomful of people, and I thought, *Yes, that's it exactly.* I dated around and had a loose group of friends, but other than my aunt, there was no one who truly understood me. And then I met Bridget.

Our once upon a time began on a Saturday night. I was twenty-two, and an exec at the PR firm where I worked was throwing a party at her house in the Annex. It was an old brick mansion with a turret and a grand staircase. There was a white tent in the backyard and paper lanterns and an infinity pool. I wore a ruffled dress and a crown made with flowers from my aunt's garden. The night felt enchanted.

In reality, it wasn't so different from the kegger I'd gone to two streets over during freshman year. A staggering amount of alcohol was consumed. Nobody had a bathing suit, but one of the guys from finance jumped into the pool, fully clothed. Others followed. When a senior associate ogled my chest, I took a giant step back, twisting my ankle. I ended up on the ground with a broken shoe. It was my cue to leave.

I was walking down Brunswick with one bare foot when I heard a bicycle bell, and then, "Hey, Cinderella."

I turned around, and there was Bridget, astride a red one-speed, wearing cutoff denim overalls, a white helmet, and not a lick of makeup. She was stunning.

We'd never had a proper conversation, but I knew her from work. She was an assistant, like me, but in meetings, she spoke with the authority of someone with twice the experience. "It's Bridget, right?"

"Yup. And you're Lucy Ashby, the girl who draws daisies in meetings."

I smiled. "I do tulips, too."

"So that party was a shit show."

"Yeah. I thought it would be a little less of a . . ."

"Giant fucking disaster?" Bridget supplied.

I nodded.

She pointed to the shoe in my hand. "What happened there?"

"I got it caught between the pavers and fell in a puddle of pool water." I twisted to show her the wet spot on my backside. "At least I hope it was pool water. My heel snapped off."

"Where do you live?"

"Jarvis and Wellesley."

"That's not far from me. I'm in Cabbagetown. Hop on."

Which was how I found myself sailing down Bloor Street on Bridget's handlebars, listening to her stories about growing up on Prince Edward Island. At one point, I laughed so hard, I almost fell off. When we got to my building, we sat on the front steps and talked for over an hour.

"I'll save you a seat in the quarterly on Tuesday," she told me as she buckled her helmet. "You're always late."

"All right." I was surprised she'd noticed. "Thanks."

She got on her bike and pushed off, calling over her shoulder, "See ya, Ashby." It's something Bridget's dad does, I'd learn—call people by their last names.

By the end of the week, we were sharing snack runs and lunch breaks and rumors, and she'd shortened Ashby to Bee. She said it suited me, the way I never stop buzzing around. I didn't

mind it, though. Not one bit. Because for the next five years, until the day she moved out of our apartment, I never felt lonely.

We're not roommates anymore. We're twenty-nine, and she's
getting married. We've both thrown ourselves into our careers.
Bridget's job interview at Sunnybrook was the reason she missed
her flight to PEI five years ago. She blew the hiring committee
away, of course, and ended up staying for hours, touring the
campus, meeting her future coworkers and her boss's boss. The
days when we swapped office gossip on our coffee breaks feel
like another life, and it's become harder to get away together.

I doze off somewhere over Quebec, but the nap doesn't last
nearly long enough. I dream of a wedding, all the flowers dying
minutes before the ceremony. We hit a patch of turbulence above
Maine, and I'm wide awake, heart thundering, palms damp.

In all the years Bridget and I have been friends, I've never
heard her sound as lost as she did on the phone yesterday. It's always Bridget taking care of me. She's picked me up after I've
fallen more times than I can count. Bridget rarely stumbles.

The practical side of my brain knows I shouldn't be on this
plane right now. When I called Lillian at Cena yesterday evening
to tell her that I had to reschedule, her disappointment was clear.
I couldn't tell her exactly when I'd be back. I sounded like a flake.
Bridget insisted on buying my ticket, but she didn't book a return. I can't imagine staying longer than the weekend. I have too
much going on, including the flowers for Bridget's wedding, but
how can I deny her anything when she's given me so much?

"Attention, all passengers," the captain says. "We're about to
begin our descent into Charlottetown."

This will be my fifth trip to the island—I came alone last
July. I peer out the window, and my stomach dips. From the
sky, the island looks like one of Bridget's grandma's quilts—a

patchwork of farm and field and tree. It may be Bridget's home, but it's precious to me, too. Some of my happiest memories are set on this gorgeous crescent of green land.

Some of my biggest mistakes, too.

But I won't repeat them. Not this time. For once, this summer will be different.

It has to be.

Because Bridget is my most cherished person. My sage. My sister. I'd do anything she asked me to, including an emergency trip. Including not falling in love.

3

Now

I've always liked flying into Charlottetown. You exit the plane right onto the tarmac, which used to make me feel like a celebrity. The airport itself is a teeny tiny delight. There's one baggage carousel, and your suitcase is in your hand within fifteen minutes of setting foot on Prince Edward Island soil.

Based on her instructions, I assume Bridget will be waiting for me in the parking lot, so I head straight for the Cows Creamery cow statue to wait for my luggage. The cow is life-size and cartoony—black and white with a pink snout—and it always makes me smile. I've been mildly obsessed with it since my first trip. But my cow is nowhere to be seen. I turn in a circle in the middle of the room, horrified.

"Can I help you find something, sweetheart?" a woman with a broom and dustpan asks. Islanders truly are the nicest humans.

"No. But thank you," I tell her. "I just noticed that the cow is gone."

"It's a shame, isn't it? Renovations. I miss Wowie, too."

"I didn't know she had a name."

The woman nods. "Wowie."

She wishes me a good day, and I take two steps toward the

baggage carousel, when I'm tackled. Bridget is a full head shorter than me, but she hurls herself at me with such force, I'm almost knocked to the ground. Her arms band around me and my face is engulfed in a cloud of blond.

We saw each other last weekend at the wedding shower her coworkers threw, but she hugs me like it's been months. Bridget seemed fine then, but I could have missed something. I was distracted that day, uneasy because I wasn't at In Bloom.

"I'm so glad you're alive," I say into Bridget's hair. "You scared me yesterday." I squeeze her tight, then hold her out by the shoulders so I can see what I'm working with. She's wearing cutoff shorts, a tank top, and not a stitch of makeup. She looks almost like she did when we were twenty-three and roommates, before she moved in with Miles.

With her mop of golden curls and pocket-size height, Bridget seems like an adorable sprite, with freckles that sprinkle her nose and shoulders with any hint of sun. But she's tough and often misjudged—she loves busting up those misconceptions. I saw it firsthand when we worked together.

Once, during a tense meeting, she turned to the guy next to her and told him his attitude was "horse shit." It was before we were friends, and the way she said *horse* sounded sort of like *hurse*. I liked it—both the old-fashioned curse and the bald confidence with which she wielded it. Bridget's East Coast lilt was most obvious after a drink or in the heat of a fight. Then her *r*'s came out of her mouth as if she was paying them extra attention.

"I'm so happy you're here." Bridget smiles, twin dimples popping.

But her cheeks are pale and dark circles hang below her brown eyes. Bridget is devoted to her sleep schedule, but there's no way she got her self-mandated eight hours last night.

"You know I'd go cliff diving if you asked."

"Maybe tomorrow." She squeezes my cheeks. Her physical affection knows few boundaries, and my cheeks take much of it. "All I want is to spend quality time with you, my dear, sweet bestie who I love so very, very much."

She sounds far more like herself than she did yesterday, but it must be an act. Bridget didn't ask me to fly to Atlantic Canada eight days before her wedding so we could spend time together. That's not what this is about. This is a rescue mission.

When I asked how long she needed me to stay, she'd said, "As long as you can." With any luck, I'll spend two nights at Summer Wind and be on a plane back to Toronto on Sunday, Bridget in tow.

She nods toward the carousel, where my suitcase has now made an appearance. "There's your bag." She loops her arm through mine. "Come on."

It's humid outside, the ground wet from rainfall. The sun shines brightly, but there are storm clouds to the east. The weather can change fast on the island.

"Do you want to tell me what happened yesterday?" I ask as I wheel my hardcase to the parking lot.

"I got homesick," she says, with a *no big deal* shrug. "With the wedding and the honeymoon and work, I didn't know when I'd be able to visit, unless I came now. I was hoping to surprise my parents. But I should have called ahead. I know how slippery they are."

I study her profile, trying to figure out how much of that's a lie. "You sounded extremely upset."

"I was. They just take off on a road trip without telling me? It's so typical."

"Your mom and dad were gone when you got here?"

"Yup. They hadn't booked their flights to Toronto, so they decided to take the scenic route. They're going to see friends in Fredericton, spend a few days in Montreal."

I can hear her annoyance. Ken and Christine are great parents, the reason Bridget and Felix are so self-reliant and sure-footed, but they have a lackadaisical approach to making plans that puts her on edge. Ken was a history teacher and Christine a large-animal vet, and now that they're both retired, they're almost impossible to pin down. They do what they want, when they want to, and they reserve the right to change their minds. I think Bridget's need for order is a direct response to her parents' more relaxed attitudes.

We're halfway across the parking lot, and I'm about to ask her again why she needed me so urgently, but then I see him.

Felix Clark is leaning against a black pickup truck, its tires covered in sienna dirt, reading a paperback. His dark hair falls in a swirling, gorgeous mess over his forehead.

I suck in a breath. Seconds pass before I manage to take another. It's been a full year since we've seen each other, and it comes back to me in a flash.

Bright blue eyes. Strong hands. Ocean breeze on sun-bronze skin. A kiss on a beach. Sand in the sheets. The day when everything changed.

I had a good time.

That I don't trip is a miracle. My stomach spins like a windmill, and my heart is doing its best to pound a hole through my chest.

Calm down, I tell it. *Behave.*

But it only quickens.

Felix is here.

4

Summer, Five Years Ago

Bridget was in the shower, singing at an earsplitting decibel, while I hid in her bedroom. Felix was downstairs, and I didn't want to be alone with him. He was Bridget's younger brother, and I was reeling. So far, since returning from picking Bridget up at the airport, I had successfully avoided him.

I doubted Bridget's room had changed since she left for Toronto to attend university. There was a puzzle of the 2010 Canadian Women's Olympic Hockey Team holding their golds, assembled, framed, and mounted on the wall, and a Team Jacob canvas tote hanging from her closet door handle. Three hockey trophies. The patchwork quilt that covered the bed was made of purple and pink squares. The space belonged to a different version of Bridget than the one I knew.

I was sitting on a pile of faux-fur pillows, flipping through a fashion magazine I'd bought at the airport, when I heard the knock.

Tap, tap. Pause. *Tap.*

I froze.

"Lucy?" Felix called.

"I'm busy."

"Can you let me in? I'd like to talk."

I closed my eyes and pressed my fingers into the sockets. I didn't want to talk. I wanted to return to yesterday afternoon, thank Felix for the oysters, and not have sex with him four times in the house my best friend grew up in

He knocked again.

But I also didn't want Bridget to catch her brother talking to me through the door, so I unlocked it and pulled him inside.

"You shouldn't be here," I hissed, letting go of his arm. "Bridget could have heard you."

A loud *Oooh-oooh-oooooh!* rang from the bathroom.

"I think we're safe," he said, deadpan. "Next time, don't leave me standing in the hall. I used our secret knock."

"We don't have a secret knock."

"We do." Felix held my gaze while he rapped his knuckles on the door. Two soft taps, a pause, and then a third, louder one.

"Well, we don't need one."

He took a step nearer.

Being this close to Felix was a bad idea. His fresh-air smell was impossible to ignore. Even without touching him, I could feel the heat of his body. The rebellious swirl of hair above his eyebrow called to my fingers. I wanted to climb him. I wanted to plunder his mouth. I wanted to slide my tongue over his dimple and sink my teeth into his bottom lip. I stepped back.

"What are you doing?" I asked. "You're not allowed to be in here. We're not allowed to do this."

His smile was as slow as molasses. "We're not *allowed*?"

"No! I'm under strict instructions!"

He blinked at me, baffled.

"Bridget has rules."

"Rules?"

"Yes. Rules. Three of them." I technically hadn't broken any, but there was no doubt in my mind sleeping with Felix would be frowned upon. To say the least.

"And they are?"

"Eat your weight in oysters." I paused. I didn't want to tell him *all* the rules. "And leave the city behind."

Felix's gaze was steady. Hypnotic. "You said there were three. What's the third one, Lucy?"

I may have been evading Felix, but my brain had been circling him all day, unearthing every single detail Bridget had ever shared about her brother. He was twenty-three, had lived on the island his whole life, and he was a competitive oyster shucker. But of all the facts I'd excavated from my memory, his ex-girlfriend, Joy, was the one that stood out most.

"Bridget asked me not to fall in love with you. It was sort of a joke, but also not? She doesn't want a repeat of what happened with . . ." I winced. "Well, you know. You were there."

A shadow passed over Felix's eyes like a rain cloud. "Got it."

"I'm sorry. I shouldn't have brought it up. Bridget told me you've had a bit of a rough time." Actually, what she'd said was that her brother had been "drinking like a fucking fish" and doubted we'd see him while we visited. Apparently, his best friend's couch had formed a Felix-shaped dent since the breakup.

"Anyway," I rushed on. "We don't have to worry about that rule. Because that's not what's happening here—not that there's anything happening here. I'm not anywhere close to falling in love with you. I don't have any interest in starting a relationship. We just met and you're okay, but . . ."

Felix's grin returned, carefree. "I'm *okay*? Wow." He ran his hand through his hair, laughing. I stared at his fingers. They'd been on me this morning. They'd been *inside* me this morning.

"You'll be happy to know I didn't come here to ravish you. I thought we should clear the air, so you don't spend the next two weeks dodging me."

"I wasn't dodging you."

He stared at me, one eyebrow arched.

"Okay, maybe a little. Felix, we had sex!"

"More than once," he said, eyes glimmering.

"How could this have happened? Bridget must have told you that she missed her flight. You must have known I was coming."

He shrugged a shoulder. "I crashed at my buddy's place and left my phone in his truck yesterday morning. I knew Bridget was coming home, but I guess I didn't pay enough attention to when."

I rubbed my forehead. "Bridget cannot find out." She'd disown me.

"She won't. Unless you throw yourself at me in front of my sister, I think we'll be fine."

"There'll be no throwing." Felix was so off-limits, he may as well have been wearing a medieval chastity belt.

He smirked. "So you say."

"You're not that hot," I lied.

"I'm kidding. I'll be on my best behavior; you'll be on your best behavior. No one needs to know about last night." A vision of Felix above me, his arm around my knee, flashed in my mind. "Or this morning."

"Agreed."

"But you should try not to blush like that," he said. I put a hand on my sternum, the skin hot beneath my palm. "Might give us away."

"There's no *us*," I said, glaring.

Felix chuckled. It was such a good sound. Throaty and a little rough.

"This isn't funny. Bridget is my best friend in the entire universe. I love her like family—better than most of my family if I'm being honest. She can't know about us."

Bridget was protective of the people she cared about, and under normal circumstances, that circle included me. But when it came to her brother, all bets were off. I didn't want to risk the most important relationship in my life.

"I'm not going to tell her," he said. "Believe me, I have no interest in discussing my sex life with my sister. Or getting involved with one of her friends."

"Thank you."

He leaned in a little closer. Dropped his voice. "That will be our first rule: We don't tell Bridget."

"Do we need rules?"

His gaze moved to my mouth, and need thrummed between my thighs. "I think we might."

I swallowed. "Okay, fine. We don't tell Bridget. What happens on the island . . ."

"Stays on the island." He nodded. "Rule two: We won't sleep together again."

"That goes without saying."

"And three's obvious."

"Is it?"

"It is." Felix's dimple winked. "Rule three: You're not allowed to fall in love with me."

5

Now

Felix hasn't seen us yet. He's absorbed in his book. There's almost always a paperback tucked into the back of his jeans. He goes through them quickly.

"I thought your family was on their way to Toronto," I say to Bridget, casually, as we walk toward him.

"Mom and Dad are," Bridget says. "I couldn't get the Mustang to start, so I called Wolf." And Felix is nothing if not dependable.

From head to foot, I devour him. The deep midsummer tan. The breadth of his shoulders. His solid arms. The fitted white T-shirt and the dark jeans. Same as when I met him. But the clothes are new, a little more stylish. He's clean-shaven—no facial hair hiding the right angles of his profile or the cleft in his chin. It's been years since I've seen Felix without a beard, not since we first met. His hair is a sexy disaster. It's grown since I last saw him. I could hold it in my fists now.

He flips a page. It's a thick thriller with a black cover and neon title, a stark departure from his usual reading material. Modern classics, classic classics.

I don't know if he can sense my gaze, but he glances up from the book and his eyes land on mine in an instant, as though we are magnetized.

It's too much—how handsome he is.

Felix's focus stays secured on me as we approach. He's as still as a mountain. But even across the parking lot, I can feel the heat rippling beneath.

I raise my hand, willing it to stop shaking. I didn't expect to see him until the wedding. I'm not prepared. But I can do this. Of course I can.

When I reach him, I paste on a smile. "Wolf, what a nice surprise."

His eyes flash at the nickname, and his dark brows crunch together.

Wolf.

I've never been able to use it comfortably, to make it fit the man I've come to know. Wolf is Bridget's little brother, a character in her stories. Felix is a different person entirely.

I step closer, arms outstretched, and give him a neighborly hug, doing my best not to breathe him in. But it's no good. Pine, salt, wind—a breeze through a coastal forest. Felix is the best thing I've ever inhaled, and it's been a full year since I've had a hit.

"Hi, Lucy." His voice smooths along my spine like a hand down a cat's back.

I pull away and make the mistake of meeting his eyes. They always get me—those two pools of unlikely blue, the smudge of brown that forms a miniature island beneath his right iris. But his expression is guarded. Felix usually sparkles like fireworks.

I don't realize I'm staring until he frowns, a pair of parallel grooves running atop his nose. Those lines weren't always there, but then again, Felix is twenty-eight now. Five years have passed since we first met. Every time I see him, he's changed. Just a little. Just enough that I find myself cataloging all the subtle differences, paying him more attention than I should. *Liking* him more than I should.

"How have you been?" I ask.

"Can't complain." Felix's smile isn't his usual open grin. It's a fortress, revealing nothing of what lies behind, which is a shame because I'm desperate to know what he's thinking.

Felix takes the handle of my suitcase and hoists it into the bed of the truck. I watch his biceps and forearm muscles tense and struggle not to think about how they felt under my palms.

"Can you believe he got rid of the beard?" Bridget squeezes her brother's cheek, though there's not much flesh there to get between her fingers. "Wolf wanted to be pretty for the wedding."

Felix ignores that. A part of me thrills at the idea that it might have had something to do with me.

"It looks good," I finally say. It's a lie. Felix looks like every ill-advised sexual fantasy I've had. "Thanks for picking me up."

He nods. "It's not a problem."

If you were to judge Felix's mood by tone of voice, you'd often find yourself guessing. He delivers almost everything in the same deep deadpan. It's his eyes that say more than the words from his lips. They whisper, they tease, they laugh. I've seen them dance in the starlight. But there's no trace of that Felix right now. The worry that's followed me since last summer— that I've ruined things between us—resurfaces.

He turns to Bridget. "I'll take a look at the Mustang when I drop you two off. See if I can get it running."

"You should sit up front, Bee," Bridget says, but I decline.

I'm prone to car sickness, but I know myself, and I should not be allowed to sit beside Felix. If history has taught me anything, it's that I need to put as much literal distance between my body and his body as possible. Felix and I are combustible in small spaces. Or we were once.

As he navigates out of the parking lot, Bridget exhales a satisfied sigh. "It's been forever since we were all here together."

I glance at Felix in the rearview mirror. His eyes meet mine for one brief moment. It's a drop of liquid turquoise, but I want the whole ocean. *No*, I tell myself. *Not one sip.*

"It'll be just like old times," Bridget says.

Felix's jaw ticks.

A steam-filled bathroom. Skin lit by the moon. A small bedroom on the eastern edge of the island. It won't be like old times. It can't be.

IT'S ALWAYS THE ROADS THAT GIVE ME THE FIRST FEELING of being away. The streetlights are different here—hung horizontally, red beside orange beside green—and there are roundabouts everywhere. The first time I drove on the island, I squealed as I steered around them.

Fields roll past. Vibrant green rows of potato plants and blinding yellow canola crops. White churches, orange barns, dappled ponies, and grazing cattle. Quaint country communities. Hunter River, Hazel Grove, Pleasant Valley, Kensington. Some are little more than signs on the highway.

I focus on the scenery because I'm getting woozy. My motion sickness is always worse when I'm low on sleep, and between fretting about Bridget and fretting about the flower shop, it wasn't a restful night. I should have taken the front seat when she offered.

"Have you eaten anything?"

I look up to find Felix studying me in the mirror.

"A yogurt, before I left for the airport," I tell him. I've been existing on a diet of Uber Eats and coconut Activia, staying at the shop later and going in earlier than I used to. I haven't been to the grocery store in over a week. More than two, maybe. I've adopted the belief that yogurt expiration dates are merely a suggestion.

Felix opens the center console. "Here," he says, passing back a snack bar that's mostly nuts, the kind I like best.

I meet his eyes in the mirror. "Thank you."

"You just happened to have that in there?" Bridget gawks at her brother.

"No," he says. "I bought it when I stopped for gas. Just in case."

"Just in case," she repeats.

"Lucy gets carsick if she has an empty stomach."

"I know that," Bridget says, suspicious. "But I'm surprised that *you* know that."

I feel like a teenager whose parents have returned home early in the middle of an unsanctioned house party. Chairs knocked over. Red Solo cups in the potted plants. Wobbly-legged sixteen-year-olds staring at the adults in horror.

We're about to be busted.

But then Felix lifts a wry brow at her and says, "She almost puked in my truck last summer."

Blue shimmers in the distance, and Bridget opens her window, filling the vehicle with ocean air. She casts me a sympathetic look as I take a bite. I chew slowly, and it does help a little.

After I've balled up the wrapper and tucked it into the pocket of my striped cotton dress, I close my eyes and press my temple to the glass.

A few minutes later, I hear Bridget say quietly, "It's nice that you two are friends."

There's a long pause before Felix replies.

"Friends," he says. "Sure."

6

Now

Friends. Sure.

He says it so softly that I strain to hear it. For the rest of the drive, I keep my eyes shut, examining those two syllables and what they mean. We had been inching closer to something that felt like friendship before I messed up.

I don't know if it's the scent of the ocean, or if my body knows the twists of the road, or if Summer Wind is imprinted on me at a cellular level, but I can feel when we're almost there. I open my eyes when the truck slows. I don't want to miss my first glimpse. The cedar shingles, the yellow door, the red dirt road snaking through the grass, the Gulf of St. Lawrence glittering behind it.

The house stands as it always has, in all her sturdy glory. Just seeing it feels like taking a deep breath. I'm here. The place that calls to me more than anywhere else.

Felix lifts my suitcase from the back and carries it into the house. Bridget wraps her arm around my waist, and as we follow behind, she pops onto her toes, kisses me on the cheek, and says, "Welcome back, Bee."

Summer Wind is as spellbinding inside as it is out. You enter through a shaggy mudroom. It smells like wood and damp wool.

There are shoes scattered over the floor, and a stratum of raincoats and scarves and umbrellas cover the hooks. It's the middle of summer, but the winter boots and jackets haven't been put away. It reminds me of the closet that leads to Narnia, and just like in the story, traveling through it makes real life feel a world away.

I unbuckle my sandals and follow Bridget into the main space, feet already gritty with sand. There's a large living area that opens into the kitchen at the far end, with tall windows that look over the wide expanse of sky and sea. The white linen couch and armchairs are rumpled and so soft, they threaten to swallow you when you drop into them. Braided rugs lie higgledy-piggledy, a patchwork of color over wide knotted floorboards. A fireplace is set into a brick wall, painted white and stained with smoke from years of use. There's a stack of logs on one side and a vintage steamer trunk that's full of blankets on the other. An upright piano stands under the staircase that leads to the second floor. There's a five-disc changer on the sideboard. Bridget's dad, Ken, is the resident Summer Wind DJ and swears CDs are coming back. When he's home, the evenings are set to a Canadian rock soundtrack. Joel Plaskett, Feist, the Tragically Hip, Sloan. There used to be books piled on every surface, but they belonged to Felix, and he no longer lives here.

Summer Wind has never been polished or even overly tidy, but it has the feeling of being wholly loved, so different from my parents' house in St. Catharines, with its colonial furniture and formal sitting room. I never really felt at home there.

When I was growing up, the Ashby family's schedule revolved around my older brother's hockey—Lyle was promising enough to capture the attention of scouts. Sometimes, on tournament weekends, my parents would send me to Toronto to stay with my aunt. Her yard was where I could get messy and be silly. Stacy showed me how to start seeds and deadhead petunias. She let me ransack her beds, picking whatever I fancied to fill a vase for her kitchen windowsill. Sometimes, if I was lucky, she'd bring me around the corner to hang out at In Bloom. With Stacy, I felt like I belonged.

Much of the Clark house is unchanged from my first visit, but the kitchen has been totally renovated. Christine had it re-done after the hurricane two years ago. I wander through the space, running my hand over the cabinets. They're sage green now, the hardware gold, and there's a large butcher block island.

I stop in front of the sliding glass door, taking in the vista. A lawn of vibrant emerald stretches to the grassy dunes that buttress the beach. The gulf unfurls in the distance, a brilliant royal blue. It still amazes me how beautiful it is here, how my chest feels like a tightly wound bobbin in the city, but just standing in this spot loosens me enough that I can feel the difference in my lungs.

"I'll see if I can get the Mustang started before I go," I hear Felix say. He and Bridget are standing by the foot of the stairs. "I put Lucy's suitcase in my old room."

"Actually," Bridget says, "I wanted to talk to you about that. I was hoping you'd stay here. With us."

My eyes fly to Felix, but he's frowning at his sister.

"Bee can sleep with me," Bridget goes on. "And you can have your old room. All of us home together, just like it used to be."

Felix rolls his shoulders. "I can't," he says. "This isn't my home anymore, Bridge."

"No, I know that. But I was hoping we could spend time together. I want my best friend and my brother with me right now."

"What's going on?" Clearly Felix is in the dark as much as I am. He doesn't play games, so it doesn't surprise me when he comes right out and asks, "Did something happen with Miles?" I can tell he doesn't like asking, that he doesn't believe anything *could* happen. Bridget and Miles have been together for three years now, and he's as solid as granite. They both are.

Bridget blinks three times in quick succession. "No, of course not."

The twin lines atop Felix's nose deepen. "So he's okay with you being here?"

She shrugs one shoulder in the manner of all Clark family members. "Sure."

I want to believe her, but I have a sinking feeling that this *is* about Miles. Bridget has a track record of chewing over her problems in silence. Sometimes she deliberates for days. She hates asking for help, and she rejects unsolicited advice. If the wedding is in jeopardy and her relationship is on the brink, there's a strong possibility she won't tell me until she has decided on a full course of action. Coming here was the right thing to do. I'll be by her side when she's ready to lay it all out.

"Wolf, come on," she says. "Who's going to keep Bee and me in oysters if you're not here? Who's going to light the bonfire?"

Felix gives his sister a flat look. "You can do both those things."

"But why should I when I have my wonderful baby brother who I hardly ever get to see around to do it for me?" Her smile is sweeter than a sugar bowl.

Felix runs his hand over his forehead. He's good at setting boundaries, but I know it's difficult for him to let anyone down, especially his sister. "I've got stuff to take care of out at the cottages."

Felix and his best friend, Zach, own a strip of land south of Souris, where they've built four vacation homes. Salt Cottages have been hugely successful. The buildings are stunning, the view is phenomenal, and their reviews are gushing. They're booked through the high season—I checked online.

Zach lives in Summerside and continues to work as a project manager for his family's design/build company, but Felix's cabin is close to the cottages. He handles everything except for the cleaning, so when he says he has stuff to take care of, he's not lying. But he's also his own boss. If he wanted to stay at Summer Wind, he could find a way to make it happen.

There's one explanation why he won't: me. I feel myself flush.

"I get it," Bridget says, squinting. "I do. But I miss you, Wolf."

"I'm sorry." His eyes skate almost all the way over to me but stop short. "I just can't."

Felix grabs a set of keys off the hook by the door, and my stomach twists. I know I'm the one who put this awkwardness between us.

I'm cautious as we follow him to the large wooden shed at the end of the driveway.

Felix opens the barn door, and pulls the cloth off a very shiny, very red car. Five minutes after meeting me, Ken brought me outside to show off the Mustang, telling me about the months he and Felix spent fixing it up.

I think it's a sixties model, but I *know* it's a stick. Bridget tried to teach me to drive it once, but I stalled so many times that it took ten minutes to make it to the end of the Clarks' winding driveway. Bridget and I were laughing like hyenas, and I had to pull over before I turned onto the road. We climbed out of the car and lay in the field, holding our sides and cackling up at the clouds.

Felix gives the car a pat hello on the hood and gets into the driver's seat. The engine refuses to turn over. He taps his fingers on the steering wheel, thinking, and I make the error of looking at his hands. Those hands. Those long fingers. Thick. Dexterous.

"Probably the battery," Felix says, climbing out of the car. "I told Dad we should put a new one in not long ago. I think he ordered it."

He pops the hood. Pokes around in an assured way that makes me avert my gaze. What's so fascinating about tendons anyway? Bridget surveys the shelves in the shed.

"This it?"

Felix glances over his shoulder. "Yeah. I'll switch it out, and hopefully that will do the trick."

I step outside. I do not need to watch Felix work on a car. When I hear the engine rumble to life, I'm hit with loss. Felix will be on his way now. He'll return to his side of the island. But it's for the best.

"I'll stop by in a couple of days. With oysters," Felix says as he hugs his sister goodbye.

He heads to his pickup, lifting his hand in my approximate direction. His eyes meet mine. But they don't twinkle, they burn. Darker than ever—deeper than before. "Good to see you, Lucy."

Bridget drapes her arm around my shoulder, and we watch the truck bump down the driveway, leaving behind a cloud of reddish dust. And me.

7

Now

I approach Felix's old bedroom with caution, afraid of the ghosts I'll find inside. When I push the door open, I'm so surprised by what I see, I double check to make sure I haven't entered the wrong room. Bridget told me that Christine had redecorated, but I can't quite believe how different it is.

When Felix lived here, the room looked like a barely crashed-in crash pad, with Blu Tack smudges marring the taupe paint, memories of hockey posters long since ripped down. But now the walls are covered in cream-and-white-striped paper and framed watercolors of flower-filled vases. There's a pink-and-white quilt on the bed, Bridget's grandma's handiwork no doubt. The windows still look onto the strip of grass that becomes sand that becomes sea, but the desk that used to sit under them is gone. The books, too.

Nothing is left of Felix's room except for the bed, a handsome wooden antique with post and spindle head and footboards. I'm not sure how I'll be able to sleep in its sheets. I can picture us there, that clueless couple, that endless night. I'll see him in my dreams tonight. His fingers, unraveling the braid in my hair. His body, moving over mine.

Felix. More.

I cross the room to look out the windows, which are now topped with roman blinds in a cherry voile instead of plain white drapes.

"It's weird, isn't it?"

I turn around to find Bridget in the doorway, studying me.

"It's hard to imagine your mom picking all this out," I agree. "It's more my taste."

Bridget gives me a funny smile. "I thought so, too." Her eyes narrow. "You're a bit flushed."

Bridget can usually read me like there are closed captions of my innermost thoughts displayed on my forehead. But she's not herself right now, and I don't think she suspects anything's off.

"Just hot." It's a half-truth. The Clarks have a thing about air-conditioning—as in, they refuse to get it. I crank open the window.

"Do you want to unpack?" Bridget asks. "Or should we head out now?" We always used to begin our vacations the same way, with a long, slow walk by the water.

"Are you up for it?" She looks exhausted, but otherwise, she's behaving as if that panicked phone call never happened, as if I didn't just put my life on hold and hop on a plane to be with her. But I know Bridget, and I know I can't push her to talk when she doesn't want to. Unless I'm ready to fight, which I'm not. When we argue, it escalates fast, like we're sisters with a lifetime of combat experience at our disposal.

Our last blowout was over her dieting. I've seen it countless times at In Bloom—brides who shrink themselves between our initial consultation and their wedding day. I didn't think Bridget would be one of them. It was one of the rare occasions I won the argument.

I glance at the bed. "I'll unpack later." My suitcase is a disaster. I used to love planning my island vacation wardrobes. But there was no careful rolling and fretting over *this skirt or that* yesterday. There wasn't any time. I poured myself a generous glass of wine, shoved everything in my bag, and ordered a take-out prosciutto and arugula sandwich, which even I could have prepared had I any food in my fridge. I remembered my nightgown only as I was zipping the suitcase up this morning.

"I should give Farah a call before we head out," I say to Bridget now. This trip has put my work stress to an eye-twitching level.

"Don't you dare. Farah can run that place in her sleep. She doesn't need you."

Farah's precise words were: "You could go and never come back, and I'd be fine." She wasn't joking.

"Thanks," I say flatly.

"You know what I mean. You haven't taken a vacation in way too fucking long. I know I've said it before, but you're doing too much, Bee."

Bridget has been encouraging me for months to hire another staff member. She minored in finance, manages a meaty budget at work, and has been filing her own taxes since she was a teenager. When I took over from my aunt three and a half years ago, she helped me clean out Stacy's office. It looked like a tipped-over newsstand, papers strewn about everywhere. Bridget was disturbed by the mess and possibly turned on by the prospect of corralling it. She's been helping me with the administrative end of the business ever since.

I know Bridget's right. I am doing too much, but it doesn't cost me anything if I work long hours. I'm terrified of overspending, of making one bad decision and bankrupting the business, of my parents being right after all. The full weight of owning In Bloom didn't settle on my shoulders until my aunt died last year.

"Bee," Bridget says softly. "I'm worried about you. I know you can manage the same amount of work as three people combined, but you're running yourself down. You're going to burn out."

"Bridget," I say, narrowing my eyes. "Did you orchestrate this vacation so you could stage an intervention?" I wouldn't put it past her. As brazen-mouthed as she is, Bridget has a sly side.

"No. But you *do* need to take a breather."

Maybe this trip can be an opportunity for Bridget and me to unwind like we used to. Gorge ourselves on oysters and vinho verde. Relax. *Talk*. Throw ourselves into rule number two and really leave the city behind.

"I guess a breather doesn't sound terrible," I say.

Her dimples pop. "I love it when you don't argue."

But it's jarring—the forced smile and the mauve crescents under her eyes—and it does nothing to conceal the worry on her face.

OUR TRADITION IS THE SAME WHEREVER WE TRAVEL: Once Bridget and I get settled, we go outside and we walk. It's our way of shaking off work and urban life. Rain doesn't stop us. Snow doesn't, either. On PEI, we head to a beach so we can drink in the Maritime air. I always search for sea glass in the sand and never find it. Sometimes we tromp down to the shore in front of Summer Wind, but today, Bridget suggests Thunder Cove. Neither of us has been since before the hurricane, when Teacup Rock disappeared into the gulf.

We park at the end of a red dirt road, take a path through the dunes, onto the beach. It's as breathtaking as it was when I first saw it. Red sandstone cliffs rising high above the sand. Caves and crevices, carved by the Atlantic, shaped by wind. Swishing grasses and soaring gulls. I still can't get over how massive it is. I knew PEI had beaches, but I hadn't known they had beaches like *this*.

I used to braid my hair into all sorts of elaborate styles to combat the humidity and wind, but I savor the feeling of the strands lashing against my face, my dress whipping around my legs. It makes me feel small in the best possible way. I've been existing on stress and spicy noodles, but that version of Lucy feels insignificant when I'm standing on the edge of the island.

The surf is gentle today, barely crashing. I feel strangely emotional when I see what's left of the Teacup—where it once rose, majestic, is only a burnished red platform of rock in the shallows of the sea. I hear Bridget sniff.

"Are you crying?"

She touches her cheek. "I guess I am." She laughs at herself, but the sound gets stuck in her throat and becomes a sob.

"Hey." I touch her arm. "Let's stop for a sec."

I've broken down in front of Bridget countless times. But she's never been much of a crier. We sit side by side on the sand, knees drawn to our chins.

"I'm sorry," she says.

"Don't apologize. You never have to apologize for having feelings, especially not to me. It's better to get it out."

Her chin begins to quake, and her eyes fill. When she blinks, big round tears slide down her cheeks. She shakes her head, bewildered at herself, and then buries her head between her legs.

I rub her back, telling her it's going to be okay. But it's almost impossible to keep myself from falling apart alongside her. I look at the sky, blinking back the stinging in my eyes. I want to be the strong one for once. Bridget cries until there are no more tears, only a runny nose.

"Want to tell me what that was about?"

For a minute, she just stares at the waves, at the blank space where a precarious rock once towered. "It's just gone. The cow, too."

"The Cows Creamery statue? In the airport?"

"Yeah," she says. "You loved that fucking cow."

"I did. But things change, Bridget. Shorelines and airports, especially. It's not all bad. It just is."

She turns to me. "It doesn't bother you that the rock has just vanished?"

"A little. But nothing is permanent. It was meant to go. Everyone knew that thing wouldn't last forever. You saw it. The top was too heavy for the bottom."

She looks back at the horizon.

"Can you talk to me about what's really bothering you?" I ask.

She breathes in. Then out. "I just want to sit here," she says. "Please. I don't want to talk."

We gaze out at the water together, and eventually, Bridget rests her head on my shoulder. A tangle of blond spirals and brown waves swirl across my vision.

"It feels like things are slipping away," she says.

I don't tell her that I feel it, too. Natural wonders. Landmarks. My aunt. Bridget, too. Ever since she met Miles, she's been a little less mine.

I picture Felix's truck disappearing in a cloud of burnt dust this afternoon.

"I'm always here," I tell her. "I'll never slip."

Not again, anyway.

8

Now

"Do you think there's any chance your parents have wine in their fridge?" I call to Bridget as she heads upstairs. She always showers after our inaugural walk. She's the most laidback, chill-mongering version of herself on the island, but her loafing still follows a schedule.

"Not at all," she says. Ken drinks beer or whiskey, and Christine mostly abstains.

"Rye and peanuts, then?"

She nods. "Rye and peanuts."

I know when she's washing her hair, because I can hear her rendition of "Un-Break My Heart" from the kitchen. I'd like to read into the song choice, but it's one of her lather-rinse-repeat standards.

I should probably make us something resembling a meal. While my greatest culinary achievement is predicting the winners of *The Great British Baking Show*, Bridget hates cooking. Miles is the chef in their relationship, a very good one. It's how he won me over—I'm a sucker for a homecooked meal. I survey the meager contents of the Clarks' fridge. We'll have to go grocery shopping tomorrow. I hunt out the rye and a bag of peanuts in the shell—two things you can always count on Ken having in stock—and pour myself a finger of whiskey.

I rarely drink brown liquor back home, but I could use the fortification. My mind has been stretching, bending, performing acrobatic feats on a balance beam, twisting to process Felix's evident discomfort with me and Bridget's runaway bride act. I take a sip, and the caramel burn in my throat grounds me. I'm on the island. Back at Summer Wind. And something weird is happening with my best friend. I've never seen her crumble like she did at the beach.

I find bread in the freezer and Cheez Whiz in the back of the Clarks' fancy new refrigerator. I've just settled the grilled cheese sandwiches into the pan when I notice photos tacked to the side of the fridge. That's new. I checked for family pictures that first summer. I wanted to see just how oblivious I'd been to who Felix really was, but there were none. At the very least, I wasn't that clueless.

The only photo of the Clarks that Bridget had on display when we lived together was a framed picture on her dresser, taken when she and Felix were children. But during that earliest visit, I forced her to give me a guided tour through the family albums Christine keeps in the TV room, so I've seen some of the ones on the fridge before. Class pictures and snapshots of family reunions and sandcastle competition winners. The Clark siblings at various ages. Bridget has looked like Bridget since she was a newborn, but Felix grew into himself. He was a wrinkly red baby with a thatch of dark hair. I know he cried nonstop—that's how he got his nickname. The howling wolf. He was a bright-eyed boy, a bit on the small side, and a cocksure teen, one of those guys who skipped the awkward phase and went straight to heartthrob. There's one of him and Bridget in their bathing suits, arms around each other. It's not from that long ago—Felix has a beard.

You need to study Felix and Bridget closely to see the resemblance—the neatly sloped nose they got from their mom, the square jaw from their dad—but it's there. They share more than excellent faces with their parents, though. The Clarks feel like they belong to each other in a way that I admire and envy. Each is unique. Christine is the bluntest. Bridget, the most orderly. Ken is the peacemaker. Felix the rock. But they're all very Clark-like. Self-actualized. Resilient. Physically affectionate. Steadfast.

It's a different family from the one I grew up in. My mom, the dentist—precise, skeptical. My dad, the mortgage broker—practical, stern. They have none of the Clarks' sense of fun. Our life was routine. Cereal for breakfast, chicken for dinner. Evening news and prime-time sitcoms. Shuffling to and from arenas for my brother's hockey games. Lyle is six years older than me, and while my brother and I look alike—deep blue eyes, straight noses, thick heads of reddish-brown hair, good cheekbones—we had nothing in common as kids. A whole evening could pass with hearing my dad say little more than a few sentences. It wasn't a terrible childhood, but it was quiet, and I was often lonely.

Aunt Stacy *felt* like family, like pieces of me came from her. She was the antithesis of my mother—exuberant and fashionable and full of stories from her acting days. She was steadfastly single, but her heart was open. Bridget was a homesick twenty-two-year-old when I introduced her to Stacy, and my aunt scooped her up, fed her take-out Italian, and turned our duo into a trio.

I flip the sandwiches, and then go back to the photos, gawking at Felix's bare chest. Maybe that's why it takes me another minute to see that I'm on the fridge, too. I haven't seen this one before. Bridget and I are in the living room, and the Trivial Pursuit board is on the coffee table. We're on the couch laughing, both of us in sweaters. It was taken the year I came for Thanksgiving. Felix is in the photo, sitting in the armchair, his eyes clamped on me. My legs bristle with goose bumps, and then I hear the floorboards shift.

"What's that smell?" Bridget says.

I sniff.

That smell is burnt cheese.

AFTER OUR SIX O'CLOCK DINNER OF BLACKENED GRILLED cheese sandwiches and gherkins, Bridget and I sit on the deck, watching the birds flit through the trees. Bridget is wearing her dad's HISTORY IS NOT BORING T-shirt and a pair of leggings she describes as lovingly worn but are actually more hole than pant. She has no time for fashion, and her design sense is atrocious. She once tried her hand at flower arranging, and when I asked whether she was color blind, she thought I was joking. Every so often, she sends me photos of bouquets she thinks I'll like. They're terrible, and I love them.

Wind tinkles through the chimes. I don't know when they arrived, but they bother me. All I want to hear when I'm at Summer Wind are the breeze and the birds.

A strong gust sends the chimes into a tinny tizzy, and Bridget jumps up to remove them from the hook.

"I hate these things," she says.

"The worst."

"I'll be back in a sec," Bridget says, stepping inside.

The ceramic toad watches me with bulging eyes while I wait. "Don't look at me like that," I grumble.

My mind, the wretch, sneaks upstairs to Felix's bedroom and back to our first night together. It feels like a lifetime ago, as if we were two other people. Sometimes I wonder if I was willfully ignorant. I didn't see the toad, but there were other clues. The fact that his parents were out of town. The impeccable flower beds—I knew Christine was an avid gardener. The piano that featured heavily in Bridget's family legends. There was a bottle of my favorite vinho verde lying on the bottom shelf of the fridge that her parents had bought for us, but I didn't spot it. Maybe if I had, I would have clued in. Or maybe not.

It's cooling off quickly, and Bridget returns with a blanket from the steamer trunk, the bag of peanuts, and the bottle of rye, which she sets on the coffee table between flickering citronella candles after pouring us each a glass. Bridget's alcohol tolerance is almost zero, and I doubt she slept better than I did last night. She'll put herself to bed before the sun sets.

"What's with the photos on the fridge?" I ask as she takes a seat at the other end of the sofa.

Christine had a thing against hanging family pictures. "I know how beautiful my children are. I don't need to announce it to the world," she told me the first summer I stayed here.

Bridget shrugs a shoulder. "My mom's gone soft in her retirement. I used to think she loved horses more than people. But she really misses us, even though Wolf visits all the time." She observes me over her glass. "Did you see the photo of you and me?"

"I did." I take a sip. "I can't believe that was only two years ago. We look so much younger."

She hums. "Did you notice Wolf ogling you?"

"What? No," I say too quickly.

"What's up with you two?" She's yawning when she asks, so it sounds casual, but every inch of me stiffens.

"What do you mean?" I've come close to telling Bridget a sanitized version of my history with Felix more than once. A few years ago, I'd resolved to come clean immediately after a visit to the island, but then a week passed, and another, and it didn't seem urgent to tell her. The excuses for keeping my hookups with Felix a secret stacked up. But when I got back from PEI last summer, I was determined to do it once and for all. I made a dinner reservation at a nice restaurant so she wouldn't lose it in public. I drank several glasses of wine, but by the time the bill came, I still hadn't mustered the courage. This won't be the first time I've chickened out.

"I can tell something's going on," Bridget says. "He barely looked at you today and—" She waves her arm around the deck.

"And what?"

"He's not here. He's usually within five feet when you're around."

"He's busy at the cottages."

In my weakest moments, I read the online reviews, scanning for mentions of Felix. There's one, written by a woman named Nova Scarlet from last fall, saying the "hot caretaker and his tight white tees" were the highlight of her trip. She put a winky face emoji at the end of the sentence. I've spent a lot of time wondering what it implied.

Bridget gives me a dubious look, then throws back the rest of her whiskey, coughs, and refills her glass. For her, this is excessive.

"So I have an idea," she says.

"Uh-oh."

"A fucking brilliant idea," she clarifies.

"I'm terrified and intrigued. Continue."

"I think we should go full PEI."

"And what does that involve? Fiddle lessons from your grand-dad? Jumping off Covehead Bridge? Eating all the seafood?"

"Definitely. That's always been rule number one."

"Eat our weight in *oysters* is rule number one."

"Oh, we'll be doing that. Wolf's shucking in Tyne Valley in two days. We're going, and you'll love it."

Felix competes at the national oyster-shucking championship every year. I've never been here to witness it, but I know he's good. He came first place in the junior division when he was seventeen. It's not hard to believe. I know what he can do with his hands.

"And if I can't pressure Wolf into staying here, he'll spend the night Sunday," Bridget goes on. "It's too far to drive back to his place after the contest."

My brain goes straight to Felix first thing in the morning. Sleepy eyelids. Pillow creases. Pajama pants. Honey in his tea and on his lips.

"Wait," I say, batting the images away. "Did you just say Sunday? I was thinking we'd fly back Sunday night."

"Wolf will be offended if you don't go."

I doubt that.

"I'll be offended, too," Bridget adds.

I sigh. If I get back first thing Monday, it'll be fine. I'll be harried, but I'm used to harried.

"Okay," I say. "You win. We'll go to the shucking thing, which means we've got oysters covered."

"Then there's rule two, obviously," Bridget says. "We leave the city behind. For the rest of the week, we do all the greatest hits. Sandcastles. Seafood. Lighthouses. Coastal drives. No wedding talk. No work talk. We pretend like we're twenty-four again."

On that first trip, Bridget and I bopped around Prince Edward Island in a rental sedan, singing at the top of our lungs. It was our first time driving together—neither of us had a car in the city—and she took me to all the big tourist spots. Green Gables, the black-and-white-striped West Point Lighthouse, a hike in PEI National Park, a feast at New Glasgow Lobster Suppers. I kept a strict seafood-only diet when we dined out, gorging myself on lobster rolls, oysters, mussels, chowder, and fish and chips. I tried (and failed) to find a piece of sea glass by the shore.

It's not like Bridget to be so nostalgic, and the *no wedding talk* provision doesn't escape me, but she hates feeling backed into a corner, so for now, I let it slide. I should be able to figure out how to crack her in the next forty-eight hours.

"We've never really committed to the full Lucy Maud Montgomery experience," I say. "Maybe we should get Anne and Diana wigs. Straw hats. Raspberry cordial. Take a carriage ride in pinafores."

"No fucking way. But I'll allow a trip to Green Gables."

"Really?" We went there during my first visit, but I would have gone back multiple times if Bridget hadn't vetoed me. I keep my map of PEI in a glass-sided box on my desk at home. I've circled the places Bridget and I visited, keeping track of what I wanted to see next time. Anticipating the island was almost as sweet as being here.

Sometimes I unfold the map and run my finger along the eastern edge of the island, over the shore where Salt Cottages stand, over the area slightly inland where Felix lives. A cabin nestled among pines and apple trees, a pond under their branches.

"Really." She unfolds the wool blanket so it covers both our laps. The Clarks have the best blankets. "One last girls' trip. We'll make it count."

I huff out a laugh. "You're getting married, not dying. We have our whole lives for girls' trips."

Her smile falters, and my stomach drops.

"Bridget. You're not sick, are you?" It happened so fast with my aunt. One day, she and I were having brunch in her garden. The following Tuesday, she was in the hospital. Four weeks after that, she died.

"No." Her hair is piled in a messy bun, and it wobbles when she shakes her head. "Of course not." She scootches across the couch and wraps an arm around me, leaning her head on my shoulder. "I'm sorry, Bee," she says, knowing where my fear comes from.

After the funeral last summer, Bridget put me on a plane to PEI. I blame what happened—the way my feelings for Felix seemed to explode out of nowhere—on my emotional state. Grief-stricken. Recently dumped. I'd been so tender.

But I don't need to worry about Bridget's health. She's not sick. Her family is well. I know she loves her job, and her co-workers love her back. The bridal shower her boss held was outrageously elaborate. That leaves only one explanation.

"Things with you and Miles: You're sure everything's okay there?"

"Uh-huh."

"Hmm." It's not exactly convincing.

"I just missed my parents and the island," she says. "And I've been stressed about the wedding. I need a break. Some fun."

Interviewing wedding vendors, collecting RSVPs, preparing a run-of-show for the day itself—that *is* Bridget's idea of fun. And I know, because her nuptials have monopolized most of our conversations since Miles proposed ten months ago.

She came to the store after closing to show me the ring. Miles works in real estate development, and he picked a diamond that proved it. I *ooh*ed and *aah*ed, because that rock is stunning, and then dug out the emergency bottle of vinho verde I keep in the flower cooler.

"It's not a lot of time to plan," Bridget had said, grinning broadly. "I can't fucking wait."

No one shivers with pleasure at the words *tight work-back schedule* the way Bridget does. So I don't buy for a second that she's stressed, or that she needs "some fun." It's like we've been cast in a play, where Bridget and I have been made to switch roles. She's supposed to be the adult in our relationship. I'm the one who runs away from my problems. I can't decide whether to be concerned about her or annoyed. Scratch that, I can be both.

"You know I rescheduled a really important meeting to be here," I say. "I'm pretty sure my contact at Cena knows she's handing me a golden egg and thinks I'm flighty for rescheduling. Not to mention I'm doing the flowers for *your* wedding in eight days."

"I'm sorry to inconvenience you," she says, suddenly snippy.

I hate fighting with Bridget. I'm not good at it, and she's exceptional. My thoughts turn mushy, and I end up forgetting why we're arguing in the first place. So even though this trip *is* a major inconvenience, I back down. Bridget needs me, even if I don't know why. And she'd be there for me. Without question.

"You're not," I say. "I love you more than anyone. You know that. I just have a lot going on."

"I know you do."

We're quiet for a full minute before she says, "We can't forget about the third rule."

"I would never."

"I might have been a little oversensitive when I came up with that one," Bridget says with a dry laugh.

What an understatement.

"Nevertheless," I say. "I think it's best if we keep that one in place."

Rule number three: Don't fall in love with her brother.

9

Now

I sit on the deck after Bridget goes to bed, watching the sky turn pink over the ocean, wondering if it's possible we won't be celebrating her wedding in a week. I've been looking forward to it. Yes, it feels like the end of an era, but your best friend only gets married once. Ideally.

The Gardiner Museum is an elegant venue, and Bridget and Miles specified a "black tie" dress code on their letterpress invitations, sealed them with *B&M* stamped in wax, but there's no way the event will be as stiff as the stationery.

I've spent enough time with the Lams to see why Bridget loves them. They moved to Canada from Australia when Miles was a teenager, and they share the Clarks' dry sense of humor, high volume setting, and lack of pretension. The combination of the Clarks of Prince Edward Island and Miles's raucous Aussie relatives will make for a fun night.

There'll be an open bar and a fiddle and a food truck with lobster rolls later at night. The dinner is eight courses, Cantonese dishes carefully selected by Miles. All I know is that it involves roast suckling pig, so I'm in. I've already written my speech. I've memorized the opening lines so I can look at Bridget as I say them.

The first time I met Bridget Clark, she gave me a ride home on her handlebars. In many ways, she's carried me since that night seven years ago.

I plan to make my best friend weep. Assuming the wedding's still on.

I lift the blanket to my nose, taking a deep whiff. The steamer trunk is lined with cedar, and the Clark blankets have a distinct Clark blanket smell. I'd bottle it if I could. The sea, the grass, citronella candles, and wool blankets from the cedar-lined chest—the perfume of Summer Wind.

I give Farah a call to check in. She tells me our part-timers were thrilled to pick up extra shifts while I'm away, and to leave her "the eff alone."

"You haven't taken a vacation in forever. I'm sick of you," she says. I haven't taken time off since last summer, and I haven't come up for air since. Work. Work. Bridget's wedding. Work. Work. Work.

"Well, I'm not sick of you."

She scoffs. "Maybe you could have found a real date for the wedding if you didn't spend all your waking hours with a pair of floral shears in your hand."

Farah claims weddings are gross, but she's coming with me, and I've long known she has a caramel center under her spiked shell. I love her, but she's right: I didn't have anyone else to bring to the wedding. It used to be that Bridget was my favorite person, but now she's my only person outside my staff. In the past year, I've been so caught up with work, I've let my friendships dissolve. My sex life, too.

"You are a real date," I tell her.

"I won't grope you on the dance floor, so no, I'm not. It's a waste of your hot dress."

It is hot. I've chosen something more Bond girl than usual—dark and slinky with a slit up one thigh and a high halter neck—I wasn't sure how I'd react to seeing Felix in formal wear, or whether he was bringing a date, but I knew I'd be as bright as a poppy.

"All clothing makes a statement," my aunt used to say. "And I like mine to speak loudly." Stacy was never without a red lip and a hit of red on her body. She owned precisely one children's book that she'd read to me at bedtime when I slept over as a child. *Red Is Best.*

If my dress could talk, I'm pretty sure it would say, "Let's find a dark corner and do bad things."

"Do not sneak roses into the Mendoza bouquets," I say to Farah, changing the subject.

"They're going to look floaty."

She tells me to stop worrying and to say hello to Bridget, which, in Farah-speak, is akin to a profession of love.

I tiptoe upstairs after the call, avoiding the creaky step that's second from the top—if Bridget is sleeping, I don't want to wake her. My suitcase is a jumble, but I find my nightgown right away. It's an ankle-length white cotton number with a ruffle around the bottom and simple embroidery at the neck. It's weirdly in keeping with the new vibe of Felix's former bedroom.

With the blanket and another finger of rye, I cozy up on the outdoor sofa and open my texts. I have to scroll far down to find the conversation I'm looking for. You can't call our messages a chain, because there are only four. I sent the first one to Felix a year ago. His reply came two days later.

Me: Sorry, I missed you. Thanks again for everything!

Felix: Always a good time.

Me: Back to real life 😭

Felix: 👍

A yellow thumbs-up. The universal conversation ender.

I'd told myself it was a good thing.

As the last blush leaves the sky and the horizon disappears into twilight blue, headlights shine on the side of Ken's work shed. My arms pebble. My skin knows.

I walk along the side of the house to the driveway as Felix's pickup slows to a stop. He takes something from the rear seat and comes around the truck, carrying an armful of groceries. Felix Clark, the most considerate man I know. He stops when he sees me.

His gaze rakes over me from head to bare toe. Despite the cool breeze, it heats me through. I've braided my hair into two plaits like I often do before bed. It's me at my least sexy, but Felix has seen it before.

"You look like an olden-days ghost," he says, eyeing my nightgown, though Felix never had a problem with the nightgown.

"Can I help?" I hold out my hands, but he moves toward the house. "Wine's on the passenger side," he says, without looking my way.

I walk to the truck as Felix heads inside. I open the door, and my heart leaps like a rambunctious, poorly trained puppy. On the seat is a paper bag with two bottles of my favorite vinho verde and an overnight bag.

Felix Clark has come to stay at Summer Wind.

10

Now

Felix is crouched in front of the fridge, stowing lemons in the produce drawer. I set his bag and the wine on the table, temporarily mesmerized—the broad shoulders, the muscles shifting under his T-shirt. I watch as he continues filling the fridge—strawberries, peaches, red leaf lettuce, green beans, shallots, Brie, cream cheese, eggs, bacon, and a pink package of Cows Creamery cultured butter. I can't get it in Toronto, and Felix knows how much I love it.

My heart is a monster, filling at the sight of it. But I know how easy it is to mistake Felix's thoughtfulness for deeper feelings.

"Wine," he says. I hand him the bottles. "They're not cold. Do you want one in the freezer for tonight?"

"No, we already got into your dad's rye."

"And the peanuts?"

"Of course."

Felix doesn't move. He stays like that, staring at a carton of milk. I can almost hear him calibrating what to say next.

"Bridget sent herself to bed a while ago," I offer.

He stands and turns to face me, stuffing his hands into his pockets. "Sounds about right."

"Thank you for bringing all this."

"You're welcome." His eyes fall to the pink ribbon at the neck of my nightgown; his jaw tightens.

"You got my butter." This feels significant, worthy of pointing out. This is why it's so hard to keep myself in check around Felix. He's not just handsome; he's *good*.

"I did. I figured you and Bridget probably spent the afternoon out walking."

"Thunder Cove. How did you know?"

His gaze finds mine. It's dark. A tropical storm charting its course across my face. "I've known you for five years now, Lucy. You'd pick adventure and fresh air over a grocery store run every time."

It could be the rye or the way he smells like the wind, but I'm certain he's even more devastating than he was last year. The beard did it for me, but the full force of Felix's face is ruthless. His jaw could have been cut with an X-Acto knife. I want to smooth my hand over his cheek, trace the contours of his chin. I want to map Felix's temples and nose with my palm so I can keep the sight of him folded in a glass box in my apartment and take it out when I miss it.

Nope. Nope. No. These thoughts are not helpful.

"So you're staying?" I ask.

"I'm staying. That okay with you?"

Absolutely not. "Absolutely."

A weekend of Felix. I can do that. I'll just have to ignore how my pulse races when we're in the same room and stop picturing the teapot-shaped birthmark on his inner thigh. I can pretend I don't want to twist my body around his like climbing ivy. Simple.

"It's your home, not mine," I tell him. "It'll be fun, the three of us together again."

"Fun." His eyes are fastened on mine in a way that makes me feel stripped bare.

I shift my weight, pink climbing from my neck to my cheeks. "Not like that. That's not what I mean."

"No?" Felix looks at me like he can see right down to the marrow. I pick up a dish cloth and begin wiping down the sink.

"Of course not."

I feel him watching, but I'm intent on scrubbing.

"Lucy." The way he says my name. It's velvet. It's chocolate. It's dirty sex in the bathroom upstairs.

I wipe harder.

Felix moves to my side, his hip leaning on the counter. I think he runs hotter than other men. I can feel the heat radiating from him. "That sink is spotless."

I squeeze out the cloth and dry my hands on one of Christine's new linen tea towels. When I finally lift my gaze to his, it's searing. As entrancing as it is perilous. Felix is a whirlpool, and if I'm not careful, I'll get sucked in. This has been my longest dry spell, so I'm at a disadvantage. I used to be a serial dater. I liked the early days. The getting-to-know-you part, the rush of the first kiss. The thrill of being desired and discovered. But I've gone twelve months without even a kiss. Maybe that's why Felix seems even more smoldery.

"I'm here for Bridget." I'm talking to Felix, but I'm reminding myself.

"Right," he says. "I'm here for Bridget, too."

I know that. Just like I know there's no way I undo Felix the way the mere sight of his hands unravels me.

I nod once and begin to back away. "Good."

Space. Ice-cold showers. Focus on my best friend. Forget all the things I like about Felix that have nothing to do with the way he looks. That's how I'll get through this weekend.

"I'm going to go to bed," I say. "I'll move my suitcase out of your room. I can sleep with Bridget."

I've climbed two stairs when Felix says, "Keep your stuff where it is. I'll crash on the pull-out in the TV room." Our eyes meet across the house, and even from that distance, a zap of electricity passes between us. "You sleep well in that bed from what I remember."

I BRUSH MY TEETH, BUT WHEN I LIE DOWN, THE NIGHT I went to him plays behind my eyelids. Felix above me, his hand on my mouth. Even with the window open, it's stifling in this room. Or maybe it's me. This damn bed. "Sleep well" my ass.

I creep to the bathroom and splash my face in the dark. I fill a glass and take a long sip, when the door opens, and a broad body strides inside. I spin fast.

"Shit that's cold."

I've spilled water everywhere, including on Felix.

"You surprised me," I say, grabbing a hand towel, dabbing it over his chest, which is very bare and very warm and very hard. I shove the towel at him. "Here, you do that."

"I didn't realize you were in here. Why is the light off?" He flicks it on.

Felix's chin is lowered to his chest, drying himself off, so he doesn't witness my jaw dropping at the sight of him. He's wearing only underwear. Boxer briefs. White. I take in the sculpted muscles, the flat stomach, the grooves of his hips, the line of dark hair that dips into his waistband. Lower. It's not the first time this bathroom has given me problems.

There's water all over the floor. I reach for another towel, and crouch down, sopping it up. But I'm right in front of Felix's bedrock thighs and teapot birthmark. That's where I'm staring when he says, "Can I help you, Lucy?"

My eyes jerk upright. Felix stares down at me, gaze heating, so still I'm not sure he's breathing. I get to my feet faster than I ever have in my life, and slip. Felix has me before I fall, one large hand on my elbow, the other on my lower back. He's hauled me close to keep me steady, and our lower halves are crushed together. Through my nightgown, I can feel how hot his skin is. His smell is everywhere. We stare at each other, my nails digging into his shoulders. The way my body demands his feels almost primal.

More, it says. *Felix.*

I'm literally panting. There's no way he doesn't notice. But he's not unaffected. I can feel him growing hard against me. My eyes widen at the press of him, and his go black, his pupils swelling. It would be so easy to give in to it. This desire that comes from a place I don't recognize, a place that isn't accessible to me unless I'm with him. But I can't be that reckless.

I clear my throat, and Felix blinks. His hands fall from my body; mine drop from his shoulders. We separate. He turns his head to the side, running his fingers through his hair.

"That was . . ." He doesn't finish.

"I'm gonna . . ." I gesture to the hall.

"Lucy." My name is gravel on his tongue. "Let's—"

But I shake my head and brush past him, hurrying back to the bedroom.

I lean against the door, taking deep breaths. But I need more than a piece of pine on hinges between me and Felix.

I need a football field.

Provinces.

A whole damn country.

But I'm not sure that would even work. Somehow, I always find my way back.

PART TWO

Everything that's worth having
is some trouble.

—L. M. Montgomery, *Anne of Avonlea*

11

Summer, Four Years Ago

I was twenty-five, and life was perfect. Bridget and I were both thriving at work. She'd been in the PR department of Sunnybrook Hospital for a year and had already been promoted to a more senior role, and I was killing it at the flower shop. My aunt had let me take over the bridal consultations, and she'd hired Farah, who was as fascinating as she was terrifying. I adored her. My parents' inquiries into when I was going to get a *real job* had been reduced from a weekly to monthly frequency. We'd given our apartment a glow-up, courtesy of Bridget's larger paychecks and a set of vintage wishbone dining chairs I'd found on a street corner. Three of my friends had sworn off dating apps, but I was on algorithmic fire. There was no one serious, but I didn't want serious. I took after my aunt—cocktails, conversation, and a bit of fun were all I was looking for.

Then, one evening, Stacy took me to her office, pulled out the pair of crystal wineglasses she kept in her bottom desk drawer, and a bottle of chianti. She was closing In Bloom at the end of the year. Business was good, but she wanted freedom to travel more, maybe volunteer at a community theater. In her words: "I'm going to enjoy my life while I'm still young and gorgeous." (Stacy was sixty, and she *was* gorgeous.) She knew a florist in Rosedale who would be happy to hire me, but I loved In Bloom. I didn't want to work anywhere else. "If there's one thing I can teach you, Lucy," Stacy said as I sobbed into my wine, "it's to live your life fully, to live it for yourself and no one else. I know how much you love this place, but I have to do what's right for me, just as you have to do what's right for you."

I cried my entire streetcar ride home, and then into Bridget's curls.

She called her mom that night. "I think Bee needs some fresh air," I heard her say. "I'm going to bring her home."

My aunt paid for the ticket.

I wasn't worried about seeing Felix again. There had been plenty of guys in the year since. Yes, I thought about that night sometimes, but we had our rules. It was a one-time thing, and I already felt weird about keeping something from Bridget. Now that I knew who Felix was, I wasn't going to repeat my mistake.

He picked Bridget and me up at the airport. I saw him as soon as we stepped off the tarmac and into the arrivals lounge. He was leaning against the cow statue, a book in one hand, a giant smile breaking across his face like a wave when he saw us.

Felix greeted Bridget with a hug and me with a wink. On the drive to Summer Wind, he was animated, telling us about the piece of land he and his best friend, Zach, were planning to buy.

I had intended to keep my distance from Felix, but over the next few days, when he wasn't watching, I studied him, tracking all the ways he'd changed. He was more confident, with newfound swagger, but I couldn't tell if it was for show or not. And he'd grown a short beard. Even though Bridget had told me about it, I couldn't have predicted how well it suited him, how it would have the effect of making his eyes shine brighter. My memory had failed to capture just how striking they were. He was thicker through the chest and arms, and he seemed so much lighter. His smile unfolded with easy optimism like a patio umbrella, no trace of sadness. And every time my gaze found his, it was pure, undiluted electricity.

"Your brother seems happy," I said to Bridget on our third day.

She snorted. "That's because he's picking up tourists like it's a side hustle."

That explained the swagger.

"Really?"

"Oh yeah. Zach told me he keeps this list on his phone of his recommendations on where to go—restaurants, beaches, coffee shops, the blueberry ice cream from Cows—that sort of thing. His move is offering to text it to every pretty woman who walks into Shack Malpeque."

I was familiar with the list, though I didn't end up getting it from him last summer. "That's kind of genius," I said. "And helpful."

"Mom and Dad say he's barely spent a night here since Canada Day. I mean, I'm glad he's moved on, but . . ." Bridget shuddered.

Twenty-four-year old Felix was hot shit, and he knew it. Twenty-four-year-old Felix was a hazard to be avoided at all costs.

But it wasn't easy.

Christine and Ken didn't chart their every move like their daughter, but there was a chore calendar. Felix and I were assigned to share grocery shopping and dinner duty for three days. We took the Mustang to the store together, and I studiously ignored how his big hand gripped around the gear shift.

I squealed when I saw the bubblegum pink package of Cows

Creamery butter in the dairy isle. It had a cartoon bovine and a map of Prince Edward Island on it. Ridiculously cute.

"I don't know what cultured butter is, but I need this in my life."

Felix extended his hand, and I placed it in his palm. "I can make that happen."

We were preparing pork chops, potato salad, and green beans when Christine saw me using a steak knife to trim the beans. She handed me an enormous chef's knife and told Felix to teach me how to use it. He stood behind me, with his hands over mine, demonstrating how to curl my fingers to keep them safe, until Bridget came into the kitchen and barked, "Get off my friend, Wolf."

Felix laughed, and I dropped the knife, red-faced.

Then I drew his name from a hat as my partner for the annual Clark family sandcastle competition. The extended family descended on Summer Wind for the tradition, with the winning duo manning the grill at the barbecue that followed (a classic Clark prize if there ever was one). When the meal was finished and the bonfire lit, Bridget and Felix's grandpa would bring out his fiddle.

I spent two hours kneeling beside Felix on the beach, watching him form towers and moats with the sand. When my drawbridge threatened to collapse, he cupped his hands over mine so we could save the thing together. But for untold seconds, neither of us moved. We were in wet bathing suits, the August sun blazing hot against our skin. A smattering of goose bumps prickled my arms, and Felix's fingers flexed against mine. I turned my head. Our eyes met, inches apart. The jolt, electric.

"Thanks. I almost lost it," I said, voice catching in my throat.

Felix smiled. I couldn't see the dimple, but I knew it was there, lurking beneath the beard. "I've got you."

I only realized I'd leaned closer when his gaze flicked to my mouth, and I snatched my hands back so fast, the drawbridge crumbled, taking the front of the castle with it. We came in last place, which seemed fitting since I was also losing my resolve where Felix was concerned.

Bridget and I were leaving in two days. I could make it two more days.

I SAT AT THE CLARK KITCHEN TABLE THE NEXT MORNING with my head on its surface.

"Too much rye last night, Lucy?" Christine's voice cut through the fog of my hangover.

"We told her to eat the peanuts," Bridget said.

"Oh, big mistake, Ashby," Ken said from somewhere. He was an attractive man, bearded and fit, with chestnut hair, dark probing eyes (Felix got his blues from his mom), and a gentle manner. "The peanuts are key."

"I know that now," I said to the table. We had spent the night sitting around the bonfire, dousing ourselves with bug spray and whiskey. Before Ken and Christine went to bed, I had delivered an impassioned, hiccup-punctuated speech about how much I was going to miss In Bloom—the doorbell, the elderly woman who stopped in every Friday morning to buy herself a fresh bouquet, the buzz of seeing a space brought to life with flowers. I'd never unload like that in front of my own parents.

I felt at home with the Clarks. They didn't care about a bit of sand trampled in the house. They spoke over one another. They teased. They asked a lot of questions, and Bridget's mom told you if she thought your answer was horse shit. Literally. "That sounds like horse shit to me," was one of her catchphrases.

"I hope you've learned that there's no use working yourself into this state over your job," Christine said.

I peeled my forehead off the table. "Maybe," I mumbled to Christine.

I hadn't told my parents yet. I could already hear my dad, "It's a sign, Lucy Goose—time to get a real job." To my parents, that meant a salary and a cubicle, but I didn't want that. I wanted In Bloom.

"Right now, it feels fresh," Christine said. "But setbacks can be chances if you look at them from the right angle."

"Sounds like horse shit to me," Bridget said, sending her mother a mocking smile.

"That's not horse shit—that's the truth. Opportunities don't fall in your lap because you want them to. You have to work to make them happen."

I took a sip of coffee. It sounded smart, but I was too queasy to figure out why.

Felix, who'd been listening without weighing in, rose from the table and returned with an ibuprofen and a glass of water.

"Thought you might need these," he said, placing them on the table in front of me. Lightning blue eyes met mine. My stomach flipped.

One more day. I could make it one more day.

12

Summer, Four Years Ago

"Bee, if you don't stop jiggling your leg, I'll tie it to a cement block." Bridget tore the husk off a corncob. "You're shaking the entire deck."

"Sorry. Sorry." My mind was a train station at rush hour. I was working up the courage to put sound to an idea so outlandish, I was nervous to voice it. I knew what my parents would say if I broached it with them. "Too risky." And I knew what Bridget would say. But being on Prince Edward Island, away from the stuffed streetcars and high-rises and noodle containers that decorated my everyday life in Toronto, made unlikely dreams seem less far fetched.

Bridget and I sat side by side on the steps, the platter of shucked corn resting between us.

"I'm thinking about asking my aunt if she'd let me take over In Bloom," I said, plucking silvery threads from sunny kernel strands.

"Whaaat?" Bridget grabbed me by the shoulders, sending the corn tumbling onto the grass. "Tell me everything. How long have you been thinking about this? Bee! This is amazing." Her cheeks were pink, her freckles darkened by the sun. She looked like part of the island—someone born of soil and sea and wind. So beautiful, my best friend.

"You think so? I'm twenty-five. I've never run a business. I've never hired anyone. Or fired anyone. The paperwork alone would be overwhelming." I pictured my aunt's bomb of an office. "I've been thinking about all the ways I could improve the shop and our online presence, but what if they don't work out? And taxes! What—"

Bridget sandwiched my cheeks in her hands, and I stopped talking.

"Breathe," she said.

I took a long inhale. "Do you really think I could do it?" I whispered.

"Yes! Of course! One thousand million billion percent! You *have* to do it." Her eyes were shining with glee. "You can do anything, Bee. And I'll help with the tax stuff and paperwork if you want."

Ugh. Bridget's faith in me was boundless. I really needed to stop eyeing her brother like I wanted to dip him in melted butter. I monitored her closely. "You'd do that?"

"Of course, you sweet potato. It will be fun for me. I love Stacy, but I'm sure her bookkeeping leaves room for improvement. We can talk to her about it at our next dinner. She will be thrilled."

Stacy had Bridget and me over for dinner most weeks. She couldn't cook, but she knew her way around a take-out menu.

Bridget shivered, giddy, then rubbed her palms together. "I've always wanted to get my hands on her office."

I fidgeted with the waist tie of my sundress.

"What's wrong?"

"My parents wouldn't be happy."

"Bee, your family sort of sucks," she said gently. "The way they treat you is not glaringly awful—they're just mildly shitty. It's almost worse because it's hard to recognize the ways they cut you down."

I took a deep breath. "I know."

"But do you?" Bridget asked as the sliding door opened behind us.

Felix was standing there, in a T-shirt and jeans, dressed the way he had been the day we met. I looked at him, and he looked at me, his smile vanishing into a frown.

"You okay?"

I took another deep breath. Other than the fact that Felix was reading me like an instruction manual, I *was* okay. I didn't need my parents' approval. I had Bridget. And Stacy. I smiled. "Yeah," I told Felix. "I'm good."

His lips curved, and my mind slipped back in time. His mouth on the moles beneath my collarbone. Mine on his inner thigh, tasting his birthmark.

"Mom bought four dozen Valley Pearls," Bridget said by way of greeting. "Bee's been given timing duties."

Felix was competing in an oyster-shucking contest in a few weeks' time and Christine wanted him to practice. It took place every year in Tyne Valley, and apparently it was a big deal.

"Oh yeah?"

"Your family's been bragging about you," I said. "I told them I didn't believe you could shuck as fast as they claimed without stabbing yourself."

His mouth inched up on one side. "I did well last year."

"Dad's already given her the full play-by-play," Bridget said. "Mom says you're clean, but not quick enough. I think it's an excuse—they're trying to feed us two weeks' worth of food in one night." After the oysters, a lobster boil, then two kinds of dessert: strawberry shortcake (my favorite) and blueberry-peach pie (Bridget's).

"Without question. We better get started. Think you can keep up, Lucy? Being a timer is a very important job." He looked right at me, eyes flaring like a warning signal. "You can't take your attention off me for a second."

I ignored the wave of heat spreading across my chest and tossed my hair over my shoulder. "You bet your shucking ass I can."

Bridget and Felix groaned.

"What?" I said. "I thought that was a good one."

"Your shucking puns are brutal, Bee. Please stop," Bridget said, picking up the scattered cobs of corn. She tossed one at her brother's head. "And *you* stop flirting with my friend."

I STOOD BESIDE FELIX IN THE KITCHEN, STOPWATCH APP at the ready. My eyes caught on the small silver scar on his wrist.

"Someone distracted me," he said, tapping his knife on the mark. I lifted my gaze to his. "It was worth it."

"She must have been cute," Bridget quipped from behind me.

He smiled at me. "The most gorgeous woman I've ever seen."

Danger. Danger. Danger.

I watched Felix shuck three dozen oysters. I stared at his bronzed hands, tracked the tendons in his forearms. I listened to the little grunts he made. After he'd finished, he passed me an oyster, and when his finger brushed against mine, I felt it low in my belly. I was so riled up, I spilled a tray of ice and shells down the front of my dress and darted upstairs to shower before dinner. I needed to collect myself.

One more night.

I'd just locked the bathroom door behind me when I realized I'd already packed my body wash in my suitcase. I wrapped a towel around myself, opened the door, spun into the hall, and ran straight into a solid wall. A wall that smelled like ocean and wind and pine. For a second, I stood frozen.

Felix's hands swept over my shoulders. "You all right?"

I kept my eyes on his chest. "Yep. Good. Thanks."

He chuckled, and the sound slipped down to my toes, warm as Ken's rye. His calloused palms moved slowly down my arms, leaving a trail of blazing skin in their wake. I remembered feeling that same scrape over my waist and thigh, pushing my legs apart.

His hands came to rest on my elbows, and my fingers found their way to his stomach. I lifted my chin as he lowered his. Our eyes collided. I stared into those blue pools, at that little smudge of brown, spellbound. Felix stepped closer, or maybe I did, until the entire front of my body was flattened against his. I moved my lips toward his, or maybe it was the other way around.

"Do you want this?" His voice was a rasp.

Ken's bellowing laugh sounded downstairs. I split apart from Felix, leaping back into the bathroom as the opening siren from Sloan's "Money City Maniacs" wailed from the stereo. Felix followed me right in.

I gaped at him. "You can't be in here."

"I can't?" He looked down to where my index fingers were hooked around his belt loops. I'd dragged him into the bathroom. I let go immediately. But instead of leaving, Felix shut the door, then stepped around me and turned on the hot water, letting the shower run. Steam began to fill the space.

"You shouldn't be in here," I said as he moved closer. "We have rules."

"I know we do." His eyes flicked to my lips, then to the three moles under my collarbone. "Otherwise things might be different."

I wiggled my towel higher up my chest. I didn't need to look to know it was redder than PEI dirt. "They would?"

"Otherwise, I would kiss you right now." His focus landed on my mouth once more. "And I think you would kiss me back. I think you were about to kiss me in the hall. I think you were thinking about it yesterday on the beach, too."

I lifted my chin. "So what if I was?"

The ends of Felix's hair were already curling in the steam, and I was fighting the urge to touch it. His eyes skated lower.

"So you'd kiss me back and then I'd unwrap that towel, and turn you around so you were holding on to the counter." He glanced at the vanity by the sink. A drip of condensation ran down the mirror.

My heart pounded wildly. There was a foot of humid air separating us, and I'd never been so turned on. "I hope you're not still dressed at this point."

The left corner of Felix's mouth hooked up. "Just socks."

I laughed, but it was frothy and nervous. I could barely feel my legs. My skin was growing slick from the steam.

"Do you want to know what would happen next?" His teeth skimmed over his bottom lip.

"Yes," I breathed.

"I'd pull your hips back, and put my hand between your thighs, and kiss the skin between your shoulder blades. And when you were close, I'd tell you to wipe the fog off the mirror so we could watch."

My gaze slunk down his body, snagging on the fly of his jeans. "If we do this, it's the only time."

Felix's eyes blazed. But he didn't reply.

"Wolf? We need to get it out of our systems, okay? Just this once."

His chest rose and fell. "I'll agree to that. I have one condition, though."

I nodded, businesslike, but I was squeezing my thighs together. "Let's hear it."

He stepped into me. His lips drifted over my ear. "When you come, I want you to call me Felix."

He drew back, opening my towel and dropping it on the floor. His eyes traveled the length of my body—the blush on my sternum, the curve of my breasts, the swell of my stomach and lower. He swallowed, then reached out, thumb brushing over a tight pink nipple.

We stared at each other for three long seconds, and then Felix's mouth was on mine, his hands cradling my face. The kiss was urgent, demanding, and when I ran my tongue over Felix's lip, a groan rumbled from his chest. I grabbed at the bottom of his shirt, pulling at it clumsily. His laugh tasted like salt and Tic Tacs. He tilted back, tugging the thing over his head. I saw the narrow trail of dark hair that ran over the smooth plane between his belly button and his waistband, but then his lips were back on mine, palms sweeping over my shoulders. He held them firm, then turned me around so I was facing the vanity. He swiped a hand over the steamed-up mirror, and our eyes met in the glass. We watched each other as he unfastened his jeans. I heard them hit the tile. I heard him open a foil packet.

His hand sailed over my rib cage. "Are you sure about rule two?" he asked, voice thick, fingers coasting down to my hip, my stomach. Lower.

"Right now, I have no idea which one that is."

A knee came between my legs, coaxing them farther apart. "Are you sure you don't want to do this again?"

A finger circled with the barest of pressure, and every nerve in my body assembled in the apex of my thighs. I closed my eyes. I felt swollen and heavy, and I wasn't sure. Not at all.

"Positive," I told him.

I felt Felix hot and hard against my backside as he pressed his lips to my ear. "I have another condition," he said, circling again, just a little harder.

"Okay," I breathed.

"Look at me." His fingers halted. I opened my eyes, finding Felix's in the mirror. "And hold on, Lucy."

13

Now

Seven Days Until Bridget's Wedding

Bridget is still in her room when I awake. I can hear her gentle snores through the door. When we lived together, she'd sleep in on weekends, and I'd sip my coffee to the tune of her little snorts. At first, I found her snoring hilarious, but after a few months, I stopped noticing it. The sound became the white noise of my Saturday mornings. I hadn't realized it before now, but I miss that sound. I miss our routines. Her Sunday evening ironing sessions. Our weekly treks to my aunt's house. Face masks, Thai takeout, and a movie—our Wednesday night plans for years. I miss the globby mashed bananas on toast she asked me to make for her when she was sick. So gross. I miss having someone to come home to.

I need a heaping dose of fresh air in my lungs and caffeine in my veins, so I fix myself a coffee and step onto the deck.

Felix is lounging outside with a mug of tea and a book, both legs flung over an arm of the chair, feet bare. He's wearing track pants and a T-shirt, and another version of Lucy peels away from me and drapes herself on his lap. The part of my brain that screams *more* whenever I'm near him hasn't faded overnight like I hoped.

"I'm sorry. I didn't know you were out here." I turn to go back in the house.

"Stay," Felix says, glancing up from the page. His stare is deadly in the daylight. He takes in my hair. I've let out the braids, and it falls in waves to just below my collarbone. And then my nightgown, which is sheer in the sun apparently. He swallows.

"I think we can handle being in the same room," he says, voice rough from sleep. "Or on the same deck."

Considering how we ended up pressed together in the bathroom last night, I'm not sure I agree. But it's better if Felix doesn't know that. So I curl into my usual spot at the end of the sofa and take a stab at normal adult conversation. I should be able to do this.

"What are you reading?" It's not the same book he had at the airport.

Felix holds it up. *Pride and Prejudice*. Is he kidding me?

"What?" he says.

If I didn't know Felix, I'd assume he was setting a thirst trap. But he's not aware his degree of hotness plus a Jane Austen novel is pornographic.

He swings his legs around and sits upright, facing me. He's so comfortable in his skin. You can see it in the ease of his movements. I remember the second summer I visited the island. Felix wore his confidence like a white tuxedo—a highly visible flex. I'd wondered if it was something of an act. But there's no faking the assured way Felix carries himself. There's no art to it. He's simply Felix. Genuine. Strong. True.

"You've read it before."

"I've read it more than once," Felix says. "I grabbed it when I was packing yesterday."

"How was the thriller?"

He gives me a look that's so plainly guilty, I'm already laughing before he says, "I didn't finish it."

"I knew it." His favorite book is *Great Expectations*, and he doesn't like gore.

"Joy gave it to me. She said I had to read it."

I don't even blink at the mention of Felix's ex. I'm a champion. "And?"

He hedges. "It wasn't bad. It just wasn't my thing."

"You're such a liar. You hated it." I love that I know his taste in books better than almost anyone.

"There were so many dead people," he says. "And body parts in cupboards, and sock drawers, and hot tubs." Felix's vibe is manly—the square stubble-covered jaw, the expanse of his shoulders. Even his fingers are hypermasculine, blunt at the ends—so when he shudders, it's in such contrast to his appearance that I laugh harder.

"So now you're soothing your mind with Elizabeth and Darcy."

He offers me a half grin. My heart squeezes at the sight of the dimple. I knew it was there, stowed away under his beard all this time, but I forgot how much I adore it. I could get lost in that crevice and never find my way out; it would be a good death.

"You got me," he says.

I do, I think. *I've got you.* A beat of silence passes, and I search his eyes for a sign that last summer meant more to him, that it wasn't just me who felt the ground shift, but all I see is a playful glimmer.

"Your sister must have perfected her guilt trip," I say. "What did she say to change your mind about staying?"

"She didn't say anything. I'm here because I want to be."

"You're worried about her?"

He gives me a long look. "Bridget's never really needed anyone to worry about her."

"I know, but that's why this is weird, right?" I gesture to myself and then him and then the deck. "This is not where any of us is supposed to be. She missed her final dress fitting. I canceled the bachelorette party I was supposed to throw tonight."

It was simple, and Bridget gave me explicit orders for what she wanted. Nosebleed seats at a Jays game followed by dinner at the Old Spaghetti Factory with a small group of her girlfriends.

"Our wedding is going to be chic as fuck," she'd said. "I want to drink beer and wear jean shorts at my bachelorette." She's been looking forward to it for months.

"She's not herself," I tell Felix.

"No, she's not." He takes a sip of his tea. Earl Grey with a spoon of honey and a squeeze of lemon. Both he and Bridget prefer it to coffee in the morning. "I tried talking to her on the way to pick you up at the airport, but she didn't give me anything. What has she told you so far?"

"Not much. Homesickness. Stress. She had a complete meltdown yesterday and said something about things slipping away, but nothing that makes sense. You know her—she hoards problems until she can solve them."

Felix nods and stares into his cup, then looks at me from beneath his lashes. "Do you think he did something?"

"Miles?" I take a deep breath, turning this question over yet again. If there's one thing I know about Miles Lam, it's that he's hopelessly in love with Bridget Clark. And I like Miles. He's been an unwaveringly good partner. He worships Bridget, supports her career, cleans up. He arranged a surprise trip to Australia for their anniversary. He asked her to book the time off work but wouldn't tell her where they were going, saving Bridget from going into vacation planning overdrive, as is her way. He makes heaps of money, but he never brags about it. And he's put up with endless shit from me.

Once, after two glasses of wine, I told him he'd stolen my friend and that I was jealous he spent more time with her than I did. It was supposed to be a joke, but it came out sour. Miles said that was the only logical response to having to share the best woman on the planet, and then he poured me more wine.

"I think this has to be about him," I say to Felix. "But I don't think Miles would cheat."

Felix runs a hand over his face. "Me neither."

Bridget and Miles's relationship progressed at warp speed. It happened exactly like I expected it would—Bridget fell fast and she fell hard. She came home after their third date and announced that he was the one. Miles was similarly smitten. Theirs was a straight path to marriage, a mortgage, and babies.

My aunt had her share of "lovers," but she never settled down. She didn't want to. Stacy believed in finding your own path to happiness, and hers didn't include a partner. But she was happy when Bridget found Miles—and thrilled that the fourth member of our family knew his way around the kitchen.

"If you don't marry him, I will," Stacy told Bridget after he'd made us a rack of lamb with herbed polenta. I'm pretty sure she was serious.

"I don't know what else it could be," I tell Felix. "Bridget has been obsessed with the wedding since they got engaged, and now she doesn't want to talk about it. She wants to explore the island and do all this touristy stuff, pretend like it's our first trip here together."

There's an asymmetry to Felix's face that I find captivating.

The lopsided smile and solo dimple. That speck of brown. Right now, a single eyebrow arches. "Oh yeah?"

"Ha, ha," I say. "Obviously not that."

"Obviously not." His eyes sparkle like they once did. "I'm not sure I can go three rounds in a night anymore anyway."

I almost spit out my coffee. It's funny, though I doubt it's true. Felix is laughing at my laughter, and for a short moment, it feels fantastic.

But then our eyes catch, and Felix's smile falls.

I can feel the way our energy shifts in the air, like the smell of rain in the distance. Felix's body runs hot, but it's the weight of his stare that has my chest heating. There's always been a charge between us, but this isn't the usual rush of desire or a flirty little glance. It's deeper than before, enthralling like a spell. Bedazzling.

The truth escapes my lips.

"I missed you."

Felix blinks, surprised. "Did you?"

"Of course," I tell him. "I want to—"

The sliding door opens, and Bridget steps out in flip-flops, a toothy grin, and a ratty terry cloth robe that has been hanging on the hook in her bedroom since she was a teenager.

"I had a feeling you wouldn't be able to stay away, Wolf."

She looks between the two of us. Felix is watching me. My mouth hangs open in the middle of what was going to be an apology for how I behaved last year. "What did I interrupt? Why are you two being weird?"

"We're not," I say.

She hums, surveying Felix and then me and then Felix again.

"You are," she says. Her eyes narrow, catlike, but before she can say anything else, Felix gets to his feet.

"I've got to get going."

"What?" Bridget says, her attention diverted. "I was thinking we could do the beach this morning, find Bee a lobster roll, and then maybe Green Gables Heritage Place in the afternoon."

"Can't," Felix says. "I'm not going to be around until tonight. I offered to pick up a shift at the restaurant."

"You still do that?" I ask.

"Not really," he says. "But I told them I was out this way if they needed help. And I could use the practice." Shucking, he means. The competition is tomorrow evening.

"In that case," Bridget says. "We'll stop in for lunch."

Felix nods at his sister, rubbing the back of his neck. "Great."

As he turns to go into the house, he looks over his shoulder at me, a question in his gaze.

Once he steps inside, Bridget spins on me. "You two *are* being weird."

I deflect. "*We* are being weird?"

"Did something happen last summer?" she asks.

Guilt rises in me like a tide. I hate lying to Bridget, but this is not the moment when I'm going to come clean. "Of course not."

"Hmm." Her gaze slits. "The Clark family theory is that Wolf made a move on you, and you turned him down."

"Is that so?"

"Yup. It would explain why he's not at your feet like usual."

I roll my eyes. "The Clark family," I tell Bridget, "needs to find a bigger island so they have something else to gossip about."

14

Now

Bridget decides she doesn't have patience for the tourists at Green Gables, and since she's craving an oat milk cappuccino, we take the Mustang down to Summerside. It's the largest city on the island after Charlottetown, which means it's still small—not quite 15,000 people. I call Farah from the car to check in, and both she and Bridget snipe at me to relax. I end our conversation quickly and text her all the things I remembered in the shower this morning.

When I look at the green and red out the window, I'm reminded of the first trip Bridget and I took here together. I fell hard for the island—both the beauty of the place and the warmth of its people. I fell harder for my friend, too. There were all these things I hadn't known about her—she loved to paddleboard, swelled up with every mosquito bite, could read sheet music, and knew how to knit a scarf. Her accent came on stronger when she was at home, too.

She seems brighter than she did yesterday, the circles under her eyes almost gone. Maybe I've been worrying needlessly. Maybe she really was homesick. When we first met, she missed her family and the island desperately. She was considering moving back home. Maybe all she needs now is the ocean and rest.

After we hit up the coffeehouse downtown, Bridget takes me on what can only be described as the Bridget Clark Nostalgia Tour. We drive past her old high school and the hospital where she volunteered as a teenager. Bridget wanted to be a doctor before her tendency to hit the floor when she saw blood had her rethinking her strategy. We visit the two-story Colonial where the Clarks lived before her parents bought Summer Wind, and the house where her first boyfriend's parents still reside. She parks on the curb opposite, and we duck low in our seats while she points out the treehouse where they went to second base.

"Where is he now?" I ask as we spy on the MacDonald home. I'm trying to gauge if Bridget's trip down memory lane will end with me talking her out of midnight-messaging her ex after she's gotten into the rye. My best friend is usually as predictable as a clock, but right now, I have no idea where her odd behavior will take us.

"He's still here, closer to Miscouche."

"Is he cute? Single?"

"Mmm . . ." she says. "I think he's divorced. Big guy. Beard."

"You could be describing a third of the men on this island." I look at her out of the corner of my eye. "Are you thinking of looking him up?"

"God no," she says. "We have nothing in common. And I doubt Miles would be thrilled about me getting in touch with my high school boyfriend days away from when we're supposed to get married."

"Supposed to?"

"Bad choice of words." She sits up and starts the car, the Mustang's thundering engine putting an end to our conversation.

I'd like to tackle her and force her to talk, but I know Bridget, and if I come on too strong, she'll go on the attack.

Our last fight wasn't that long ago. It was one of the few evenings recently where it was just the two of us, with no wedding-related crafting or planning involved. I'd brought a homemade caramelized onion and Brie dip to her condo, along with a fresh baguette and wine. Bridget refused to let any of it pass her lips, despite the fact that the dip was a personal triumph. She poured herself a vodka-soda, saying something about photographs and "feeling confident," and I scoffed. Bridget never needed help feeling confident. I launched into a tirade about unrealistic body standards, and as I scolded her, her face turned crimson. When Bridget gets mad, she looks like a pissed-off angel, and sometimes it's cute enough that it takes the steam out of my anger, but not that night.

"If you have to be a stick to walk down the aisle, I'm never getting married," I announced, with my hands on my hips. Not that I was looking to get married. My aunt's independence appealed to me far more than my parents' humdrum coexistence.

She pointed her finger at me. "You're never getting married because that would mean you'd have to care about someone more than you care about your job."

I'd stared at her in stunned silence, the statement sitting between us like a grenade. Despite my preference for casual relationships, I have had one long-term boyfriend. Carter. Who dumped me a year ago precisely because of my work.

Bridget apologized quickly. "I didn't mean it," she said, roping her arms around me. "I'm sorry. Carter was a potato. And you're right—diets are dumb, and I miss carbs. Let me try some of that dip."

But the truth of what she said about Carter stuck with me. I'd like to think he broke up with me because he wasn't secure enough to be with a career-minded woman, but some of the things he accused me of rang true. I was always running late. I was always on my phone, checking In Bloom's social media. I canceled plans if a venue had accidentally broken the centerpieces or if the bouquets had unexpectedly wilted.

Bridget started eating bread and cheese again after our fight, but it was one of the few times I've managed to change her mind. Usually our arguments end with me frustrated and saying a variation of, "I don't even know what we're mad about anymore."

I don't want to go down that road with Bridget now, but I can't ignore that there's something wrong. I'm nervous that the weekend will come and go, and I'll still be on this island without answers.

"If there's a problem, it might help to get it off your chest," I say to Bridget now. "I won't judge. I won't tell you what to do. I hope you know you can talk to me about anything." I realize she doesn't like getting advice from anyone ever, but sometimes it feels specific to me.

Bridget's distracted, her attention on the road, so it surprises me when she says, "I know, Bee. I trust you. More than anyone." But she doesn't say anything more.

My guilt fills the silence that follows. I'm such a hypocrite. There are things I haven't told her, too.

I TEXT WITH LILLIAN, MY CONTACT AT CENA RESTAURANT Group, on the way to Shack Malpeque until Bridget reaches across and takes the phone from my fingers.

"Your phone has been attached to your hand all morning. Unplug for a little while, okay?"

I was trying to set a new time for our meeting about the contract next week. This is a big opportunity that's on the line, and I'm worried I've started my relationship with Lillian on the wrong foot. Besides, Bridget's one to talk. She's been messaging all day, too. Presumably with Miles.

Bridget finds the last parking spot at Shack Malpeque. The restaurant looks over a bay that shimmers blue like it did the day I met Felix. There's a boat out at the mussel floats, two farmers inspecting the ropes. The parking lot is full, and so is the patio that looks over the water. But unlike the bay and the boats, it wasn't here five years ago, and the building is less shack-like than it used to be. It's had a fresh coat of sea blue paint, and there are window boxes planted with red impatiens.

But stepping inside is like traveling through a time portal. Suddenly I'm twenty-four, Bridget has missed her flight, and I'm fresh off an argument with my parents about leaving my PR job to work for my aunt.

Bridget takes my elbow, snapping me back to reality. "Oh good. There are spots at the counter." She points to the row of stools where Felix is working.

His head is tipped down and his hair topples over his forehead. With every twist of his knife, his forearms flex. And just like that, I'm thrown into the past again. When he glances up, his eyes find mine. For a fleeting slice of time, Felix looks at me almost like he did back then, with fire in his eyes, and my heart thuds happily in my chest. But then Bridget pulls out a chair, and the flame is extinguished.

Bridget orders mussels and I order lobster and shrimp tacos with French fries, and the three of us chitchat about vacations past while Felix pries open one oyster after another. Trivial Pursuit tournaments won and lost. The year Zach brought a diagram of how to replicate the Panmure Island Lighthouse to scale for the sandcastle competition. There's none of Felix's usual flirting. There's no teasing, no shimmery eyes. But when our gazes snag, I feel it like a shock—longing and heat and something else more treacherous.

Bridget is doing an impression of her grandma's failed attempt to teach me to square dance—"You don't just have two left feet, Lucy; you've got three!"—and Felix is chuckling. It strikes me how the two of them connect in a way I never have with my brother. It could be that Lyle is six years older, or it could be that we don't have shared interests. He's a dentist like my mom and a jock, and even though I love him, I also find him a little boring. His husband, Nathan—a chatty real estate agent with a Harry Styles obsession—is the most interesting thing about him. But unlike our parents, Lyle is vocally supportive of what I do.

Stacy believed she was the reason my parents didn't approve of my becoming a florist—that it was about her rocky relationship with my mom and not about job security, as they claimed. I suspect it was both. Over time, they've grudgingly accepted my career, but they're not exactly enthusiastic, and they don't attempt to mask their anxiety about my life as a florist. I try to brush their worrying off, but I've never managed to escape it entirely. It's Bridget I turn to when I need reassurance.

When the lunch rush passes and Felix's former boss hollers at him to take a break, Bridget and I relocate to the patio while he fixes himself something to eat. I send Lillian another message about our meeting.

Would Monday evening work?

If we fly out Monday, I could meet her later in the day. Otherwise I'll have to push it until next week to give myself enough time to prepare for Bridget's wedding on Saturday. *If* there's a wedding. Tension knots in my neck, and I rub my shoulder.

I close my eyes and try to enjoy the salt air, the rumble of boat engines, and my one-beer buzz. Bridget is similarly lizard-like. We stay that way until her phone rings. She frowns at the name on the screen, then looks to me.

"Take it," I say. "I'm happy sitting here on my own for a bit."

She exits the patio and makes her way toward the beach, out of earshot. She's facing the water, so I can't see her expression. I'm trying to read her body language when Felix sets a dozen oysters on the table, along with a basket of onion rings.

"So you don't have to watch me eat," he says, biting into a tomato and cheese sandwich. But I love watching Felix eat. Even his sandwich chewing is hot. Ugh. I'm the worst.

"Is she speaking with Miles?" Felix says, turning to look at Bridget.

We observe her for a minute. "I'm not sure."

I face Felix again, and there's an awkward pause. "I wanted to apologize to you," I tell him.

He sets his sandwich down, his focus on me fully. There's no feeling like it—the rush of holding his total attention.

"This morning on the deck, that's what I was trying to say." Felix is perfectly still, but his eyes sail across my face, waiting for me to go on. "I'm sorry for how I left last year. You were so good to me, and I didn't have a chance to thank you properly. Or say goodbye." I hold up my hands. "So this is me saying thank you."

He studies me for a moment, his gaze softening. "You're welcome, Lucy."

It feels good to clear the air. "I owe you big-time."

"You do." A smile creeps over his lips slowly. "A breakfast, if I remember correctly."

I look over his shoulder. Bridget is striding toward us.

Felix follows my gaze, and says, "You can pay me back later."

15

Now

I'm sitting in a Muskoka chair by the bonfire pit at Summer Wind, but instead of watching the setting sun cast the cliffs in an even more spectacular shade of red, I'm texting with Lillian about our meeting, away from Bridget's judgment. We're turning our expensive breakfast into expensive cocktails Monday evening.

I'm so looking forward to this, Lucy, she writes. Let's get this done!

So this is good news. Great news. I could double the business in a year. But there's that quiet, questioning voice. Can I handle that? Do I want to? Who is my success for?

I set my gaze on the horizon, where the sun is dropping quickly. It will take the warmth with it when it dips below the horizon.

"Live your life for you, and no one else" was one of my aunt's signature pieces of wisdom. But what if you aren't sure what you want? Or what a full life looks like? I wish I could ask her.

I return to the house, melancholy, but then Bridget waltzes into the kitchen. She tells me that Felix will be home soon with oysters. He needs to practice for the shucking competition to-morrow night, and he's invited Zach to help us eat them. She's wearing sweat shorts and a tank top. There's a mustard stain on her left boob.

"There's a mustard stain on your left boob," I tell her.

She looks at herself and shrugs. "Meh. It's only Wolf and Zach."

I met Zach on my first trip to the island. He'd introduced himself as Bridget's future husband and, when she wasn't looking, gave me squiggly eyebrows that let me know he had a fairly accurate idea of what had happened between Felix and me. They're business partners, but they've been inseparable since they were in diapers. Zach is basically the third Clark sibling, and Felix tells him everything.

Bridget takes the rye out of the cupboard. "I'm looking forward to having a bit of fun," she says. "The four of us haven't hung out in years—it's a special occasion."

"True," I say, watching her pour two generous glasses.

For a second, I let myself imagine what it might be like to spend all my nights like this, here with these people. Drinks with my best friend. A fully stocked fridge. Waiting for Felix to return home with seafood. It would be a nice life.

Bridget lifts her glass to mine as the mudroom door opens. Felix walks in, carrying several boxes of oysters. His eyes meet mine, and my heart hums happily.

Felix is home.

I give my head a shake because I will never spend all my nights like this. There can never be anything deeper between Felix and me. I don't *want* anything deeper. He's my best friend's brother. He lives on Prince Edward Island. My life is in Toronto. Felix has a track record of sleeping with tourists, and I'm simply one of them. I'm here to support Bridget and nothing else. I should memorize it, repeat it at the top of every hour, tattoo it on my forehead so I don't forget.

"What's going on here?" Felix asks, eyeing our drinks and then the two of us. "Lucy looks like she's seasick, and you look like you're up to no good," he tells Bridget.

She tilts her head to me, eyebrows lifted. It's a silent, *You okay?* I nod.

"We're celebrating," Bridget says, turning her attention back to Felix. She takes out another glass and fills half of it with rye, handing it to him.

"What are we celebrating?" he asks, assessing his very large tumbler of brown liquor with skepticism. The stubble on his face is darker than it was yesterday. I wonder what it would be like to see him every day, to watch his beard grow in. I need to stop this.

I take a long sip of the rye. Maybe I can whiskey my fantasies into oblivion.

"You and me and Bee and Zach," Bridget says. "All of us together."

Felix and I lock eyes.

Bridget clinks her glass against ours. "Cheers."

Her phone pings, and she scowls at the screen. She types furiously, muttering to herself, then sets the device onto the counter with such force, I check whether she's broken the screen. She hasn't, but I see Miles's name at the top of a text chain, and a message that reads:

This is crazy. We should talk it out in person.

I look to Bridget.

"It's fine," she says.

"Umm . . ."

"I don't want to discuss it right now."

Felix leans over to peek at her screen.

"Stop looking at my phone." She snatches it away.

"I don't like it when the Clark family parties without me," Zach calls from the door.

"What timing," Felix says under his breath as Zach strides across the living room.

He's a tall Black man with close-cropped hair and dressed in a polo and khaki shorts. He's so preposterously handsome that the thought of him and Felix bashing around the island together as two single guys makes me want to put them both in a corner and give them a time-out.

He hands Felix a bag of peanuts and a bottle of rye "for the stash," then holds his arms out for Bridget.

"It's been too long," she says.

"Your fault," he tells her.

He greets me with a short "Lucy."

"Good to see you again," I say.

Zach stares at me, unblinking. "You too."

"When was the last time you were home?" he asks Bridget as we gather around the kitchen island.

"I was out for a week at Christmas."

"That's right," he says, as if he's only now remembering. Felix rolls his eyes. Zach's crush on Bridget began before his seventh-grade growth spurt, and he's not subtle. "Wolf and I slaughtered you and Miles in Trivial Pursuit."

Bridget looks out the window, and Zach winces. Felix has obviously filled him in on the little we know about Bridget's situation.

"I'll marry you, Bridge," Zach announces after a minute.

"Obviously," Felix and I chime at the same time.

The room is silent for a moment, and then everyone laughs, even Bridget.

"I mean it, though," Zach says after we quiet down.

"We know," Felix and I say in stereo again. I glance at him, and he's smiling, not exactly at me, but at least in my general direction.

"I don't think Lana would mind, Bridge," Zach goes on. "She's pretty liberal-minded."

"Who's Lana?" I ask.

"New girlfriend," Felix says.

"Not that new," Zach corrects. "But definitely out of my league."

"Is Lana aware of your crush?" I ask, pointing between him and Bridget.

"Of course." Zach claps his hands. "But it's not a crush. Loving Bridget Clark is a lifestyle."

"I can't wait to meet her," Bridget says. "Wolf said she's a nurse?"

"Best one in Montreal," Zach says. "But she's coming out in September. Trial run. We'll see if she still loves me after living with me for a month."

"Of course she will," Bridget says. "Hopefully the island wins her over. I don't think many people from away can picture what it's like to live here after Labor Day."

Prince Edward Island is swarming with tourists in the summer, but just as people "from away" come and go with the warm weather, so do a lot of the businesses, which close for the off-season.

"It's better after Labor Day," Zach says, and Felix nods.

I pour Zach a drink while Felix begins lining up oysters on the counter. Zach is showing Bridget photos of his girlfriend.

"Can I help with anything?" I ask Felix. I will be the most normal, least thirsty version of myself around him, if it's the last thing I do.

He glances at me. "Want to do the lemons? And grab the hot sauce from the cupboard?"

I'm slicing the citrus when Felix says, "You're chaos with a blade."

"Hey," I say, pointing it in his direction. "I've improved. At least it's not a steak knife."

"You'll take your fingers off. Do you remember how I showed you?" His voice is low, and it rasps from his lips to land right between my thighs.

I nod. "I can't do it the way you do."

"Like this." His fingers curve over mine, and I hope he can't tell that they're shaking. "You need to protect yourself." He adjusts my grip, then steps back, satisfied.

"Stop telling secrets over there." That's Bridget. "Wolf, are you ready or what? I'm hungry."

He looks at me. "You're on."

As Clark tradition dictates, I'm the newest guest and am therefore assigned stopwatch duties. It's a specific form of agony to stand directly across the kitchen island from Felix, staring at his fast hands, trying not to think about the other things they can undo. It's cool this evening, but after the first round, I'm so overheated I have to strip off the fuzzy pink cardigan I've put on over my white sundress.

"You've lost your touch," Zach says to Felix. "Two minutes and forty-five seconds? Pathetic."

"Shouldn't have had that whiskey," Felix says. "Let's go again."

He's halfway through the next batch, and Zach's heckling so loudly I have no idea how Felix manages to better his time. "Two minutes and twenty-nine seconds," I say.

Bridget pulls a face. "You're out of practice."

"Apparently."

"And with added penalty time." She clucks her tongue.

"Penalty time?" I ask.

Felix explains: "The judges add additional seconds onto your time for any mistakes, like if there are bits of shell or grit left behind."

Bridget wiggles her fingers in Felix's direction, and he hands her his knife. She bends close to the platter, narrowing her eyes as she studies the oysters. She pokes at each with the knife and wrinkles her nose.

"This one isn't fully severed from the muscle," Bridget says, peering up at Felix. "And there's grit in two of them, some shell in another . . . So that's twelve seconds of extra time for a total time of . . ." She points at Zach as if they've played this game many times before.

"Two minutes and forty-one seconds," Zach says.

Felix runs his hand through his hair. "Not good enough."

"What's the goal?" I ask, realizing how little I know about this part of Felix's life.

"One minute and thirty seconds. A minute forty, max."

"If Wolf shucks them cleanly, that should get him in the top five," Zach says.

Felix glances my way. "I'm very clean."

I don't know what it says about me, but I find these three words intensely sexual.

We finish the tray of oysters, and Felix pulls another box from the fridge, picks out eighteen, and arranges them on the wood surface. When he's suitably pleased with his setup, he meets my eyes. He's so focused on me, it's like Bridget and Zach aren't even in the room. He gives me a nod, and I count him down from three.

I can feel Zach watching me watch his best friend. Felix

finishes the batch, and everyone breaks for another round of drinks and oysters. When Bridget steps outside with her phone and Felix excuses himself to the bathroom, Zach turns to me and says, "What's the situation with you two?"

"What do you mean?"

He gives me a steely-eyed stare. He knows I'm full of crap.

"There's no situation, Zach."

"That's what Wolf says, but I don't think that's true. You're single. He's single."

I have to school my expression at this news. "How do you know I'm not seeing anyone?"

"I have my ways." I lift my eyebrows. Zach shrugs, then says, "Bridget."

Before I can interrogate him about that, he adds, "And I've seen the way you look at each other—you're both so obvious."

I cannot fathom what he thinks is obvious.

"There's nothing between us," I tell him. "Same as always."

He snorts. "I can't tell if you're lying to me or lying to yourself."

I ask Zach a question about outdoor living walls because I know it'll distract him. Zach has more hobbies and interests than anyone I know. He's telling me about biodiversity in urban environments when Felix returns to the kitchen, and my eyes find his across the room.

"See, that," Zach hisses. "It makes me want to take a cold shower."

TRIVIAL PURSUIT COMES OUT SOMEWHERE BEFORE Bridget's fourth glass of rye and after she holds Zach's cheeks between her hands and says, slushy-mouthed, "I missed you so much."

Zach is trouncing the rest of us. He's the reigning champion and takes sick pleasure in making everyone else look like fools. When he scores a fourth piece of pie and runs around the room with his arms above his head, Bridget throws a pillow at him. "You're an overgrown encyclopedia."

"I have to impress you somehow, Bridge," he says, flopping on the sofa between us and slinging an arm around her shoulder. "So tell me—is this wedding happening or not? No pressure, but Lana and I have our hotel room booked, and I need her to see me in my suit."

Bridget's shoulders inch toward her ears, the pink of her cheeks deepening as she stares down at the game board.

Felix and I share a look, and I know by the determined set of his eyebrows and the steadiness of his gaze that he's done giving her space.

"What Zach is trying to say," he starts, "is that you have guests traveling from as far as Australia in a couple of days, and if you're backing out of this thing, it would be considerate of you to let everyone know sooner rather than later."

Bridget cuts Felix a razor-edged look. "I *do not* want to talk about the wedding."

He leans forward in his chair, hands clasped between his knees. He looks straight at Bridget. "You made Lucy drop everything and fly out. I'm staying here because you asked me to. You can at least do us the courtesy of letting us know why you've summoned us."

Felix doesn't raise his voice, but he speaks with quiet force. I've never heard him talk like that to Bridget. Or anyone.

The Clarks stare at each other, neither one speaking.

"We're just worried about you," I try. "The wedding is a week away. Did something happen between you and Miles?"

"Can I not, for once, let loose?" Bridget says, her voice shaking. "Am I not allowed to do something spontaneous?"

"Of course you can," I say. "But, Bridget, this is obviously not about being spontaneous. If something's wrong, maybe we can help you figure it out. You don't have to solve all your problems on your own."

Her eyes begin to well, and I motion for Zach to get off the couch.

"Talk to us, Bridge," I say, putting an arm around her. "Or I can send these two hooligans away, and you can talk to me. I'm worried about you."

She looks at me, her deep brown eyes glistening, and shakes her head.

"I can't," she says. "I'm not ready to tell you."

16

Now

I blink at Bridget. The rejection smarts. So much so that it renders me speechless.

"It's not because I don't trust you, Bee," she says.

I swallow. "Sure."

She sighs, then kisses my cheek. "I'm going to go up to bed."

I stare at her back as she climbs the stairs, stunned. After she's disappeared, I rise.

"I'm going to clean the kitchen." I'll scrub my hurt away.

Felix stands, too. "I'm going to talk to her."

Zach joins me at the sink. Bridget's and Felix's voices are loud enough that we can hear them arguing upstairs, but they're muffled, so we can only make out a few words here and there.

Felix: "You're kidding."

Bridget: "I wish I was."

It doesn't take long for the Clark family feud to go quiet again, but neither sibling returns. I rinse the last of the dishes, looking out the window at the silver streak of moonlight on the water.

"The silence is slightly unsettling," Zach says. "You think Bridget's bleaching her crime scene?"

"I've never heard them fight. Felix is so even-keeled. Nothing seems to bother him."

Zach looks at me.

"What?"

"You called him Felix. No one calls him that."

I don't reply.

"Huh," Zach says. He squeezes his bottom lip between his thumb and index finger. And then, "He's not as easygoing as you think, Lucy. He has feelings."

I frown. "I know that."

Zach stares at me for a long moment, but all he says is, "Good."

Felix's voice, gruff, interrupts us. "I'm taking a walk."

He's already out the sliding door by the time I turn around.

"I think he swiped the bottle of rye," Zach says.

I look out the window and watch Felix make his way to the water until he disappears.

Twenty minutes later, when he still hasn't returned and Zach is arranging the living room for bed, I throw on my cardigan and grab the nearest warm thing, a blanket from the steamer trunk, and head into the night.

The beach is empty, but the sky is full of stars, a glittering cloak of diamonds over a shimmering black sea. I walk along the shore. The air is thick, but it's cooler than I expected, and I fold my arms against the chill.

I'm thinking of turning around, but then I see him in the distance, his white T-shirt glowing under the moon. As I get near, Felix takes a sip from the bottle, wipes his mouth with the back of his hand, and without looking at me, says, "Hey." His voice is ragged.

"You still have four limbs," I say.

He huffs out a dry laugh. "Barely."

When I edge closer, I can see that his jaw is rigid. He takes another drink.

"Here." I hand him the blanket. "It's cold out."

He takes it from me, but instead of wrapping it around his shoulders, he passes me the bottle of rye and lays the blanket on the sand, straightening it until he's satisfied with the edges.

He's kneeling on one side, looking up at me. We watch each other, unblinking, and then Felix holds out a hand. Time hangs suspended as I stand before him, staring at his palm. My pulse ricochets, faster, then faster still.

"Sit down, Lucy." His voice is rough, worn from arguing with Bridget. I know how much effort it takes to go into battle against her.

With hesitance, I take his hand in mine, and when his finger-tips fall on my wrist, I'm certain he can feel my heartbeat. It's a heavy, ceaseless thud.

He tugs me a step closer.

"I think we can handle sharing a blanket," he says.

So I sit, knees drawn up, next to Felix.

We look out at the inky gulf in silence, the bottle between us. Felix is warm beside me, and the cool air doesn't feel so chilly anymore. The breeze feels like whispered sweet nothings against my cheek.

Eventually Felix holds the whiskey out to me. I meet his side-ways gaze as I reach for it and take a sip. When I hand it back to him, he does the same. It feels strangely intimate.

"Did you get anywhere with Bridget?" I ask after we've passed the whiskey back and forth a few more times.

Felix doesn't answer for such an expansive stretch that I wonder if I articulated the question. "She really was homesick," he says finally.

"You must have been talking for almost an hour. What about the text from Miles? She didn't give you anything more?"

There's enough light that I can see his eyes moving around my face, catching on my nose, my lips. "She's worried about you."

"She's always worried about me."

He shakes his head. "No. I don't think she's ever worried about you much until now."

"Well, right back at her," I say.

Felix takes another sip, then says, "Do *I* need to worry about you?"

It catches me off guard. Does he *want* to worry about me? Do I need to be worried about?

"After that fight with Bridget, I should ask you the same thing," I say. "What were you two arguing about?"

Felix stares at me for a moment before answering "Her secret keeping."

I reach for the bottle and take a drink, though I already feel the rye buzzing in my limbs.

"Tell me how you're doing," Felix says.

I peer at him. "I'm fine."

"Lucy." His gaze travels my face, and I feel like he's drinking me up. "Really tell me. Tell me what's happening at the store. Tell me about Farah and what poetry she's working on. Tell me about flowers." He sounds a little desperate, and his words run together.

"Felix Clark, are you drunk?" I don't even think I've seen him tipsy before—he holds his liquor well.

"Maybe a little," he says with a half smile that's definitely intoxicated. "But I also want to know, Lucy. Talk to me."

I study the beautiful planes of his face, the way the moon refracts off his cheekbones and hides in the hollows below, and even though I know talking to Felix could get me into more trouble than pressing my lips to his, I say, "Farah's writing elegies."

The dimple fires. "Poems about the dead."

"Yeah, but I think they're kind of sexy. I've heard her reciting lines about unyielding flesh and honeyed nectar."

Felix lies back on the blanket, hands under his head, biceps popping. "What else?"

"Hmm." I lie beside him, and we stare up at the stars. "I think she's sick of me. I've been spending a lot of time either at the store or doing event installs."

"How much time?"

"All of it."

He tilts his head to me. "Do you still love it?"

I gaze at the galaxy, and my throat goes tight. It's both the question and the moment—being here, in my favorite place, with one of my favorite people. I wish I didn't like him so much.

"I don't know," I tell him. "I love so much of it. I love the creative parts. I love working with flowers, but I don't love everything that comes with it. Managing people, business strategy, more emails than you would think. I became a florist because I hated my desk job, but I'm finding myself behind one more and more." I watch a satellite blinking its way toward the Big Dipper.

"Sometimes I worry that as I've got older, I've shrunk my

world instead of making it grow," I admit. "Picking flowers, making floral crowns, mucking in my aunt's garden—those things used to be my hobby, but now my aunt is gone, and my hobby is my job, and work is my entire life."

I feel his fingers twine around mine, and for a moment, my whole heart is held between our palms. He squeezes once, then lets go. I want it back immediately.

More, my heart says. *Felix.*

"Tell me about your farm."

Your farm. Felix is the only person who knows about it, and I like how he makes it sound—like a real thing.

"There's no farm," I say, tipping my head to him. I haven't fantasized about it in such a long time. It's no use dreaming about things that will never be—there's too much reality to contend with.

"Not yet. Describe it to me, Lucy."

Felix can say my name a thousand different ways. A *Lucy* that vibrates in the back of his throat, gritty with desire. A *Lucy* that sounds like sun showers. A *Lucy* of smug amusement. A *Lucy* that's more a sigh of relief than a name. A *Lucy* that's all awe and wonder. This *Lucy* is a gentle command.

In one breath, it all comes back to me. The thing I've secretly wanted for so long—a cut flower farm.

"I don't think about it much these days," I tell Felix. "But I always pictured a greenhouse."

"What else?"

I first imagined having a small garden, but it grew every time I envisioned it. It became a rectangular plot of nutrient-rich soil somewhere outside the city with enough flora to stock a farmer's market stand through summer. Then a flourishing farm, with blossoms as far as the eye could see. Sunflowers following the light. Rivers of blue salvia. Delicate pink cosmos, swaying in the breeze.

I turn my face back to the stars, smiling up at them. "A field with rich soil. Sunflowers. Salvia. Cosmos."

"Dahlias," he says. It's not a question. Felix knows.

"Dahlias," I repeat.

"Tell me more, Lucy," he says. "Tell me everything."

17

Thanksgiving, Three Years Ago

I became the owner of In Bloom at 12:01 a.m. on January 1. Stacy and I threw a party at the shop, a New Year's Eve open house, where friends and customers dropped in and out. At midnight she made a speech and concluded it by taking a bow, handing me her keys, and declaring, "What's mine is now yours."

I had hoped to return to Prince Edward Island in the summer, but I wasn't confident enough to leave the shop yet. Bridget was dating Miles, so she brought him home with her instead. Not wanting to miss our girls' trip entirely that year, she convinced me to join her for a few nights over the Thanksgiving long weekend in early October.

I'd never been to PEI in the fall before, and Bridget said to bring sunglasses, a hat, and my warm sweaters. It was a sunny autumn, but it could get chilly. As I rolled up my clothing, I couldn't help but think about seeing Felix again. It had been a year and a half since I'd seen him, and I wanted to look good in an effortless, breezy way. Not that we'd be repeating what happened the last time I visited. I would avoid narrow hallways, looking at his hands, and steam-filled bathrooms. I would keep my clothes on—and my towel on, too—no matter how suggestively his eyes sparkled or what words came out of his hot mouth.

Besides, I had just ended a four-month thing with a firefighter, and for all I knew, Felix was seeing someone. What I did know about him from Bridget didn't involve his love life. He had scored a cheap flight to Lisbon and taken off with a backpack. It was his first trip overseas, a short holiday before he and Zach began to work in earnest on the design plans for Salt Cottages. Our flight landed Friday morning, Felix's that night.

Five minutes before Bridget and I left for the airport, I removed my nicest lace underwear from my suitcase, and then threw them back in again. Always good to have an extra pair. It had nothing to do with Felix. I was committed to rule number two—Felix and I would not be sleeping together again. This trip would not end up like the last one.

As soon as we stepped onto the tarmac, Bridget sprinted toward the bathroom. She had a bladder the size of an acorn and refused to use the toilet on the plane. While she waited in line, I went straight to the Cows Creamery cow, giving the statue a pat on its pink snout.

Ken drove us to Summer Wind. It was a postcard-perfect fall day. The roads were lined with pumpkin stands and the yellow and orange leaves that still clung to their branches shone in striking contrast to the sky. Most tourists to Prince Edward Island visited in the summer. They roamed Green Gables Heritage House, stuffed themselves silly with lobster, wiggled their toes in the sand at Cavendish Beach, bought tickets to *Anne of Green Gables—The Musical*, golfed. But early October was so stunning, I couldn't imagine a more beautiful time or place. The colors of the island always astounded me—how green the grass, the neon canola fields, the rich rust of the soil and sand, the purple streaks of lupines. But under the bright blue fall skies, everything seemed more vivid. It felt like after the clammer of the summer high season, the island began to flat-out brag.

"I'm so glad I live in a world where there are Octobers," Anne Shirley said, and now I knew why.

Christine welcomed me with the same rib-squeezing hugs she gave Bridget, and I was directed to carry my bag up to Felix's bedroom. He'd bought his own place on the eastern side of the island, and his bookshelf was gone, but otherwise the room looked the same. The antique post and spindle bed with a red-and-blue quilt folded at the end. A small desk under the window. Zero artwork. I unpacked my things and with them a memory of my last night here—the hard thrust of Felix's hips, the heat of his eyes on mine in the mirror, the ends of his hair curling in the steam. His Tic Tac kisses.

I want you to call me Felix.

I pushed it all aside, then went to the bathroom to douse my face in cold water. I needed to pull myself together before he arrived.

Bridget and I had just returned from a walk on the beach when Christine announced, "Bad news. Wolf's flight was canceled. Mechanical issues. The earliest one he's found is Wednesday morning."

My stomach dropped. Bridget and I were leaving Tuesday. I shook off the disappointment. I should be celebrating—no Felix meant I would get through the weekend unscathed. This was a good thing. This was great.

"IS YOUR BROTHER SEEING ANYONE?" I ASKED BRIDGET as I applied liquid eyeliner on Saturday night. Zach was throwing a party, and we were invited. Now that I wasn't going to see Felix, I was hungry for details.

Bridget was pulling her hair into a slightly less haphazard bun. She paused and narrowed her eyes. "Why?"

I narrowed mine back. "Because I'm planning to fall madly in love with him and just want to make sure I'm in the clear before I do," I said, face heating despite the joke. "Also, just curious."

She glared. Bridget loved a good glare, but then she rolled her eyes. "He hasn't mentioned a girlfriend to me," she said. "If there was someone in the picture, he would definitely tell Zach, and Zach would want to gossip about it with me. So unless he's got some secret side piece, he still hasn't seen anyone seriously since . . ."

"Joy," I finished. Bridget avoided saying her name. Before Joy broke up with Felix, she had been Bridget's best friend and was now her sorest spot. They were joined at the hip from preschool through to Brownies then Guides, figure skating then hockey. Felix was the annoying baby brother, until he wasn't annoying. He was Joy's secret crush, and then her not-so-secret boyfriend.

"Yup." The *p* came out of her mouth with a *pop*. "Rotten potato."

ZACH LIVED IN A CHEERFUL BLUE-SIDED BUNGALOW IN Summerside, which belonged to his grandmother before she had moved into a retirement home. We were greeted by an overstuffed hall closet, a pile of boots, ballet flats, running shoes, and a grinning Zach.

"It's my favorite Clark," he said, wrapping his arms around Bridget and then turning to me. "And Lucy! Welcome, welcome."

Zach instructed Bridget and me to take ourselves on a tour. I bit back a smile at the mishmash of furniture—the dark polished-wood pieces he must have inherited from his grandmother and the stuff, like his gargantuan television, that screamed twenty-five-year-old *dude*.

We found the rest of the party in the kitchen. There were about twenty people jammed into the space. Zach stood next to the fridge, talking to a woman with long strawberry-blond hair.

I felt Bridget tense beside me.

"Is that?" I asked.

"Yep. That's—" I watched her swallow.

"Joy."

If I had really looked at Joy, I would have noticed that her features were delicate and angular, but her mouth was round and sweet. I would have noticed that she'd slicked her lips with juicy cherry red gloss and that her bangs fell in a flawless heavy fringe to her lash line. I would have envied how she'd managed to make a Fair Isle sweater and jeans look alluring. But I wasn't looking at her, not really. I was looking at my best friend, who had gone white.

As Joy and Felix got older and grew more serious, Bridget and Joy weren't just friends; they were family. There was talk of weddings, and babies, and Auntie Bridget. There was a ring and a party with a surprise proposal. There were *plans*.

Bridget sucked in a breath.

"Do you want to go?" I asked. "I won't mind."

She stared at Zach and Joy, shaking her head. "No. I can do this."

We wove our way toward them and Bridget offered a shaky "Joy, hey."

She turned toward us, and I almost recoiled with a hiss. Joy's eyes were the most stunning amber, like fall in a bottle. Old-fashioneds and pumpkin spice and leaves crunching underfoot.

"Joy, this is Lucy, Bridget's best friend and roommate in Toronto," Zach said when Bridget didn't.

Hurt, clear and quick, flashed in Joy's gaze, but then she smiled. Oh god, she was even prettier when she smiled. "It's so nice to meet you," she said, offering her hand.

"Classic Zach," called a man over my shoulder. "Always with the prettiest women in a room."

I turned around and found myself facing a burly ginger. He wore a toque pulled over his forehead, red hair curling out the bottom.

He shook Zach's hand and gave Joy a kiss on the cheek. "Hey, Colin," she said.

"We all went to school together," Zach explained as Colin said hello to Bridget.

Colin gestured at Joy with his beer can. "I'd heard you and Wolf were back together. Is he here?"

Scarlet spread across Joy's cheeks. She shook her head. "We aren't together."

Colin scratched his beard, and I thought he looked relieved. "Sorry about that," he said. "I heard yous were talking again, and my brother said he ran into you together at Upstreet Brewing."

"We're just friends," Joy said. She turned to me. "I follow In Bloom on Instagram. I love that wedding bouquet you posted last week. The one with the cabbages?"

I stared at her open-mouthed. The bride wanted something "unique" and "not girly," and I responded with purple and green kale, sedum, amaranthus, sage, and rosemary. Even Farah was impressed.

"It was kale," I said to Joy.

"Yes, that's right," she said. "And the herbs? Genius. You're so talented. And your shop looks so amazing. I want to stop in the next time I'm in Toronto."

I was stunned. After everything Bridget told me, Joy was not what I expected.

Felix was twenty-two when he proposed. He and Joy had been together for seven years, but she broke off the engagement a week after saying yes. Bridget and I were newly minted roommates back then, and she was shocked by the sudden way Joy dropped her brother, but she thought their friendship would endure. It had made it through Joy quitting hockey to get her grades up. It had weathered Bridget moving to Toronto and Joy to Nova Scotia for school. But it didn't survive Felix, and Bridget was devastated.

The twin breakups—Joy's with Felix and Joy's with Bridget—brought us closer together. A good friendship origin story involves a villain. Ours was Joy.

"I need to find myself" and "I don't know who I am"—two things Joy told Felix when she gave him back the ring—soon became part of our lexicon. As in:

"Can you take out the recycling?"

"I wish I could, but *I need to find myself.*"

I glanced at Bridget now, bewildered. Joy was lovely.

"Thanks," I said. "I have a lot of help, especially from this one." I bumped Bridget with my hip. "She's the reason my accountant loves me."

"Lucky. There's no one who loves a spreadsheet more than you, right, Bridge?" Joy looked at Bridget with a shy smile.

Bridget didn't reply. She blinked at Joy with a pained expression, like she was fighting back tears. She grabbed my arm and squeaked, "We have to go." She yanked me to the other side of the room to get ciders from an ice-filled cooler on the mahogany dining table.

"Are you okay?"

"Yes," she said, though obviously she wasn't. "I can't believe she and Wolf are friends again. *We* were friends first, and she abandoned me like I meant nothing. Obviously he always mattered more to her."

"I'm sure that's not true. I'm sure she misses you. You're the best. But it's been a long time. Maybe she thinks you wouldn't be interested in a relationship."

"I'm not."

"Really? She seems nice."

Bridget peered around me, taking a long sip of her cider. "I can't go there again."

I followed her line of sight. Zach and Joy were deep in conversation.

"Traitor," she grumbled.

I finished my drink almost as fast as Bridget did hers, but I cut myself off on the next round because Bridget was throwing back ciders with slaphappy enthusiasm. I'd never seen her this thrown off by another person.

"Joy broke both our hearts." That's what she told me back then. But I hadn't realized until now that there was only one ex in Bridget's life who really mattered, and that ex was Joy. The person who held her childhood memories. The woman who saw her through braces and first boyfriends, who witnessed her break an arm on the ice, who helped skate her off, who came with her parents to the hospital. Her oldest friend.

An hour and two more ciders later, Bridget rejected my suggestion she switch to water. Another hour and one more cider after that, she was asleep on the pile of coats on Zach's bed.

When the rest of the party had cleared out, Zach, Joy, and I sat Bridget up, got her to take a drink of water, and helped her into the passenger seat of her parents' car.

"Do you want me to follow you home?" Joy asked. "I can help you get her up to her room."

Blah. What an angel. "Yeah. That would be great."

18

Thanksgiving, Three Years Ago

The Clarks' Thanksgiving Day dinner preparations began shortly after breakfast. Bridget and I were on mashed potato casserole duty, still dressed in our jammies. She in a hockey jersey and hole-ridden leggings, I in a long-sleeve flannelette nightgown covered in tiny flowers that the firefighter I'd been sleeping with referred to as a boner killer.

Bridget peeled and I sliced the potatoes into large hunks with the oversize chef's knife Christine forced into my hands.

"I don't see what's wrong with a paring knife," I said to Bridget when her mom was busy making the stuffing.

"Welcome to the Clark family," Bridget said.

I smiled. "I like it here. Aside from the knife."

We were halfway through the potatoes when I heard the mudroom door swing open. It was almost like the atoms in the house had rearranged. I knew Felix was there before he called out, "Happy Thanksgiving."

I turned around slowly, my pulse rocketing.

Felix was walking across the living room, a large canvas backpack over his shoulder. His hair was longer than it had been when I saw him last. He still had the beard, a little shaggier than before, and he wore a nubby oatmeal wool sweater that I bet his grandma had knit. Bridget had one just like it. His jeans were cuffed over a pair of scuffed gray suede boots. He looked cozy and a little rumpled. Autumn Felix.

"Wolf!" Christine and Bridget cried out in unison, crossing the floor to meet him.

He dropped his bag and hugged his mother, then his sister. I couldn't look away.

"Hi, Lucy," he said when he let Bridget go.

I don't know how he made my name sound like foreplay. I took a shaky breath. "Hey, Wolf."

His eyebrow arched, but he was smiling. God, he was glorious.

"How are you here?" Bridget asked.

"Found an earlier flight. Thought it would be fun to surprise everyone."

I returned to the potatoes, my hands far less steady than before. I felt the heat of him before he spoke.

"You haven't been practicing."

"I am now. Your mother is a tyrant," I said, glancing over my shoulder. Our eyes met. *Snap.*

Felix chuckled. "That she is. May I?" He gestured to the knife. I passed it to him, but he shook his head. "Try it again."

He adjusted my hand, and I felt the electricity zip from the pads of his fingers down to the base of my spine. "Good."

Felix stepped away, leaned his hip against the counter, watching me. It didn't help with the wobbly fingers.

"Are you going to stand there and lord over me?"

"I'm not that much taller than you. I can't lord."

I turned to him. "Your shoulders are like six feet wide. You're lording."

"It's true," Bridget said, picking up the vegetable peeler. "You're lording."

Felix scoffed. "I'll go take a shower, then."

I should have kept my gaze on the knife, but I met Felix's eyes. They were dancing, not heated exactly, but definitely teasing.

"Not happening," I mouthed to him, and he laughed. Because it wasn't happening. This time was *still* going to be different—it didn't matter that Felix had waltzed in looking like sex.

"Suit yourself," he whispered, leaving me to the potatoes and the image of Felix Clark in the shower.

He stayed close most of the day, helping with the cranberry sauce, setting the table with Bridget, telling us about the hostel he'd stayed at in Lisbon, the castles he'd visited in Sintra, the cherry liqueur and vinho verde. When Bridget asked about the plans for the cottages, he described them in such vivid detail that I could imagine myself walking around the rooms, stepping onto the deck. Felix had a way of painting pictures with words that I hadn't noticed before, and he sounded different than he had the last time I'd seen him, more mature.

For dinner, there were baked oysters with bacon and Worcestershire sauce (an Aussie preparation Miles had introduced to the Clarks on his maiden visit that summer), followed by turkey, stuffing, acorn squash, mashed potato casserole, green bean casserole, mashed turnip, and Brussels sprouts—a laughable amount of food. I had extra helpings of everything.

A bigger crowd than usual was gathered around the table— two sets of grandparents, two cousins, and an aunt—and the space was tight. I was acutely aware of Felix sitting beside me. Of our elbows knocking as we ate. Of the way our fingers touched when he passed me the platter of turkey, how a current pinged from his pinkie to mine. I could think of little else aside from how good he smelled, how warm his body was next to mine, how well that body worked with my body. When his knee bumped against my knee, an accidental nudge, I almost jumped out of my chair. He laughed quietly.

The volume setting of a Clark family gathering, the number of voices competing to be heard, overlapping in happy arguments and in-jokes, made it so that only I could hear when Felix leaned toward my ear and asked, "Do I make you nervous, Lucy?"

"Not at all," I replied, keeping my attention on my dinner.

"Hmm," he said, then took a bite of stuffing.

"Hmm," I said back, spearing a bean with my fork.

We didn't speak more than a few sentences here and there ("pass the gravy," "hand me the salt") for the rest of the night, but I could feel his gaze on me when we cleaned the table and got out the board of Trivial Pursuit. When Bridget sat down at the piano around midnight, and everyone gathered around her with their glasses of rye to sing "Let It Be," I found myself staring at him openly, and him at me. Felix had a good singing voice, deep and clear, and our eyes didn't leave each other for the rest of the song.

I had offered to give Felix his old room back, but he said he was happy to sleep on the pull-out sofa in the TV room. I washed my face, changed into my nightgown, and braided my hair with trembling fingers. I lay down, but I couldn't be still. Felix didn't sleep in this bed anymore and I had been the one in it the last few days, but I swear I could smell him on the sheets. I must have tossed and turned for an hour. I felt like an everlasting sparkler, sizzling and sparking in the dark, no end to the burning. I hadn't been this sexually frustrated in . . . ever? I had never craved another person the way I craved Felix. The house was silent, everyone having long since fallen asleep. I threw back the sheets and paced the floor of the bedroom.

Would it really be so wrong if I crept downstairs and slipped into bed with Felix? It's not like Bridget had told me explicitly not to sleep with him. The rule that we had agreed on was that I wouldn't *fall in love* with him. I had no interest in falling in love with Felix. Having his mouth and hands all over me, however, I was very much in favor of.

I walked to the door but hesitated, wondering whether I should turn around.

"Fuck it," I whispered to myself. I deserved an orgasm or seven.

I flung open the door, tiptoed downstairs, quiet and quick. I knocked the way he'd shown me two years earlier. *Tap, tap,* pause, *tap.*

Felix was pulling a shirt over his head when the door opened. He wore pajama pants and a surprised expression. For a second, neither of us spoke.

Now that I was standing here, I wasn't sure what my move was. "I used our knock," I whispered.

Felix grinned. "I'd forgotten about the knock. Something on your mind, Lucy?"

"Yes." I cleared my throat. "You."

We stared at each other for a slice of a second before Felix wrapped his arm around my waist and brought his mouth to mine, his lips urgent. It was exactly what I wanted, but I was still so shocked by the suddenness of the kiss that my knees began to buckle. His arm tightened around my middle, holding me firm. I moaned.

He pulled back an inch, breathing heavily, a smile slinking across his lips. "Should we take this inside?"

It was only then that I realized we were standing in the doorway. I looked into the TV room over his shoulder. "I've never been able to say no to a pull-out couch."

Felix laughed, tugging me into the room. He shut the door and drew me closer. I melted into his chest as we kissed again, my hands compassing his shoulder blades. His found the back of my head, confident, angling my face, his tongue hot on mine. There was no space between us, only layers of fabric and him, already hard. It felt like sex, the way he devoured me, the way I squirmed against him, my body seeking friction, seeking *him*. I'd been kissed by Felix, but never like *this*.

Felix ran his fingers along one of my braids, then set it behind my shoulder. He worked at the lace at my throat, untying the thin satin ribbon, moving much slower than he had seconds ago; then he lowered his mouth to my collarbone.

"We're terrible. We said we wouldn't," I said, shuddering at the graze of teeth and then the soft sweep of lips coasting up my neck. My pulse thudded under his mouth.

"We can stop," Felix said, his lips moving back to mine. But he didn't kiss me. He waited.

"No," I told him. "I want more."

His thumb swept across my bottom lip, and I sucked it into my mouth. He groaned.

"I haven't been able to stop thinking about you. How you look when you're naked. How you sound when you come. I've had a hard-on like a fucking fourteen-year-old since I walked in the door." His nose slid along mine. "You're a goddamn wonder."

His words were gas on a flame. Felix opened his mouth to speak again, but I put my lips on his, smothering the sentence. Hours of pretending I didn't want every inch of his body pressed against mine vanished. The kiss was frantic. Greedy mouths and desperate tongues. Hands cuffed around backsides. Hips rocking.

I scrambled to get his T-shirt off, my nails scraping over his skin. I ran my fingers through the soft dusting of hair on his chest, over his strong shoulders, then pressed my mouth to his neck. I shivered at the drag of his rough palm along my rib cage, over my hip, to the top of my thigh.

"Can you do me a favor?" Felix asked.

"Pretty sure there's nothing I wouldn't agree to right now."

He inched up my nightgown, then led my fingers to the hem. "Hold this for me?"

"I can take it off."

"I like it," he said, kneeling. "I like imagining everything that's hidden underneath."

I laughed, but then he traced a line on my inner thigh with his mouth, and every muscle I owned clenched. Felix nipped at the flesh, his beard tickling and scratching. He held me open, pushing aside the lace of my underwear, flicking his tongue until I started to wobble.

"If you think my core strength is good enough for me to stay standing for this, you have seriously overestimated my fitness level," I whispered, and felt his chuckle roll through me.

"I'm serious," I said, pulling on his elbows. "I have the exercise routine of a starfish."

He stood, grinning. "Shush."

Felix planted messy kisses to my temple, cheek, the corner of my mouth, as we lifted off the nightgown and stumbled to the mattress. We collapsed onto the pull-out together, and the springs let out a loud *eeeeerrrrrch*. We froze, Felix on top of me, smiles smooshed together.

Felix stayed still for another few breaths. His hand coasted over my thigh, and as if he could feel how tense I was, he said, "The door's locked, Lucy. The worst that could happen is someone will knock."

"That would be extremely bad." But Felix's fingers moved between my legs to where my every nerve was screaming to be disrupted, and then his mouth followed. When he pulled my underwear off, lifted my leg over his shoulder, and told me he loved how I tasted, I forgot where we were. I put my hand over my mouth when I came, but Felix stayed where he was, sucking and kissing, until I reached for him. He stood with a satisfied grin, digging a condom out from his backpack. I wondered how many he'd used on his trip.

"I like to be prepared," he said, seeing my expression. He lowered his pants, dropping them onto the floor. He stood naked before me, skin glowing silver in the moonlight.

My throat went dry at the sight of him. The totality of Felix shirtless was so extravagant that I might have laughed if I didn't want to touch every part of him. His shoulders were obnoxious—sculpted with intent, or at least I assumed so. I didn't think you could look the way Felix did without putting in time at the gym. But he was muscular in less obvious places, too. The space beneath his armpits on either side of his chest was built up, like a pair of sexy wings might reside there. And he had those twin lines that ran on diagonals above his pelvis.

I reached for his hand, and he climbed over me, bending to my chest, seeming to get lost there. I wiggled beneath him, wanting him now. In whispered pleas, I told him so. He rose to his knees between my legs, rolling on the condom, eyes on me.

"Sit up for a sec," he said, and I did what I was told, lifting myself onto my elbows as Felix, one by one, unfastened the elastics around my braids and raked his fingers through my hair.

I lay back, hair spilling across the pillow, eyes not leaving his. Cloaked in midnight, he surveyed me, swallowing once, and in that moment, I felt a shift. The charge was still there, but instead of sparking and sizzling, it was heavier somehow. Felix smoothed a palm down my side. He tugged my hips closer, until he was nudged against me, and he lowered himself onto his forearms until our noses were almost touching.

"I forgot how good this felt," I told him.

He pressed his lips to mine, once. "I didn't."

We stared at each other, and time seemed to stop.

"Don't fall in love with me, Felix Clark," I whispered. "Rule three."

"I wouldn't dream of it."

Felix began inching inside me, a slow stretch that called a whimper from my throat. He paused, brushed a strand of my hair behind my ear.

"Shh, Lucy."

He took his time easing deeper until his hips were pressed fully to mine. He was still, but I felt him throb inside me.

"Okay?"

I wrapped my arms around his shoulders. "More."

He pulled almost all the way out, and then with the same unbothered pace, returned to me. It was the best kind of torture. When he rose to his knees, rubbing two fingers against me, I shuddered out a surprised breath—my body usually wasn't ready for a second round so quickly. Only with Felix. He cupped his other hand over my mouth, and I tilted my hips at the unexpected thrill of it. The bed squeaked.

"Think you can stay still, stay quiet?" he said.

I mumbled a yes, but when his fingers moved between us, I moaned against his palm. Felix grinned, cocky and one-sided.

Nothing had ever felt as good as his hand on my mouth, his fingers between us, the rhythm he set. I felt like the sand the surf crashed over. When he spread my legs wider, pushing deeper, I whispered his name into his palm.

"I love hearing you say that." He circled his hips. I closed my eyes at the sensation, and Felix's hand moved from my mouth to my breast, taking my nipple between his thumb and index finger. I bit my bottom lip. "Say it again, Lucy."

"Felix," I whispered. "More."

We stayed wound together after, catching our breath, Felix smattering kisses to my lips and cheeks. He shifted onto the mattress beside me, bringing me with him, folding me against his chest. It wasn't long before we were both asleep.

I woke to the soft toll of bells. It was a pretty sound, a quiet twinkling, like stars coming to life. The bed shifted, and Felix unwrapped his arm from my waist and his leg from between mine. He shut off the alarm and sat on the edge of the mattress, his exceptional back to me.

"What time is it?"

"Four thirty. I thought you might want to get upstairs before anyone wakes up."

More, my body screamed. *Felix*.

He peered over his shoulder, and I sat, bringing us face-to-face.

"Okay."

Felix's hand coasted to my cheek. His thumb passed over my lip, his mouth moved closer to mine. "It's nice to see you again. We always have a good time."

My laugh came out as somewhere between a snort and a guffaw. "A very good time."

Felix smiled. "Best time I've had all year."

"You've just come back from Portugal. Surely traveling was the highlight."

His eyes danced, beautiful. "Lucy . . . Lisbon . . . It's hard to say which experience is more memorable."

"If that's the case, I think you need to improve your travel itinerary."

He nudged his nose against mine. "This itinerary suits me just fine."

We were kissing again, losing track of the hour, of sense, of anything that wasn't our lips and hands and tongues. When we finally pulled apart, our gazes remained tethered. Felix's palm came to rest on my cheek, his fingers tangled in my hair. It felt new and tender, and it made me nervous.

"We're good, right?" I whispered. "We can be normal around each other?"

Felix's hand fell from my face, and he smiled. "Yeah," he said. "We can be normal."

19

Now

Six Days Until Bridget's Wedding

When I wake up in Felix's old bedroom and the room is bright and the clock says ten thirty, my first reaction is panic.

I call Farah immediately.

"This better be important, Lucy," she says when she answers. "We're in the middle of getting our deliveries ready."

"I overslept. I wanted to make sure I didn't miss anything."

I hear her mutter under her breath. "Did you find another time to meet with Lillian about the restaurant contract?"

"I did. Tomorrow evening. I'll be back in time."

"Great, so until then, I need you to start behaving like you're on vacation. Enjoy your last day. Forget about us here, and for the sake of my sanity and yours, will you please kindly fuck off?"

She hangs up, and I stare at the screen. I don't think Farah's ever told me to fuck off before. Overt displays of frustration fall outside the narrow range of emotions she allows others to witness.

I find Bridget and Felix in the kitchen, sitting across from each other at the table, drinking their first cups of tea and speaking in hushed tones. Felix sees me first.

We stayed out on the beach last night, talking, until I began to shiver. I would have lain there all night if Felix hadn't noticed. I would have stayed beside him until my teeth chattered and my fingers turned to ice. It was almost two a.m. when we whispered good night in the kitchen.

"What's wrong?" he says now, and Bridget turns around in her seat.

"Are you okay, Bee?"

"I slept in. Went into a minor tailspin that the store was on fire, or our delivery guy canceled, or our website crashed, or the cooler broke in the night, or Farah got a stomach bug, or any multitude of disasters that could happen before ten in the morning."

Felix and Bridget stare back at me with worried expressions, looking more like siblings than ever.

"But everything was fine?" Bridget asks.

"Yeah." I take a deep breath, put on a smile that Bridget must see through, because she gets to her feet and throws her arms around me. "Poor sweet potato." She leads me to the table. "Let's get you something to eat. Wolf offered to make breakfast."

"Did he offer, or did you refuse?" I glance at Felix, who's already getting out of his chair.

"Little bit of Column A, little bit of Column B," Bridget says.

No one is dressed for the day. Felix is in soft pants that are obscene if you choose to look closely, and she's in shorts and another one of her dad's T-shirts. This one reads, HIS-TORY TEACHER. NOUN. JUST LIKE NORMAL TEACHER, BUT COOLER.

"I don't mind cooking breakfast," Felix says. He's moved to the coffee maker.

"I can do that," I tell him, reaching for the box of filters in his hand. Our fingers touch, and for a second we stand there, holding the box between us. It's the smallest slice of his skin against the smallest slice of mine. Innocent. A nothing of a touch. Except my heart speeds up and my breathing does, too. Felix shifts his index finger, drawing a line over mine, and then releases the little yellow box of paper filters. It happens so fast that I think I may have imagined him touching me, but it's also possible he didn't notice that he was doing it. That his finger wandered of its own volition. Maybe his body betrays him the same way mine does. But now my nerves are frayed and I'm picturing Felix naked and kneeling over me in the TV room, and I end up spilling coffee grounds all over the counter and floor.

I'm filling my mug after cleaning up my mess, my free hand unconsciously rubbing the knot between my neck and shoulder when I feel him watching me. When I check, he's closer than I expected. I could reach out and touch him. I automatically glance to see if Bridget's noticed, but she's not at the table.

"She's in the bathroom," Felix says. He nods in the direction of my shoulder. "What's going on there?"

"Seventy-hour workweeks."

"Want me to massage it?"

I go from a normal Lucy shade to hibiscus red in the second it takes me to say, "Umm."

"I'm not going to bite." His eyes are sparkling. Sunbeams on ocean waves. This Felix I'm used to. He's good at flirting. A natural. It takes nothing to be drawn in.

"You've been known to bite," I find myself saying.

He throws his head back and laughs.

"I'll take a rain check," I tell him. Felix's hands on my body are one of the things I want the most and need the least.

Bridget lays out the agenda for today while we eat the scrambled eggs and bacon Felix prepared. The three of us will visit Green Gables Heritage Place in Cavendish and have lunch at Blue Mussel Café in North Rustico. I'm ordering the beer and lime mussels *and* the seafood chowder poutine. Bridget is already dreaming about the seafood bubbly bake. Then we'll head back to Summer Wind for some downtime before we trek out to Tyne Valley with Zach for the oyster-shucking championship.

But when we're showered and dressed and it's time to get on our way, Bridget is buried in her phone.

"I'm going to hang back," Bridget says.

Felix and I share a glance. "Are you sure?" I ask.

"You should get out of the house for a while," Felix says.

"I'm fine," she says, stating the not-at-all obvious.

"Bridget," I try. "I want to do this with you. For old times' sake."

She peers up at me. "I can't right now. You guys go without me."

"Really?" Felix says. "I'm not sure I'll appreciate Lucy's argument about why no performance of Gilbert Blythe will ever be better than Jonathan Crombie's as much as you do."

"Jonathan Crombie was magic," Bridget says.

"Come on, Bridget," I plead. "It'll be fun. We can do our favorite Anne and Diana lines. I'll let you take Anne." I read *Anne of Green Gables* so many times when I was a kid, I know the best quotes from memory.

She laughs, and for a moment I think I have her, but then she shakes her head.

"We'll watch the movie later," Bridget says. "The DVD is kicking around somewhere."

"The shucking competition is later," I say.

"We'll watch it another time, then." A text lights up her phone, and Bridget glances at the screen. "I need to take care of this. You two go."

So we do.

20

Now

Felix is quiet on the drive except for the *tap, tap, tap* of his fingers on the steering wheel. He isn't usually fidgety.

"So Bridget was being weird, right?"

I glance at him, but I don't think he's heard me.

"Felix?"

His eyes flick to mine. "Sorry, I missed that."

"I said, Bridget was being weird."

"With the texting?"

"Yeah, with the texting. But she didn't seem upset. Do you think they're working it out?"

Felix shrugs. His tapping resumes.

"Is everything okay?" I say when we're pulling into the parking lot.

His brow furrows. "Why wouldn't it be?"

Tap, tap, tap.

"You seem nervous."

In seconds, the tips of his ears blush rose.

"I hope it's not me."

Felix shuts off the engine and turns to face me. His eyes are hooked on mine. "You don't make me nervous, Lucy."

"Okay," I say. I know there's something else coming. I want to drop his gaze, but it's impossible to look away. That speck of brown isn't just brown, I notice. There's a little green in it. That speck is hazel.

He leans in. "You make me a lot of things, but nervous isn't one of them."

My jaw drops, but then Felix pulls back with a one-sided grin and says, "I do get a little anxious on competition day, though."

"So," I say, regrouping. "I don't make you nervous, but oysters do."

He laughs and opens his door. "Exactly. Never underestimate a bivalve."

GREEN GABLES HERITAGE PLACE IS A WHITE FARMHOUSE with a green roof and shutters, sitting atop a grassy hill. There's a barn and a little trail that runs through the trees, and the rooms of the home are done up to look like they would have in the late 1800s, with flourishes inspired by the *Anne* books. The house was owned by Lucy Maud Montgomery's cousins. When she wrote *Anne of Green Gables* in 1905, Lucy was only thirty-one, just two years older than me. She drew on her childhood visits here for the setting.

You enter the property through a visitors' center, and Felix and I take our time wandering around, reading the placards about the author's early life. Her mother died of tuberculosis before Lucy was two and she was raised mostly by her grandparents.

"I forgot how sad her story is," I say to Felix as we leave the building and step into the sun. Lucy's best friend, her cousin Frederica, died of pneumonia at age thirty-five, and Lucy's marriage to a Presbyterian minister was a challenging one—both struggled with their mental health and addictions to prescription drugs. Lucy is believed to have taken her own life.

"But look at this," Felix says. We gaze over at the farmhouse. There are people everywhere—picnic tables where families stop for snacks, a couple taking turns posing in front of the building, and a stream of people waiting for a turn to walk through the home. Felix nods toward a lanky teenage girl. She's holding a periwinkle blue hardcover of *Anne of Green Gables* to her chest and openly weeping. "Look at how many lives she touched. This is a happy ending."

It's so bright, I have to cup my hand over my forehead so I can see Felix properly. "You're right," I say. "I like your way of looking at it better."

He grins. A big one. A single, perfect dimple one. "Let's go explore."

Still, I'm feeling a little blue. I've seen the eighties CBC film and its sequel at least twenty times, half of them with Bridget. It would have been nice to have come together. I miss her. I've been missing her since she moved out of our apartment. But as we shuffle through the house, Felix whispers into my ear, "'Tomorrow is a new day with no mistakes in it.'"

I look at him, surprised.

"I've read the book," he says. "And when we were kids, Bridget made me watch the movies a thousand times."

It's amazing how small the rooms are, how outlandish the wallpaper. Even though I know the movies weren't filmed here, I picture Megan Follows as Anne and Colleen Dewhurst as Marilla, churning butter in the dairy porch.

"'I'm in the depths of despair,'" I say as we tour the kitchen.

"'My life is a perfect graveyard of buried hopes,'" he replies.

Soon my cheeks begin to hurt from smiling.

"Would you rather be 'divinely beautiful or dazzlingly clever or angelically good'?" I ask Felix as we head upstairs.

He chuckles, then says quietly, "'Kindred spirits are not so scarce as I used to think.'"

The bedrooms are decorated to make you feel like you're snooping through the Cuthbert home—a man's vest and hat in one room, a dress with puffed sleeves hanging in the closet of another.

Outside, Felix and I trek down the slope, down Lover's Lane, and over the wooden foot bridge through the Haunted Wood. We don't speak, but the silence is comfortable. The path is narrow enough that, every so often, our shoulders brush, but Felix doesn't jump back at the contact and neither do I.

The feeling of wanting to hold his hand seems to come from nowhere. It startles me how strong it is. It's almost all I can think about as we meander through the forest. It's like I'm twelve all over again, that summer at camp when I had an epic crush on a sixteen-year-old counselor. He sat beside me on the bus that took us to the river for swimming, and I put my hand on my knee, making it available for him. When we got off the bus, my hand still unheld, he said, "Nice riding with you, Lisa."

Seventeen years later, I'm attracted to a guy I probably shouldn't be attracted to, wondering how disastrous it would be if I reached out and took his hand. He held mine so briefly last night, and I want to twine our fingers together, feel his large palm in my small one. But this is never happening. Holding hands with Felix would be bigger than anything we've done. Holding hands is for boyfriends, not former lovers.

By the time we're climbing the knoll to the house, my left foot is throwing a tantrum. My right isn't great, either. In a moment of style rebellion, I decided not to put my running shoes in my suitcase—I'm so sick of wearing them every day at work.

"Do you mind if we rest for a bit?" I gesture to a patch of lawn beneath a tree.

We sit, legs stretched in front of us. Felix is in jeans, per usual, and I'm wearing a yellow spaghetti strap sundress with buttons down the front and gloriously generous pockets.

"Tired?" he asks.

"My feet are." I lift an ankle and point to my strappy silver sandals. "I love them, but they don't feel the same about me. Horrible, beautiful shoes."

Felix tips his head, studying them. "They're very pretty," he says. "The pink buckles are a nice touch, and they look good with your dress. But they're probably not worth losing a foot over."

There's something about Felix assessing my footwear that's deeply funny.

"What?" he asks as I'm laughing. His smile is mystified.

"Felix Clark, fashion critic—I had no idea."

"I'm full of surprises." He motions to my foot. "Let me see it."

"You want to check the quality of the craftsmanship?" I ask, shifting so that I'm facing him, my knees folded up and my feet next to his thigh.

"Something like that." His hand wraps around my ankle, and he brings my left foot onto his lap. He unfastens the buckle, fingers grazing my skin. When I shiver, he lifts his eyes to mine.

"That was involuntary," I tell him, and he smirks.

He takes off the shoe, setting it on the grass. When his hands close around my foot and begin rubbing the arch with his thumbs, I tell him my feet are gross. They're dirty from our little hike.

"Shush," he says.

So I shush. I lean back on my elbows, and let Felix have his way with my toes. I close my eyes, and tilt my face to the sun, because Felix is about to give my foot an orgasm, and I can't look at him or what his hands are doing.

"Other one," he says eventually, taking hold of my right ankle, unbuckling the strap. Both feet are in Felix's lap, and even though I'm consciously making an effort not to shudder, I haven't felt this relaxed in a long time. I haven't had such a fun day since . . . since the day I spent with Felix on the beach a year ago. My bones are liquid gold. The tightness in my chest, gone. It can't just be the coastal air. Or the massage.

"This is nice," I say, prying an eye open to gaze at Felix. And even though I know I shouldn't, I picture another, impossible world, where Felix and I belong to each other. His useful hands. Oysters on ice. Nights in his solid embrace.

He looks at me curiously. "Prince Edward Island?"

Umm. "Prince Edward Island," I repeat. Sure. "And resting for a minute. I'm probably working too much."

"So why don't you rest for a minute?"

I look at the sky, squinting. "I can't. It's not the time. I feel like I've been running a marathon at a sprinter's pace, only there's no finish line." There are hardly any clouds today. Just a few wisps of white in the distance. "We have this huge opportunity at work—a contract that would mean big things for us. Getting everything set up so we can pull it off is going to be . . . a lot."

"You can do it."

I meet Felix's gaze. So steady. So sure. So like his sister in that way. "I can."

"But you're not sure you want to."

"How can you tell?"

He shrugs a shoulder. "I know you, Lucy. I know what you sound like when you're excited about something."

"You know what I sound like when I'm excited."

He laughs. "I know both those things. I know more than that, too."

Felix holds my eyes with his for a moment. "What would it feel like if you said no to the contract?"

"Terrible," I tell him. "Impossible. I'd feel like I'd failed the business, failed Farah—she's really excited about it. I've always wanted to prove myself with In Bloom. I've always wanted it to be a success, but it felt so much more important after my aunt died. Like if I lose it, I'll lose her altogether." I feel myself getting choked up, so I smile. Sometimes the act alone can make me more cheerful. "But I won't lose it. I've got Bridget in my corner, and she'd never let that happen."

A flicker of something crosses Felix's eyes. "*You'll* never let that happen. I'm sure Bridget has been a huge help, but you don't need her."

I'm about to protest, but he picks up my left foot again. "I had no idea you were so good at this," I say, closing my eyes once more.

"There's a lot you don't know about me, Lucy," I hear.

On our way out, we walk past a display of small white cards with messages from visitors, standing in metal holders. English. French. Japanese. German. Childish scribbles. I pause when I come to the one that reads, *I am here now, and everything is okay.*

It feels like it's written just for me.

From the corner of my eye, I see Felix pick up a pen and write something on a blank card. He sets it in an empty holder.

This is Lucy's happy ending.

I look at him, and then at the dozens and dozens of messages.

I am here now, and everything is okay.

21

Autumn, Two Years Ago

Bridget moved into Miles's condo that fall, and the transition was harder than I'd expected. As roommates, we spent countless nights dancing in our socks in the kitchen, talking until our voices grew hoarse and our eyelids drooped. I made hot toddies and mashed bananas on toast when she was sick; she held my hand while I cried. But now she had her big job and her live-in boyfriend. As the future sprawled before us, a tendril of fear curled around my spine. We were getting older. We were growing up. The day had come when we wouldn't dance in our socks in the kitchen anymore.

I decided to cut back on takeout and fancy coffees and manicures and keep the apartment. It would be tight, but I could make it work. I convinced myself I'd enjoy living alone. I could turn the spare room into an office. But when Bridget and Miles pulled away in the moving van, I lay on the floor of her empty bedroom and sobbed.

I was so lonely with her gone. I wanted someone to fill the emptiness she'd left behind. Until that point, I had approached my dating life like a buffet, never committing to one dish, never settling down with one person. Carter was a friend of Miles's, and we'd been on a few dates that year, but after Bridget moved out, we started seeing each other more often.

He was a few years older than me and worked in sales for a tech company, a job he mildly detested but earned him a hefty enough salary that he didn't complain. He had good manners, a nice watch, and a financial advisor. And he was handsome, in that tall, slim, and smacking of success type of way. My mother approved of him, which pleased me more than it should have.

Stacy was confused about why we were spending so much time together, and she told me so over spaghetti and meatballs with Bridget. We were sitting in our regular spots around my aunt's kitchen table when she, out of nowhere, said she hadn't pictured me with someone so drab.

"He's not drab," I argued. "He's fine."

"He's a little drab," Bridget said, her mouth full of pasta. "He kind of reminds me of your dad."

"Not helping," I told her. "And gross."

"Lucy, you deserve so much more than *fine*," Stacy said. "You should have a partner who sets you on fire."

I pictured Felix instantly.

"I don't need fire right now," I told her. "I need company."

"They make vibrators for that," Bridget said.

"Ha. That's not what I mean."

Stacy kissed my forehead. "I know."

For the rest of that evening, I couldn't seem to push Felix from my mind. I fell asleep, thinking about the way he kissed me last Thanksgiving, hearing him whisper, *You're a goddamn wonder.*

And then the storm came.

AS HURRICANE FIONA PREPARED TO RAVAGE PRINCE EDWARD Island that September, I tracked it on my phone, my fear growing with every article that predicted it would be the worst that Atlantic Canada had ever faced. Power outages. Rainfall warnings. Wind warnings. Surge warnings. Potential shoreline erosion.

Because Summer Wind was on the coast, Ken and Christine were leaving the house to stay with Bridget and Felix's grandparents. But the eastern side of the island, where Felix lived, was supposed to get the worst, and even Bridget seemed fretful. Carter and I had tickets for the symphony the evening Fiona hit. Roy Thomson Hall was a large venue, but I felt trapped. The music sounded ominous, the performers' black clothing, funereal.

Through Bridget, I learned how Felix's home had shaken the night of the storm. He was without power for weeks. But he was okay. His house was okay. Salt Cottages were well under construction, and they, too, were unharmed. There were trees down everywhere. One narrowly missed his truck. A neighbor's roof had been torn off. Felix was lucky.

Summer Wind was less fortunate. The windows on the north side of the building had been shattered; the rooms facing the sea soggy with water damage. Cedar shingles were torn off the side of the building.

Once Felix's power returned, Bridget told him to get his ass on a plane and come for a visit.

IT WAS A WEDNESDAY EVENING IN OCTOBER, AND WHILE it wasn't face masks and Thai, Bridget and I were together. We sat on the pretty back patio of a snack bar in the west end with Miles and Carter, one of the rare occasions when all our schedules aligned. The space was enclosed in glass for the cooler months and full of plants, like a greenhouse that served burrata. A fifth chair sat empty at our table. Felix would be arriving any minute.

This would be his second trip to Toronto. He and Ken had driven Bridget to the city for her first year of university. They'd shlepped her stuff into the residence hall, ate wings at a pub near the campus, spent one night at a hotel in the north end, then hightailed it out of there. Rush-hour traffic, a late-summer garbage day, and the disaster that is frosh—Toronto hadn't made the best impression.

According to Bridget, Felix was now dating a paramedic named Chloe. The news had surprised me. Felix hadn't seen anyone seriously since he and Joy broke up four years earlier.

"Bee," Bridget said. "Leg."

I apologized. I hadn't realized I'd been jiggling it. I shouldn't have been anxious to see Felix again. For the first time since I met him, we were both in relationships. And while the night Felix and I spent together over Thanksgiving last year had felt *more* than ever before, we were back to normal the next day and parted with a friendly hug at the airport. This time would be different. Good different, I told myself.

"Wolf! You made it," Bridget said, looking over my shoulder. She got to her feet and squeezed his cheeks. Felix dropped an overnight bag on the floor. I hadn't seen him in twelve months, and he looked great. More mature. His beard was still short, but his hair was, too, cropped close on the sides, the waves no longer crashing over his forehead. He wore a leather jacket that looked new, a white Henley underneath, and jeans cuffed over his suede boots. He was casual compared to the rest of us—Miles was in a business suit and Carter had a cashmere sweater over his collared shirt—but on someone as attractive as Felix, it read like a power move. We gave each other a polite hug, I introduced Carter, and Felix took the seat next to me.

"How long are you staying?" I asked, doing my best not to

stare. It felt like a magic trick. Felix here. In the city. On this patio.

"Just a few days," he said. "The bathroom tile for the cottages is finally being delivered Saturday. I want to install it soon so we can get a photographer out. We want the website ready when people start booking their summer vacation."

I needn't have been nervous. Dinner was easy. Fun. Natural. There weren't any awkward moments or sex-eyes. Felix described flying into Toronto, how the lights glowed orange and white in the night sky and then he noticed fireworks bursting across the entire GTA. The woman beside him explained they were for Diwali, but it felt like a special welcome. Just once, when Carter had his arm around my shoulder, did I notice Felix watching Carter's fingers twiddling the ends of my hair.

Carter had an early client presentation the next morning and left while we ordered a last round.

"You should come by In Bloom tomorrow if you have time," I told Felix as we said our good nights in front of the restaurant. "I'm there all day until we close at six."

He said, "Sure, maybe I will." And when we hugged, he held me just a little tighter than he had earlier in the night.

The next day passed with no sign of Felix—not that I was surprised. I had offered him a tepid invitation, and he had given me a noncommittal response. Farah left early to prepare for a spoken-word performance at an upscale essential oil retailer in the Eaton Centre. "It pays," she explained.

I locked the door at six, closed out the cash, put the till in the safe, and was about to begin sweeping when I heard the knock.

Tap, tap. Pause. *Tap.*

My hands froze, but I didn't look up until it sounded again.

I lifted my eyes. Felix was standing on the other side of the door, a toque pulled low over his ears. His breath left his mouth in misty puffs.

Before I met Carter, I had fantasies that started this way, with Felix showing up at the shop after hours. I imagined letting him inside and him kissing me before I had a chance to say hello. I'd bring him to the office and unzip his jeans and use my mouth to show him how much I wanted him.

I raised my hand, and Felix raised his, but I didn't move. For untold seconds, all I did was stare. I didn't think he'd come.

"It's cold out, Lucy," I heard him say through the glass, and I gave my head a shake.

We didn't break eye contact as I crossed the store toward him. I'm not sure I even blinked. I unlocked the deadbolt and Felix stepped inside.

"You're here," I said.

"Is that okay?"

Normal, I told myself. *Be normal.*

"Of course, yes. Come in." I waved an arm behind me.

I completely redecorated after I took over from my aunt. I was going for urban farmhouse—shiplap walls painted Cloud White, matte black fixtures, the oversize oak table near the back. I displayed the flowers in galvanized steel sap buckets, arranged by color on the wall opposite the front door so customers were greeted with a rainbow of flora as soon as they stepped inside. On a sunny day, light would stream through the windows, and I thought there was no prettier space in all of Toronto. But it was even more incredible when the sky was gray and the city felt dingy.

"So this is it." Felix surveyed the space, turning in a slow circle. "It's beautiful, Lucy. It's like stepping into spring."

It was one of the loveliest compliments I'd received, but all I could think to say in response was, "Thanks."

"Did you do these?" He was standing by the bucket of bouquets. There were two left. The flowers got an update when In Bloom became mine, too. Stacy preferred dense, dramatic arrangements. If there was a calla lily in sight, my aunt had it in a vase. She was the showstopping Butchart Gardens, but I was a rambling English flower bed—unfussy and romantic.

"This one," I said, pointing to the bundle of pale yellow and peach ranunculus and roses.

"How much?"

"Oh." I was already blushing. "I've already shut down the cash, but it's all yours. Consider it a 'welcome to Toronto' gift."

"Deal," he said. "Dinner's on me, then."

"Dinner?"

"Yeah. Unless you have plans?"

I did. And she was staring at us through the shop window, eyebrows raised. I waved at Stacy, gesturing for her to come in. She still had a set of keys. I watched Felix take in my aunt. She wore her salt-and-pepper hair cropped short, her lips painted crimson. Stacy was my mom's older sister by five years and had the same cheekbones we did. She was dressed in head-to-toe red—trousers, cashmere turtleneck, wool coat all in the same shade of scarlet. She was striking, and I could see from Felix's expression that he thought so, too.

"Darling," she said, giving me a kiss on each cheek, her hazel eyes on Felix. "What have I interrupted?"

"Stacy, this is Felix, Bridget's brother. Stacy is my aunt," I told Felix.

"Oh, how fun." She kissed the air beside his face. "Your

sister is my surrogate niece. I love that girl. Foul mouth, but what a spark."

"It's nice to meet you," he said. "Lucy was giving me the tour. It's incredible."

Stacy assessed him. "It is," she agreed. "Though I can't take credit for it. This is all Lucy."

He nodded. "It feels like Lucy."

Her eyes narrowed, a sly smile playing on her full lips. "Hmm."

I felt a pronouncement coming, possibly a dangerous one. "Felix, my aunt and I had dinner plans tonight, but you're welcome to join us." I cast Stacy a look that I hoped conveyed that I needed her to be on her best behavior.

Stacy glanced between Felix and me. "You two go enjoy yourselves without me tagging along."

"We don't mind," I said. "Do we?"

"Not at all," Felix said. "Lucy talks about you all the time."

I tilted my head. He'd noticed that?

"Hmm." My aunt's lips were curled in mischief. "Very tempting, but not tonight. Lucy, I'll see you and Bridget for dinner this Sunday. I've ordered a lasagna."

I nodded. "We'll be there."

"It was lovely to meet you," she said to Felix. She turned to me. "Darling, walk me out."

"He's edible," she said once we were outside. If Felix hadn't been watching us through the window, I think she would have been rubbing her hands together and licking her lips.

"He is." It was an undeniable fact.

"You've slept together."

I flushed immediately. It wasn't a question. She knew.

"I haven't told Bridget."

Her grin fell. "You must."

"It wasn't serious, and it's over. There's no point upsetting her."

"Lucy, I very much doubt that it's over. There was enough tension between the two of you to bounce a coin off. That gorgeous creature is smitten, and from the way you're blushing, I'd say you're also taken with him."

"It *is* over. He was just a *lover*, as you would say. Nothing more. I don't understand why you're making a big deal out of this. You've been so opposed to me seeing Carter."

Stacy sighed. "I'm worried I've rubbed off on you so much that you can't see what you really want. I've lived my life for myself. I love my independence. I don't believe in one true love. For *me*. We have so much in common, but I don't think we're the same this way. You crave people, taking care of others, and being taken care of."

"That doesn't mean I need a man."

"Of course not." She thought for a moment before she spoke. "I think you'd like having a partner. But you've chosen to date someone you'll never fall in love with. Carter is a waste of your time."

"You don't know that," I said, though I knew she was right.

"I do." Stacy gave me two kisses, then met my eyes. "Whatever happens, don't keep secrets from Bridget. Trust me on this."

I returned to Felix after she left, shaken.

"I have to finish closing here," I told him, walking straight to the back to get the broom. "But if you don't mind waiting, we can head out after."

Felix followed me, asking if he could help, so I handed him the broom while I moved the flowers into the cooler. Before we left, I wrapped his bouquet with brown paper and a wide black-and-white-striped ribbon.

I handed him the flowers, meeting his eyes for the first time since coming back inside. I was relieved to find there was no electricity there. My aunt was wrong about Felix. He had Chloe; I had Carter. Maybe this could be the beginning of something new. Something safer. More like what it should be.

"You okay?" he said.

"Yeah. I'm good." It felt like we were finally on solid ground.

I gathered my coat, and we walked along Queen Street East, toward the cozy wine bar Farah and I liked to visit after work. As we passed the windows of an independent bookstore, Felix paused.

"Let's go in," I said.

We browsed around separately. I went to the home and garden section, and Felix presumably went to find something published before the invention of the automobile. I was flipping through the pages of *Floret Farm's Cut Flower Garden* when he found me. He was holding his flowers and a tote bag with the store's logo on the front.

"That was fast," I said, closing the book. Felix peered at the photograph on the cover. It was of a woman walking through a field in rubber boots, an armful of orange dahlias thrown over her shoulder.

He read the subtitle aloud, "*Grow, Harvest, and Arrange Stunning Seasonal Blooms.*" Then looked at me. "May I?"

I handed him the book, and he turned through the pretty pages.

"The author owns a flower farm in Washington," I told him. "It started as a tiny backyard garden, and she and her husband turned it into a massive teaching farm and seed company."

I followed them on Instagram and scrolled through the feed with envy and admiration.

Felix went back to the beginning, eyes moving quickly over the page titled, "Key Cutting Garden Plant Types." He read fast. I'd noticed it that first summer.

"A cut flower farm," Felix said after a minute. "Is this something you'd want to do?" He glanced at me.

I used to think staring into Felix's eyes was like staring at an ice floe. But I was wrong. They were warm, not glacial. Staring into Felix's eyes was like floating in a blue lagoon.

I shrugged. "It's silly."

"I don't think so," he said back.

"I think I'd like to grow my own flowers one day," I said. I hadn't told anyone this before, not even Bridget. "I'd like to have a farm."

Felix held my eyes for three long seconds. I looked at that little dot of brown in his right eye.

"See, it is silly."

"It's not," he said. "It's perfect. I can picture it: you on a farm, surrounded by flowers."

"It's just a dream."

"It's a good dream," he said, then walked toward the cash register. He passed the clerk the book.

"You don't have to do that. I don't have a garden, and my balcony doesn't get enough light for me to grow much of anything on it."

"Dream big with me, Lucy."

22

Autumn, Two Years Ago

As we walked to the wine bar, I pointed to my favorite neighborhood landmarks. The mural on the side of the butcher shop. The coffee shop with the best salted chocolate chip cookies. Felix had a shopping bag in one hand and the bouquet of flowers in the other. It was a good look.

"So what did you get?" I asked him once we were seated on stools around a horseshoe bar.

He pulled a copy of *White Teeth* out of his bag and placed it on the counter.

"That's not like you. You usually read stuff written decades before we were born."

He blinked at that, like he was surprised I'd noticed. "I'm making my way through a list of modern classics."

"Ah," I said, surveying the wine list.

"They have a vinho verde." Felix pointed to the menu, and I smiled. I guess he'd picked up on a few things about me, too.

We ordered tapas. I told him about Carter, and he told me about Chloe. She'd recently moved to the island from Ottawa. They'd met in Charlottetown, when she asked him for directions to Water Prince Corner Shop, and they had now been dating for a couple of months.

"Finally ran out of tourists, huh?" I joked as the bartender delivered two glasses of the crisp white wine.

But Felix didn't laugh. He tipped his head. "There weren't that many."

"Oh, come on," I said, taking a sip. "I'm not offended I wasn't special. I know how you used your recommendation list as a way of getting someone's number."

He studied me in a way that made my chest prickle. "I sent that list to a lot of people. I started compiling it because I knew I wanted to put it into a brochure for guests at the cottages one day."

"That was three years ago. I didn't realize you and Zach were thinking about Salt Cottages back then."

"Yeah," he said. "We started planning a few months before I met you. I know I seemed like a loser oyster shucker—dumped by his fiancée and living with his parents—but I was saving."

"That's not how I saw you," I said. "Not at all."

Felix shrugged a shoulder, and I wasn't sure if it was because he didn't believe me or if he didn't really care what I'd thought of him.

"Anyway, I didn't run out of tourists. That's not what I'm looking for. I was never really a casual fling kind of guy."

"But Joy threw you off course?"

"Partly," he said, gaze fixed on mine. "And it's hard to resist a woman in a tablecloth who tells you she's wide open." His eyes shimmered. Teased.

"Ha. With a line that smooth, how could you resist?"

"I couldn't. It was impossible."

"Have you always been a reader?" I asked. I thought about

the copy of *Wide Sargasso Sea* that lay on his nightstand that first night.

"You know that I didn't go to college?"

I nodded. "How come?"

"I didn't see the point of it. I thought I had my future all figured out. Zach went to Dalhousie in Halifax, and when he'd come home, he had so much to talk about—new ideas, new people, new bits of trivia. Even the way he spoke changed slightly—I think he probably enjoyed showing off his vocabulary." He smiled. "But I felt like I was missing out, so I asked him to share his English reading lists with me. I made my way through those books, and then I kept going. At the beginning, it was about not being left behind, but I discovered how much I love reading." His voice had deepened, turned a little hoarse. "My parents both had year-round work and steady incomes, but that's not a given on the island. Other than Portugal, I haven't traveled much because I've been so cautious with money, but I love how books can transport you almost anywhere."

"Have you ever considered writing?"

He looked surprised by my question.

"I bet you'd be good at it."

"I have a journal, but most of my writing is in the margins of books."

"Defiling your precious novels? Felix Clark, I'm shocked."

He chuckled, and when our eyes met, I flushed with warmth. The spark, it was there, but different. Less of a dangerous crackle and more like a comfortable hum.

"So you've done Portugal. But what's next on your list?"

He ran his teeth over his bottom lip. "I couldn't pick. Everywhere, anywhere. France or Italy. A backpack, trains, baguettes, a good book in a big park. Or England. So much literary history there. But there's so much *history* everywhere. Germany. Turkey. India. I'd love to see Japan and now Australia, thanks to Miles. Scotland. Brazil."

I started laughing. "You're just naming all the places."

"I'd see them all if I could. But I'd always go home. I'd always go back to Prince Edward Island."

I sighed. "There's nowhere I love better, either. It feels like home to me when I'm there, too."

"Maybe you should make it home one day. You could find a few acres of land for your farm. It's not as expensive as it is here."

The thought had crossed my mind, but only as a fleeting fancy. My life was in Toronto. The shop, my aunt, my best friend. I could never live so far from them. And I didn't know the first thing about managing a farm. I was still finding my feet running the flower shop.

"Can you do me a favor?" I said later, as we finished a plate of manchego drizzled with honey. The past few hours with Felix had been a relief. Maybe we could start over as friends and put the past behind us.

He looked at me from the corner of his eye. "Of course."

"Don't tell your sister about the whole flower farm thing."

"How come? I mean, I won't if you ask me not to, but why wouldn't you want Bridget to know?"

"Have you met your sister? If I mentioned the idea to her, she'd be dragging me to see acreages within a week. If she thought I was sitting on a dream, she wouldn't let me get away with not seeing it through." I loved Bridget's encouragement, but I needed to do things at my own pace.

"All right. I promise I won't say anything to Bridget about your farm." His mouth hooked up on the left side. "I'm good at keeping secrets."

The following evening, Miles cooked something compli-
cated that no doubt required going to thirteen specialty grocers
and the fancy butcher. His idea of heaven. Felix and I washed up.
It was simple, all four of us together. It felt like family and friendship and something else I wasn't sure how to name.

I saw Felix again Friday morning, a breakfast before his
flight. Bridget had a six a.m. yoga class and was happy to leave
her brother in my care. We ate eggs Benny, and he told me about
all the work he'd done at Salt Cottages. He wanted my advice on
social media and his website and took my answers seriously, pulling out his phone to type a few notes. He even listened to my
soliloquy about online reviews.

"You should come see the cottages when you're on the island
next," he said. "It's a bit of a drive from Summer Wind, but you
and Bridget could make a day of it. Hit up Basin Head and Souris.
We can do a barbecue at my place."

"I'd like that," I told him, grinning. This was friendship,
coming into bloom. New buds on old wood, like a hydrangea
plant in spring. "You got to see my baby. I want to see yours, too.
And I'll need to snoop through your bookshelf. I'm sure it's
epic."

His smile was warm. "Maybe next summer."

THE FIRST PACKET OF SEEDS ARRIVED THE FOLLOWING
week in a yellow envelope. My name was on the outside, but
there was no note, only a paper sleeve with a picture of dahlias
on the front. I brought it to the office and pulled the book Felix
bought me off the shelf. I studied the woman on the cover of *Floret Farm's Cut Flower Garden* and the bouquet of orange dahlias
flung over her shoulder.

After we closed that evening, I walked to the bookstore. I wandered around, not sure what I was looking for. But then I saw a beautiful clothbound edition of *Wide Sargasso Sea*. I mailed it to Prince Edward Island the next day. I didn't write a note. I didn't need to.

My gift said, *I'm thinking of you,* all on its own. Just as his did.

23

Now

Six Days Until Bridget's Wedding

"What are the chances your sister has used her time alone to figure her shit out, and now she'll tell us everything?" I ask Felix on the drive back from Green Gables.

We've been chatting today like we did when we spent time together in Toronto two years ago. I'm vaguely aware that I've been enjoying his soft chuckles and thoughtful questions a little too much. His smile, now readily available, makes my chest *feel* things. But he's not the Clark I should be focusing on.

Felix hasn't responded to my question, so I press on. "Do you think it's possible she's had a breakthrough? Maybe when we show up, she'll be ready to tell us what the problem is and how she plans to fix it?"

Felix glances my way. "I really hope so."

"If not, I'm going to have to talk to her. I need to sort out her wedding order before we watch you shuck your heart out at the competition tonight." I don't want to beg Bridget, but she's getting married in six days, and there's a time crunch. The flower auction is less than forty-eight hours from now. I have to force the issue.

"I think that's a good idea," Felix says. "She's had long enough."

When we arrive at Summer Wind and Felix shuts off the truck, he turns to me. "Once you have a chance to speak with Bridget, let me know?" He opens the door. "I need to take a nap before I shuck. Someone kept me up late, talking on the beach last night," he says, climbing out with a smirk.

Felix retreats to the TV room pull-out sofa, and I find Bridget pacing by the fire pit, phone to her ear. I wait until she's done, then attack.

"We need to talk."

WE HEAD TO THE WATER, THROUGH THE DUNES, AND AS soon as we step onto the sand, we take off our shoes and leave them on a rock while we walk.

"It hurts that you haven't told me what's going on," I say. Bridget stares at her feet. "And I can't make you, even though, if our roles were reversed, you'd drag it out of me."

She looks at me then, squinting. "Would I?"

The question sits there.

And then she says, "You don't think if you were keeping something from me, I'd respect that there was a good reason, and let you tell me in your own time?"

My stomach lurches. It's a familiar feeling, the one I get when I think about the secrets piling up between us. If Bridget ever finds out that I've slept with her brother, and not just once by accident, the length of time I've been withholding is only going to make it worse. I should have told her already.

"I think you would tempt me with Miles's paella and wine and weasel it out of me."

"Maybe."

"Definitely." Bridget wouldn't let it go if she suspected I was hiding something. "I just need to know if I should order your flowers. At the minimum, tell me that."

"Yes," she says quietly. "Order them."

"Okay. Good." I study Bridget. She has none of her usual sparkle. "Right?"

Bridget links her arm through mine. "Let's keep walking."

We stroll in silence, and I tuck her against my side.

We used to tell each other everything, but a crack has formed between us. It felt easier to keep pieces of myself from her. The flower farm. Felix. I'd tucked away my doubts about Carter, knowing she'd pounce. I stopped sharing the minutiae of my days—a delayed floral shipment seemed too small to bother her with. But only now do I see that everything I've hidden has put a wedge in our relationship, robbed us of the uncomplicated intimacy we once had. I wonder whether Bridget has been squirreling bits of herself away from me, too.

I hold her tighter. "I'm here," I tell her. "When you're ready."

But she doesn't speak.

And I can't go home until she does. Our friendship is fractured, and I need to repair it—there's nothing more important than Bridget. Not a restaurant group contract. Not my stress. Not even flowers. Which means I can't leave until Bridget tells me her truth. I can't leave until I tell her mine.

24

Now

Felix is a mess—jittery and uncharacteristically clumsy. In the five minutes before we're supposed to leave for Tyne Valley, he manages to knock over Christine's Christmas cactus, shatter a water glass, and misplace his keys.

"He's always like this on competition day," Bridget says as we search the living room. "He's also got these random superstitions, like wearing the hat and the shirt."

I peer at Felix. He's lying on his stomach, looking for his keys under the sideboard. When he stands, I see that the gray shirt he's put on is almost transparent. I can barely make out its faded white lettering, but I'm sure one of the words is OYSTER. His olive green baseball hat also has an ancient-looking patina. It's mesh-backed, with McINNIS SEAFOOD written across the front. I know from extensive social media creeping that it's Joy's family business.

"Wolf wore that hat when he won the junior shucking championship a million years ago," Bridget says.

"Eleven years ago," Felix corrects.

"I think you wear it to make Joy's father cry," she says. "The son he always wanted."

Felix gives her a flat look, and then Zach calls from the kitchen, "Found them." He holds up the keys. "They were in the cupboard with the glasses."

Felix stumbles over a corner of a rug on his way to retrieve them.

"You're even more of a disaster than usual, Wolf," Bridget says.

"I'd say he's about the same," Zach says.

Felix shoots him a half-hearted glare. "It's important to me."

"We know," Bridget says. "It's your thing. Your only thing."

"Not true," Zach says. "He has two things: oysters *and* books."

"I have more than two things."

"Name them," Bridget says.

"Get lost." He turns to me, laughing. His gaze is warm—it feels like swimming in paradise. "Anything you want to add?"

"Try not to stab yourself."

He winks. "No promises."

"WHY DON'T I DRIVE?" I SAY TO FELIX WHEN WE HEAD out to the truck, but he shakes his head.

"I'm fine."

He's not. He drums his fingers on the steering wheel the entire forty-five-minute drive to Tyne Valley. He takes a break every so often to wave hello to an oncoming vehicle, or lift his hat, wiggle it around, and set it back on his head.

There's a community supper at the fire hall, and we stuff ourselves with fried oysters and potato salad and coleslaw and lemon pie. Well, Bridget, Zach, and I do. Felix mostly pushes his food around.

We walk across the street to the arena, where people are streaming inside. Felix is so distracted, he trips over his own feet.

"Whoa there, son," a large man says, holding Felix's arm to keep him upright.

"Ray," Felix says, giving him a hug. "Good to see you."

Ray has an auburn beard sprinkled with white, sun-worn skin, and bourbon eyes. His T-shirt is the same green as Felix's hat. It takes me a second to see McINNIS SEAFOOD written across its chest, and another to put it all together. Ray is Joy's dad.

"Look who's here," Felix says.

Ray's smile grows as he pulls Bridget to him. "It's been too long, girl. But you're too thin," he says. "They don't feed you back in Toronto?"

Bridget pats his belly. "Not as good as they do at home." Ray lets out a deep laugh, as if it comes from the bottom of a well.

"Good to see both young Clarks here. Brings back memories," Ray says after Felix introduces me. "I'll never forget the night you took home junior shucker. You were, what, eighteen?"

"Seventeen," Felix says.

"Seventeen." Ray shakes his head. He puts one large hand around Felix's shoulder. "Watching you win was one of the proudest moments of my life."

"Mine, too," Felix says solemnly.

"Well, I better find the wife. She gets antsy before the grading contest. Good luck tonight, son."

"Thanks, Ray," Felix says. "Break a leg."

"So that was Joy's dad," I say to Felix as we head inside the arena behind Bridget and Zach.

"Uh-huh." He's preoccupied, his gaze pinging around the crowd.

"And the founding member of your fan club. He really likes you."

He looks at me then. "Yeah," Felix says. "Ray's all right."

The arena is already half-full when we get inside. Everyone is gathered on the concrete surface where the ice will become winter. There's a stage at one end, a couple hundred folding chairs arranged in front. Canopied stalls are set up at the back of the space—a bar, an oyster station. Guns N' Roses plays over the sound system, and volunteers mill about in bright red TYNE VALLEY OYSTER FESTIVAL T-shirts.

I am absurdly overdressed. Most people are in cotton tees and shorts. Flip-flops or sneakers. I, on the other hand, have put on a silk smoking dress covered in oversize poppies, which I'd tucked into my suitcase on the unlikely chance Bridget wanted to go into Charlottetown for a night out. I did a cat eye.

"Why didn't you tell me this was a casual event?" I say to Bridget as we pass a young woman wearing a tiara and a sash that reads MISS OYSTER PEARL—even she's wearing denim cutoffs and a tank top. Bridget has on something similar, but I thought that was just Bridget being Bridget.

"What about an oyster-shucking event in a community arena suggested not-casual?" She scrunches her face. "Why do you care? You look the way you always do when you go out."

It's true. I've been the dressiest person in the room many times in my life. It's kind of my thing, and it's never bothered me before.

"You're right," I say. "I don't care." But I think maybe I do. This is Felix's world, and part of me is wondering if I could ever fit into it.

Felix is pulled aside by one person, then another. A man a bit younger than his father claps him on the back and asks about his grandparents. A guy our age asks him why he hasn't seen him at the gym this week. A couple—who by their matching ISLAND SPUDS hats I assume must own a potato farm—invite Felix to their home for dinner next week. Many of those who stop him are women. Many of them beautiful. I watch a brunette put her hand on his chest, over his heart. My belly pinches strangely. Which is silly. I have no claim on Felix.

The emcee is already onstage—bearded, ball-capped, and wearing a shirt that reads LET'S GET SHUCKED—going over the rules.

"After the juniors shuck, it's the grading contest," Bridget explains. Felix has vanished into the crowd. "And then the national shucking championship is after that. We have a couple hours before Wolf competes."

"What do we do until then?" I ask as Felix reappears, clutching three cans of beer.

He passes one to each of us. "Drink."

"What about you?"

"No alcohol before I shuck," he says. "Then . . . a lot of it."

"I'll drive us home," Zach says. "I won't drink anything after this."

I see her over Felix's shoulder just before she gives it a tap. Her hair is such a pale shade of red, it's almost blond. It extends to her mid-back, and her bangs are immaculate. Joy is even more stunning than when I met her three years ago.

I watch Felix hug his ex, holding my breath. I've never seen Joy and Felix in the same room, and it's staggering how easy they are together. After they embrace, Bridget holds her arms open and proceeds . . . to . . . hug . . . Joy?

"Joy! I'm so glad you're here." She nods at the stopwatch around Joy's neck. "Wolf didn't tell us you were volunteering."

It's like I've entered an alternate dimension, one where my best friend wouldn't be the primary suspect if Joy were found murdered in her sleep.

"Surprise," Felix says, giving Joy a grin and a dimple.

"You're looking at one of the official timers for this year's Canadian Oyster-Shucking Championship," Joy says, puffing out her chest in jest.

"You should be shucking yourself," Felix says, his voice fond.

She rolls her eyes. "Yes, Dad."

I'm mostly at peace with my curves, but Joy is so toned, she makes me feel like a moose in a maxidress. Her hair is in a high ponytail, and she's in a red volunteer shirt and bike shorts that treat her thighs with the adulation they deserve.

"Hi, Lucy." She leans in to embrace me. And ugh, she smells amazing, too. Like a butterscotch sundae. But an elevated one. One that would cost twenty dollars in Toronto. "It's so nice to see you again."

"You too," I tell her, though frankly, I would have preferred not being reminded how perfect and genuinely nice the woman Felix wanted to marry is. Or seeing how relaxed they are with each other.

She nods at the stage. "I gotta get up there. Lucy, I have a question for you about peonies later, if you have a sec? Mine are unhappy."

Blech, she's wonderful.

"Uh, sure."

She turns to Felix. "Mrs. Stewart is looking for you. She wants to set you up with her granddaughter in Borden-Carleton."

He looks at Joy, disturbed, and she laughs.

"I'm just warning you," she says.

Felix winces. "Thanks."

I watch them with a feeling not unlike dread. Or maybe it's a form of jealousy. It's not about the prospect of Felix being set up. Or even about Joy. It's realizing that he has a reason to fear Mrs. Stewart's granddaughter, and I don't know what it is. But Joy does. Because Joy knows Felix. He has friends who understand him and exes who he bumps into on occasion. He has people who see him year-round, not just when the weather's warm, who see him at the gym and know when he's off his routine, people who can invite him for dinner on a random Wednesday evening.

"Well, I gotta get back to it," Joy says. And then off she goes, ponytail swishing.

I must be wearing my feelings on my face because Felix gives me a questioning look. I smile, ignoring it, and turn to Bridget. "I never thought I'd see the two of you so chummy. Care to explain?"

"She reached out to me a while ago."

"Really? That's great. Why didn't you tell me?" It's another thing gone unshared between us.

"It's no big deal, Bee. We've just been texting a bit."

I make myself smile. "I'm going to need to read the entire exchange later. This is a very big deal."

We take our seats as the first heat of teenage shuckers are called onstage—two boys and one girl. There are three timers standing behind them, including Joy, one per shucker. Felix's leg bounces up and down when they start, fingers tapping on his knee.

"Cut it out," Bridget says.

"Makes me edgy to watch," he says.

"Take a walk. Bee, go with him. You're not good at sitting still, either."

We can't move three feet without someone saying hello to

Felix. He's shaking hands and making small talk like a politician. The conversations are brief, but each is a reminder: Felix Clark does not cease to exist when I leave the island. I knew that, of course, but it's been easier to imagine him tucked safely away in his cabin in the woods—busy with work the way In Bloom consumes my days in Toronto. But Felix has a whole life I know nothing about.

"Well, aren't you the prom king," I say after we finish chatting with friends of his parents'.

We're studying a table of wooden oyster crate dioramas that have been decorated by children—an octopus's garden, a bubblegum pink hair salon, a trio of baby sharks dressed for school. There's a fiddler onstage now—the juniors have finished, and their oysters are being scored by the judges.

Felix smirks. "I was."

"Of course you were." Joy and Felix, the perfect couple. "Although you don't strike me as someone who loves the spotlight."

"I'm not. But community matters to me."

"That's why you do this?"

"Yeah." He offers me a dimple. "Ego might have something to do with it, too."

"But you love it."

"I love it." He looks around the arena. "Even though I sometimes feel like I'm seventeen when I'm here."

"And that's bad? I seem to recall you were a seventeen-year-old shucking champion."

His laugh is soft. "I was a seventeen-year-old jackass."

"Somehow I doubt that." I nudge him with my elbow. "Ray said watching you win was one of the proudest moments of his life."

"Yeah. Did you know that I used to work for him?"

Felix and I haven't really talked about his history with Joy and her family. "I don't think so."

"Ray taught me everything I know about oysters, including how to shuck them. He was my boss, but he was a mentor to me, too. There were years when I spent more time with the McInnis family than my own." He shrugs. "When I won, I competed on behalf of their family business. It meant a lot to him."

"How long did you work for him?"

Felix adjusts his hat. "Pretty much the entire time Joy and I dated, so almost seven years—part-time during high school and full-time after. When Joy was away at university, I saw her parents more than I did her."

"Wow." It seems unfair that he lost his fiancée and his job in one day. "Did you ever consider staying on?"

Felix shakes his head. "It would have been too hard, and I needed to put that part of my life behind me."

I nod. "It's impressive that you and Joy are friends."

"We agreed to make an effort and be civil. We know all the same people."

He steps closer, holding my gaze with an intention that has me shifting. "And I thought life would be easier if we could be in a room together."

Before I can reply, someone else taps him on the shoulder.

We find our seats when the grading contest begins—apparently watching people sort a pile of oysters by size doesn't give Felix heart palpitations. My eyes keep wandering to Joy onstage, and I don't miss that hers travel to Felix and me between rounds. They would make sense as a couple. There's a history there. I know their families used to be close. They're more than just civil—they're friends. And they live in the same province. Move in the same circles. Joy is part of the community Felix loves.

Zach and Bridget are cheering on Joy's mom, a petite blonde who's putting her fellow graders to shame. I whisper to Felix, "Have you ever considered giving it another shot with Joy?"

Narrowed eyes move around my face, like he's trying to read an upside-down map. His gaze clears, as if he's tracked down the truth from the labyrinth of my mind. He moves toward my ear so no one else can listen and says, "Are you jealous, Lucy?"

My chest heats, and Felix pulls back. I stare into his eyes, trying to read what they're saying, but then Bridget leans over my lap.

"I think it's time for you to go do your thing, Wolf," she says. "The shuckers are gathering over there." She points to where a large group is assembling at the back of the space.

Felix gives me one last look, like he knows every single dream and doubt and dangerous thought that lies beneath my skin. And then he's gone.

25

Now

A bagpipe sounds from the back of the arena, and we turn in our seats. The musician begins a slow walk down the aisle toward the stage. He's in his early twenties, wearing a newsboy cap and a short-sleeve plaid shirt, trailed by a group of about forty people. Directly behind the bagpiper, a man hoists an enormous wooden trophy over his head, a large oyster at its center.

"I didn't realize there would be so many of them," I say to Bridget as I watch Felix. He's near the end of the procession, head tilted down so his hat covers most of his face. Ray walks alongside him, one arm slung over Felix's shoulder.

"It's a big deal," Bridget says. "The shuckers come here from across the country, and the winner competes at the worlds in Galway."

"So your brother would go to Ireland if he wins?"

"Theoretically, yes. But he won't," Bridget says. "Don't give me that look—he knows he's not going to win. That's not what this is about. It's tradition. Pride."

"Community," I murmur as Felix passes us, lifting his chin in our direction.

Bridget cups her hands around her mouth and yells, "We love you, Wolf."

"We shucking love you," Zach calls out.

Bridget and Felix have no time for my shuck puns, but if we were playing a drinking game based on the ones uttered tonight, we'd be facedown on the concrete.

"What the shuck?"

"Shucks to be you."

"Aww, shucks."

Felix's ears are bright pink by the time he reaches the stage. The competitors gather for a group photo, and Ray pulls out his phone to take selfies with Felix, both pointing to their McInnis Seafood swag.

The troupe is shuffled off, and the emcee goes over the rules. Each shucker gets twenty oysters and chooses eighteen to shuck as fast as they can. Afterward, judges assess the bivalves, adding penalty time for any errors.

"There's a thirty-second penalty for any oysters out of their shell," he says. "If there's blood on the oyster, that's also a thirty-second penalty."

"I didn't think oysters had blood," I say to Bridget.

"He means the shucker's blood," she says, and I grimace.

"All right, Tyne Valley," the emcee calls. "Let's! Get! Shucked!"

He calls out the first four competitors, Ray among them, and they sort through their box of Malpeques, arranging them before they begin. A timer stands behind each. Joy is assigned to a woman who has brought a small wooden platform to rest her oysters on. Two shuckers wear a glove on one hand. Ray has placed a folded tea towel at his station. I had no idea there were so many methods. Felix uses his bare hands and the tabletop.

"Timers, are you ready?" the emcee calls. The shuckers lean over the table, palms raised above their heads. The timers nod.

"Shuckers, are you ready?"

None of them look up.

"Tyne Valley, are you reeeeaaaaaaaady?"

The arena erupts in cheers.

"Then let's count them down. Three. Two. One. Shuck!"

I watch Ray work. He sets his oyster on the tea towel and sinks his knife into the hinge of the shell, twists his wrist to open it, then runs the blade along the inside of the top shell, removing it in one swift movement.

I look for Felix beside the stage. He's there with his arms folded across his chest, Joy's mother beside him.

As soon as Ray sets his eighteenth oyster on a salt-filled tray, he taps the butt of his knife against the table three times. He's the first to finish.

"Two minutes and twenty-two seconds for Ray McInnis," the emcee calls. "Good time."

Ray walks off the stage and heads straight to Felix and his wife. But he doesn't hug her first. He throws his arms around Felix, the two of them laughing.

"They're close, huh?"

Bridget follows my gaze. "Used to be," she says. "I feel sorry for him."

"Your brother?"

"Ray," Zach and Bridget say at the same time.

"He was counting on Wolf joining the family business," Bridget says. "I think he was as devastated as my brother was about the breakup. God, that seems like a long time ago, doesn't it?"

I dig into my memory. The October many years ago when Bridget and I first moved in together, before I met Felix. She had come back to the city after visiting her family for Thanksgiving, and I could tell she was upset. I wanted to cheer her up, so we went out.

Bridget takes her eyes off the stage and turns to me. "Remember that bar we went to? The one with the tiki drinks?"

"We drank a giant volcano bowl of punch."

"And you told me about Thanksgiving dinner with your family. I think your aunt and mom got into a fight?"

"My mother wanted Stacy to take off her heels in the house."

"And we were laughing so hard because your aunt—"

"Threatened to fill her shoe with gravy and put it on the table—she said it was too fabulous not to be appreciated." I smile. "And then you suddenly started crying. It was the first time I'd seen you cry."

Bridget told the whole story through tears and hiccups.

"That time was awful—for Wolf and for me. But I guess now that I'm older, I can appreciate that it must have been just as hard for Joy, too."

I've always thought so, but I'm surprised to hear her say it. Zach, who's sitting on Bridget's other side, looks at me over her head, wide-eyed, and mouths, "Ohh emm gee."

"Joy lost her boyfriend and her best friend," I say. "It would have been awful. But maybe you can start over."

Bridget studies me, her head tilted. "I thought you might think it was a bad idea," she says. "That's sort of why I didn't tell you we'd been texting."

Bridget has completely misjudged my reaction. "I think it would be good for you to patch things up. It's not too late."

"Maybe." She sighs and leans into me. "No guy is worth losing a friend over."

I glance at Felix at the side of the stage, and then at Zach. He gives me a pointed look.

"No," I tell Bridget. "They're not."

FELIX'S NAME ISN'T CALLED UNTIL THE EIGHTH AND final heat of shuckers. Only a few finish with times around one minute thirty, which is what Felix is aiming for. A restaurateur from Vancouver is the fastest so far, at one minute and twenty-seven seconds.

When Felix walks across the stage, my stomach knots. Joy stands behind him, slightly to the right. She's his timer.

Felix sorts through his box of oysters before they start, hands steady. There's no trace of nerves now. Zach and Bridget are already hollering, but I'm not sure he hears them. Once he's arranged the bivalves into tidy rows, he flips his hat backward.

Something about the movement, the boyishness of the gesture, the familiarity of his fingers, tugs at me. He leans over his workstation, hands raised over his head, eyes down.

When the emcee calls out, "Timers, are you ready?" Felix lifts his gaze. He finds me in an instant, and I'm right back in the restaurant where we met five years ago, with Felix looking at me from across the room, a shock of electric blue beneath black lashes.

"Shuckers, are you ready?"

We stare at each other, and I'm hit with a feeling so powerful, I put my hand to my chest. My heart is screaming at me. *Him*, it says. *More*.

"Tyne Valley, are you reeaaaaady?"

Felix lowers his eyes as the audience shouts the countdown.

Felix pries open an oyster, then another and another, faster than I've ever seen. Bridget is yelling at the top of her lungs, but then falls quiet. I hear her say, "Holy shit," and I know he's moving quicker than she's ever seen, too.

I peel my gaze from him only for a moment to watch Joy. Her eyes are narrowed on Felix's hands, cheeks flushed. Her lips are moving.

"Go, go, go," she's saying.

At the one-minute mark, Felix has shucked more than half his batch.

He sets his final oyster on the tray of salt and slams the handle of his knife against the table once. Joy lets out a yelp and shows her stopwatch to the emcee.

"Felix Clark taps out at one minute and thirty-three seconds," the emcee calls, and Felix's eyes expand.

We're out of our seats, clapping and cheering as Felix raises his hands above his head. He looks skyward, turning with a breathtaking smile across his face, and then Joy launches herself at him, circling her legs and arms around his waist like a red-headed monkey. Felix spins them in a slow circle, his hands gripping her thighs. They're both laughing.

My heart falters. *Mine*, it says.

I think my lips may have said it, too, but I can't hear over the whoops from the audience.

Joy slides down Felix's front, then drags him off the stage. He's greeted by her parents and some of the other competitors. He stumbles as he moves, stunned. Bridget leads our group toward them.

"You did it, Wolf. You fucking did it," she says.

I stand back as everyone has their moment with Felix, and when it's my turn, I give him what I intend to be a loose hug, but he draws me against his body, so we're lined up, chest to chest and hip to hip. I glance at Joy over his shoulder. Her brows rise up in surprise.

"Let's find drinks," Joy says, tugging Bridget along with her. I watch them go, former best friends, snaking their way through the crowd hand in hand, then I turn back to Felix.

"Congratulations! You were incredible," I tell him, pulling away. "You should be slurping oysters out of a mermaid's belly-button and doing backflips into a pool of champagne."

Felix's mouth inches up at one edge. "I haven't won, Lucy."

"Incorrect. You set your best time. If that's not worth celebrating, I don't know what is." I nod toward the bar. "Come on."

Felix downs three cans of beer as though they're thimbles of water and he's been lost in the desert with nothing to drink. At one point, I watch the brunette from earlier whisper something in Felix's ear that makes him laugh, then shake his head.

Zach catches me glowering. He follows my gaze to Felix and the brunette, who is now biting her bottom lip. "Interesting," he says.

By the time the judges have finished scoring, Felix has one arm around Zach and another around a guy they went to high school with. His eyes are at half-mast, but he straightens as the top ten are announced. When the sixth place shucker walks on-stage, it's obvious that unless Felix racked up some serious penalty time, he's earned a spot in the top five.

Fifth place is called, and a chef from Vancouver hops on the stage to receive her plaque.

Fourth place is called, and we all freeze, except for Felix, who creeps closer so we're standing side by side.

His hand brushes mine, and then he laces our fingers together. I take a shaky breath. I hate how good it feels to have his palm against mine. I hate that I never want his hand to touch a woman who isn't me. More than anything, I hate that Felix's hookups never bothered me as much as realizing that it doesn't matter whether I fit into his world—I'm only a temporary guest. I *can't* belong here.

"In third place," the emcee announces, "with eighteen seconds in penalties for a total time of one minute and fifty-one seconds is Felix Clark of Prince Edward Island."

Bridget jumps up and down, and Zach claps his hands over his head, but Felix remains still.

"Go," I tell him. "Get up there."

He faces me, bringing our joined hands to his mouth. With his eyes on mine, Felix presses his lips to my knuckles. Everything fades away. The cheering. Bridget's gasp. Even my pulse, a booming drum, is silenced. My awareness is isolated to my fingers, to the sliver of skin beneath Felix's lips. It lasts for only a heartbeat, and then Felix leaves us.

Bridget looks at me, her eyes bulging. What her brother just did was more intimate than if he'd smacked a quick peck on my mouth.

"What was that?" she asks.

I have no idea. I stare at Felix, making his way across the stage to claim his plaque. "I think he drank too much."

Felix is lost to revelry for the next hour. Every so often, our eyes meet through the sea of people, and he stares as openly as he smiles. The dimple is a permanent exhibit. His happiness, unbound, is intoxicating. Everyone around him basks in his warmth.

When the partying dies down, Felix climbs into the back of the truck clumsily while Bridget gets into the front. She and Zach are in the midst of a heated debate about a Trivial Pursuit game I gather took place when they were teenagers. She must have forgotten about my motion sickness.

In the darkness of the back seat, I feel Felix's gaze on me. When I meet his eyes, he reaches across the bench, linking our fingers together. He rests his head back and falls asleep moments later. I stare at our joined hands. It would be all too easy to get caught up in the feeling of his hand in mine, to grow used to it, to miss it once I'm gone. But after last summer, I know what it's like to feel the warmth of his attention and then go without it. Every part of himself that Felix offers up, every piece I allow myself to savor, is just another thing I'll have to say goodbye to. Because even if Felix weren't Bridget's brother, I'm not part of his world, and that's never going to change.

So I pull my hand away. I ignore my heart's protests.

Him, it says. *More.*

THE NEXT MORNING, I'M AWAKE FIRST. ZACH PEELS himself off the couch when the coffee's brewed. Felix is sprawled on the pull-out, still in last night's clothes.

For a few hours yesterday, I had a reprieve from the constant toll of work stress. I barely checked my email. But now Felix's confusing hand-kissing and Bridget's looming wedding day have me wanting to tear my eyeballs out.

"Thank you?" Zach says when I pass him a mug. "You look pissed, Lucy."

"Just tired."

"Uh-huh," Zach says. "That scowl has nothing to do with Courtney?"

"Courtney?"

"The woman I saw you shooting daggers at last night," he says. "Brown hair. Pretty."

I'm about to tell Zach I don't know what he's talking about, but I change my mind. I've woken up cranky, and I'm running with it. "How many women did he sleep with in the past year?"

Zach blinks at me. "You mean the past year when you and Wolf were *not* in a relationship?"

I grit my teeth. Good point. "Yes."

"That's not my information to share. But he's not a monk, Lucy. He's been dating, looking for someone who he could see a future with."

My throat goes tight. I have no idea what I wanted to hear, but that wasn't it.

Zach's eyes soften. "Do you want to talk about it? If you want to get anything off your chest, I won't share it with him. I'm a master of keeping secrets."

I shake my head. "But thanks." Zach is good people, but if there's anyone I should talk to, it's Bridget.

Zach shrugs. Just one shoulder. Like a Clark. "Have it your way. You two have been dicking around like a couple of assholes for years now. Who am I to stop you?"

"Again, thanks."

Bridget tromps downstairs, ordering us to get dressed for our trip to North Cape.

"What's with your face, Bee?" she asks before marching into the TV room to rouse Felix. She's peppy and bossy and smiling, and her mood swings are wearing on me. I have no clue what's going on, and despite what she says, I don't trust that she's getting married in five days. And I'm about to drop thousands of dollars on her flowers.

I step outside to call Farah. She'll have to handle the auction tomorrow. I've sent her my order list, including what I need for Bridget's wedding. I hate delegating such a crucial task, but there's no other option. I can't go back to Toronto without setting things right and telling Bridget about Felix.

Farah answers with her signature, "This better be important."

"I know I said I'd be on a plane today, but—"

"You're running off with Bridget's brother and never coming back?"

After my aunt met Felix two years ago, she explained to Farah, in extraordinary detail, how handsome he was. "That's funny," Farah said. "Lucy's never mentioned that he's a hottie."

"It's not like that," I say now.

"You don't sound like you've been relaxing," Farah says. "You sound like a sewer rat."

"I don't know what that means, but it was a late night. I'm tired."

"You know you're a walking tire fire when you don't get enough sleep," Farah says.

"How's Sylvia? I miss her." Asking about Farah's dog is the best way to change the subject.

"She's a goddess," Farah says, and then puts Sylvia on the phone so I can say hello.

After I hang up, I call Lillian. I've already texted to say that I need to reschedule yet again, but I want to get a read on where we stand.

"I'm sorry," I say, freezing at the sight of a skunk waddling across the lawn and into the shrubs. "You're probably beginning to question whether I'm reliable, but I promise you I am."

"It's fine, Lucy. I understand," Lillian says, though I can hear that she doesn't really. "We all have personal lives."

An "urgent personal matter" was how I characterized my sudden trip.

"Yes, well, I'd be on a plane to Toronto right now if I could. This is the last place I want to be."

"Why don't you let me know when you *are* back, and we can make plans then?"

"Sure," I tell her, stomach wrenching. When I first met Lillian, she was so enthusiastic about working together, but I can hear her confidence in me slipping. "Again, I'm so sorry, Lillian. You'll have my undivided attention when I'm back. Work is my only priority." But the truth of it leaves me feeling a little hollow.

"Perfect," she says. "We'll talk soon."

I hang up, and I turn around, surprised to find Felix standing in the doorway. Blue jeans. White T-shirt. Bed head. Fresh shave. What was he doing, kissing my fingers like that last night? Holding my hand? I don't think he was purposefully trying to confuse me, but he did. I'm angry with myself, but I'm angry with him, too.

"Good morning," he says.

"Hi." I look at a spot on his shoulder.

"Are you feeling okay? Hungover?"

"I'm fine."

"You don't seem fine," he says. "You musn't have slept well. I can tell you're tired by the look on your face."

"Why does everyone have a problem with my face this morning?"

"Lucy." He tips his head. "What's wrong?"

I meet his eyes then. Dangerous, gorgeous man. "Nothing," I tell him.

"Come on. Something's bothering you," he says, stepping closer. "Want to talk about it? Maybe I can help."

"No." I lift my chin. "You really can't."

26

Summer, One Year Ago

My life fell apart in a series of three events. I arrived at In Bloom one morning to find the front window shattered. Inside, the store had been ransacked. Flowers dumped in the cooler, water pooling everywhere. The shelf of vases, toppled. Shards of glass and porcelain littered the floor. My office was torn apart. I sobbed when I saw my aunt's crystal wineglasses lying broken on the floor. The police suspected it was just kids wreaking havoc, but it felt like a personal attack, a violation of what I'd devoted my life to.

The next morning, Carter broke up with me. He said I hadn't shown him half as much devotion as I did the shop.

"I know you don't love me as much as your business, but do you even *like* me?"

His words cut. It wasn't that I'd been dumped, but why.

I didn't love Carter. I didn't need him. And I'd treated him like a lounge chair—a soft place to land, part of the decor of my life, entirely replaceable. I hadn't noticed, but he had.

Three days later, I got the call from my aunt. She was already in the hospital. Her cancer was quick.

"At least I'm going out while I'm still young and beautiful," she said as I applied her lipstick with a thin brush, the way she'd taught me. I swept blush over her cheeks generously—her skin had gone dull, gray. Farah covered for me at the shop, and I spent visiting hours at my aunt's bedside, holding a can of ginger ale while she sipped from a straw, too weak to lift the drink herself.

A week after Stacy was admitted to the hospital, I was surprised to hear my mom's hoot of a laugh and my aunt's responding honk coming from her room. They never laughed much together. I stood outside the door, listening to Stacy telling Mom a story about the last man she'd been seeing, how he'd stand at the fridge, squirting sriracha and hoisin onto a spoon as a midnight snack. The next morning Stacy would find orange and brown splatters all over the floor "like bad abstract art." "Good in bed, though," she added.

I heard my mom sigh. "It sounds fun. You've had so much fun."

"I have." There was a shuffling of sheets, and then I heard my aunt say softly, "Don't cry, Cheryl. I'm the one dying."

There was a long silence. "You were right, you know," my mom said.

"I know."

A chair scraped over the floor, and I peeked around the corner. My mom was leaning over Stacy's bed, hugging her sister. My aunt had tears on her cheeks.

"You still shouldn't have told me the day before my wedding," my mom said, her voice muffled. I had no idea what they were talking about.

"I admit my timing was poor." Stacy saw me in the doorway then and gave me a sad smile. "I should have said something sooner."

She was gone four weeks later.

She left me a note. It wasn't in her handwriting—one of her nurses must have helped.

I loved you like you were my own.

Bridget felt Stacy's loss like she was family. She worked through her grief by helping my parents with the funeral arrangements. I wasn't sure when Bridget called her brother, whether it was when Stacy was in the hospital, fading before my eyes. Or if it was after the funeral, when she found me crying on the floor of the shower. And I didn't know how Felix had freed one of his cottages for me. According to Bridget, they had been fully booked. But Ken and Christine were renovating Summer Wind in the wake of the storm damage. They weren't ready for guests.

"I'm getting you out to the island," Bridget told me through tears. "I wish I could go with you, but I can't swing it with work. Wolf and I have it all figured out. You don't have to do anything. Just get there. You need some fresh air, Bee. You need time to recover."

I hadn't seen Felix since his visit to Toronto last fall, but every month, a yellow envelope of seeds arrived at the store. I had ten packets now. Zinnias and snap dragons and daisies. And every month, I sent him a book back. A self-help about becoming a hotel magnate as a joke. An illustrated children's book called *Felix After the Rain* that turned out to be more emotional than I'd anticipated. I wondered what his girlfriend, Chloe, thought of the books. I wasn't sure what our exchange meant or how to explain it. Books and seeds felt like our secret language. Something just for us. I didn't know how it fit into our rules. Maybe we didn't need them anymore.

Felix was waiting for me in the terminal. There was a plane full of people between us, but I spotted the loveliest flecks of blue between the shoulders of strangers. He bundled me in his arms, swaying back and forth like a ship on tranquil waters, whispering, "I'm so sorry."

The drive from Charlottetown to Salt Cottages seemed to take a lifetime. In reality, Felix and I were on the road for about an hour, but as the sea slipped away and the woods grew dense, it felt as if we were traveling to the end of the world. I told Bridget I would rent a car and chauffeur myself, but she said Felix insisted he pick me up, and now I was glad he had.

It wasn't like the trip to Summer Wind, where the landscape was dotted with barns and churches and cattle, the roads brimming with signs of life, a potato truck here, a tractor there, a pickup shuttling a boat on a trailer. My vision was hazy from the tears I'd shed on the plane. It was as though I was viewing the spruce and birch through a warped glass bottle.

We barely spoke, but I was aware of Felix's worried gaze shooting to me every few minutes.

"Why don't you shut your eyes for a little while," he said, and I leaned my forehead against the cool window.

I tried to nap, but my stomach turned over. I hadn't eaten that day. I wasn't sure if I'd eaten the day before. The farther east we went, the deeper into Kings County, the worse I felt. I became so nauseated, I had to ask Felix to stop the truck. He held my braids in one hand, rubbed my back with the other, whispering, "Good girl," as I retched into the scrub on the side of the road.

I felt a bit better, or at least less pukey, by the time we passed the sign for Salt Cottages and Felix said, "We're here now, Lucy."

I straightened as he turned down a long driveway. Four identical houses stood in a row in the distance. Set back from the ocean, each had a peaked black metal roof and vertical wood siding painted bright white. Paths of gravel and flat stepping stones I knew Felix had laid himself led to each entrance, where ferns in black planters sat beside the doors. Felix parked beside the cottage on the far left, and we climbed out of the truck.

He brought my suitcase inside and said he'd let me rest, but I shook my head. I knew how important the cottages were to Felix. "Give me a tour?"

As he led me through the house, a strange feeling unfurled in my chest. Windows looked onto the deck and over the surrounding fields and ocean. There were gorgeous hardwood counters in the kitchen and high-end appliances. The shower was tiled in turquoise glass, a similar shade to Felix's eyes. There were three bedrooms—not huge but spacious enough to be comfortable—decorated in white and seafoam.

Felix pointed out all the little details he was pleased with—the fancy showerhead, the dimmer switches on all the lights, the way the windows were arranged for optimal views and privacy, the backsplash he'd installed in the kitchen.

I kept saying "Wow" over and over, grief and car sickness temporarily forgotten. I knew Ken was handy and had taught Felix how to use a table saw and lay flooring, and the importance of precision. Bridget told me how much of the work Felix had done himself, but I was blown away. He was so skilled.

Felix pointed to the dining table, where a welcome basket sat at the center. Inside: a bag of Covered Bridge chips, potato fudge, a map of PEI like the one I had at home, two Red Island ciders, and a small booklet, bound with blue string. *An Islander's Guide to PEI* was printed on its brown card stock cover. I flipped through the pages, scanning the suggestions for restaurants, lobster suppers, shops, cafés, ice cream, kids' activities, beaches,

locally made beer and cheese and soap. Each included a thoughtful sentence or two explaining what made it special. He was a
beautiful writer. I turned back to the first page, reading the par-
agraph that welcomed the reader to the island and to Felix's favorite spots on it—recommendations he'd collected over his
twenty-seven years of living on PEI.

I glanced at him.

"Told you," he said, smug.

"I still don't buy it that you weren't trying to pick up dozens
of tourists a season."

He smirked. "Only one or two."

Much like at Summer Wind, there was a sliding door that led to
a deck. We stood side by side in front of it, staring out at the view.
The sky was indecisive today, changing in minutes. Cloud, rain,
sun, a watery rainbow in the distance, the ocean shining silver.

"I'd like to do more landscaping—add a fire pit and some
gardens," Felix said. "It'll be more work, but I don't mind. We're
really going to go for it at Christmas, too. Lights everywhere. I
was thinking of building a skating rink out there." He pointed to
the field. "We'll get the photographer here again. I want to build
our winter business. What do you think?"

I gazed at Felix. He surveyed the green that spread before us.
So proud, so handsome. So smart and talented and sure. He'd
become such a man since I met him four years ago. Here he was,
in the life that he had built for himself, more solid than ever before. He was fully formed, grown into the person he was meant
to become. No longer the sullen twenty-three-year-old, licking his
wounds after Joy broke up with him. No longer the teasing flirt.

"Sorry," he said, ears blushing. "You're not feeling well, and
I'm boring you."

"No." I put my hand on his arm, ignoring how hot his skin

felt beneath my fingers. A personal fireplace. "I'm sorry. I want to hear all about it. It's been a long time. But I'm not a very good conversationalist right now," I admitted. "I haven't been sleeping. Or eating, which makes the car sickness worse. I feel like I've been hit by a truck."

"How about I make you something? I went grocery shopping this morning—the fridge is full. A sandwich maybe? I got the butter you like."

"Thank you, but that's okay. You've done enough for me already."

Felix studied me, head tilted to the side.

I stamped on a smile. "Let's do something before I go back to Toronto. I'll take you out to dinner as a thank-you." Chloe could spare him for one night. "The Inn at Bay Fortune maybe? I've always wanted to go."

His mouth turned down at the corners. "I can stay if you want. Keep you company."

"Felix, you don't have to babysit me. I don't want to be any more of a burden than I've already been."

"You're not a burden, Lucy."

My eyes began to sting. I was too raw for his kindness. "Thanks," I whispered.

"Plus my sister threatened bodily harm if I didn't take care of you."

I sputtered out a laugh, wiping my cheeks. I couldn't believe I was crying in front of Felix. We'd opened the door to friendship when we spent time together in Toronto, but we hadn't reached the level of comforting each other during moments of crisis. "Sorry—I'm super emotional right now. I'm not very fun to be around. You go do your thing, and I'll text you when I'm in better shape." Bridget had put Felix's number in my phone.

After assuring him I was okay once more, he left me alone. I stared out at the sea, listening to his truck rumble to life, and the sound of the engine receded. Then I dropped onto the couch and sobbed into a pillow.

ONCE MY TEARS DRIED, I LOOKED AROUND THE EMPTY house, alone. Lonely. I thought about texting Felix to see if he wouldn't mind hanging out with me for the evening, but I couldn't force myself to ask that of him. He had a girlfriend, and I wouldn't be thrilled with that if I were her.

I inspected the kitchen. There was a bag of coffee on the counter from the good roaster in Charlottetown. A bottle of vinho verde in the door of the fridge. Eggs, Avonlea cheddar, a rainbow of produce, a fresh loaf of bakery rye, a box of my favorite snack bars, and a pink package of Cows Creamery cultured butter. I didn't know whether Bridget had sent Felix a shopping list, or if in the four years that we'd known each other he had absorbed what I like to eat the way I had absorbed what he liked to read. I had a slice of buttered bread for dinner, standing over the sink.

When Felix knocked on the door the next morning, I was surprised to see him. I was still wearing yesterday's clothes and hadn't looked in a mirror, but I could feel that my eyes were puffy. My mouth tasted like I'd sucked the metal off a flagpole. I hadn't washed my hair in days. When I stayed at Summer Wind, I would do my makeup first thing so Felix wouldn't see me without it, but I hadn't bothered packing more than lip balm, and I couldn't find the energy to care.

But I did notice things about Felix I hadn't yesterday. His jeans were fresh, the deepest shade of indigo. His sneakers were leather and also new. He wore a black V-neck shirt, different than his usual white tee, made from a thicker cotton. He'd done something to his hair to put the waves in their place.

He was doing a similar inspection, a frown knitting his brows. "Why don't you go take a shower, Lucy," he said. "And I'll make breakfast."

I didn't bother telling him to go. I had a feeling he wouldn't have even if I'd asked, and I didn't want him to. I still wasn't used to living on my own, and I liked having someone around. I liked having *Felix* around.

He stayed all day. We ate fried egg and cheddar sandwiches on toasted rye and watched *The Great British Baking Show*, my preferred comfort viewing. We walked to the shore in the late afternoon. I was briefly revitalized by the wind, the feel of sand underfoot, and the sound of the surf, but I tired quickly. I fell asleep, my head on Felix's lap, somewhere between the technical (baguettes) and the showstopper (3-D bread sculptures), and woke up to darkness, my cheek on his thigh, a blanket tucked around me. Felix sent me to bed. I found him asleep in the bedroom next to mine the following morning.

I felt guilty for monopolizing Felix, and after he cooked breakfast for me for the second day in a row, I told him so. I was okay, I promised him. I liked his company, knew I'd miss him when he left, but I told him that I was on the mend.

And I was. I read on the deck, took long strolls along the beach and through the woods, sometimes weeping, sometimes smiling into the sun. There were so many birds flittering through the treetops—redstarts, yellow warblers, vireos. I grew accustomed to their song, my solitude not as keen in their company. I picked armfuls of wildflowers and filled the cottage with the kind of unstructured arrangements my aunt would have lovingly called "common." I felt her with me while I worked. And day after day, the tightness in my chest eased. But I knew it would be hard to go back to the city. I would be more alone than ever.

Me: I'm not sure I want to come home.

Bridget: Wolf must be treating you well.

Me: He has. But I hate the idea of going back to my empty apartment. No you. No Stacy.

Bridget: There's always me.

If I could have stayed on the island forever, I think I would have. Being on PEI had a way of making life feel simpler. I breathed easier. Began to sleep better. Slowed down in a way I never could in the city.

Over the next few days, I saw Felix around the cottages, gardening, checking on guests, cutting the field on a ride-on mower, shirtless, his bronzed skin beaded with sweat. He played soccer with the kids in the cottage next to mine, waving at me from the grass. He stopped in every day, making sure I was okay. One evening, he arrived with a box of oysters and a knife, and we ate them on the deck at sunset with the vinho verde.

Felix told me that he and Zach were looking for another property. Felix's preference was for the east, Zach's for the north shore. He wanted to know my thoughts. He asked me about the shop and about my favorite flowers and Farah, who he wished he'd met while he was in Toronto. He didn't know any poet-florists.

Sometimes our eyes would catch, and the air would crackle, and I remembered him saying "*I want you to call me Felix*" three years ago. But then one of us would look away, and the spark was forgotten, though it hadn't escaped me that not once did Felix mention his girlfriend. And I didn't ask.

On my second to last day, he showed up in the Mustang.

He was smiling bright, and so was I. Felix loved that car, and I loved that fucking dimple.

"What's this?"

"We're going for a ride. Thought you might appreciate doing it in style." He handed me the keys.

"I can't. It's a lost cause. Bridget tried to teach me to drive a stick once."

He smirked. "I'll show you how to handle it."

"Ha," I said. "But seriously. My parents didn't want me to get my license—they were convinced I was going to wreck their Volvo. They offered to double my allowance if I'd hold off on taking my test." When my aunt caught wind of this, she and Mom had an epic fight. In the end, Stacy drove from Toronto to St. Catharines to give me lessons herself.

Felix's gaze hardened. "That's messed up. Anyone who can turn plants into large-scale pieces of art can drive a stick."

Ten minutes later we were shuddering down the driveway, Felix coaching me on when to use the clutch and shift. I yelped with every jerk of the vehicle, terrified I'd ruin the thing. Until I was doing it, driving through the countryside, fields and farmhouses whizzing by.

"Maybe I should get a dog," I said, smiling.

"What?" Felix asked, baffled.

"I always wanted one when I was a kid, but my parents wouldn't let me." Instead, I tied a skipping rope around my toy poodle's neck, dragging her around the house. I rubbed her belly, fed her invisible kibble, and pressed her nose into a bowl of water. "They said I wasn't responsible enough, but they also didn't want me to get my license, and look at me now."

"Should we find a pet store? I'll buy you a dog right now, Lucy."

I laughed. "I don't think I have room in my suitcase."

"I learned how to drive before it was legal," Felix said. "I convinced my dad to show me. We went up and down the driveway. Back and forth, back and forth. I could parallel park at fourteen."

"Why were you in such a rush?"

"I thought it looked fun, but I also wanted to be able to ask a girl out as soon as I got my license and take her on a date without our parents having to drop us off. I had a lot of ideas about sex in back seats."

"I bet." I glanced at him. "And did that happen for you?" Felix would have been with Joy by the time he got his license.

He smiled. "Maybe a couple of times."

"Hmm," I said, though it sounded like a growl.

We drove to Point Prim Lighthouse, the oldest on the island. Of the many, *many* lighthouses I'd visited over the years, I decided it was my favorite—tall, round, and painted bright white—and that Point Prim was one of PEI's loveliest spots: a peninsula of gorgeous farmland jutting into the ocean.

"I could live here," I said to Felix as we ate lunch at the chowder house that sat on the edge of the rocky shoreline beside the lighthouse.

He leaned back in his chair, eyeing me in a way that made my stomach flip. "I can see it," he said. "The island suits you."

"CHLOE DOESN'T MIND YOU SPENDING SO MUCH TIME with me?" I asked as we drove to the beach the following day. We took the truck this time.

"Uh, no." Felix cleared his throat, then glanced in my direction. "Chloe and I broke up."

"What? When? Bridget didn't tell me."

"Not that long ago. She wanted to move back to Ottawa, and I didn't want to go with her. Neither of us wanted to do long distance. She said I didn't let her get close enough when we were living in the same place anyway." He shrugged. "Maybe I didn't."

"I'm sorry," I told him. "I thought it was going well. I had no idea."

"It's fine. You've had a lot going on—I'm sure that's why Bridget didn't mention it."

"I guess. Carter dumped me last month, too."

"I heard," he said, his gaze flicking my way. "That's too bad."

Felix told me how much he loved the island's east coast. He said it was quieter than the north shore, wilder, and that the beaches were beautiful. Souris was good for sea glass hunting, and Bothwell was one of his favorites, but we went to Basin Head, where there were changing rooms and a canteen housed in little wooden buildings by the shore.

The sand was pale white, stretching as far as I could see to the north, swaying dune grass and scraggly pines running its length. To the south was a rocky red cliff crowned with evergreens. We took our shoes off and walked up the shore, where it was quieter, the sand squelching strangely under our feet.

"It's called the singing sands," Felix said. I rubbed my toes back and forth, trying to make a melody. It sounded like an out-of-tune seal.

We laid down a blanket and ate our picnic of baguette, cheddar, ham, olives, and Red Island ciders. I searched for a piece of sea glass in the little clumps of seaweed that had washed ashore but, as always, found none.

"I'm beginning to think sea glass is a prank islanders play on tourists," I said, plunking down beside Felix.

He grinned. "Nearly forgot," he said, reaching into the pocket of his bathing suit and pulling out a milky white stone that looked like a small piece of quartz. "This is for you. I saw it the other morning. You must be good luck—I haven't found a piece in ages."

He placed the sea glass in my palm. "White's not as rare as some of the other colors. Orange, red, and blue are tough to find now."

I studied the little treasure, then lifted my gaze to his. Electricity ran from his eyes to mine and back again. Something was happening between us, but I wasn't sure what it was. I knew how Felix flirted, and this wasn't it. This was tender. This was sweet.

I thanked him, smiling a nervous smile and laughing a nervous laugh, then dug out my sunscreen.

"Here," Felix said when I rubbed it over my shoulders. "I'll do your back. Your dress is low."

"Sure," I said, voice husky. "Thanks."

I turned around, and Felix moved my braid over my shoulder. His palms coasted over my skin, and I closed my eyes. It was unfair how good his hands felt, how his touch sent blood flowing from my head to between my legs. But I needed to ignore how his body did things to my body. I didn't want to mess with what we had going. This tentative friendship that began when he visited Toronto, that I believed had grown with every book I'd sent him, every package of seeds he'd mailed to me.

We spent hours reading on our bellies, kicking our feet, me scouring a stack of magazines and Felix with his nose in *Beloved*.

In the midafternoon, he stood, peeled off his shirt, and extended his hand to me. I'd neglected to pack a bathing suit, but it was hot enough that I held up my dress and waded in to my knees while Felix swam. The beach was busy, but when he emerged from the ocean, I forgot about everyone around us. He walked through the surf, water running down the tanned expanse of his torso, orange swim trunks clinging to his hard thighs. This friend thing would be easier if he didn't look like *that*. I stared at Felix, my dress slipping from my fingers, as he made his way to me. He glanced at the lilac fabric swirling around my legs, and then up at me, a smile growing when he caught the red blaze across my chest.

We dried off, drank our ciders, and Felix asked about my aunt. I told him all about Stacy's garden and how it had been my happiest place when I was a kid. I told him how she was the only person in my family who understood me. I told him how much Bridget missed the island when I met her, and how Stacy scooped her up into our little family. Old movies. Pasta from the restaurant down the street. Boozy lectures about living life to its fullest. Outings to the theater.

I wiped my tears with the damp hem of my dress, and Felix put his arm around me. We stayed like that, side by side, staring at a ship in the distance, and eventually I set my head on his shoulder.

We were watching a Great Dane try to capture waves in her mouth when Felix asked gently, "What happened with Carter?"

I blew out a breath. "I thought things were going okay, but he said he hadn't seen me half as emotional about him as I was about the break-in at the store."

I hesitated before telling Felix the next part. I didn't want him to think less of me. "He said I was"—I made air quotes with my fingers—"'kind of a shitty girlfriend.'"

"What a dick," Felix said.

"I know, but he was right in some ways. I did care more about the business than him."

"Of course," Felix said. "It's a part of you. He should have realized how lucky he was."

I sat upright so I could look at him. We were so close, I thought I might be able to count every one of his ebony eyelashes. Felix reached for my braid, pushing it behind my shoulder so it fell down the center of my back.

"He wasn't the right guy for you."

His fingers skated over my spine, featherlight, and my breath hitched at his touch, at the way he looked at me, his desire laid bare, there for the taking.

"Sometimes I wonder if I might not want to find the right one," I whispered. It's something I'd worried about—if I dated Carter because I knew we'd never last. My aunt thought I should be open to a meaningful relationship, but the only man I seemed to be drawn to time and time again was sitting next to me. And he lived eight hundred miles away and seemed as reluctant to commit as I was. I could never have him. "I think I might be broken."

"Lucy." That's all Felix said. Only my name, but I felt it *everywhere*.

Something had shifted between us since I'd arrived, an awareness that was now impossible to ignore. Felix had become so much more to me than a casual hookup, but I didn't know what to do with this knowledge. All I could do was address my loudest, most urgent need: I'd been craving Felix's mouth and hands and wind-kissed skin since the moment we met. I felt like a bottle of champagne, shaken and ready to pop.

"You're not broken," he said. The space between us narrowed. "You're p—"

I pressed my lips to his. "I want you," I whispered against them.

He smiled against my mouth, his hand wrapping around my braid. "I want you, too."

"Yes," I told him.

More.

27

Summer, One Year Ago

Felix was lying beside me when I woke up, sunlight streaking his dark hair with gold. I gave myself a moment to drink in the sight of him—naked, chest bare, the sheet around his waist—then sat, taking in my surroundings. I was in Felix Clark's bedroom. In his house.

There was just enough space for a queen-size bed, two nightstands, and a four-drawer dresser, which sat underneath a window overlooking the back of the property. Despite its size, the room was stylish, with a deliberate color scheme I doubted Felix was responsible for. The walls were two-tone—matte black from the floor to waist height and light brown on the upper portion—the bed linens gray and toss pillows tan. Black swing-arm sconces were installed on either side of the bed, and a vintage map of Prince Edward Island hung on one wall in a handsome frame. The only thing that didn't coordinate seamlessly was one of his grandma's patchwork quilts, folded across the bottom of the bed.

I'd barely paid attention when Felix carried me in here yesterday. We'd come straight from the beach and spent the rest of the day and night twisted together like two ampersands. We were covered in sand, and after round two, Felix sent me to wash off while he stripped the sheets and remade the bed before joining me in the shower. We'd slept together before, of course, but it felt different. We were learning each other in a way we'd never been able to. The first time was slow, Felix's forehead on mine, his kisses like confessions. His words, too.

You, he kept saying. *You.*

Felix, I kept saying. *More.*

My chest ached with finally having him again, and when he was kneeling in the shower, my hands in his hair, I had a fleeting thought that I might be in trouble. But there was no stopping us. We were loud and greedy and giddy. I felt like a squirrel—that I wouldn't survive winter if I didn't get all of Felix in my system before I returned to the city.

I stared down at him now. He looked almost innocent while he slept, but his lips were swollen, and my thighs were chafed from where his beard had scraped against them.

Stomach rumbling, I slipped out of the bed, threw on one of his T-shirts, and found my way down the hall to the kitchen. His place was small but well cared for. It had smart slate gray siding Felix had replaced himself and a pond that sat to one side, spindly old apple trees behind it. There were no neighboring homes in sight. Felix had redone the bathroom, replaced the windows and furnace, reshingled the roof. He hadn't gotten to the kitchen yet. He told me all this on the drive from the beach.

"It's not much," he'd warned, fingers tapping on the steering wheel. Nervous.

"I'm sure it's great." I put my hand on his thigh. "But let's save the tour for later."

We were tearing off our clothes before we made it over the threshold.

I placed a slice of bread in the toaster, studying a photograph on the fridge of Felix and Zach standing on the doorstep of one of the cottages while I waited. Zach's arm was around Felix's shoulder, and they both grinned broadly. I wandered over to the living room. It was painted a dark mossy green, the furniture caramel leather. There was a cute cast-iron fireplace in the corner. I wondered if Chloe had been his interior decorator, or maybe Joy. I knew she'd helped with Salt Cottages, knew Felix and his ex were friends, but I was surprised by how the thought made me feel. Itchy and uncomfortable.

There was a large bookshelf that couldn't contain all of Felix's books—they were stacked in neat piles over every surface. I picked up a copy of *White Teeth* off a teak end table and flipped through it. Felix had written in its margins, black ink marking favorite passages.

The toast popped, but my gaze had snagged on the bookshelf. They were all there. *Wide Sargasso Sea*, *Felix After the Rain*, *Great Expectations*, the silly hotel self-help. The ten books I'd sent Felix, all in a row. They sat on a shelf of their own, showcased like treasures between brass book ends.

I ran a finger over the spines, heart racing. There was *The Light We Lost*, which I bought in April because my favorite bookseller, Addie, said that I should try something written this century. She thought I might like it. I read the jacket copy and thought Felix might, too. I chose *Happy Place* in May because the idea of Felix holding that bright pink book delighted me to no end and because I could think of no happier place than PEI. I pulled out *Great Expectations*. It was a beautifully designed hardcover, which I'd sent because I'd heard Felix say once how much he loved it. I turned it over in my hands, opened it to a random page. My breath caught at the sentence he'd underlined.

"I loved her against reason, against promise, against peace, against hope, against happiness, against all discouragement that could be."

I quickly tucked it back on the shelf, feeling like I'd been caught reading Felix's diary.

"Good morning."

I spun around. He was wearing loose cotton pants, slung low on his hips. He hadn't put on a shirt. A pillow crease ran from his temple to his cheek, disappearing into his beard. His gaze met mine. It wasn't a spark that struck me. Or the snap of electricity. It was all the moments we'd shared, all the things I'd noticed about Felix, admired about him.

I kept the ten packets of seeds he sent me in the glass box with my map of PEI, but I'd also collected every scrap I knew about Felix, storing them away without intending to. Now they were all pieced together, a scroll of memories unspooling infinitely. The covert glances. The stolen kisses. The books tucked into his jeans. Felix's quiet ambition. The way he drank his tea in the morning, blowing into the cup to cool it down. The speed at which he could shuck a dozen oysters. How he'd handled my body last night like it was precious, like it was *his*. The way he listened, with his head tilted to the side, eyes slightly narrowed. His calloused palms. How the muscles in his back moved under his shirt. How he helped with cooking and cleaning and went to the store to buy Portuguese wine when Bridget and I ran out. His easy confidence. The lovely things that came out of his mouth.

I knew Felix at twenty-three—brokenhearted, putting his life back together—and I knew him now, at twenty-seven—determined, solid, the kindest man I knew.

I stared at him, lungs squeezing tight.

"Lucy," Felix said, and I blinked. He strode across the room, setting his hands on my hips, searching my eyes. "Looks like you went somewhere there for a second."

I glanced at the shelf of books I sent him, panic gripping me. I heard my aunt's voice, the night she met Felix. *That gorgeous creature is smitten.*

But he couldn't be. We'd been careful. We'd kept feelings out of it. I *had to* keep feelings out of it. My aunt was gone, and I had In Bloom to protect. I had to stay focused. I couldn't have *more*. Not now, and not with Felix of all people. He lived on Prince Edward Island. I didn't have time for a relationship, let alone something long distance. And even if I did, Felix was Bridget's brother. I pictured her tears when she told me about his breakup with Joy, thought of the night where she laid out the rules for our first PEI vacation.

Don't fall in love with my brother. I couldn't deal with losing you, Bee.

Bridget, who I loved more than anyone. Bridget, who I needed more than ever now that my aunt was gone. Bridget, who I would do anything for.

There were two pillars in my life that I needed to guard. In Bloom and my friendship with Bridget. I may have liked Felix more than any man I'd known, but he was an impossibility.

"You," Felix said with a lazy grin. "Your hair." He pushed it behind my shoulder and kissed my temple. His lips coasted to my neck, sucking on the flesh beneath my ear. He groaned. "Your skin. I don't think I will ever get enough."

I felt like I couldn't breathe. This thing between us was getting away from me, but what if I wasn't the only one?

"Lucy?" Felix's gaze returned to mine. He traced my cheek with his thumb. "We didn't eat much yesterday. You must be starving. I'll make you French toast and bacon."

My favorite breakfast.

What did he say when he was in Toronto? "I was never really a casual fling kind of guy."

My heart was a rocket. "I have to go," I said. "I can't be here."

"What? Why? Is everything okay?"

"No." I shook my head, grabbing for the first lie I could think of. "It's work. Our online ordering system crashed. Can you drive me to the cottages? I need to use my laptop."

Felix stared at me for a long moment, brows pinched, his gaze moving around my face. He'd never looked at me with that kind of intensity before, with eyes so dark. But he nodded and then, like a switch flipped, he was light again.

"Of course." He took a step back. "No problem. Let's get you back."

If Felix could see through the lie, he did me the courtesy of keeping it to himself. We dressed, and on the short drive, he kept glancing my way. But I couldn't look at him. I needed to not be beside Felix, smelling him, wanting him, worrying. My feelings were bursting from me like fireworks, an explosion of respect and affection and longing. But had this become something more to him, too?

"I'm going to be busy all day with this," I said as he parked. "But I'll see you tomorrow, okay? We can grab breakfast before you drive me to the airport. My treat." I jumped out of the truck.

I was halfway to the door when Felix called my name. He was standing next to the vehicle. "You forgot your bag."

He held up my purse.

"Oh."

Felix walked toward me. He slipped the strap over my shoulder. "All set."

"Sorry I have to cut things short." I felt like I'd fallen off a cliff, into the ocean, plunging deep, deep, struggling for breath. But Felix smiled, eyes shimmering.

"There's no need to apologize, Lucy." He winked. "I had a good time. That's what we do, right?"

It was like being doused in cold water. *A good time.* That's what this was to Felix. That's all it ever was. Felix hadn't lost control. I had.

I forced myself to smile. "Yes. So did I. This was fun."

He kissed me on the cheek. "It always is."

"I'll pick you up before your flight tomorrow," Felix said, leaning out the truck window before he pulled away. "I'm holding you to that breakfast."

But it wasn't Felix who arrived at the cottage the next day.

"Something came up," Zach said when I opened the door. "Wolf can't make it."

28

Now

Five Days Until Bridget's Wedding

We're soaring up the coast on the edge of the cliffs. The land to our right drops off abruptly into the gulf. White windmills rise in the distance. Lobster traps are stacked beside barns and out-buildings.

The trip to North Cape, the tippy top of the western side of the island, is well over an hour, too long for Zach's legs to be squished in the back seat. I'm looking out the window to try to keep my stomach from turning over—the majesty of the scenery is lost on me. Bridget says the view is worth it. We're going to get food after—there's talk of a good lobster roll in Tignish.

"There are sixty-one lighthouses and range light buildings on the island," Zach declares from the passenger seat.

"I have no idea what a light range is," I say, voice flat. I'm annoyed with everyone. Bridget. For dragging me to the Maritimes and making me cancel my meeting with Lillian. Felix. For kissing my hand. For wanting to find someone to build a future with here on the island. For the thumbs-up emoji he sent me and the year of silence that followed. Zach. For being smart. And myself. For being so very stupid.

"A range light," Zach corrects. "They're sort of like lighthouses—they're used for marking the entrance to a harbor, so there's always two of them. There are twenty pairs on PEI."

"Thank you for that, Zachary," Bridget says, and Zach turns around, batting his eyelashes at her.

Every so often, Felix glances at me in the mirror, but I won't meet his eyes. I let myself fall into Felix's orbit, let him slip under my defenses. It's last summer all over again. I need to keep my distance.

I look out the window, taking deep breaths. It's more than motion sickness making me nauseated.

"You okay?" Felix says.

"I'm not going to vomit in your truck, if that's why you're asking."

"Let us know if that changes."

Zach holds up the box of nutty snack bars Felix brought. "Wolf's an excellent Boy Scout. We come prepared."

We off-load in front of a large building perched on the lip of the peninsula—the North Cape Wind Energy Interpretive Centre. It earns its name as soon as I step outside. The skirt of my sundress blows around my calves, and I have to hold my hair out of my face as we clamber over red boulders to the rocky shore. An octagonal lighthouse stands in the distance, its white paint faded. It's overcast today. The wind tastes like rain.

"It's more than one hundred and fifty years old," Zach says. "Built in 1865. It's not the oldest one on the island. That would be Point Prim Lighthouse, which is one of two round brick lighthouses in Canada."

Point Prim. The reminder of last July, when Felix and I visited the lighthouse, and the following day when we spent hours entangled in his bed, has my chest heating. I can feel him watching me, but I keep my focus on the water.

"All right," Bridget says, giving Zach a tap on his arm. "We get it. Your brain is *huge*."

"Have you noticed the tides?" Zach asks me.

I look to where he's pointing.

"Under there is a rock reef—the longest in North America."

"Hence the need for the lighthouse," Bridget says. "You can walk on it when the tide is low. But right now . . . can you see it?"

"The waves?" They're rolling in gently, crashing against each other in a line that stretches out from shore. "What is that?"

"Two tides come in from opposite directions and meet here," Zach says. "The Gulf of St. Lawrence and the Northumberland Strait."

I cup my hand over my brow. "I've never seen anything like it." I step closer, able to make out a strip of rocks between the tides. I watch, mesmerized, for minutes.

"It's incredible," I say eventually. "But it looks strange—tides shouldn't come together like that." It's like an optical illusion.

"And yet they do," Felix says, his voice almost next to my ear. Only when I look over my shoulder do I realize that Zach and Bridget are wandering along the beach. It's just Felix and me.

"They're pulled together," Felix says, voice low, eyes latched on to mine. "They can't help it."

The skin on my arms pebbles, and for a moment, I can't seem to look away. But then I shake my head and point at Zach and Bridget.

"I'm going to go find them."

I turn and walk down the shore, leaving him staring at my back.

WATER SLIDES DOWN THE WINDSHIELD IN A WALL OF wet. Felix shuts off the truck engine, and the four of us sit inside, fogging up the glass. The distance to the front door of Summer Wind seems a lot farther than it does when the sky hasn't opened its belly on the world.

Bridget spent the entire ride back from North Cape texting with Miles while Felix shot glances at me in the mirror and Zach attempted to crack the tension by explaining the power dynamics of his fantasy basketball league. I'm tired of all three of them. I want out of this truck. I want off this island.

"This rain isn't going to let up for a while," Zach says as thunder rumbles. "We should make a run for it."

Bridget's phone rings. Miles's name is on the screen. "Hey," she answers. "I'll call you back in a sec, okay?"

I gape at her when she hangs up, and Bridget gapes back.

"So," I say to Bridget.

"So," she says back.

Outside, lightning snaps, and so does my patience.

"So your wedding is in less than five days, and we're sitting in a truck in the middle of a storm, on Prince Edward Island." My volume increases. "I have a life, you know. And it's not here."

"I know that," she says quietly.

"For the sake of my sanity, would you please tell me what the hell is going on?"

Bridget's face has gone bright red. But she doesn't look like an outraged angel. She looks like she's about to cry.

"I'll get you back to Toronto, Bee," she says, tapping her

phone. "If that's what you're worried about, I'll book our tickets right now."

"You know that's not all I'm worried about."

She ignores me, focusing on her screen.

"Tomorrow is sold out."

I pinch the bridge of my nose. Shit.

"But there's a flight Wednesday morning."

"Thank god. I need to get out of here."

"Ouch," I hear Zach say.

"This is not how I wanted this trip to go," Bridget murmurs.

"How *did* you want it to go?" I say. "*Pleeease* tell me. I'm dying to know."

She glances up from her phone, her eyes glassy. "I just wanted to spend time together."

"We can spend time together in Toronto!"

"I'm sorry," she says softly, not fighting back. This isn't the Bridget I know. With a final pleading look, she opens her door and hurries toward the house.

I can't share the same air with her right now. Or Felix. "I'm going for a walk," I announce.

Not waiting for a reply, I step into the storm. The rain is coming down so hard, it stings my skin. It feels good. It feels like the weather has tailored itself to my mood. It takes seconds for my dress to become saturated, the skirt sticking to my legs. Red mud splatters my shins. I make it to the shore before I hear him.

"Lucy, stop."

"Leave me alone," I call. I feel like the lightning that splits the sky. I feel like the thunder that's shaking the ground. I am a black cloud ready to erupt. I turn left and keep walking.

"It's too wet to be out here." He's closer.

I get another dozen paces before I feel his hand on my wrist.

I spin around. Felix's shirt is plastered to his chest. Droplets fall from his eyelashes and the ends of his hair.

"Are you okay? Talk to me, Lucy."

"You're the last person I want to talk to." Felix flinches, but I don't give him a chance to reply. "Why are you following me? Why are you pretending to care? I don't need you to be nice to me, Felix. I need you to leave me alone."

His frown carves grooves between his brows. "What makes you think I'm pretending? I just followed you into a storm." He gestures to his soaked-through shirt as evidence. "I do care about you, Lucy."

"You care about fucking me." That's where this always leads.

"I care about *you*."

Another branch of lightning fractures the sky. I think of that text he sent me last year. "Oh please. I know I'm just a good time to you. Don't pretend I'm something more than that."

His lips press together as he stares at me. "That bothers you."

I blink. Once, twice, a third time. Felix steps closer. I'm looking straight into his eyes, trapped. I want to reply, but I don't trust myself to sound steady.

"It does," he says. "I can tell. But I want to know why. I thought this was about having fun, Lucy." He studies my face and takes another step closer. "That's what we've agreed to from the beginning. That's what you wanted."

I wipe the rain from my eyes. "Well, it's not fun for me anymore."

He brushes a piece of hair away from my face, and I turn my cheek. "Lucy." The gentlest *Lucy*. The word echoes around us, reverberating over the fields, rolling around with the thunder.

"Don't *Lucy* me. Don't say my name like that."

"How do you want me to say it?"

"Truthfully. Like I'm just a hookup. Like I'm the person you sent that stupid thumbs-up emoji to. Like I don't mean anything to you." My voice breaks, giving me away.

"You're upset about an emoji?" He's fighting back a smile, and it only makes me angrier. "Lucy," he says again. It's a hopeful *Lucy*. A *Lucy* that sounds a lot like delight.

"That," I say. "Don't say my name like that. Like I'm important. Like I make you happy. Like we're friends. I know I'm insignificant. I know you've been dating other women, and whatever! I don't care." I throw up my hands to underline the lie. "We went a year without speaking. We're not friends. I get it. We're not anything."

Felix takes another step forward, crowding my space, suddenly serious. "Friends," he says. "Is that what you thought we were?"

I stare at him, breathing heavily, not sure what to make of the way his gaze heats. It's fastened to mine, snapped in place like the final puzzle piece. I swallow. "I thought we could be."

"Lucy." It's a growl, a vibration deep in his chest. "I don't want to be your friend."

I jerk my head back, but Felix's hands come around my face as he captures my mouth with his. His grip falls to my waist, hauling me tight against him. He sucks on my bottom lip, groaning. Despite common sense, the sound is my undoing. My lips part, letting him in. I curl my fingers into his hair, locking him to me, and our kiss becomes an urgent collision of hot tongues and wet flesh and frenzied fingers. The warmth of his mouth, the *taste* of him, sends a shudder through my body. He pulls back only enough to rest his brow on mine, eyes closed. His nose brushes mine, and he swipes his thumbs over my cheeks.

"What is this?" I whisper. "What's happening right now, Felix?"

"I'm sorry," he says. "I'm so sorry. I thought you realized. I thought that's why you left so suddenly that morning a year ago. It hurt. That's why I didn't take you to the airport. That's why I dated women who weren't you this past year. I've been trying to get over you, Lucy. You mean so much to me that I can't think, can't even breathe properly, when we're together."

He inhales through his nose, steadying himself. I can feel the restraint in his body, like he's barely holding himself back. His gaze finds mine. It's *burning*.

"Tell me you want me so I can kiss you again," Felix says. His fingers flex at my sides.

"I want you," I say. "You already know that."

He shakes his head slightly, water dripping from his brow. "No, tell me you want *me*. Not just having sex with me. *Me*."

"You?"

"Me."

Awareness washes over me. "This isn't just a fun time for you?"

His hands cup my cheeks. "No, this isn't just a fun time for me." His eyes are anchored to mine. "If I'm honest, it probably hasn't been for a while. Last summer, I thought you may have felt something for me, but the way you left . . . I figured I'd been kidding myself. I thought you knew how I felt about you. All that time we spent together. The day on the beach, the night at my house. Lucy," he says, his thumb tracing my jaw. "Tell me I'm not alone in this. Tell me you feel something, too."

I survey last summer with new eyes. How Felix freed up one of the cottages for me. Filled the fridge. Got the wine I like. Hugged me at the airport. Held my hair back when I was sick. He stayed with me. Checked in on me. And then there were the hours we spent together in his bed. *You*, he kept saying to me.

I've buried my feelings for Felix in a secret garden beneath my rib cage. I didn't think he'd done the same.

"I did," I whisper. "Last year, I felt it, too. You're not alone," I tell him. "I want *you*, Felix."

His fingers tunnel into my hair, a smile forming on his lips. He kisses me, sweet.

"For more than one night, Lucy," he says. "I want you for more than one night."

"For two?" I grin.

"More."

"More," I agree. As soon as the word leaves my lips, his are on mine. But *kiss* isn't a strong enough word for the way Felix claims my mouth. It's sucking and biting. His tongue, indecent. His hands, gripping my backside, moving me against him.

"You," he says. "You feel like you were made for me."

Thunder shakes the earth, and I reach for his belt.

"More." The word has many meanings.

"Here?" I feel his chuckle, but his fingers move to the bow on the shoulder of my dress. He pauses, then looks around. "Maybe not here."

Felix takes my hand and leads me around to where the rock and cliffs create a private cove just for us, and then we're kissing again. Soaked through to our skin. But I'm not cold. I'm not sure I'll ever feel the cold again. I could taste the rain on Felix's tongue forever.

I unfasten his jeans, and he unties the bows that hold my dress up. He's so hard in my hand. Heavy. Thick. Perfect. His mouth moves from my neck, down my chest. My bra is tossed to the sand, and he sucks on one nipple, then the next, the way I like. Hard, then harder, then teeth. His hand grapples with the skirt of my dress, pushing it up my thighs. I'm helpful. I take my underwear off myself while he digs a condom out of his pocket.

"Always prepared," I say as he hooks his arm around my leg, holding me tight, opening me up for him. And it feels so good, the slow stretch. Bliss. I arch back, tilting my chin to the sky. But when he begins to move, it's too much. My leg goes weak.

"I can't do this standing up."

"Fair enough," he says, gripping my ass, and lifting me clean off the ground. I yelp and snap my thighs around his waist.

"You can't hold me up like this." We're so slippery.

"Try me."

I squeeze him with my legs like a stress ball, afraid I'm about to crash to the sand.

"Relax, Lucy. I've got you."

"You better," I say, loosening myself. Felix adjusts his stance, and then he sinks so deep, I suck in a loud shock of air. He thrusts once, and I have to close my eyes.

"You okay?"

I mumble out a "Fantastic."

His replying laugh is strained. I tuck my face into his neck, holding him close. With every sound I breathe into his skin, his fingers tighten on me. It feels unreal, like every time we've been together before, but new, too. More primal. Unrelenting. Too much. Not enough. I come so fast, I'm a little annoyed with myself.

"What's that face?" Felix says, slowing his pace, kissing me softly.

"Too soon," I say.

He hums. "Feel like getting sandy?"

And then he's lying back on the wet beach, and I'm on top of him, kissing him, savoring him, relearning every inch of him. It's still raining, but it's gentler now. The water warm. This time when I come, Felix does, too, his mouth on my moles.

I lay strewn over him like a blanket, out of breath. He runs a hand over the pebbled skin on my arm.

"Let's go back to the house. Let's get you dry."

Felix helps me off the ground, reties my dress, and tucks me against his side. We make our way back to Summer Wind. Happy, laughing, and covered in sand.

29

Now

The house is empty. Felix and I call out for Bridget, but she's not in her room, the bathroom, the kitchen. She's not watching TV. She's not anywhere. I check the driveway. Zach's truck is gone, and Felix's is, too.

"Um . . ." I say, stepping back inside. "I think we've been ditched."

Felix stands beside the coffee table, a sopping wet mess. We brushed ourselves off as best we could, but we still dragged half the beach back with us. I think my dress might be ruined. I begin to laugh, but then I see a sheet of paper in his hand.

"What's that?"

Felix passes it to me. My name is at the top in Bridget's handwriting.

"I haven't read it," he says.

Bee,

I know you're upset with me, and I'm sorry. I know you put your life on hold to come here for me, and I'm grateful for that. I've bought our tickets for Wednesday morning—they're on me. Flight leaves at ten.

*I'm meeting Miles in Charlottetown. He lands this evening.
We have some things we need to work out in person, but I promise
you I'll explain everything to you when we're back tomorrow.
You are the very best friend, and I love you.*

—B

P.S. Tell Wolf I borrowed his truck.

I hand it to Felix after I'm done. As his eyes move across the
page, they harden. A muscle in his jaw ticks. But when he lifts his
gaze to mine, the ice melts. He throws an arm around my shoulder, drawing me to him. He brings his lips to my forehead. It's so
casually affectionate, and the ease at which he does this is a little
staggering.

"I hope you don't mind being stuck with me for the night,"
I say.

"I can think of worse things." He looks at the letter again.
"Should we call her?"

"No. Let's leave her alone." I'm baffled by what "everything"
could be, but I'm also hopeful that if she's meeting Miles, the
wedding is on. "I love her, but this trip has been chaos."

His thumb brushes over my bottom lip. "It's not all bad."

Felix's eyes are on me. And I know that look. That blue fire.

"Shower?" he asks.

"Shower," I say.

WE SPEND THE AFTERNOON SO TIGHTLY KNIT TOGETHER
that I can't say for sure where Felix ends and I begin. When my
stomach grumbles, Felix pulls me from his old bed.

"Let's go out."

We dress, and Felix tosses me the keys to the Mustang. I almost trip on the rug trying to catch them.

He picks up the keys off the ground and hands them to me. "You drive."

After some jerky shifts and a few reminders from Felix, I have the hang of it again. The rain has stopped, but moody clouds linger, the departing sun slung low and plump between them. Shadows grow long, and the fields glow gold. The ocean is dark, twinkling with promise. Felix's profile is washed in orange and gold. We crest a hill and are met with a stunning vista of cliffs and sea. I let out a long exhale.

I follow Felix's instructions to a roadside fish and chips stand and fold the towels he packed over the damp picnic table bench. We sit side by side, thighs kissing, ankles twined.

Without asking, Felix opens a couple of ketchup packets and squirts them on my fries. It's how I like to eat them—uneven dollops of red sauce, some bites sweeter than others. These details we've stored about each other.

I press my lips to his when he's done. "Thank you."

"For the ketchup?"

"For the ketchup."

I open three more packets and squeeze them into a puddle for dipping on the side of his basket, the way he likes.

"I can't believe you have to leave in two days," Felix says. "I've just got you."

"I know." But I'm grinning. *I've just got you.* I don't know what this is, but I like it already.

"I'll be in Toronto later this week for the wedding."

"I'm very aware."

"I've booked a hotel room." His eyes ask the question.

"Cancel," I say. "Stay with me."

His smile is magnificent. "Is your bed pink?"

"Does that matter?"

"I like your pink." His gaze drops to my mouth.

"You make that sound dirty."

"It might be."

"Well, the bed is white. The walls are pale pink."

"Perfect."

"Felix Clark among the streetlights and traffic and skyscrapers. You are made for the East Coast, but I like picturing you in the city."

He hums, then swipes his thumb over a dot of ketchup at the corner of my mouth. He sucks it off his thumb. "I'm made for a lot of things."

I'm going to miss this place. I'm going to miss this man.

On the way back to Summer Wind, we stop at a market and Felix buys oysters for dessert.

"You never get sick of them, huh?" he says after I've polished off my eighth. We're snuggled on the outdoor sofa. Citronella candles flicker in jars around the deck.

I squeeze a lemon wedge over my ninth. "Never."

"You still eat like you're from away," he says with fondness.

"I *am* from away."

"You've been here so many times, you're practically an islander."

"I think island regulations stipulate you have to spend at least three winters on PEI before you can claim that title."

Felix smiles. "Five, actually. I like oysters, but they're not my favorite."

I jerk my head back, eyes wide. "Excuse me? I don't think you're allowed to talk like that. They might not let you compete next year."

"I prefer my seafood cooked. I'm more of a fish and chips guy."

"I find this highly offensive, borderline scandalous. No wonder it's taken you so long to come clean."

Felix laughs, then prepares an oyster for himself, shaking a bottle of hot sauce on top. "There's a lot about each other we don't know yet."

"Hmm . . . That's true. Important things. Your favorite color, for instance."

"Pink."

"That's *my* favorite color."

"Mine, too," he says. "Pink like your suitcase. Pink like your lips. Pink like that striped dress with the buttons and the buckles on your sandals. Pink like the ribbon on your nightgown. Lucy pink."

I don't even think he's joking. "Lucy pink. You're . . ." I shake my head. "You *like* me."

"I do."

I take a deep breath. "It's going to take me time to get used to that. It feels . . ."

"Like a dream?"

"Or an explicit fantasy."

He chuckles.

"Favorite number?" I ask.

"Ah, the tough questions. Six."

"Because?"

"When I turned six, I announced that it was my favorite number, and my dad said when I turned seven, seven would be my favorite number. I decided right then that I'd never let go of six."

"So committed. Mine is thirteen. I feel the need to show it love."

"Very generous. Very Lucy."

"Middle name?"

"Edgar."

"Felix Edgar Clark," I repeat. "I can work with that."

"And yours?"

"Beth. Not as exciting as Edgar."

"Lucy Beth Ashby." He cocks a brow. "Sounds *very* exciting."

"Ha. If you could go anywhere in the world? Just one place."

He stares out at the water. "Australia. I've heard so much from Miles, and I'd like to see it for myself." His voice has gone soft. When his gaze returns to mine, it looks . . . I'm not sure. Sad? Hesitant?

"It's a very long flight," I say.

"It is. Maybe you could keep me company. We could go together one day, stand on a different beach, facing the Pacific."

"One day." I like that—the idea of a future with Felix in it.

"Can I ask something more personal?"

Felix turns his attention to me. "Okay."

"I've heard Bridget's version of your breakup with Joy, but not yours. And I'm curious."

He slides an oyster between his lips and chews it slowly. "Is there anything specific you want to know?" he says after a minute.

"Whatever you're comfortable sharing."

"You probably know most of the story." He rubs the back of his neck. I can feel his reluctance, sense that wound hasn't healed completely. "I was fifteen when we started dating. Joy was sixteen. But we had known each other most of our lives. By the time I was twelve, my crush was fully realized. The way Joy played hockey . . ." He drifts off, shaking his head as if he's still amazed.

"In some ways," Felix goes on, "I think that was our problem. When Joy and I started dating, it was very serious very fast. The way it progressed felt like an inevitability rather than a choice—we followed the path we thought we were supposed to. She went away to university and I stayed here. We spent our weekends visiting each other when we could, and we both missed out on other things. I'm not saying we didn't love each other. We did." He shrugged. "But we grew up."

"But the breakup was hard."

"Harder than hard. My mom and dad were in on the proposal. Joy's parents, too. The four of them organized this big party for all our friends and family, and I got down on my knee in front of everyone. Joy burst into tears. I thought they were happy ones. She said yes, and then broke up with me not long after. It was shocking . . . and so painful."

He looks lost in the memory, the lingering hurt.

"I'm so sorry."

Felix sets his hand on my knee. "It's okay. There's nothing there anymore. Joy is seeing someone, and . . ." He kisses me once. "Maybe I am, too."

He lets that sit there.

Maybe. Maybe it could work.

"What is it that you're looking for?" I ask. "From this. From us."

Felix sets his plate down, then takes mine from my hands and puts it on the coffee table. He leans over me, bracketing my head with his arms.

One kiss. "This."

Then another.

"But not just this?"

He shakes his head, moves his mouth to my ear. "No. More than this."

I tilt my head to the side as his lips find my chest. "I think I need to go slow," I say. And I definitely need to tell Bridget. "I'm not good at this. I'm not good at more."

Felix lifts his head, bringing his eyes to mine. Steady. "I am."

WE SPEND THE REST OF THE EVENING ON THE COUCH IN the TV room under a blanket. I'm wearing one of Felix's sweatshirts, black with a hood and white drawstrings, and nothing else aside from my prettiest pair of underwear and a thick pair of socks. He's in sweats. I am addicted to Felix in sweats. I am addicted to Felix in everything.

Felix has put *The Great British Baking Show* on, but we're not really watching. We're smiling at each other, kissing, twisting our fingers together.

It feels as if we're playing, testing what a relationship could be like, but I'm so at home. So comfortable.

It's like we've had a thousand nights like this one.

I lift the blanket to my nose, take a deep whiff. I want to remember everything about this moment.

"What's with you and the blankets?"

"Ugh. They're just the best. The wool is so soft. The color." This one is a lemony yellow. "I love how they smell like this place."

"They're made on the island," he says, pointing to the tag at the edge of the blanket. MACAUSLAND'S WOOLLEN MILLS. "Up in Bloomfield. I can take you there tomorrow if you want."

"Yes. Really?"

"Sure. I've never seen someone so excited by a blanket."

"I'm going to need you to roll around in it so it can soak up the full Felix scent."

He laughs. "Excuse me?"

"I'm hooked on it," I tell him. "I could bottle it and make a fortune."

"You," he says, "are an odd woman, but I'll happily roll around on your blanket."

"Good man."

We kiss, we whisper, we hold hands.

"I can't decide if I like you better with or without the beard," I say, narrowing one eye. "You're almost too hot like this." Felix smiles, and I touch his dimple. "But I feel like the beard makes your eyes stand out even more."

"My strongest feature."

"They're lethal." I heave an exaggerated sigh. "It's a real conundrum."

"Let me know when you solve it. I was trying out the clean-shaven thing for the wedding. I wanted time to grow the beard back in case it was a mistake."

"That's shockingly vain of you, Felix Clark."

"Well, I was going to see *you*." He pulls me, hauling me over his lap so I'm straddling him. He squeezes the backs of my thighs. "I wanted to look my best."

"I bought a very sexy dress, with an extremely high slit, but the neckline goes up to here." I point above my collarbone. "I didn't want you to see . . ."

He finishes my sentence. "You blush?"

I feel my chest heat. "Uh-huh."

"It's happening right now, isn't it?" He dips his hand under the bottom of the sweatshirt. His fingers creep up my stomach.

"No." A pinkie grazes my nipple.

Felix places his palm flat on my sternum. "I can feel how hot your skin is. Your heart is beating so fast."

"You're imagining things," I say as the flush spreads beneath his fingertips.

"Really?" He arches a brow. "Arms up, then."

I pause, then raise my hands over my head. Slowly, Felix works the hoodie off, sucking air between his teeth. I watch him soak me in, first with his eyes, then with his hands, following the scarlet with his fingers.

I dip my head so I can kiss his cheek and mouth and neck. When I pull the collar of his shirt to the side so I can taste his skin, he lets out a low moan. I reach for the hem.

"I showed you mine."

When I've got his top off, I shimmy from his lap, bringing him with me. I lie back, wanting to feel his bare chest against mine. I love how he's hard where I'm soft. He traces my moles, he kisses the indent at the base of my throat, then, eyes finding mine, positions himself between my thighs. Even though he's still half-dressed, the way he's pressed against me—all of him and all of me—and even though I'm sore from the beach sex and the shower sex, I'm already throbbing.

"I want to make something clear." He rocks his hips against me, and my eyelids flutter closed.

"Mmm?"

"Look at me, Lucy."

My gaze finds his.

"You and me—we're very good at this, but we're more than this."

"Okay," I whisper.

He strokes my cheek with his thumb and then my bottom lip.

"I'll go as slow as you want." He kisses me once, brushes his nose against mine.

"Thank you," I tell him. I snake my legs around the back of his thighs and give him a long kiss. "But right now, I'm not interested in slow."

30

Now

Four Days Until Bridget's Wedding

There's no four thirty alarm. No sneaking out. There's only me and Felix in a bedroom dappled in dawn. His body is wrapped around mine, naked. Memories of last night stir as Felix kisses my shoulder good morning.

His tongue and mine. Palms on flesh. His hands on my waist.

I've waited so long for this.

You feel so fucking right.

Muscles shaking. Eyes meeting. Ecstasy. Relief.

"Stay here," he says now. "There's no rush. There's nothing to do. There's nowhere to be."

I fall back to sleep, and he's gone when I pull myself from the bed and slip on my nightgown. I feel stomach muscles I thought you had to pay a trainer to identify. My thighs ache. Felix's head and hips were between them countless times yesterday.

I find him in the kitchen, hulling strawberries. There's an empty milk glass vase and a heap of flowers on the counter.

"What's all this?"

"Good morning to you, too." He holds a strawberry to my lips, and I open my mouth. I taste the berry, that burst of summer, and then his finger.

"Lucy." He's biting his lip, and I'm thinking about how dropping to my knees first thing in the morning sounds like a very good way to start my day when he says, "Later. I brought you supplies. I liberated them from my mom's garden, and they'll need water."

I let his finger go, and survey the delphiniums, snap dragons, sweet peas, and daisies.

"Your mother wouldn't be happy about this," I tell him. Our love of gardening is something Christine and I bonded over. I helped her divide and replant peonies when I visited at Thanksgiving three years ago. But I know she prefers seeing her blooms outdoors, rather than on her table.

"If I were the one putting her flowers in a vase, she'd kill me. But you? She'd be thrilled."

"Really?"

"Really." He kisses my temple. "I have an idea." A Clark sentence if there ever was one.

"Uh-oh."

He grins on the left side. "I thought we could cook tonight, for Bridget and Miles. I have a feeling everything will be okay there, and we can tell them about us. Toast the future."

"You," I say, kissing him, "are a very thoughtful man. I'd forgotten Bridget and Miles existed. I forgot the rest of the world existed." But it does, and Felix and I are going to be together within it. We're going to tell Bridget the truth. There's nothing left to hide. It's hard to fathom how different things will be.

I look at the flowers again. "Thank you for this."

Felix brushes my hair to the side and kisses my neck. "You're welcome.

"I'm making bacon and French toast," he says.

"Of course you are."

He smiles. "Meaning?"

"Meaning French toast is my favorite."

"I know."

"Meaning you're perfect."

"I'm really not."

I begin to pull my hair back so I can get it out of my face, but Felix tells me to turn around. I face the cupboards, giving him my back. His fingers skim my spine as he gathers my hair in his hands. I feel a gentle tugging.

"What are you doing?"

"Helping." More tugging. He's braiding my hair.

"How do you know how to do that?"

"Barbies."

"Barbies?"

"Mmhmm. I grew up with a very bossy older sister."

There's one final tug, and then his fingers are at my wrist, slipping off the hair elastic I've stored there.

"That's better," he says, kissing my cheek. He nods at the flowers. "Now get to work."

As Felix makes me coffee, I trim the stems. As he begins to cook, I fill the vase. But Felix has brought me so many flowers, I hunt for more of the milk glass vessels Christine keeps in the hutch. I arrange half a dozen before breakfast is ready. I love how the shears feel in my hand, how satisfying it is to clip each stalk at just the right length using only my eye, balancing the arrangements so that they look precisely as I want them to. Wild and flowing, tumbling over the lip of the vase as if there's no way to contain them. But I am. I am containing them. They are my pastels, and I am the illustrator. They are my clay, and I am the sculptor.

I'm here and nowhere else. It's me and my hands and these

flowers that Felix picked for me. There's no bride I'm worried about pleasing. No client I'm trying to impress. I'm not rushing to get it done before the delivery van pulls up.

This is what I love. Creating. Shaping. Building.

For the first time in so very long, I lose myself in imagining a cutting garden of my own, the way I used to, riding the streetcar to and from work, doodling in my sketchbook.

When I'm done, I set the arrangements on the table, with the biggest in the middle, the rest surrounding it. It's nowhere near my most elaborate grouping of arrangements, but it might be the most beautiful. I look at Felix, who's standing over a pan of sizzling bacon, and think, *More. Felix.*

"What time does your flight land on Friday?" I wrap my arms around his middle as he's at the stove and bury my face against his spine. I breathe him in deeply.

"Eleven something," he says. "Are you okay back there?"

"I don't think I can exist without this smell."

"Lucy." He turns his face to kiss my temple. "The things that come out of your mouth."

"The things that go into my mouth." I clamp my teeth around his earlobe.

He laughs, but it turns into a groan. "Shush," he says. "I'm trying to feed you."

I trail my hand down his torso.

"Lucy." He turns his head, looks at me over his shoulder. My hand dips lower.

He shuts off the stove. Turns around, his grip firm on my waist, bringing me snug against him. I plait my arms around him.

"I've imagined this," he says, palms skimming up my back. "You and me, in the kitchen together."

I push a wayward lock of hair off his forehead. "Cooking?"

"Cooking. Kissing. Fucking on the table."

"I like these sexy stories you tell," I said. "Is it an East Coast thing—like a sea shanty?"

"Of course. Every islander has an erotic shanty up their sleeve." He puts his lips to my ear. "Although in my version, we're not in my parents' kitchen."

"Fair. Get back to breakfast, then."

We eat on the deck, plates on our laps. He's in his armchair and I'm in my sofa nook. The maple syrup is the good kind. The French toast tastes better when Felix makes it. There's a square of Cows cultured butter melting over the thick slice of bread. The sun is so bright, it puts Felix's profile in shadow. I can only make out the glorious shape of him. I can't see what his eyes are saying. But now I don't need to. Now I know.

It's a gorgeous day. Sky blue sky. Green, green grass. Red cliffs. Birds. Breeze. There's a fox slinking across the grass, unbothered by our presence.

This is the place I love.

I spoke to Farah earlier this morning to make sure all went well at the flower auction and texted Bridget to ask when we can expect her and Miles today, but she hasn't replied. I'm nervous to tell her about Felix, more so now that there's a possibility of an us. I *want* there to be an us. But I also feel like I've been carrying a heavy parcel for five years, and I want to set it down. I want to talk to my best friend about the guy I like.

"How is this going to work?" I ask when we're done. My guess is that Bridget will freak. My hope is that she won't disown me. If that's the case, she'll want to know our plan.

Felix arches a brow.

"You and me," I clarify.

He rises, catlike, and sits beside me, pulling my feet onto his thighs, kneading the sole of my left foot with his thumbs.

"How do you want it to work?"

"I don't know. Your sister will ask. I thought it would be smart to have an answer."

"Well, for starters," Felix says. "I know how close you and Bridget are, but you don't owe her an answer if you don't have one."

I take this in.

"But you want to have an answer," Felix says, studying me.

I nod. "A loose one?"

"Okay."

"I want to know if you're going to keep seeing other people."

"Are you going to see other people?"

I chew on my cheek.

"What are you thinking, Lucy?"

"I'm trying to decide how honest I should be."

"Completely," he says. "I can handle it."

I watch his fingers working the arch of my foot. "There hasn't been anyone in a long time."

Felix's gaze is scorching. "Define *long*."

"For the past year there hasn't been anybody else. But I'm not you," I rush on.

"Lucy, for the record, I dated two women over the past year. I was trying to move on." He gives me a meaningful look. "No one comes close to you."

"But let's say you do meet someone you're interested in."

"How about we don't say that? I'm not interested in other people."

I smile. "Me neither."

"All right," he says, squeezing my foot. "Our rules are very out of date. So this can be our first one. It's just you and me."

"And what do we tell our friends and family?"

"We say we're together and request they back off while we figure it out."

It feels radical. "You are great," I tell him, poking the cleft in his chin. "I wish I was like you."

"We've already got one of me. We need you to be exactly like you."

I stare at him. "Are you real?"

He looks down at himself. "I think so, yes." He pats his chest. "I feel real."

"Well, you don't look or sound real, Felix Clark."

"I can show you how real I am."

"Right here?"

His eyes flare. "Right now."

"You," I say, "are indecent."

"Very."

"But you're also the most thoughtful, steadfast, unreasonably attractive man I've ever met."

His lips twitch. "'Unreasonably attractive'?"

"Yes," I say, nudging him with my toes. "It's rude. I thought so our first night together."

Felix's mouth sneaks up at its corner. "I can show you rude."

"Let's see it, then."

Felix stands, taking me with him. He undresses me carefully, like a beautifully wrapped gift. He sets my braid behind my shoulder, then unties the ribbon at my neck, eyes on mine. That look. I feel it between my legs. He opens every one of the buttons lining the bodice and slips it off. The nightgown falls to the wood. I'm naked, dressed only in sunlight. There are houses in the distance, perched atop the cliffs, but unless they have binoculars, we have privacy.

I reach for his shirt, and Felix gives his head a shake. "Lie down, Lucy."

WE WANDER DOWN TO THE SHORE MIDMORNING. FELIX brings an old quilt, the one the Clarks use as a beach blanket, and we rest our sex-slack bodies on the sand.

I don't want to go back to work. I've never felt it as sharply as I do right now. I want to arrange flowers. But the rest of it—the Cena meeting, the never-ending emails, the positions I'll have to fill—right now, I could leave all of it behind. I hadn't realized it until now, but I've burned myself out.

Felix and I are lying facing each other, and he's skating his fingers along my arm.

"Tell me your flaws," I say. "You must have some."

"I have plenty."

"Such as . . ."

"I'm not always great at handling my emotions. Sometimes I get overwhelmed, and it seems easier to shut them out, pretend like what I'm feeling isn't there." He pauses. "And I'm not a big fan of risks."

"What kind of risks?"

"Any. All. I've been burned in the past, which you know. I rebuilt my life once. I can't rebuild it again. I make sure I get things right the first time. Going slow is good for me, too."

"That can be our second rule," I say. "We'll take it slow."

He kisses me once, softly. "I have an idea."

"Uh-oh."

"For how this could work. We got sidetracked earlier. It's straightforward. Do you want to hear it?"

"Of course."

"I'll come to Toronto for the wedding. We'll have four nights together. You've spent a lot of time in my world; I want to spend more in yours."

"You do? You hate the city."

"I don't hate it," he says. "I want you to show me your apartment. I want to know where you keep the seeds I sent."

"They're in a glass box on my desk in your sister's old room."

"I want to see the box on your desk. I want to watch you arrange flowers and then go to the wine bar. Instead of saying goodbye at the end of the night, we'll go back to your place and wake up together in the morning. I want to see what type of coffee maker you have."

"My coffee maker?" I'm laughing now.

"Yes. I want to be able to picture exactly where you are when we're not together."

"I'll show you my sketchbook. The one with all my ideas for the farm."

"That's the first thing I want to see."

"I like this plan."

"Good. So I'll come to Toronto for the wedding, and then we'll save so we can go back and forth. You'll come here in September. I'll go there in October."

"But I love the island in October. I want another Clark family Thanksgiving feast."

The dimple surfaces. "So I'll come to Toronto in September. And you'll come here in October. My parents would love to have you."

It could work. We'll text, we'll talk, we'll send tasteful nudes. We'll send distasteful nudes. "We'll see each other once a month?"

"If we can afford it. If not, as often as we can. It's a short flight. You'll bring me a book. And I'll bring you a packet of seeds. We spend a few days together. We don't see other people."

"What will you tell your parents?"

"What *should* I tell them?"

I push a lock of hair off his forehead. "I think you should tell them we're dating."

He smiles. "Dating."

I smile back. "Dating."

"I think you should be there when I do. I want you to see my mother's face."

"Why's that?"

He looks surprised. "Don't you know? Christine Clark is the president of your fan club."

I kiss his ear. "Mmm. I think maybe I did know that. She sent me a knife once." It arrived after my first visit. An enormous Henckel. *Use it*, her card read. I found it odd since Bridget already owned one, but I guess Christine knew we wouldn't be room-mates forever.

"I know," he says. "Have you ever taken it out of its case?"

"Never."

He laughs. "I think she decorated that guest room especially for you."

"No."

"Just a hunch."

"My parents aren't like yours. They might not be so excited." Bridget's brother, long distance . . . "They'll have doubts."

"I'll comb my hair when I meet them."

"Ha."

"Would that bother you, if they had doubts?"

"Is it terrible if I say yes? I'd want them to see how great you are. But they're not the most encouraging people. They're very safe, and I think this would seem risky."

His eyes move between mine. "They don't want you to get hurt."

"No, never. But they overcorrect."

"Because you're the baby."

It took my parents years to stay pregnant after Lyle was born. It was my aunt who told me there was more than one miscarriage, and that when my brother took to skating at three, they poured their grief and love into his hockey. I was a complete surprise, one they treated like blown glass.

"Always and forever. They still call me Goose." When I was a toddler, I was always falling, always getting into mischief, breaking things. I became Lucy Goose. "Unlike you, I don't appreciate my nickname."

His fingers sweep to my shoulder, then back to my wrist. "Have you ever thought about telling them that?"

"My aunt said I should. I just don't want to offend them, you know? My mom is sensitive, and she shuts down when she's upset. She can be a bit icy."

Felix took this in. "What's your brother like? He's older, right? Lyle?"

"Yeah. I'm pretty sure he didn't know I existed when we were kids. But we're okay now. I did the flowers for his wedding." He and Nathan got married two years ago. "He lives in St. Catharines, but we have dinner when he's in the city. I think you'd get along. He'll talk your ear off about hockey, and Nathan's sweet."

"I'm glad I got to meet your aunt," he says after a moment. "Even if it was just for a few minutes."

"Me too."

"She was your mom's sister?"

"Mm."

"Are they similar?"

"Oh god no. I thought they hated each other until my aunt got sick."

Felix is silent for a moment. His fingers, which had been traversing up and down my arm, rest on my elbow. He's waiting for me to continue.

"Stacy and my mom were never friends the way some sisters are, and I never understood why. But when my aunt was sick, I heard them talking, and . . ." I take a breath, remembering what Stacy told me in the hospital after my mom left that day. "My aunt wasn't a fan of my dad when my parents started dating. She didn't think they had chemistry, and she kept hoping my mom would realize that they weren't a good fit. She thought my dad was more boring than dry toast, that he didn't make her laugh. But she didn't say anything, and then the day before the wedding, she just unloaded it all on my mom."

"Bad timing," Felix supplied.

"Exactly. I always wondered why their relationship was so tense, but now it makes sense. And my dad knew Stacy had questioned their relationship, so that added to the strain."

A cloud passes, muting the sun. I get lost in Felix's face. The lines that have deepened. The brow that arches. The tiny spot of hazel on his eye.

"My mom visited a lot when my aunt was sick. They laughed more than I'd ever heard them in my life."

"Do you think your mom forgave her?" Felix asks me.

"She did," I say. "In the end. But they let this one thing come between them and they lost so much time. It wasn't soon enough."

31

Now

Felix and I drive to Bloomfield and back in the Mustang, windows down, so I can buy a pink wool blanket. There and back, it's more than two hours, but I savor being close to him. His hand on the gear shift, the wind ruffling his hair. I like Felix. And he likes me. It's as fresh as a crocus in spring, but it's never getting old.

By the time we get back to the house, it's late afternoon. Felix assigns me as his sous chef, and I peel the husks from sunny cobs of corn while he scrubs new potatoes. We don't talk much, but the way we navigate the kitchen in tandem feels like a conversation. A dance. A song. The lyrics say, *We're good together.*

Bridget should be here any minute. Hopefully Miles is with her.

When Felix hands me a tomato and an enormous knife, I scowl. He knows I prefer when he does the cutting-up.

"You need practice," he says, and because his eyes are soft and glowy, I take the knife and slice the tomatoes. What I wouldn't do for those eyes.

Without Felix asking, I prepare them the way he does, overlapping the rounds on a plate, drizzling them with olive oil, sprinkling on the sea salt. I pluck basil leaves from Christine's herb garden and tear them into strips to scatter over top. I hold the dish out to Felix with a smug grin. But I catch an odd look on his face.

"What?"

He blinks. "You're so fucking hot. That's the sexiest plate of tomatoes I've ever seen." He takes my face in his hands and crushes his lips to mine quickly.

"The words that come out of your mouth," I say, laughing.

I chop dill for the potato salad. Felix stands beside me, whisking a marinade for the steak.

I've just finished setting the table when the door to the house opens.

"There you are," I say to Bridget when she enters the kitchen. I'm smiling because Miles stands beside her, holding her hand.

He's a good-looking man. Tall. Dark hair always neatly combed. He's elegant and polished, but he's not as reserved as he looks. His smile is wide. His waist is narrow. He looks like he could swim a mile, but he's not very confident in the water. Bridget's working on it.

"It's the future Mr. Bridget Clark," I say to Miles before I realize that he's wearing an unusual expression.

"Lucy, hi." He sounds off, too.

Bridget has moved into the kitchen, studying the flowers on the table. I've set it with Christine's nice linen napkins and got out the special plates from the hutch, the ones with the gold band.

"You got out the good china."

"I did. We're throwing you a celebration dinner," I say. "Felix and me."

I see his dimple from the corner of my eye, but I'm lasered on Bridget. She doesn't react to me calling her brother by his given name, like I thought she would. She touches a daisy petal and bursts into tears.

I rush to her side, sending a worried look to Felix. But he doesn't seem shocked by what's happening to my best friend.

"What did you do?" I ask Miles.

He holds up his hands. "It's not what you think."

"I will kill you, Miles Lam. Don't think I won't. I have a very large knife, and I know how to use it."

Bridget laughs, then begins to sob harder. I hug her close. "What is happening right now? Can you please tell me?" I usher her over to the sofa, glaring at Miles.

"Bridget. Talk to me."

She nods through her tears. Swats them away with her hand. "Okay." But she doesn't speak. She pushes a curl from her face, and it falls right back.

When we were roommates and Bridget's hair was annoying her, I'd weave it into a French braid. We've had a lot of talks while I plaited her hair.

"Turn around," I tell her. "I'll get it out of your way."

Miles joins Felix in the kitchen. Felix says something quietly in his ear, and Miles nods. I get the feeling I'm being left out of something. They watch as I separate Bridget's hair into sections, both looking concerned. Only when I'm finished does Bridget speak.

"Can we take a walk?"

WE GO TO THE BEACH.

"I'm not sure where to start," Bridget admits.

"Is there a beginning?"

She takes a deep breath. "I think so. It's also the middle and the end."

"Okay," I say. "Start there."

She stops walking and looks at me. Her chin quivers. "I don't want to say it. If I say it, then it's true."

My stomach dips. "Is the wedding off? Because if it—"

"No," Bridget interrupts. She swallows twice before saying, "Miles has been offered a job in Australia."

Everything goes blank. My mind, offline. My body, frozen.

"Bee?"

I focus on Bridget, on her brown eyes, which are beginning to well up again, and it all makes sense. Bridget has spent the past few days working through the biggest decision of her life. And I know my friend. I know she's already made it.

It takes me a full ten seconds to speak. "You're moving to Australia."

She nods, and twin tears fall onto her freckled cheeks. "I'm sorry, Bee." She wraps her arms around my waist, burying her face on my shoulder. Bridget is crying, but I stand there, arms limp at my sides. I think my brain is broken.

"I don't want to go," she chokes out.

Her body begins to shake. Her sobs come harder, like they're ripped from her soul. It wakes me up. I'm Bridget's best friend, and I need to act like it. I circle my arms around her shoulders, holding her tight. "I don't want you to go."

"I know," she says. "I know. Please don't hate me."

"I could never," I say, squeezing her to me. "Never, never."

We cry into each other's necks, and when the sobs turn into sniffles, we sit side by side on the sand, knees drawn up, so Bridget can tell me the full story. With a voice that sounds like it's been churned in a concrete mixer, Bridget explains that Miles's employer is opening a satellite office in Sydney. He's been tasked with running it. It's a significant promotion.

"How long have you known?"

"Just a few days. He got the offer last week, and I freaked."

"That's why you came here."

"Yeah," she says. "I just wanted to hug my parents and my brother. And you. I needed space to figure out what to do. I've turned it over one hundred times, but there's really no option."

"You have to go."

"I have to go." She sighs. "I've always wanted to go back to Australia. To stay longer than we did last time, but I never wanted to move there. It's so fucking far."

"It's as far as there is."

Bridget tells me they've committed to going for two years, and then they'll reassess. "We leave in October."

My mouth opens. That's only two months away. "But you love your job," I whisper. It's the only counterargument I have.

"I *really* do." Her chin is wobbling again.

"So why go? Why does Miles's career take priority?"

"It doesn't. He would turn it down if I asked. But it's an incredible opportunity, and I don't want to hold him back. And part of me can see what a once-in-a-lifetime experience this will be for me. I've only ever lived here and in Toronto. I'd like to get to know the place where Miles grew up. It's only two years."

"You sound like you're trying to convince yourself."

She laughs. "Maybe."

"Do you think your boss would let you stay on remotely?" I want to climb into bed and hibernate for two years until Bridget comes back, but I've switched over to best friend autopilot, attempting to be supportive.

She sucks in a deep breath. "I don't know. I still haven't figured that part out yet. I like going into the hospital, having colleagues, feeling like I'm part of a community. I love my coworkers. I love what I do. But I'm not sure it would make sense with the time difference."

"What is the time difference?"

"They're sixteen hours ahead."

"Wow. You're going to be living in the future. Can you tell me the winning lottery numbers?"

"Absolutely. That's exactly how it works. We'll be rich."

A couple walks by us on the beach, nodding as they go.

"I can't believe it," I murmur. "I think I may have to live in denial until you get on a plane. Even then, I'm not sure I'll be able to accept it." I turn to her. "Bridge, you're my everything."

She tucks my hair behind my ear, then holds my cheeks in her hands. My tears threaten once more.

"I love you," she tells me. "But I can't be your everything. Nobody can. And I'll still help with the shop—I can do the accounting stuff. You don't have to worry about that."

Something about her offer bothers me, but I can't put my finger on why.

We go quiet and watch the waves, letting it all sink in.

Bridget is moving. To another continent. Another hemisphere.

"I think you're brave," I say eventually. "What you're doing is brave."

"Thank you."

"But I wish you would have told me sooner. I get that you don't appreciate unsolicited advice, but this is a really big thing to hold back from me."

"I was trying to protect you. You lost your aunt last year, and

I know how much you miss her. Plus, you're already so stressed—
I didn't want to add to it. But it also felt like if I told you, it would
feel real, you know? And I didn't want you to try to talk me into
staying before I'd made a decision."

"Bridget, I can't even talk you into buying a new pair of leggings. And you keeping secrets *is* stressful. You're always helping
me but never let me help you. It sometimes feels like our relationship is one-sided because you don't need me."

Her brows lift. "You really think that? Bee, of course I need
you. Why do you think this is so hard for me? For years after I
moved to Toronto, I felt so alone. But then I met you, and I met
Stacy. I wouldn't have survived without you and all that pasta
your aunt fed us. Our Wednesday movie nights. Our kitchen
dance parties. The flower shop. Our excursions to the theater
with your aunt. I would have moved back to the island. I wouldn't
have met Miles. I wouldn't have my job. I owe you everything. I
love you, you potato."

I begin to cry again. "I love you, too."

She rubs my shoulder until I meet her eyes and brush my
tears away. "And you know my parents adore you," she says.
"They'd have you here anytime, and it will make me feel better if
you'd visit them."

"Have you told them yet?"

"No," she says. "I'd like to put that off forever. They already
think Toronto is too far."

I think of the way Felix glared at the letter Bridget left yesterday. "Your brother knows, doesn't he? Is that what you were arguing about the other night?"

She nods. "He wouldn't leave me alone until I told him. Wolf
can be pretty headstrong. And he was pissed that I was keeping
it from you."

Bridget told Felix before she told me. My first reaction is hurt, but I know it's hypocritical. I've been keeping secrets from Bridget, too. For years.

"I'm sorry, Bee," she says.

I know it's time to confess, but I'm terrified. Bridget's moving to the other side of the world, and it would be so easy for her to cut me out of her life. I'm losing her to Australia, but if she feels betrayed, I'll lose her all over again.

"I . . ." I hesitate. Because there's something I haven't considered before. What if Bridget isn't upset? What if she thinks Felix and I wouldn't work as a couple? Felix may not care about her opinion, but I do.

"Bee?" Bridget asks when seconds pass without me speaking.

"I have to tell you something." It comes out in a rush. Six words in one.

"What is it?"

I feel like I might vomit. "Please don't hate me." I repeat her plea.

"It would be impossible to hate you."

"I—" I've tried to do this before, but I've never got this far. I feel like I'm sprinting toward the edge of a cliff. I take her hands in mine so I don't have to jump alone. This is it. I take a deep breath, then fling myself into the air. "I like your brother." I let it hang there for second. "A lot."

Bridget frowns, confused.

"And he likes me." I sound like I'm thirteen. I try again. "Bridget, I have feelings for him. Real ones. We—" Her eyes widen, and I go on. "We are kind of . . . um . . . Well, there's kissing."

"You and my brother?"

"Yes."

"Are kissing." She speaks slowly, processing.

"Well, it's more than kiss—"

"Stop." She cuts me off, and I hold my breath. "I don't want to hear whatever you were about to say. He's my *brother*, Bee."

"I know. I'm sorry. Please don't hate me."

Her nose scrunches. "Why would I hate you?"

"You told me not to get involved with him."

"I told you not to fall in love with him. Wait, are you in love with Wolf?"

"I *like* him a lot. More than anyone. In a way that scares me, to be honest."

"Huh." A smile begins to blossom on her lips as she shakes her head. "I can't believe it. I mean, I knew you'd fooled around, but—"

"Wait." My jaw hangs open.

Bridget looks at me, smug.

"You knew?"

"I knew."

"Did Felix tell you?"

"Is that what you call him? That's so weird," she says. "And no, he didn't tell me. Although, when you came back from PEI last summer, he stopped asking about you, which was such a dramatic change from his regular pestering for Bee-related intel. And you got this weird look whenever I mentioned him. I knew something had gone down—I told you that."

I'm speechless.

"I remember being suspicious the second time you came here," Bridget says. "You and Wolf kept staring at each other. But it was that trip we took at Thanksgiving—I went to the bathroom in the middle of the night, and your bedroom door was open."

"Oh my god," I murmur. I can't believe I didn't close it when I went to find Felix downstairs.

"And you weren't in bed."

I rub my eye, not sure whether to be ashamed, embarrassed, or relieved—all those things, probably.

"And I heard the pull-out sofa make a very loud screech."

"No," I say.

"Yes," she says. "I'd like to scrub that from my brain."

"I'm sorry. I'm so, so sorry." I take a deep breath.

"I'll send you my therapy bill."

"So Miles knows?"

"Yes, Miles knows. I assume Zach knows since he and Wolf don't keep secrets. My grandparents definitely know—Grandma was the one who first mentioned to my parents that she thought you were more than friends. And I'd put money on my mother redecorating Wolf's old room specifically with you in mind. Christine Clark doesn't do girly, at least she didn't used to. This entire family has been secretly shipping the two of you for years."

This is dizzying. "Why didn't you say anything?"

"Why didn't *you* say anything?" she counters.

I'm defenseless. "I didn't know he was your brother. Not at first. I met him at the restaurant when you missed your flight that first summer." I will never share the rest of that story with Bridget. "We promised it wouldn't happen again. I'm sorry I kept it from you, but it wasn't supposed to mean anything. For a long time, I didn't think it did. I didn't want it to."

"Wow." She pauses, gathering her thoughts. "This has been going on for five years?"

"Not the whole time. I'm sorry I haven't told you until now. I've tried, but with what happened with Joy, I just couldn't do it."

"Well, I would very much appreciate if you don't break my brother's heart and then ignore me in the aftermath." She says this deadpan, but there's a small smile on her face.

"But what if it doesn't work? If I fuck it up, I'll lose you both. You'll hate me."

She scoffs. "If you fuck it up, then I'll love you. It's Wolf who needs to watch out."

She stares out at the water, chewing on her lip, for a solid minute. "I can see it," she says, sounding decisive. "He'll steady you, and you'll pull him out of his shell. He's always more talkative when you're around, and you'll both take care of each other. I think it could work." Bridget falls silent again, then shakes her head. "Wow. You and my brother, huh?"

"Yes," I say. "Me and your brother."

32

Now

Bridget and I stay on the beach for a long time. We don't say it, but I think we both feel that reality awaits us at the house, and neither of us wants to face it. We make our way back slowly, one heavy step at a time. My brain feels like mashed bananas on toast. Bridget is moving, and as that truth settles, I know it will knock me over. I see it coming like a train. Panic. Loneliness. All the ways I'll miss having her close. I can feel it in my lungs already.

But then I spot Felix. He's on the deck with Miles, and I can tell when he notices us. His body goes still. And then it goes fast. He races toward us, and as he gets closer and our eyes meet, I know it's only me he sees. It stops me in my tracks.

"Whoa," Bridget says.

"Whoa," I agree.

When Felix reaches me, he picks me up, clean off the ground, hugging me tight. I wrap my legs around his waist and press my face into his skin, the bronzed curve where his shoulder meets his neck. Salt and sun and wind and trees.

"I'm sorry I didn't tell you," he says. His voice vibrates through me, and I grip him tighter. "It wasn't my news to share."

"I know. I'm not angry."

I can feel the tension leave his body.

"Are you okay?"

"No." I smoosh as much of me into as much of him as I possibly can. Forehead. Cheek. Eyelid. Nose. Lips. "I feel like my heart has been torn from my chest, but if I can stay right here in the crook of your neck, it would help."

I feel his chuckle. "I think I'll have to put you down eventually. I'm strong, but I'm not strong enough to carry you indefinitely."

Bridget pipes up, "It's a good thing Bee told me about the two of you or this would be weird. Actually, it's still weird."

"I think you better put me down," I say. Bridget's not ready for PDAs.

I unwind my legs from Felix, and when he sets me on my feet, Bridget shoves her brother's shoulder. "Wolf, what did I tell you about flirting with my friends?"

He raises a brow. "I hope you're not expecting an apology."

"Be careful," she tells him. "I know where you live."

"How are you really?" Felix asks as we walk to the house. His arm is wrapped around my waist, keeping me close to his side.

"Devastated. But I'm not sure I can talk about it without breaking down again." Even at that, my voice catches. "I'm sort of panicking."

"Don't panic," he says. "Nothing good comes from panicking."

"I know," I tell him.

But two months from now, Bridget will be in Australia, Felix will be here, and I'll be in Toronto. The ache in my lungs begins to burn.

Felix kisses my temple. "We'll get through it together, Lucy," he says.

Together. I like how it sounds.

33

Now

Bridget's Wedding Day

My alarm goes off at five. I need to be at the Gardiner Museum early. I've rallied the whole team today. But I can spare a few more minutes. I hit snooze, but big hands grip my waist, and Felix rolls me on top of him.

"No fair," I grumble.

"You told me not to let you sleep in." He kisses me. "This is your wake-up call."

Having Felix in my bedroom is magic. A new first. I show him how to use my coffee maker, and he fixes me a pot while I shower. Finding him in my kitchen, blowing into his cup of tea, is surreal. My apartment will never be the same. From now on, I will always picture Felix Clark drinking Earl Grey in this kitchen.

HE COMES WITH ME TO THE MUSEUM—HE WANTS TO WATCH me work and he wants to meet Farah. I introduce him to her, Rory, and Gia, then start on the archway, but my gaze keeps slipping to him, distracted.

"Your heart's leaking out your eyeballs," Farah says from across the space.

So I kick Felix out. It's my best friend's wedding day, and I need complete focus.

I returned to Toronto seventy-two hours ago, but I've slid right back into overdrive—long hours at the shop, a newly signed contract with the restaurant group, full-time positions for Rory and Gia, a raise for Farah, and two more job openings ready to be posted next week. Work is how I coped with losing my aunt, and it's how I'm coping with Bridget moving. She's leaving a big hole in my life, and I need to fill it somehow. Job stress I can handle. Saying goodbye to Bridget in two months . . . I can't even think of it.

All of it slips away as I begin to fix stems of magnolia leaves into the foam base of the arch. I enter the singular place where my mind is quiet and my fingers take over. Halfway through, I have the notion that if I could do this every day—work with flowers and cut the other stuff out—I would be happy. This is the thing I love doing. I was made for this work. And Bridget's wedding will be my best work yet.

I stand back when I'm done, surveying the structure, assessing the balance. There are branches of blackberries and globes of hydrangea, fresh and dried. Creamy ranunculus, roses, magnolia leaves, and seeded eucalyptus. My arches are usually seven or eight feet high. This one is ten. It's partially because Miles is a very tall man and the venue is open and airy, all glass and sharp edges. But it's also because I'm showing off. By the time we finish, the museum looks like a fairy tale, the aisle lined with blossoms, chair backs swagged in blooms.

I MAKE MY WAY DOWN THE AISLE, FINDING FELIX AT THE front of the room, standing with Miles and the best man. We blatantly stare at each other until I take my place as maid of honor and shift my gaze, waiting for her. When Bridget walks toward us on Ken's arm, I can't take my eyes off her. She glows. She's radiating from within, reflecting light all around. The dress is white. Simple. Scoop neck, sleeveless, a column of silk caressing her skin and falling to the floor. There's no lace or beading or embellishment of any sort. There's no underwear, either. Bridget tried a thong, but even that showed through. Her heels are delicate, pearlescent, and I doubt they'll make it past tonight's dessert course. Her hair is pulled back into a low, perfectly imperfect bun, and the greens in her bouquet trail almost to the floor. Her dimples are on full display. She's gossamer. She's wind and air and cloud. The embodiment of happiness. So beautiful, my best friend.

I stare directly at her because I don't want to miss a thing, but I can feel Felix's gaze. I know if I look, I'll see the dimple. He hasn't stopped smiling all day. When Bridget joins Miles at the altar, my eyes slide to Felix.

"Hey," he mouths.

"Hi," I mouth back.

"You look hot."

"You too." Felix in a tux is criminal.

He nods his head at the archway. "Also hot."

I know it is. But I love that Felix thinks so, too.

Before the rehearsal dinner yesterday evening, he told his parents we're dating. I stood beside him, but Felix did the talking. Christine gripped Ken's forearm like she might fall over, but then she let out a whoop.

Bridget and Miles's first kiss as a married couple lasts so long, there are hollers from the audience.

"Get a room, mate," one of the Aussies shouts.

When the newlyweds make their way down the aisle, Felix whispers something to the best man, and switches positions with him. We turn toward each other. He wipes a tear from my cheek with his thumb and then offers his arm.

"I know you," he says.

"We've met before."

"But never like this."

"That suit should be illegal," I say when we're halfway down the aisle.

He chuckles, then whispers, "Tonight. You, me, that dress, your dining table. I'm going to bend you over it."

I lean into his ear, my heart racing. "Not if I bend you first."

THERE ARE PHOTOS WHERE WE ARE POSITIONED BESIDE each other. A dinner where we are seated next to each other. Felix invents ways to keep touching me—his hand wanders to the base of my spine as I move, his fingers skim over my shoulder when I laugh. At one point, his palm coasts under the slit in my dress and takes up residency on my thigh. I didn't let Farah off the hook—she's still my date for the evening—but Felix talked her into swapping seats. I'm sandwiched between the Clark siblings, and I can't stop grinning.

When it's time for my speech, I rise to the microphone. My hands are shaking. Even though I can feel Felix watching, it's only Bridget I see. I've been planning to make my best friend cry since the moment she and Miles got engaged. But now that I'm looking at her, the person dearest to me, it's my eyes that are stinging.

"The first time I met Bridget Clark, she gave me a ride home on her handlebars." I sound shaky, so I take a deep breath. "In

many ways, she's carried me since that night seven years ago."
My voice cracks in the middle of the sentence. I've been avoiding
thinking about it for days, and now the truth bashes against me.
Bridget is moving to Australia, and I don't know how I'll survive
without her. I scan the page, knowing I'll never be able to say
everything I've written without a spectacular display of sobbing.
But I do it anyway. I cry my way through the speech.

"Miles, take good care of her," I finish. "There's no one more
precious to me."

I turn to my best friend, her cheeks streaked with tears. "You
are the love of my life, Bridget."

THE WEDDING CAPTURES HOW BRIDGET'S WORLD IS SPLIT
between city and coast. We're downtown, near the corner of
Bloor Street and Avenue Road, Toronto rushing by outside. Inside, there are courses upon courses of food, the finest you can
ask of any caterer. Roast suckling pig. Deep-fried crab. A whole
white fish with ginger and scallions. The bubbly is the good stuff,
the string quartet plays Vivaldi. Everything runs on a precisely
considered schedule. But there's also dancing, kicked off by
Bridget's grandfather on the fiddle. Her shoes come off at this point.
Zach loosens his tie. The gift he brought is suspiciously Trivial
Pursuit–shaped. At eleven, a food truck parks outside the venue
with buttery lobster rolls. The dance floor is never empty. I don't
think a group of one hundred people have ever had such a fun night.

Shortly before midnight, the music stops, and Miles takes the
mic from the DJ and says, "This one goes out to my wife."

And then, at the top of his tone-deaf lungs, Miles Lam sings
"Un-Break My Heart."

It's a bizarre choice for a wedding and exactly right for Bridget.

Miles puts his entire soul into it. Fist pumps. Chest whacks. Eyes shut and chin raised to the ceiling.

And the whole night, Felix by my side. Felix's hand in mine. Felix's lips on my lips. We dance, and we laugh, and we can't stop touching each other.

"I'M RELISHING YOU," I TELL FELIX, TIPSY, AS WE MAKE out in the stairwell. I'm addicted to how he tastes. Salt and Tic Tacs.

He laughs into my mouth. "Relishing?"

"Yes, and I don't think I've ever relished anyone before. But I relish you, Felix Edgar Clark."

Felix takes my head in his hands. "I relish you, too, Lucy Beth Ashby."

After the kissing, when I return to the party from the bathroom, I catch Felix standing next to the floral archway. He looks surprisingly at home in his tux, like he could walk out into the night of the city and look like he belonged.

Mine, my heart says. *Felix.*

He runs his fingers along one petal, then another, his expression awed. I relish him from across the space, and then I haul him back to the dance floor so I can enjoy him in my arms.

The DJ is playing something slow and old, and my head is on Felix's shoulder, and I'm certain this curve of muscle and bone was made for me. Zach and his girlfriend, Lana, are close by, and he gives me a thumbs-up. It feels so good, being with Felix, surrounded by our friends and his family. It feels perfect. It feels like I should be with Felix always. For a little while, I pretend that he isn't leaving on Tuesday.

Mine, my heart keeps saying. *Felix. More.*

34

Now

We stumble into my apartment, drunk. The champagne is only partially to blame.

"I think this has been one of my top best favorite nights ever," I say between kisses.

Felix laughs. "It's up there for me, too."

I growl and give his bottom lip a little bite.

Felix pulls back, looking into my eyes with total seriousness. "You should know that you're competing with the night Zach lost a bet and pierced his nipple."

I nod. "Fair."

We haven't left the hallway, haven't taken off our shoes. We just keep kissing. I'm overcome with the need to make this moment last forever. I want to hold it between my hands like dough and stretch it out slowly and carefully so that it never ends. I feel a flutter of panic at the idea of going back to the ceaseless grind. I don't want to come home to an empty apartment. And I don't want to be without Felix. I want to be back on the island.

I pull away from him suddenly, digging my phone out of my clutch.

"Was it something I said?" Felix says behind me.

I peer over my shoulder. He's looking at me, amused, tie askew, hair mussed from my fingers. Wonderful, gorgeous man.

"I'm getting organized," I tell him, pulling up my calendar app. "I want to plan this out."

"This?"

"Us. I don't think I can wait a full month before I see you again."

I frown at my screen.

"That's a lot of pink and orange and green," Felix says. "What does it all mean?"

I sigh. "Meetings, event installations, staff schedules."

"Wow."

I flip through to September, and it's worse. "Everyone assumes summer is our busy time," I explain when Felix's eyes widen. "But things pick up in the fall in Toronto." And I need to start interviewing for the new positions, and then train those people. "I'm never going to be able to leave the city," I murmur absently.

We look at October. "Farah has time off over Thanksgiving this year. I forgot. I won't be able to come to the island then." My heart sinks. This is going to be a lot more challenging than I thought. I signed that contract with Cena without considering how it would impact Felix and me.

"I'm stressed just looking at this," I say. "Why have I done this to myself? How are we going to make this work?"

"Maybe seeing each other every month was too optimistic. But we don't need to book any flights tonight," he says. "We'll be okay, Lucy. We'll both be busy. I've promised Zach I'd scope out some new properties this fall. Time will fly."

I don't think that's true.

"I know we said we'd take things slow, but this feels like taking things nowhere." I hadn't thought it through before, but having Felix with me in Toronto has underlined how much long distance is going to suck. "You being there, me being here. It's going to be hard."

It's going to be even worse when Bridget leaves in October.

I look around the apartment. The small kitchen that opens to the living and dining area. The round white table and wishbone chairs I made Bridget carry home with me all the way from Richmond and Bathurst. The pink sofa I bought after she moved out. The rose-colored glassware on the brass bar cart. It all looks like me, but this place hasn't really felt like home since Bridget left. She's what gave these walls meaning. Without her, it's a book without words, a vase with no flowers. I don't want to come home to this. I turn back to Felix. Maybe I don't have to.

The idea bursts from me like a rocket.

"I should move to PEI," I blurt out.

Felix laughs, surprised, until he sees that I'm not kidding. "Maybe one day—"

I cut him off. "No. Like, now. I should move in with you."

"Uh."

"Think about it. It's perfect. I love it there, and I love being with you. I can't face my life right now, Felix. Bridget's leaving, and I'm burnt out, and it's only going to get worse. Look at this thing." I wave my phone in the air. "I think I might need to blow it all up. I want to go back with you."

"Lucy." He's looking at me carefully. "It's always hard to go back to normal life after a trip. I think you might be suffering from a severe vacation hangover."

"No, I think I might be having an epiphany. I signed the restaurant contract, but I don't even know if I really wanted to. I don't know what I'm doing. I need to figure out what I want my life to be so I can live it fully."

Saying the words out loud makes me miss Stacy all over. I want Italian take-out nights. I want her to take me to a play. I want her arms around me. I want dancing in the kitchen with Bridget. I want to grasp on to those moments, to wrap myself up in them. I want a soft place to land, and more than anything I don't want to spend my nights alone. Here.

"You can't do that, Lucy. We can't do that." Felix looks stricken.

"Why not?" The lines above his nose are deepening, but I press forward. "Farah can take over the store for however long I need her to. It would be like . . . an extended vacation."

Felix blinks. "Living on the island isn't an extended vacation. I'm not one, either."

"No, I know." I blow out an exhale. "Of course I know that."

"We both said we wanted to take things slow. It's too soon to move in together. We haven't even talked about our future together, not really."

"I know, but we can sort that out, right? It'll be easier if I'm there, without the rest of my life to worry about." My brain is fuzzy but some part of it must know what I sound like. But the brakes have fallen off, and for some inexplicable reason I barrel on. "Felix, I just need some time to figure things out. I need to find myself, you know?"

As soon as I say it, I know I've made a mistake. And not just because Felix flinches.

"I'm sorry," I say quickly. "I shouldn't have said that."

For a few seconds, he can't speak. He swallows. "Lucy. I—" A shadow passes over his gaze.

I put my hand on his shoulder. "I'm not her," I say quietly, but I don't think he hears.

"I—" Felix closes his eyes. One inhale through his nose. "Lucy, I don't think this is going to work."

My lungs stop. "What?"

"Not right now."

My lips part, but I can't get words to come out.

"Lucy, I want to be with you." He cups my elbows, face close to mine. "But I need to know that you want to be with me for the right reasons—not because you need a break from your life."

"It's not just that, Felix. It's you. I don't want to be alone. I don't want to be without you."

"I want that, too." His hand finds my cheek. "I want you in my home, in my bed. I want us to have our own full days and come back and talk about them together. But I can't start this unless you're certain about us."

"I am," I tell him, louder. "I'm not sure what I want, but I know I'm happy when I'm with you. Work, living here, being lonely when Bridget moves away—that's what I need to sort through."

"And that's okay. You don't need to know what you want yet, and you *should* take time to figure that out. But I don't think I could handle it if you came to the island for the wrong reasons and then decided I don't have a place in your life after you've had time to reflect. If we do this, I want to do it properly."

I take a beat to listen to what he's said. This is the most important fight of my life, and I don't want to get confused. "I need to think for a minute." I stare into his eyes, desperation rising. I can feel the tears coming. "Don't leave. Please stay."

"I'm not leaving. Let's sit down."

I get to the sofa. Felix brings two glasses of water, and I sip at mine until I can untangle my thoughts, repeat in my mind what Felix has said so that I can try to understand.

"I've never wanted to be with another person the way I want to be with you," I tell him. "I've never liked anyone the way I like you."

He swallows, then reaches for my hand. "Can I?"

I nod, and his fingers fold into mine. I squeeze.

"I can't be your escape route." He pauses, letting this sink in. "I don't want to be a stop along your journey. I want to be the destination."

"You're scared."

"Lucy, I am *terrified*. The way I feel about you . . ." His eyes are fixed on mine, pleading for me to understand. "You could break me so easily."

The way he says it makes my heart ache. Felix deserves a relationship that starts from a steady place, and I can't give him that today or tomorrow. It's not the right time for him, and maybe it's not the right time for me, either. I have a history of turning away from my problems instead of confronting them, and moving to PEI would be no different. And is it what I want? I can't say I'm 100 percent certain. I need time to figure me out.

"I'm scared, too," I tell him. "I don't want to lose you."

"I don't want to lose you, either."

"We can't do this now," I say. I know he's right. I can't run away from my life—I owe that to myself, but I owe it to him, too.

When the tears come, Felix bundles me against his chest. I try to soak up the smell of him, imprint it on my soul.

"Lucy." His voice is thick. "There's a reason we keep coming back to each other. We can come back to each other again."

I burrow farther into his warmth. "What if we don't?"

"I think we will." Felix takes my shoulders in his hands, and gently leans me back so I can look at him. His cheeks are damp. "But if we don't, then we know it wasn't meant to be."

"I don't like that," I tell him. "I'm mad at you," I say with no heat.

"I know."

I stare at him, this beautiful, caring, brilliant man. A man I admire more and more every moment we spend together. Even now. I want him to know. I *need* him to know. "Can I tell you something?"

"Anything."

"It's going to sound corny, but I feel like I should say it in case I don't get another chance."

"I'm a big fan of corny," Felix says, voice rough.

"I've always thought what you did was impressive—the way you started over. The life you'd planned was knocked off course, but you picked yourself back up. You and Zach had a dream, and you worked hard to make it a reality. And the cottages are incredible—I don't know if I expressed that last year. I've always found it inspiring."

Felix tries to smile. "That's funny," he says. "I've always thought what *you* did was impressive. You left your job, defied your parents, carved your own path. Corny or not, I think *you're* inspiring."

My chest hurts with how badly I want to hold on to him, to never let him leave. "We've been good for each other, I think," I whisper.

"I think so, too."

"Can you stay? Just for tonight? I sleep better when you hold me."

He shakes his head, eyes glassy. "I'm going to go. If I don't, I'm not sure I ever will."

"Now?" I say, my throat going tight again.

"Yeah," he says gently. "I think I better."

He gathers his things from my bedroom as I wait near the door.

"Where will you go?"

"I'll get a cab. Head to the hotel where everyone's staying. Don't worry about me."

"But I will," I tell him. "I'll think about you all the time, and I'll worry."

"You don't need to." He looks at me like he's trying to memorize me. "Worry about you."

"I don't want to go another year without talking," I say. "I want more than an emoji."

He turns around. "I can do that."

I nod, and he opens the door. I know this is the part where we say goodbye, but I don't think I can manage the word. So I lift my arm to wave.

But Felix captures my hand and presses a kiss to my palm. "I relish you, Lucy Beth Ashby."

He doesn't say goodbye, either.

35

Now

Felix has been gone for ten minutes, but it's almost like none of it happened, as if it was all too perfect to be real.

My tears are dry. The champagne buzz has faded to nothing. My thoughts have, too. I wash my face and braid my hair and change into my nightgown, numb.

But my sheets smell like him, and as soon as I set my head on my pillow, it comes rushing back. The days Felix and I spent basking in the glow of each other on PEI. Felix lying here next to me last night. Felix squeezing ketchup on my fries. Felix and I kissing on the beach last summer. Felix meeting my aunt, Felix at Thanksgiving, Felix in the bathroom, Felix the first time I saw him. A crackle of blue, a flash of an oyster knife, fast hands, messy hair.

I push him out, but my mind wanders to Bridget. My best friend who's leaving in two months. I picture Teacup Rock before the hurricane swept it into the ocean. That magnificent red formation of sandstone carried away by the wind. I hear Bridget, whispering, *"It feels like things are slipping away."*

And I cry.

I AWAKE WITH A STIFF NECK AND EYES THAT FEEL LIKE sandpaper. I head directly to the coffee machine, and while it brews, I text Bridget. She's packing for her honeymoon today, but I need my best friend.

Do you have time to come over? Or if not, then a call?

Bridget shows up that evening, a grocery bag in her hands. She holds it up. "I brought ice cream.

"I've already talked to Wolf, but I want to hear from you what happened," she says when we're on the couch, bowls of Moose Tracks on our laps.

"He ended things." The back of my nose starts to tingle. I shake my head. Then take a deep breath. Bridget squeezes my shoulder. "Or I guess we both did."

"He put it differently. He used the word '*breather*.'"

"Maybe that's what it is. I've been thinking about it all day, and I do think I need some time. I can't go on the way I have been—I don't want to dread going into work. I don't want to lie in a puddle of my own tears when you go to Australia because I have no other friends to spend time with. Part of me still wants to get on a plane to the island and never come back, but I know that would only make things worse. For me, and for Felix. I really like him, Bridget."

Her smile is soft. "I know you do."

"I want to make it work, but I know that would be impossible if he's worried I'm a flight risk. And I guess I can admit that it isn't an ideal time for me to jump into a relationship with everything that's going on at work. He'd probably feel ignored the way Carter did."

"That doesn't sound like Wolf. Nor does it sound like you." She studies me. "I haven't seen you this worked up about a guy before."

"No," I say. "Me neither."

"Have you talked to him today?"

I shake my head. "I'm a little nervous to get in touch. I'm afraid he won't write back or that he'll be cold. What if he was breaking up with me in the gentlest way possible, and I never hear from him again?"

Bridget laughs. "I'm sorry," she says. "But I saw Wolf. I know that's not what happened. You should reach out. When you're ready."

"I don't know when I'll be ready."

Bridget hums. "It's not a bad plan, you know? To take some time to think about yourself—what you want, what you need— that can only be a good thing. I approve. And if it makes you feel better," Bridget says, "my mom gave Wolf an earful when he told us what happened. Apparently she doesn't believe in 'breathers.' And you know what Christine Clark is like when she's salty."

That does make me feel better. "How many *horse shits*?"

"All of them," Bridget says. "I think she ran out."

My apartment seems quieter than ever once Bridget leaves. She's not moving for another two months, but I can feel her absence already. It's only when I'm serving myself another bowl of ice cream that I remember her offer to keep helping me with the flower shop. It nags at me as I braid my hair before bed. I'm lucky my best friend has acted as my professional safety net, but I've been running In Bloom for more than three years—I should be my own safety net.

I'm so tired. I feel like I've been running for too long. I need space to ask myself big questions and quiet so I can hear the answers. I need a fresh start.

But I don't need it right now. Right now I need my bed.

THE FOLLOWING DAY, FARAH TAKES SYLVIA FOR HER AFternoon walk and returns with coffee. We sit at the table, the dog's muzzle on my foot, and she tells me for the sixth or seventh time how smoothly everything ran while I was gone.

"It was fun," she says, her pointy neon green nails curved around a paper cup. "I'm good at bossing people around. You should go on vacation more often."

I make a noncommittal *hmm*. Stepping back from work, even for a few days here and there, isn't feasible. I can't believe I thought for even a second that it was a good time to run away from my life.

I can tell Farah wants to push the issue, but her eyes narrow as she studies me. She waves her finger in a circle in front of my face.

"You look like an anal gland."

"Thank you so much."

"Are you okay?"

"Not right now," I say. I have no capacity to say otherwise. I miss Felix like an organ. "But I will be."

"Do you want to talk about it?" she asks.

"No." But I decide to anyway. Farah pulls out the emergency bottle of vinho verde from the cooler, and I tell her everything that's happened since the very first summer. I'm through with secrets.

36

Now

October

Bridget boards flight AC119 to Australia on October twenty-ninth. Miles is already in Sydney, house hunting in the inner west suburbs, so I ride with her to the airport. It's the only time I've wished for heavy traffic on the way to Pearson, and the only time the roads are empty.

As we sail up the highway, I hold her hand so tightly, she complains she can't feel her fingers but I don't let go. Right now, holding Bridget's hand is the only thing keeping me together. If I let go, I'll shatter into a million jagged pieces.

Once we arrive, I load her luggage onto a cart and lift her suitcases onto the baggage scale, because Bridget is six weeks pregnant.

I walk with her to the security gate. I stay with her until the very last moment. And then I hug her until we're both crying in the middle of the terminal and an elderly woman passes us each a tissue.

I tell Bridget she's my best friend. I tell her that I'll miss her. I tell Bridget that I love her more than anyone.

And then I let go.

PART THREE

I don't want sunbursts and marble
halls. I just want you.

—L. M. Montgomery, *Anne of the Island*

37

Now
October

"You seem surprisingly stable considering Bridget just left," Farah says the day after I take Bridget to the airport.

"I'm never stable enough for you to quit, if that's where this is headed."

"No," she says. "But I do want to talk about something. It's been two months since you went to PEI, which means it's been two months since you took a vacation day."

"I know. We've been busy."

"We have, but we have more help now. Things are going well. You could breathe for a minute, and we'd be okay." She frowns, but not in the way she does when there's a tiny dog in a customer's handbag. She looks surprisingly vulnerable. "Do you . . ." She rolls her eyes. "I don't know . . . not trust me?"

"What? Absolutely I do. Why would you think that?"

"You waited a year to take a holiday and only left because Bridget was in crisis. You're here all the time. You show up on your days off."

"I—" I take a beat to figure out what I want to say. When I used to compliment Farah's work, she'd hike her shoulders to her ears like she was in pain. Over time, I stopped doing it. I assumed she knew how much I value her. "I trust you," I tell her. "You're organized, reliable, and unbelievably talented. I'm sorry for not letting you know."

Farah squirms in her seat but says thanks. Just as I think we're done, she clears her throat. "I understand that this is your business and that nothing is more important to you, but I care about it, too."

"I know that." I saw past Farah's apathetic veneer a long time ago.

"Lucy, you're a micromanager."

I swallow. That's hard to hear.

"If you can step back a bit and let me help more, I'd appreciate that. I'd like some room to grow."

I take a deep breath. "I get it." *Room to grow.* "I think I need that, too."

38

Now
December

I spend my evenings curled up with the Floret Farm book, reading about how the author's now-famous flower farm began by growing two rows of sweet peas in her backyard. I read about how that little garden became a bigger garden and about the greenhouse her husband built. I learn about seasonal blooms and local varieties, about soil tests and succession planting and the importance of growing not just flowering species but ones that provide other material for arrangements—greens and seed pods and twigs. On my streetcar rides to and from the store, I begin to imagine.

I slowly dial back my hours at the shop. I give myself time in the workday to take care of paperwork, prepare quotes, and review my orders, and I find that it's not so arduous now that I have more help. I take a day off and see a matinee performance of *Les Misérables* by myself. I sit in the dark theater, missing being here with my aunt and Bridget so badly, I'm not sure whether it's the play or the longing that makes me weep. But when I'm back on the street, out in crisp daylight, I feel invigorated. I didn't think I was the kind of person who could go to a show on her own. It turns out that I like surprising myself.

Bridget and I stay in touch through a constant exchange of emails and calls and texts. She sends me photos of flower arrangements she thinks I'll like. They're all hideous, and I love them. I think about what she once said—that no one can be my everything, not her, not a partner—and I begin to reconnect with old friends. We meet in cafés and I apologize for being absent over the past year and a half.

I'm walking home from a coffee with a former colleague from back in my PR days and decide to stop by a small organic seed shop. When I see the packet of forget-me-knots, I know exactly what to do with them. Felix and I haven't spoken in more than three months, not since the night we decided to put a relationship on hold. My first step toward him is cautious, and just like before, I don't write a note. I mail the seeds to Prince Edward Island the following day.

The next week, a yellow package arrives to the flower shop. It's heavier than the ones Felix used to send, but it's his handwriting on the label. I recognize it from in the margins of his books. I've seen it on ten other envelopes. I pull out a copy of *The Secret Garden*. He hasn't written a letter, either. I stare at the book, smiling, and then I reach for my phone.

I love it.

I'm not nervous that Felix won't reply. I'm becoming more certain of myself, and I'm ready for whatever comes next, thumbs-up emojis and all. But not even a minute goes by before his message lights my screen.

Yours doesn't have to be a secret.

I laugh. I told Bridget about the farm before she left. She was looking at properties online before I finished speaking.

Classic.

I leave the conversation at that, but I'm warm all over. Felix is there—as a friend or more, I'm not sure. But he's a part of my life now—I won't let him go.

I go to the seed shop after work. It's snowing, but the flakes melt on my cheeks. They turn to water on the pavement, impermanent, like winter. I buy dahlias, similar to the ones he first sent me, though these are a different variety. Sweet Nathalies. Felix texts me when they make their way to him.

Felix: The internet tells me they make good cut flowers.

Me: The internet knows all.

Felix: How are you?

I think about it for a minute.

Me: I think I'm good. I miss Bridget terribly.

I don't tell him that I miss him, too. This time, I'm going slow.

Me: Can you believe you're going to be an uncle?

Felix: Can you believe you're going to be an aunt?

Me: Yes! I was born for aunthood.

Felix: You had a good role model.

Me: The best.

It's only a few days before another book arrives. *The Language of Flowers.*

Subtle, I write to him. I don't hear back until I'm at home in the evening.

I like to keep you guessing.

Three dots wriggle on the screen, and then disappear. Then appear again.

Can I call you?

My heart races at a speed only Felix makes it race.

"I'm not really a fan of texting," he says when I answer.

"Are you a fan of talking on the phone?"

"I'm a fan of listening to your voice."

I smile. "Can you tell when you're flirting, or is it so ingrained that you don't notice?"

His laugh—soft, short—fills my ears, my lungs, my heart. "I'm only telling the truth."

"I like your voice, too," I say, rummaging through my fridge.

"What are you doing?"

"Trying to figure out how I can turn two apples, a carrot, and a jar of mustard into dinner."

"Do you have a pork chop?"

"Afraid not."

"Then I can't help you." He pauses. "We should cook dinner together another time. I can walk you through making something."

"You'd be walking me through burning something," I say, though I love this idea. "But I'm game if you are."

I send Felix carrot seeds next, and he sends me back a cookbook of recipes from PEI called *Canada's Food Island*.

"I think this might be too advanced for me," I tell him on the phone that night.

"Nah," he says. "We'll start easy. Page thirty-three."

"Chipotle Mussel Salad does not sound easy."

"Saturday night," he says.

On Wednesday, I prepare files for my accountant—I made Bridget go over everything before she left so I can do it myself. On Thursday, I spend hours building a wall of flowers and hanging chandeliers for a holiday party. I notice that my body aches more than it used to. So, for the first time in my life, I decide I should go to the gym. I splurge on six sessions with a trainer. I don't want to lose weight, I tell her. I want to be strong. I start out on the elliptical on Friday after work and spend my thirty minutes there, dreaming about my make-believe flower farm. It's grown into three acres of greenhouses and fields and row upon row of flora. I tell Felix all about it Saturday evening as we're cleaning mussels together.

"What about a vegetable garden?" he asks. I have him on FaceTime, propped on the counter.

"I hadn't thought of that."

"It might be nice to grow your own food. I know where you can get some carrot seeds."

Nothing gets burned, and we eat our dinner with beer and

tortilla chips. Even though it's not a date, it's the best date of my life.

I TRAVEL TO ST. CATHARINES TO SPEND CHRISTMAS DAY with my family, and when my parents suggest that I sell the flower shop while business is good, I tell them to back down. I tell them I know what I'm doing. They say nothing more on the subject. Lyle bumps my hip when we're clearing the table and whispers, "That was awesome."

I visit Stacy's grave on New Year's Eve—it was her favorite holiday—and then hit the bars with Lyle and Nathan, who I convinced to come to the city and crash at my place for the night. We down toxic-looking green shots and can't get a cab home, so the three of us amble, arm linked in arm linked in arm, to my apartment. It's the most fun I've had with my brother.

One morning in early January, Bridget FaceTimes me to tell me she's having a girl. I cry with happiness. I cry because she's so far. I want to hold my best friend's baby in my arms.

"What did Wolf send you last?" Bridget asks when I've regained my composure.

"Another cookbook," I tell her.

"And you sent him?"

"Rose seeds." A buttery yellow variety for friendship.

With every envelope I send to Prince Edward Island, my dream flower farm has become more detailed. I draw diagrams of garden plots and plantings. I sow the seeds Felix sent me years ago in imaginary earth, and they become rows of dahlias and zinnias and snap dragons. Sometimes I arrange the flowers in bunches right out in the field, but on hot days, I take them into the shade of the barn and work at an old harvest table. There's a dog on my farm, running between the plants, and a swimming hole with reedy banks and a deep center. I want to be near a body of water, even a small one.

"How long do you think you'll keep this up?" Bridget asks for the gazillionth time.

I tell her I don't know. I've been doing well on my own, thriving in a way I wouldn't have thought possible. Though sometimes I miss Felix with such force, I need to place a hand on the wall to keep steady. It sneaks up on me in the dairy aisle of the grocery store when I'm picking out butter. It slams into me when I'm making coffee, knocks me about when I'm braiding my hair before bed. But I take strange comfort in these waves of heartache. They're like annotations in a book, a note in the margin that reads, *This is important.*

"I have news for you," Bridget says. "Joy is engaged."

My stomach drops. My reaction an irrational knee-jerk. "To Felix?"

Bridget looks at me as if I've spoken in Latin. "No, you potato. To Colin Campbell. I think you met him at Zach's party years ago. Big guy. Red hair. Red beard. Smiley."

It takes me a minute to drum up the memory of Colin in Zach's kitchen. "Wow," I say. "That's great."

Bridget smirks. "Mmm. They've been together for over a year. I'm thrilled for her. Word is that Colin Campbell eats pussy like a champion."

I spit out my coffee. "Bridget."

She rolls her eyes, smug smile firmly in place.

"What?"

"I have more news."

"I hope it doesn't involve the sex lives of islanders."

"Liar," she says. "But no. There's a piece of land for sale I thought you might like. A few acres out Point Prim way," she goes on. "Zach sent me the listing. It's near the lighthouse. Gorgeous spot. Goes right to the water."

"You have Zach scoping out property for me? In PEI?"

"I have, and it's a good one."

I look at the listing Bridget sends me. Every few days, I check it again to see whether it's still for sale. It's a strip of green land, a stand of trees at its farthest edge, the ocean beyond. It's just a field, but it could be a farm.

BOOKS COME AND SEEDS GO.

Sunflowers. Salvia. Cosmos.

To the Lighthouse. Tomorrow, and Tomorrow, and Tomorrow. A collection of Maya Angelou's poetry.

"I didn't know you liked poetry," I say to Felix one Saturday evening in late January.

"I like poetry."

We're making chicken and couscous from the *Seven Spoons* cookbook he gave me. I wanted to learn how to roast a whole bird, and Tara O'Brady promises that this is a "mostly hands-off dinner."

"I'll have to report this development to Farah," I tell him while I set the chicken in the oven.

We drink wine while we cook, chat while we wait, and eat together when it's ready. We spend countless nights like this. Not just Saturdays.

I like this little world we've built. But I exist outside of its comfort. I exist outside of work, too. I go to galleries and movies and restaurants with friends. But in February, I decide to spend my thirtieth birthday alone. I buy a bottle of champagne and order my favorite spicy noodles and watch a wonderfully mediocre rom-com with a clay mask on my face. And even without Bridget next to me on the sofa, I have a great night. I'm evolving.

My apartment is, too. My office looks like a vision board sprung to life. There are books about perennials, a brass watering can, and a potting table stocked with gloves and terra-cotta planters. I've got everything I need for a garden of my own, but nowhere to grow. I search for a new apartment—maybe the main floor of a renovated Victorian, one with a flower bed the owner might let me tend. I even go see a few. But then I realize: I want to put roots into my own soil.

"You're thirty," Felix says when we speak next. It's Tara's Bee-Stung Fried Chicken night—I've been working up to this. I covered my chicken pieces in the dry rub yesterday and took them out of the fridge an hour ago. I'm determined to get it right.

"I am," I agree.

"How's it going so far?"

"On this, the third day of my thirtieth year?"

"Yeah," he says. "Tell me how you're doing, Lucy."

I pause, my fingers covered in a buttermilk cornstarch paste. I hold up my hands to the screen. "Right now I'm a mess. But otherwise, I'm sort of great."

I miss you, though. I miss you so, so much.

"I miss the island," I tell him. Because that's true, too.

He smiles softly. "The island misses you back."

Felix and I fry the chicken pieces at the same time. We've become experts at cooking in tandem. The dish is a masterpiece. Crunchy and juicy. The hot honey butter a revelation.

"I can't believe how good this is," I say, licking my fingers. I don't think before I say it. "I wish you were here so we could enjoy it together."

I glance up at my screen, worried I've ruined whatever this new thing between us is, and find Felix smiling. "I wish that, too. But we're enjoying it together now."

"You're right," I tell him.

But it's not enough.

THE NEXT WEEK, I MEET MY MOTHER FOR LUNCH AT A café in the department store where she's shopping for her vacation to Mexico. She's cranky, bemoaning the death of customer service, so I wait until the cappuccinos are delivered following our meal, then ask, "Can I talk to you about something?"

"This sounds serious."

"It is," I tell her. "I think I'm falling in love."

My feelings for Felix have been growing for years now, and I know there's no stopping them. I can't dream about my farm anymore without seeing Felix there with me.

My mother straightens her shirt collar. "What's his name?"

"Felix," I say. "Felix Clark."

She blinks at least ten times. "Bridget's brother?"

"Yes."

"How long have you two been together?" She sounds hurt. She thinks I've been keeping this from her.

"We're not. That's what I wanted to talk to you about."

I give my mother an abridged version of our history, and when I'm done, she lets out a long sigh.

"Oh, Goose. I don't know what to say. I've only ever wanted

you to be happy and comfortable, and it doesn't sound like you're either of those things."

"I'm getting there," I tell her. "I feel better than I have in a long time. I know what I want." I clasp my hands together under the table. "One of those things involves you."

She looks surprised. "Oh. And what's that?"

"I'd like you to stop calling me Goose."

I MAKE A CALL AFTER LUNCH.

"You don't want to see it?" Zach says.

"I trust you," I tell him. "I'm doing it."

39

Now

March

The cow is gone but Felix is here, waiting for me in the terminal. I spot him just before he sees me. He's reading, of course. When he glances up and finds me, his eyes spark, but his feet stay planted as I make my way to him.

I've arrived with a book in my bag and my heart in my hand, and I have no idea how he'll react to everything I'm planning to share with him, but I hug him close to me and breathe him in. Wind. Ocean. Trees.

"You have a problem," he says. He's wearing a heavy coat, but I can feel his laughter rumbling through his chest. I've heard it so often over the last five months that we've been talking and cooking together and learning each other, but there's nothing like feeling it in my body.

"I know," I say. "I've been in withdrawal."

"Hi," he says when I loosen my grip.

"Hi," I say back, getting lost in his face. His beard is back. His eyes are as bright as I've ever seen them.

"You're here."

"I'm here."

I told Felix I wanted to visit so I could cook with him in real life. It's not a lie, but it's not the complete truth, either. He's booked me in one of the cottages for the week. I hope that's because he's being chivalrous, not because he doesn't want me at his house. It's better this way. If things don't go how I want them to, I couldn't manage staying with him.

"I want to show you something," I say when he pulls out of the parking lot. The snow has melted in Toronto, but it still blankets the ground here.

He lifts an eyebrow. "Oh yeah?"

"Not like that." But god, just like that, too. I recite the address from memory.

"Point Prim Road?" Felix asks, confused.

"Point Prim Road. Want me to put it in your phone so you can use the GPS?"

He shakes his head. "I know my way." He glances at me. "Do you want to fill me in on what this is all about?"

"Not yet."

I'm too nervous to say much the rest of the drive. When Felix pulls up to my dream, which amounts to little more than a metal gate across a snowy path, I'm breathing heavily. Perspiration beads at my hairline.

"What is this, Lucy?" He looks at me. "Are you carsick? I have a snack bar in here." He reaches into the center console, but I put my hand on his wrist.

"Let's take a walk," I say, digging the book out of my bag.

We get out of the truck. I climb over the gate, and Felix follows.

"I didn't take you for an outlaw," he says once we're walking across the field. Snow crunches under our boots, our words turn to fog from our lips.

"I'm not," I say. I take a deep breath. "I own this land."

Felix stops walking. "You what?"

I turn to face him. "I bought it," I say. "For my farm."

He blinks like he's misheard me. "For your farm?"

I nod. "This is the first time I'm seeing it," I tell him. "I had Zach check it out."

"You had Zach check it out?"

I nod again. "He's been really helpful."

"Zach," he says slowly. "Has been really helpful. To you. While you were buying a farm. Here. On Prince Edward Island."

I look around at the plain of white, the snow-covered pines that surround it. "I wouldn't call it a farm. It's more of a field, really. But it goes all the way to the ocean."

"To the strait, you mean."

I smile because islanders are so particular about how they label bodies of water. "Yes, it goes all the way to Northumberland Strait."

He still looks stunned. "Why? Why would you do this?"

"Because," I tell him. "I love Prince Edward Island more than I love anywhere else, and I want to make it my home one day. I want to build a life here. I want to grow flowers here." Even if Felix doesn't want to do it with me, this is where I want to be.

Felix is staring at me with big blue eyes, but he hasn't spoken. Before I lose my courage, I hold the book up. "I brought you something." I wrapped it in pink paper because this book is a gift as much as it is a message. "I wanted to give it to you in person."

If I weren't wearing mitts, Felix would see my fingers tremble when I pass it to him. He pulls off his gloves and removes the paper, turning the novel over in his hands, then looks up at me.

"*Anne of the Island*?"

"It's the third one in the series," I say. I annotated it on the plane, underlined all my favorite parts, wrote notes in the margins for Felix to read.

He tilts his head. His eyes search mine for meaning.

"Have you read it?" I ask.

"No," he says. "Only *Anne of Green Gables.*"

"With all the reading you do, you should have finished the complete works of Lucy Maud Montgomery by now." I tap the cover. "In this book, Anne leaves Prince Edward Island and goes to college in Nova Scotia. Gilbert proposes twice. The first time Anne's not ready and takes up with a man who is completely wrong for her. In the end, though, she realizes that the island is her home and Gilbert is her true love."

"Smart woman, that Anne Shirley," he says, scanning my face.

Nerves zip through my limbs, ripple in my chest. They aren't going to stop me. I'm afraid, but I'm not going anywhere.

"Felix, I brought you here to tell you that you are in every one of my dreams. I came here to ask whether I'm in any of yours, too."

I barely have time to register before his mouth is on mine. I rope my arms around his neck, pulling off my mittens so I can slide my hands into Felix's hair. My fingers curl into the thick strands at the nape of his neck like they've always belonged there. His lips are reverent, the most devout kind of worship, as slow and sweet as jam. My lips part and a sob escapes, but it dissolves on Felix's tongue. Warm like hot honey butter, even in the last weeks of winter. When he pulls back, he rests his forehead on mine.

"All of my dreams, Lucy. Every single one."

I kiss him again because I've missed how he tastes, and I haven't had nearly enough. One hand tilts my head, the other finds my waist, towing me to him. I melt into his mouth, his chest, his hips, and a familiar growl sounds in the back of his throat. I devour it. I devour him. Felix's mouth coasts along my jaw.

"I didn't know if I'd ever feel your skin again," he rasps against my throat. "I missed you. I missed this neck."

I take his face in my hands, bring him back to me. "The neck is all yours."

He runs his nose against mine. A thumb traces my cheek. "I've always thought we fit perfectly together," he says.

"You haven't always thought that," I say, smiling. I don't think I knew what happiness was until this moment.

"I have." He pushes a stand of hair off my forehead. "And I loved your smile. It's as bright as sunshine. I loved your lips, and your breasts, and your hips. I loved your thighs." His mouth trails south. He unbuttons my jacket and kisses the trio of moles. "I loved these three dots." He kisses his way back up, his face returns to mine. "Are you following?"

"I think I am."

"Let's make sure, Lucy." His eyes sparkle. So does the dimple. "I love your name. Lucy Beth Ashby. I love the feel of it in my mouth. I love the way you braid your hair before bed. I worship the nightgowns. And your dresses. The one you wore when we met. The purple one with the bow around the middle." A finger steals across my cheekbone, over my bottom lip. "Your skin. It's so soft. The way your lipstick tastes, like wax and honey. The way you taste when you come."

"If you keep talking like that, I might ask you to ravish me right here in this frozen field."

Felix's hands travel to my lower back, crushing me to him. I go willingly.

"I'd ravish you anywhere, but I'm not done yet. I love how much you love my sister, and your shop, and that cow statue."

"Wowie," I say.

His smile grows. Blossoms to its fullest. "Wowie," he says. "I love your strong opinions on butter. And the things you can do with flowers. You're an artist, Lucy. I love how you hold a knife, and I love watching you eat. I love the way you blush. Fuck, the way you blush. I love how you ask questions and really listen to the answers. I love every book you sent me, every package of seeds. Every look you've given me. Every touch. Every kiss. You could throw up in my truck a dozen times, and I wouldn't mind."

I laugh, but my heart is singing, *More. Felix.*

"How can you make that sound romantic? I love the things that come out of your mouth."

"Your mouth is exquisite. Lusher than any garden. More gorgeous than any rose."

"Your words," I say. "So beautiful."

I map his jaw with my fingertips, then set my palm on his chest. He places his hand atop mine.

"There have been times when staying away from you has felt as impossible as not breathing. I think I'm made for you, Lucy," he says. "Since the first day we met, I think a piece of my heart has belonged to you. Every year, it just got bigger and bigger. I don't know when it became more. Maybe when you put that pink package of butter in my hand. It could have been when we watched each other in the bathroom mirror. Or when you came to me that Thanksgiving. Or when I saw your shop. Or when you sent me that first book. Or when we went to the lighthouse at the end of this peninsula, and you looked like you'd never been happier to be anywhere or with anyone. I don't know when it happened, but the whole thing is yours, Lucy. My entire heart if you want it."

I press a hand over his lips. "That's enough talking."

"I have more to say."

"I know you do." I loop both arms around him. I look into his eyes, the most radiant of all the blues. "But I traveled across the country so I could tell you, and you're not beating me to it. I love you, Felix."

Felix blinks, and then tips his head back. A laugh, glorious, erupts from him, and then he plants his hands on either side of my face. "You." He kisses me once. "I am so in love with you. Wildly. Deeply. Unrelentingly in love with you."

Felix's mouth is on mine again, and it's not a polite kiss. There's sucking and biting and big hands all over.

"Home," he says. "I want to take you home."

A BOOT ON THE DOOR MAT. A COAT FLUNG ONTO THE couch. My sweater littering the hallway. We are giddy and frantic, just like the first time. Our kisses are sloppy. Our smiles are, too. But when we step into Felix's room, his mouth slows down. I have no idea where my skirt went.

I tell him over and over, "I love you. I love you." It slips off my tongue easily. Holding it back was the hard part.

We kiss, and touch, and roll around until Felix makes his way down my body. He runs his tongue over the pink bands my bra has stamped into my flesh, following the grooves. I feel his callouses over my ribs. I love these hands. I admire the golden brown of his forearms. I love this skin. His palm slides down my torso, along my stomach, and between my legs.

"You look like a dream," he says before his mouth follows.

After I come so loud that I'm thankful Felix doesn't have neighbors, I pull him back to me. Kiss his mouth, tell him how much I love it. I make him lie down, so I can get on top. I look at him beneath me, lips slick, eyes hooded. When I fit myself around him, he lifts his chin to the ceiling.

"I might not last long," he says, voice ragged. "It's been a while."

"That's okay. We have time for a second round."

He takes a deep inhale, and I circle my hips once. His eyelids flutter, so I do it again. This will be fun.

"What's that look?" he grits out.

"I was wondering how fast I could end this." I reach behind me, running a hand along his inner thigh, over his birthmark. He groans and closes his eyes. I watch his chest rise and fall, but when he meets my gaze again, he's wearing a look of total determination. I know this look. I'm in trouble.

Felix grips my backside as he sits upright, pulling me onto his lap.

"Do your best, Lucy." He moves his lips to the moles under my collarbone, then lower. "And I'll do mine."

We have sex once, twice, three times. We break for food and water and for Felix to start a fire in the living room. My mouth can't form any shape but a smile. I press my face into the pillow, laughing as Felix sinks his teeth into the flesh of my backside.

Once we've fully exhausted ourselves, he tucks me against his chest, hugging me close. It's where I feel safe. It's where I feel cherished. It's my whole world, right here, wrapped up with Felix.

THE SUN HAS LONG SINCE RISEN BY THE TIME I WAKE UP. Felix is fast asleep, a boyish grin on his lips. I slip on one of his shirts and sneak out to the kitchen. I make myself toast and Earl Grey tea because Felix doesn't own a coffee maker. There are two photos on his fridge now. The one I saw the last time I was here—Felix and Zach at Salt Cottages—and one of me. It's from Bridget's wedding. I'm on the dance floor, the only person in focus, watching Miles sing. I have my fingers pressed over my smile.

While I wait for the toast to pop and the tea to steep, I inspect Felix's books. The ones I've sent him are displayed on a shelf along with the seeds. I pick up *Great Expectations*.

"Good morning," I hear Felix say.

I turn around to look at him across the room. He's wearing underwear and a white T-shirt. He looks rumpled and gorgeous and mine. I think of all the things I love about Felix, and this time I don't run. I cross the floor, throw my arms around him, and say, "Good morning, my love."

40

Now

Spring and Summer

I know where I want to end up, but I'm not ready yet. So Felix and I go back and forth. April in Toronto. May on Prince Edward Island.

Felix discovers my world. We have sex in my pink bedroom, on my white sheets, and when we're cuddled together afterward, he asks to see my notebook of flower farm ideas.

"Do you think I'm too ambitious?" I ask as he flips through the garden diagrams, the sketches of arrangements, the lists of imaginary supplies.

He kisses my temple. "I think you're brilliant. A dreamer with beautiful dreams."

I keep the Earl Grey he likes in the cupboard next to the fridge, and he masters my coffee maker. I let him inspect my medicine cabinet and my magazine collection. He makes bouillabaisse in my kitchen, familiarizes himself with where I keep the corkscrew and the good knife his mom gave me. He insists on meeting my parents, so we drive to St. Catharines, and I introduce him to my mom and dad, my brother and his husband.

"He's very handsome, I'll give you that," my mother says

when it's just the two of us in the kitchen. "But are you sure it's a good idea to be involved with Bridget's brother, Goose?"

"Mom," I say. "Please don't call me that. And yes, I'm sure. I've never been surer of anything."

"Then I suppose you have my blessing."

I take a deep breath. "I'm thirty years old, Mom. I'm an adult. I didn't ask for your blessing."

She flinches, surprised. She studies me like she's seeing me for the first time. "You have my best wishes, then." She sets a piece of orange cake on a plate. "You seem happy together."

"We are." I hesitate for a moment. "Are *you* happy?"

She pauses, assessing me.

"I heard you and Stacy talking once, at the hospital."

"Ah." She sighs. "I'm happy enough, Lucy. Your aunt thought life should be full of fireworks, but I'm content—that's enough for me."

My aunt wouldn't be satisfied with *content*, but I know I won't get anything else from my mother. "Stacy met Felix once," I tell her. "It was only for a few minutes, but I think she liked him."

My mom smiles, wistful. She slices another wedge of cake, and I think that's the end of the conversation. But then she says, "Your aunt would call him *edible*."

"That's the exact word she used."

She laughs, pressing a finger to the corner of her eye. "She would have liked him, Lucy. She would have liked him a lot."

I wrap my arms around my mom's waist, my eyes stinging. "Thanks," I whisper.

There's a day during Felix's visit that I can't swing taking off. He rides with me on the streetcar in the morning, kisses me goodbye, and returns after the store is closed and everyone has gone home. I hear his *tap, tap,* pause, *tap* on the door. I unlock it, and drag him into the office, and act out one of the fantasies that involve me and him in this small room.

It's painful to say goodbye, just like I knew it would be. But it isn't too long before I'm back in Felix's world. I spend a week there in June. He picks me up at the airport and we drive east. He buys a coffee maker for me and shows me how to make a perfect cup of tea for him. We cook together. I choose a book of poetry from his collection, and he reads it to me in the evening. But he doesn't read for long, because poetry from Felix's lips uncoils me in a brand-new way, and I'm on my knees after only a few stanzas. I choose Austen the next night. It's no better.

We have dinner with his parents at Summer Wind, and sleep in the guest room, the one Christine decorated with me in mind.

We walk through the field where we want to build a life together one day. We imagine what our house might look like, we discuss where the dahlias should grow. Felix has grand plans for a vegetable patch.

"Carrots," he says, "are very good for you."

"You," I tell him, "are very good for me."

In August, Felix meets me in Toronto, and together we fly to Sydney so we can hold Felix's niece in our arms. Bridget and I hug and cry and cling to each other for five minutes in the airport, and when we part, I find Felix with a baby nestled to his chest.

"Hi, Rowan," he says. "I'm your uncle Felix, but everyone calls me Wolf."

Felix brings the baby to me, cradles her in my arms with the utmost of care. Rowan's eyes are squeezed shut. She's all nose and cheek, with wisps of black hair sticking out from under her knit hat. I run my finger over her nose. Felix's nose.

"Rowan," says Bridget. "This is your auntie Lucy. But us girls call her Bee."

Bridget kept her job and was managing it remotely before Rowan was born. But she's taking a full year leave, and we have whole days to spend together. We take a lot of walks with the baby. We stroll the harbor, past the Opera House, and into the Royal Botanic Gardens. We shop at Paddy's Markets and have fish and chips overlooking Watsons Bay. It's winter in Australia, but it's warm on the weekend, so Miles drives us to Palm Beach.

I stand on the shore with Felix behind me, his arms around my waist. We stare out over the Pacific, with Bridget, Miles, and Rowan sitting on a blanket, brushing sand off watermelon slices. I want this forever, I think. Felix holding me against his chest, looking out at the sea.

I turn to face him. "I have an idea."

"Uh-oh," he says.

"A fucking brilliant idea."

Dimple pop. "Give it to me."

"I don't want to spend another autumn alone. I want to be with you for Thanksgiving. I want to be with your family at Christmas. I want to see Salt Cottages with all the twinkle lights. I want to go skating with you. I want you to build me a fire so we can curl up next to it. I want to wake up together every day. I'm ready to live our dreams instead of talking about them. I want to build our house."

"*Our house.* I like how it sounds when you say it."

"Is that a yes?"

He holds my cheeks between his palms. "I have some ideas, too."

"Do you?"

"I've been sketching."

"Sketching?"

"Drawings of houses. Ran a few ideas by Zach and the architect at his company who designed Salt Cottages."

"You sneak. I had no idea."

"They're just preliminary. A house. A barn. A greenhouse. I didn't want to get too far ahead of myself until you were ready to look at them."

"You've been designing my farm?"

"I have. I took a couple photos of your notebook, and I've got some thoughts. It's all up for discussion. I want to do this together."

"Together," I repeat.

"You and me," he says.

"In PEI."

"If that's what you want, Lucy."

"That's what I want." Felix and me, on another beach, one with red sand and cliffs and a view of a different ocean. I want cold February nights with him reading me books. I want July mornings in a blossoming garden. Felix will be my home, and I will be a place for him to return to. He'll be my oasis, and I'll be his. He'll save his best words for me, and I'll save mine for him. "It's exactly what I want."

EPILOGUE

The Following Summer

We've propped all the doors open, and people roam in and out of the house, from the living room to the kitchen to the stone patio. It's not a farm yet, but it's not far off. Felix and his dad built the greenhouse this spring. The foundation for the barn has been poured. A narrow stream winds its way through birch and white spruce at the back of the property, and there are rows of turned soil.

We haven't had time to finish decorating, but even without curtains, our home is perfect—a modern farmhouse, with a charcoal exterior and a gabled roof. We've named it Primfield House.

Like a man possessed, Zach oversaw every detail of the design and construction, swearing it would be ready by the beginning of the August. And he was right. It was a good thing, too. Felix sold his place, so we were staying at Summer Wind, and he was getting grouchy about sharing a roof with his parents.

My life is almost unrecognizable from the day Felix and I stood on a beach together in Australia and decided to knit our lives together. I moved to the island in December. I gave up my apartment. I travel to Toronto once a month, and Farah is managing In Bloom. She says she's "considering" my offer to buy in as a co-owner. I think she wants to do it, but I *know* she likes to keep me in suspense.

There are so many guests at our housewarming and so many questions. What are my plans for the Farm at Primfield? How am I liking life on the island? Where did I find that light fixture? I lose track of Felix within an hour. I suspect to find him in the kitchen with the teenager he hired to shuck for the evening, but he's nowhere to be seen.

I'm putting out a tray of miniature fish cakes when Zach's girlfriend, Lana, corners me to tell me she suspects Zach is going to ask her to marry him. Lana moved here from Montreal a few months ago, and I know for a fact that Zach has a ring. Their relationship is charmingly competitive, and she wants to propose first. She asks for my help brainstorming ideas. I don't see it for the distraction that it is until I hear a clinking sound on the other side of the room. The crowd is so thick, I'm not sure where it's coming from.

But then I see her on the staircase, a champagne glass and spoon in her hand. Our eyes meet. It's been a year since Felix and I visited her in Sydney, a year since I've seen my best friend, and I'm already blinking away tears.

Bridget looks the same as she always has. Her cheeks are pink, and her hair is in a tizzy. She's wearing a pair of old jean shorts and a sleeveless shirt. But there's a floral crown around her head—the kind I wore the night we became friends. She made it herself—it's wilted, lopsided, and in a discordant combination of orange and purples. It's ugly as sin, and it's spectacular.

I can't pull my eyes away from Bridget.

"What the hell?" I mouth to her.

She blows me a kiss, then clinks her glass again. Between the chatter and Ken's playlist, only a few people twist their necks toward her. Bridget sets down her glass, puts two fingers in her mouth, and whistles.

Her gaze travels to her right, where Miles is stepping out of the reading room, Rowan in his arms. They must have snuck in while Lana was showing me a video of a flash mob proposal. Rowan is trying to keep a hold of the *Anne of Green Gables* alphabet book Felix bought for her a few weeks ago. He claimed he was mailing it to Australia.

An arm falls across my shoulders. "Surprise," Felix says.

I turn my head. Felix is clean-shaven and dimpled. His beard comes and goes with the seasons. Here for the winter, vanishing with the snow in the spring.

"You," I say to Felix. "You tricked me."

"Uh-huh." He kisses my cheek, and then smiles at his niece.

"Now I know why I couldn't find you earlier," I say.

He kisses the side of my head. "I asked my dad to keep the music loud so you wouldn't hear Rowan."

Bridget waves her hand. The room waves back.

"Wow," she says, surveying our faces. Her parents. My brother and his husband. Her grandparents and various Clark aunts and uncles and cousins. There's a handful of Guinness World Record–holding oyster shuckers and half of Felix's high school graduating class, Joy and Colin among them. Bridget's eyes land on my parents, and her smile broadens. "It's so good to see you all, and it's so good to be home. Actually . . ." She looks at Felix and me. "It's even better to be right here, in Wolf and Bee's home. And what a lovely one it is."

"I helped," Zach pipes.

Bridget raises her glass in his direction. "Of course you did, Zach." She pulls in a breath. "I'll be honest: Seeing my best friend and my brother standing over there"—she nods toward us—"holding each other, seems both completely natural and totally weird."

Felix is fast. A palm turns my face to his, and the other hand burrows into my hair. He kisses me the way he does when we're alone. There are whoops and whistles, and I can feel my chest heating, but I loop my arms around his waist, and draw him closer. We don't have to hide our love from anyone, including ourselves.

"I guess I was asking for that." Bridget's voice is dry, but her smile cuts dimples into her cheeks. She takes a sheet of paper from her pocket.

"I was desperately homesick when I met Bee. As you all know, I'm an islander at heart, and I liked Toronto well enough, especially at night. Back when I was in my early twenties, I'd ride my bike through Cabbagetown, catching glimpses of people inside their homes. I loved seeing the city lit up in the dark. But I missed my family. I missed the island—the wind and the water and Mom's cooking. I was lonely. And then I met Bee.

"The night we became friends, she was wearing a floral crown, made with real flowers." She points to her head. "Much nicer than this one. I used to be wary of women who looked like her—feminine and stylish, with cheekbones people pay for. At work, her makeup was always flawless. I thought she was probably all frills and gloss. I was wrong.

"She looks sweet, with those dresses and that smile, but Bee is tough. Tougher than she thinks. She hates fighting, but she won't stand down when it matters. It's one of the things I admire most about her. I used to wish that we had met earlier in life, when we were kids or teenagers, but now I think we found each other at the right time. We became adults together. Our friendship is how I learned to compromise. It's how I learned that the families we make are as significant as the ones we're born into. It's how I learned that the greatest loves are not always romances."

Bridget's speech is far longer than the one I gave at her wedding, and by the time she's almost finished, I've ruined one of my good napkins with my mascara. Felix stands behind me, arms banded around my middle, chin resting on my shoulder. Every so often I feel his laugh on my back or his smile against my cheek. I turn to look at him when Bridget speaks about what a wonderful brother he is, and I see that his eyes are shimmering.

"It's so wild, the things we do for love," Bridget says, looking right at us, her chin trembling. I put my hand on Felix's cheek. It's damp now, like his sister's. He turns his head and kisses my fingers. "Sometimes where we find it is even wilder."

Bridget raises her champagne flute, and the rest of the room follows. "To Lucy and Felix and their new home." She winks at us. "It's about time."

EVERYONE HAS CLEARED OUT EXCEPT FOR THE SIX OF US. My family is staying at Salt Cottages, and Christine and Ken are babysitting Rowan at Summer Wind. Bridget and I sit side by side on the back steps. It's growing dark, but we can see Miles's and Felix's silhouettes. They're lighting a bonfire in the field. Zach and Lana are already settled by the pit, wool blankets across their laps. We're having a sleepover tonight, although one couple is on an air mattress. Our third bedroom has no furniture.

"This place is unreal, Bee. I can't believe everything you've done," Bridget says. "You and Wolf are a good team."

My gaze drifts to Felix. "We are."

I had a stall at a farmer's market for two weekends earlier this month. I didn't have a lot of material, but I managed to pull together bouquets with this year's annuals. It seemed like a good idea, but it was a lot to take on with the construction and the flower shop. Felix found me crying in the field, one of several of my "I'm in over my head" moments.

He held me and whispered, "You and me, Lucy. We've got this." I focused on the weight of his arms and the smell of his skin, and I knew he was right. We ended up sprawled on the grass, my dress pushed above my waist, his pants around his ankles, laughing and covered in petals. Afterward, Felix watched me arrange a few bouquets, then asked to do some himself. He has a better eye than his sister.

"I didn't know it would feel so nice," I say to Bridget now.

"What's that?"

"Having a partner." I used to think doing things on my own was the highest of achievements, and it is fulfilling, but asking Felix for help doesn't make me feel smaller. When I'm with him, anything seems possible. It's almost drugging, how powerful I feel. How sacred and adored. On the evenings when we're so tired all we can do is curl up on the couch in silence, Felix reading while I watch TV, I don't worry that we're tiptoeing toward monotony. I don't feel like a piece of furniture. I just feel lucky.

"But I do miss my best friend," I say. "Another two years Down Under, huh?" She and Miles have decided to extend their stay.

"Yeah, and then back to Toronto, although I'm not sure how I'll ever cope with winter again."

"I would prefer you to be right next door, or at least in Charlottetown, but I'll take what I can get."

"The flight here will feel like nothing after traveling to and from Australia," Bridget says. "We'll come out so often, you'll be sick of us."

Felix is crouched, crumpling newspaper and arranging kindling in a pyramid. A flame begins to flicker.

"You better. I caught your brother watching a video tutorial about swing set construction. He's going to build a playground out there for Rowan and the kids who visit the farm."

"And for your own kids one day?" Bridget gives me a guilty smile.

"Maybe," I say. "Or maybe not. We're not really thinking about that yet." Felix and I have taken the questions of marriage and children off the table, at least for now. I give Bridget a flat look. "Funny, I thought I'd mentioned that to you. On multiple occasions."

She gives me a sheepish grin. "Noted." Bridget hops up. "Wait one sec."

I watch Felix while she's gone. He's waited, patient, until the flame burns steady to set small logs onto the fire. I can see his satisfaction in the orange glow. He turns toward me, his eyes finding mine. My stomach dips. It still catches me off guard—how clear his love is—how openly he offers it up.

Bridget returns holding a round wooden tray. On it is a bottle of expensive rye and six glasses that look like vintage crystal. A bag of peanuts is tucked under her arm.

"Your housewarming gift," she says. "Like old times."

I rise and kiss her cheek. "Almost."

When the fire is strong and everyone has a drink, I snuggle on Felix's lap. The conversation is one born of friends old and new—stories that slip into nostalgia and inside jokes that get translated for those who don't know them yet.

Bridget forcing Felix and Zach to do her Barbies' hair.

The night my aunt tried to replicate her favorite restaurant's pasta alla vodka, and we ended up drunk on the sauce.

Felix stabbing himself with an oyster knife when we met.

"So you really didn't know who the other was?" Lana asks Felix and me.

"No," we reply in unison.

"Really?"

"Really," we say.

"My best friend and my brother. It's mildly disturbing, but I wouldn't have it any other way," Bridget says.

I throw a peanut at her.

It's the kind of night where I can feel something lock into place. *This is it,* I think. *This is everything I want.*

At one point, Zach retrieves a gift-wrapped box from his car and hands it to me. It's a game of Trivial Pursuit.

"Is this for me, or is this for you?" I ask.

"Don't raise questions you don't want answers to," he says, taking out a box of cards. "I'll just ask a few to the group."

Zach and Bridget are debating the validity of one of her answers when I feel Felix's fingers in my hair. He's braiding it down the center of my back. When he finishes, he wraps the end around his hand and gently tugs my ear to his lips.

"I've been waiting to get you alone all day." He kisses my temple, then slides a hand toward my inner thigh.

"You go first," I say. "I'll distract them."

I stand to let Felix out of his chair.

"I need to take care of something in the house," he announces.

"He'll be right back," I say.

Felix looks at me over his shoulder as he's walking away, and even in the dusk, I can see the mischief in his eyes. After a minute, I tell everyone I'm going to get a sweater. Zach snorts.

I use our knock. *Tap, tap,* pause . . . But I don't get to the third tap before Felix opens the door, laughing.

"They all know what we're doing, right?" I ask as he pulls me inside and shuts the door.

"Of course," he says. "But now no one will come inside for at least thirty minutes. Until then, it's just us, Lucy."

Felix backs me against the wall, and we kiss. He tastes like good rye and woodsmoke and the sweetest end to the best day of my life. When we part, he takes my hand and tugs me toward the stairs. Fingers laced, we climb up to our bedroom in the home we've built together. A house full of books. A field full of flowers. Our own special island.

At last Felix. At last mine.

ACKNOWLEDGMENTS

Fun. That was my singular goal for this book. I wanted to have fun crafting this story. I wanted you to have fun reading it. I *needed* a better experience writing *This Summer Will Be Different* than I had with my previous novel, *Meet Me at the Lake*, which kicked my ass and my ego and my brain. I must have manifested it into reality because I had a blast writing this book. I loved every moment I spent with Lucy, Felix, and Bridget on Prince Edward Island, even my third draft, where I started over with zero words, and even my six, seventh, and eighth drafts, where I kept tearing Lucy and Felix apart in various ways, over and over. From start to finish, I had fun.

Fun is underrated. Fun takes a backburner as we grow up. Fun is frivolous. But what's so wrong with frivolous? Fun, I think, is something most of us need more of. We should cherish fun—it's not something that's available to everyone in this world.

According to my therapist, fun is experienced in the body, with movement. So, before I began writing, I played music throughout the house, dancing as I washed the dishes and dressed and picked up after my kids—and it helped me start my workday in a lighter headspace. I began actively pursuing fun outside of writing, too. Watercolors. Pottery. More time with friends. Red lipstick. Purple pens. A vase in the shape of a bum. Bangs. Magazines. Chatting with readers on Instagram. So much Harry Styles.

Fun is often sweeter when shared with others, and not a day goes by that I'm not thankful for the people who make my job such a tremendous pleasure. There's . . .

Amanda Bergeron, who delivers her editorial feedback with the sharpest, most thoughtful notes about character development, stakes, and structure while also advocating for hotter heroes and steamy shower scenes, and with whom I get to spend long calls discussing the intricacies of relationship arcs, our children's gastrointestinal mishaps, and hairstyles. (I'm very excited about your curtain bangs!)

Taylor Haggerty, who I'm convinced is the savviest person in publishing, who is as smart as she is fast-talking, who honestly makes me smile solely by me thinking about her, and who brings fun to her work—sometimes quite literally. When something good is happening, Taylor will say, "This is fun!" And it always is.

Deborah Sun de la Cruz, who makes my books so much stronger with her extraordinarily keen insights and careful edits, who continues to make me laugh with the things she finds hot, and who makes a truly excellent book launch speech.

Emma Ingram, who throws one heck of a party, who appreciates book-themed cocktails and clothes, and who takes such good care of me always, especially on tour.

Heather Baror-Shapiro, who hustles to have my books published all over the world, and who is the reason I wake up to messages from readers across the globe.

Carolina Beltran, who makes me think bigger, who is as delightful as she is intelligent, and who we can all thank if one of my books makes it onto the screen.

Kristin Cipolla, who is responsible for my late-to-the-party *evermore* phase.

Chelsea Pascoe, who brought me to her lovely family's home in New Jersey.

Jasmine Brown, who sent the loveliest, gushy note after she read this book.

Bridget O'Toole and Anika Bates, who patiently explain Tik-Tok memes to me.

Daniel French, who rescued me when I was stranded in a Mississauga parking lot.

Elizabeth Lennie, who has graced us with another stunning cover painting that so perfectly captures the spirit of this book.

AJ Bridel, who brings my audiobooks to life and who could definitely star as a grown-up Anne Shirley.

My colleagues at Root Literary, Berkley, Penguin Canada, Penguin Michael Joseph, Penguin Verlag, and beyond, who work so hard to put this book in your hands and who have made this journey an extraordinary one.

The booksellers, librarians, journalists, podcasters, Booksta-grammers, and BookTokers who connect people with books, who fight to keep our stories in your hands, and whose passion and dedication continues to humble me.

I was worried about setting a book on Prince Edward Island. I hesitated to tell my editor, Amanda, about the idea—which amounted to little more than "best friends girls' trip to PEI"—because *I knew* she'd want me to write it. Setting is so important to me. It's been the starting place for all three of my books, and I didn't want to get the island wrong. I've traveled there three times now—the first trip was with my best friend, Meredith, years ago, and twice more to research this book. I adore the island (I'm visiting again this summer), and I hope I've done this magical place and its wonderful people justice.

I'm grateful to Prince Edward Island's Jessica Doria-Brown, who kindly read this book to help ensure I captured the island as accurately as possible. She even took it upon herself to poll island men to find out whether they find Anne Shirley attractive. Thank you so very much, Jessica. Jeff Noye is the mayor of Tyne Valley, the owner of Valley Pearl Oysters, and the chairman of the Tyne Valley Oyster Festival (home of the Canadian Oyster Shucking Championship), not to mention a Guinness World Records–holding shucker. Thank you, Jeff, for letting me ask you a bunch of weirdly specific questions about oysters, shucking, and the championship. Any mistakes about the island and oysters are my own.

On that note, there's real debate about whether to use "on PEI" or "in PEI" in this book, and I've learned that, depending on the context, even islanders don't fully agree. I've mostly gone with "on," but sprinkled in a few "ins" where it felt more natural. Thank you to all my PEI-based readers who weighed in on this on Instagram, and an even bigger thank-you for all the excitement you've shown this book ahead of its publication.

Thank you to Amy Kain, owner of the floral boutique Pink Twig in Toronto, for taking me through the ins and outs of life as a florist. I had no clue how physically demanding the work is, how competitive the business is, or how organized you must be to succeed. Any mistakes I've made here are on me.

This book is dedicated to my best friend, Meredith Marino. Meredith sends me emails that read, "I cannot believe that my favorite author is also my best friend!" I can guarantee Meredith is crying as she's reading this. There's a good chance that she's currently standing in a bookstore on publication day, buying a stack of copies, even though she's already pre-ordered it. As Meredith was reading the first draft of *This Summer Will Be Different*, she sent me texts like, "I'm on page 15 and I'm smiling ear to ear" and, "67 pages in and it's a certified smash" and, "Who would have thought when we wandered into that oyster competition that it would be in YOUR THIRD BOOK years later?" After draft one, Meredith declared it to be her favorite book of the year and "perfect," which was both incorrect and exactly the kind of best friend energy I so cherish. I hope everyone has a Meredith in their life.

But as Bridget says, no person can be your everything. Thank you to my fabulous friends who have been with me from the get-go and my fellow authors who have offered me your precious time, advice, and generosity. You know who you are. Thank you to my mom, dad, and brother for supporting me in so many ways, including but not limited to childcare, hot meals, and stair repair. Thank you to the educators who care for my children, keep them safe, and teach them to grow into curious and kind humans. Thank you to our babysitter, Micaela, for helping us have a life. Thank you to Bob, always, for the lake.

To my boys. Max, who runs sweet or salty, and Finn, who's either sweet or sour. You are (almost) seven and two and a half as I write this, and you give your father and me such profound joy that sometimes we look at each other to silently say, *I can't believe how great these kids are.* I think Max will remember our epic flight to PEI when he's older, but I don't think you will, Finn. It took thirteen hours, door-to-door, instead of five, and the two of you faced it like champions. Thank you. (You were monsters on the way back, but let's forget about that.)

To my love. Marco, I can't do it without you. You are a true partner in every sense of the word. There's no one I'd rather raise children with or grow old with or stay up late listening to music with. You are my secret weapon, my rock, my sweetheart. You are steady when I am not. You make me breakfasts, and lunches, and dinners, and deliver them with a kiss. You are the perfect end to every one of my days. And, best of all, you look phenomenal in an apron.

And to you, my reader, if you're still with me. Thank you for buying, borrowing, and listening to my books—that means I can keep doing this, the thing I love doing more than anything else. I write for myself. But I'm grateful I have the privilege of writing for you, too.

THIS
SUMMER
WILL BE
DIFFERENT

Carley Fortune

READERS GUIDE

BEHIND THE BOOK

In 2008, my best friend, Meredith, and I took a trip to Prince Edward Island. We drove our rental car (a PT Cruiser that didn't exactly scream *girls' trip*) straight from the airport to the wharf in Charlottetown, sat at the bar of a restaurant, and ordered a dozen oysters from a cute guy behind the counter.

"Where are you in from?" he asked us.

"Toronto," we told him.

"I'm sorry," he said with complete sincerity, and we laughed. It's a truth widely known that the only Canadians who like Toronto are Torontonians. And then he looked me in the eyes and said, "Welcome home."

While I didn't hook up with the charming islander, I did fall in love with Prince Edward Island, and more in love with Meredith, too. We had been friends for six years at that point, but it was our first vacation together.

We stayed with Meredith's aunt in Summerside, committed to a seafood-only diet, and drove all over the island. We visited Green Gables Heritage Place, stuffed ourselves silly at New Glasgow Lobster Suppers, and attended the Canadian Oyster

Shucking Championship in Tyne Valley. All of it stuck with me: the shucking puns, the lobster rolls and mussels and chowder, the torrential rain that had us pulling over on the side of the road with our hazards on. We had fried oysters at the fire hall in Tyne Valley, then walked across the street to the arena to watch the shucking championship, ate an ungodly number of oysters, and then got lost in the dark on the way back and ended up down a dirt road in the woods. Much to Meredith's dismay, one of the most memorable moments from that trip did not make it into the book. When we ventured to North Cape to see the tides, there was a horse walking through the surf, a man riding atop. A tween boy (adorable, bespectacled, rosy-cheeked) stood on the shore, loading what looked like seaweed into the back of a truck. Meredith and I had a good chat with him about what they were doing (collecting Irish moss), and I thought it was so cool and romantic—like something from another time. When we walked away, Meredith started cracking up. She asked whether I'd noticed what was written on the kid's shirt. I had not, so I looked at him over my shoulder. FBI: FEMALE BODY INSPECTOR. So much for romance!

Each of my books is a love letter to a place. *Every Summer After* to Barry's Bay. *Meet Me at the Lake* to Toronto. And *This Summer Will Be Different* to Prince Edward Island. But this one is also a love letter to Meredith. I took so much pleasure in writing this book, but it was a tough time at home: My children were constantly sick, and it was tremendously difficult to work while parenting. I had my own share of health issues and was in a scary car accident. A close family member was diagnosed with cancer. It all just felt like too much. Meredith and I live in different cities, and my best friend had never felt so far away. I didn't know Bridget was going to move to Australia when I was writing my first draft, but as soon as the thought came to me, Lucy's grief resonated so deeply. I miss my best friend all the time.

But back to the happy stuff: I've known that I wanted to set a book on PEI since I began writing fiction. It's a truly special place, and of course, I have a deep love of *Anne of Green Gables*, both the book and the CBC movies, starring Megan Follows, Jonathan Crombie, Colleen Dewhurst, and Richard Farnsworth. When my husband and I began dating and he told me he'd never seen them, I went straight to the video store to rent the first. He applauded at the end, and in that moment, I knew he was the man for me. There is no improving upon *Anne* and my writing cannot compare to Lucy Maud Montgomery's, but I liked being able to look at the island through a contemporary point of view. I also got a kick out of writing my steamiest romance in the place famous for such a wonderfully chaste one.

I traveled to PEI twice more while I wrote *This Summer Will Be Different*. The first was in October 2022, shortly after Hurricane Fiona caused such tremendous destruction, and then again in July 2023. Each time I've gone, I've become more infatuated with the island. I've never met warmer people, had such consistently delicious food, or been so awed by the grandeur of a beach (and I grew up in Australia). Those red cliffs are spectacular. The oysters are phenomenal. And if you ever get there, you must take a trip to MacAusland's Woollen Mills to get yourself a fabulous blanket. Or five.

But if you can't make it, I hope I've transported you there, with Lucy, Felix, Bridget, and Zach. And I hope you had as much fun reading this story as I did writing it.

DISCUSSION QUESTIONS

1. What's your most memorable vacation, and why?

2. Lucy feels a sense of belonging when she's in Prince Edward Island. Have you ever traveled to a place that felt like home?

3. If you were in Lucy's shoes, would you have told Bridget that Lucy had slept with Felix that first time?

4. If not, is there a point where you think Lucy should have fessed up?

5. Who do you think "caught feelings" first: Lucy or Felix? What do you think that moment was for each of them?

6. Bridget and Lucy's friendship is tested as they grow into their adult lives. Do you think it's possible to maintain the same depth of friendship as we get older?

7. Aunt Stacy advises Lucy to live her life for herself and no one else. Do you agree with this advice? Why or why not?

8. After Bridget's wedding, Felix and Lucy decide that it's not the right time for them to begin a relationship. What did you make of this choice?

9. What's your relationship to *Anne of Green Gables*, if any?

BOOKS I READ (AND LOVED)
WHILE WRITING
THIS SUMMER WILL BE DIFFERENT

Tomorrow, and Tomorrow, and Tomorrow by Gabrielle Zevin
Fourth Wing by Rebecca Yarros
The Whispers by Ashley Audrain
Tom Lake by Ann Patchett
Sunshine Nails by Mai Nguyen
Same Time Next Summer by Annabel Monaghan
Hello Beautiful by Ann Napolitano
Life and Other Love Songs by Anissa Gray
The Paper Palace by Miranda Cowley Heller

CARLEY FORTUNE is the *New York Times* bestselling author of *Meet Me at the Lake* and *Every Summer After*. She's also an award-winning Canadian journalist who has worked as an editor for Refinery29, *The Globe and Mail*, *Chatelaine*, and *Toronto Life*. She lives in Toronto with her husband and two sons.

VISIT CARLEY FORTUNE ONLINE

CarleyFortune.com
CarleyFortune
CarleyFortune

Learn more about this book
and other titles from
New York Times bestselling author

CARLEY FORTUNE

SCAN ME
or visit
prh.com/carleyfortune